TAJI'S

HARPER ROSS: He had seen it destroy his son and tear apart his family. Now he is obsessed with hunting down the carriers of the disease— and terrified by the answers he finds.

—

MAXIMILLIAN KLAUSEN: He was the old fashioned doctor who had lost everyone he ever loved to the syndrome. Now he's fighting to find its cure—and he's running out of time.

—

IRENE CHANNING: She was the strong and beautiful woman who was the first known survivor of Taji's Syndrome—and the first to discover the bizarre and powerful changes it had left behind.

—

JEFF TAJI: He must discover the cause of the plague and stop it. But then he faces an even more baffling mystery . . . what is happening to the survivors?

Also by
CHELSEA QUINN YARBRO

To the High Redoubt
Firecode

Published by
POPULAR LIBRARY

TAJI'S SYNDROME

CHELSEA QUINN YARBRO

POPULAR LIBRARY

An Imprint of Warner Books, Inc.

A Warner Communications Company

This is a work of fiction. None of the persons or events portrayed is real. Any relationship to actual persons or events is wholly coincidental. Locations are either the product of the writer's imagination or are used fictitiously.

POPULAR LIBRARY EDITION

Popular Library® and the fanciful P design are registered trademarks of Warner Books, Inc.

Cover illustration by Richard Newton

Popular Library books are published by
Warner Books, Inc.
666 Fifth Avenue
New York, N.Y. 10103

A Warner Communications Company

Printed in the United States of America

First Printing: March, 1988

10 9 8 7 6 5 4 3 2 1

This book
is a gift for
Larry
(without bows and ribbons)

Acknowledgments

The writer wishes to thank the following people for their generous assistance in the preparation of this novel:

Mr. R. Burr
Dr. N. T. Denning
Dr. O. Galt
Ms. A. E. Oldani
Ms. D. L. Pedderson
Dr. T. Ryan
Mr. J. Santiago
Dr. R. Whitty

Any errors in fact or procedure are those of the writer, not these most helpful persons.

PROLOGUE

January and May, 1982

Someone was careless.

Ever since the hospital called, Melinda Gower was increasingly unable to concentrate. Her scattered thoughts kept going over the smooth reassurances of the admissions nurse who had repeatedly said that Bill's condition was not critical, each time finding more questionable inflections in what she had been told: was it "and we think he'll stabilize *quickly*" or had the the emphasis been different—"and we *think* he'll stabilize quickly"? No matter how she tried, Melinda could not decide how to interpret what she had heard.

"Just finish up and get out of here," said her boss, Julio Mendez, who was senior laboratory technician on the swing shift. "Get to the hospital. Give me a call when you find out how Bill's doing."

The laboratory was a forty-five-minute drive from the hospital in Salinas, most of it over a two-lane blacktop road that skirted the edge of the gulleys at the eastern side of the valley before crossing the flat agricultural land that spread out toward the coast range. It was not the sort of road that tempted drivers to speed, except for the assistant director of research who liked showing off his Ferrari.

"Thanks," Melinda said as she went about cleaning up the material left for disposal. Her sterile lab suit felt too hot and too tight as she worked, and for the first time her face mask fogged as she hurried to the sink to complete what would have been her first round of chores on an ordinary night. She was so distracted that she dropped one of the little flasks into the stainless steel sink, drawing back as it shattered.

"What's happening?" Julio called to her.

"Dropped something," Melinda said breathlessly.

"Anything important?"

"I don't think so," she answered as she looked at what was left of the flask.

"Where?" Julio was in the middle of transferring some new slides and so could not risk interrupting the delicate work to come and see for himself.

"In the sink."

"Filter in place?" He took a chance and glanced at her long enough to satisfy himself that nothing too dreadful had happened.

Though she had not checked it, Melinda said "Sure," while she hurried through the cleaning procedures, cutting what few corners she dared and cursing Isobel Merriman for being home with an asthma attack. If Isobel had been here, Melinda could have left as soon as the call had come from the hospital. As it was, she could not leave until the first cleanup was over.

"Whose is it?" Julio asked, still concentrating on his own work.

"I . . . guess it's Hale's," said Melinda, trying to make out the name on the torn label. Hale was working on a project to come up with an ecologically safe way to get industrial wastes out of rivers and streams.

"Sure it's not Katz?" Julio said, just to be careful, since Katz was the virologist purportedly trying to develop a way to mutate cancer cells so that they would serve as an antibody against themselves, a project which had been disappointing in its results.

"It's Hale," she said with more certainty as she glanced once again at the smeared ink of the first three letters.

"Okay. No worry, then." He could think of nothing more to say to her that would not interrupt her work and slow her down. "Just so long as it's Hale's." He concentrated on the slides.

"Julio," she called, as she drained out the first cleaning

solution and started to mix the second with hot water, "do you mind if I call the hospital before I leave?"

"Go ahead. Call right now, if you like." He was working with the third rack of slides, watching them with fascination, for he could not imagine what lurked on them.

"I will in a minute." Melinda was rushing, but she could not stop herself. The thought of Bill collapsing in the middle of a softball game, possibly from a "mild" heart attack, was too incomprehensible, too horrible to shove aside. Bill's only thirty-six, she repeated over and over like a prayer.

"I'll give you a hand as soon as I can," Julio promised Melinda. He sensed that her worry was turning into panic.

"Fine, fine," Melinda replied. She was already draining the second sinkful of liquid when she realized that the two lower filter traps were not in place, and that the effluvia from the glassware in the sink—to say nothing of the contents of the broken flask—were flowing into the drain. She stared in disbelief, aghast that she could do such a thing.

A jangle from the phone distracted her and she moved away from the sink to answer the summons, dreading what she might learn when she answered it.

The impossibly minute particles of DNA continued to run out the drain, into the landfill that was used as an additional and theoretically redundant filter.

The news from the hospital was less confident than before, and Melinda put down the receiver with trembling hands. "I have to go, Julio. Now."

He did not argue. "All right. I'll handle things here. Tell Bill I—" Then he saw her face and stopped. "Don't forget your umbrella," he said in a clumsy attempt to comfort her.

Not only did the heavy storm close the road from the laboratory to the freeway, in less than twelve hours it saturated the landfill so that the material from the broken flask washed into the rising waters of the nearest river, but when it overflowed its banks, the modified DNA from Dr. Katz's most recent efforts spilled into a field just planted with lettuce.

Prompt action on the part of the lettuce-grower saved more than two thirds of his crop, and in a few months his harvest was shipped, some to markets, some to restaurant suppliers, some to institutions. Most of those people who ate the lettuce from that particular field experienced nothing more than a day of upset stomach and abdominal cramps, though a few of the elderly were ill somewhat longer and their ailment was assumed to be some new sort of intestinal flu.

But there were exceptions. For these six the coiled alteration in the lettuce brought much more than flu.

_____ *Cesily Harmmon* _____

"Have some of the salad bar," Erin Donnell suggested to Cesily as they stood in line for the buffet. "It doesn't look too bad."

"You'd think they could have some decent food at a fundraiser," Cesily said lightly, her complaint hardly more than an excuse for conversation. "Or do they want us to ante up more and then they'll bring out something worth eating?"

Erin laughed dutifully and helped herself to a small, hard section of corn-on-the-cob. "How does Brandon feel about the new baby coming?"

"He's very pleased with himself," Cesily said, reaching for the serving tongs in the lettuce bowl. "I think you're right about the salad. I don't think they can ruin raw veggies, can they?"

Erin shrugged, her expensive dress glistening with the movement. "Don't bet on it." She sneered at the various offerings in hot trays, all covered in brown sauce. "I haven't seen mystery meat like that since college."

"Have salad with me," suggested Cesily. "Say, how did you handle telling Mike about a new baby coming? I've tried to break it to Eric, but I'm not certain he understands."

"Oh, don't worry about that. Just answer his questions when he asks them. And he'll ask them, never fear. Both of mine were unstoppable when I was carrying Maude." She took a little of the pickled beets. "How's Brandon doing with the new firm?"

"Very well," Cesily said with pride. "He's being offered a partnership already, and with the clients he brought in when he went with Becker and Jackobsen, he's one of their most valuable assets, or so they've told Brandon. Do you think the buttermilk dressing would be too fattening?"

"Anything to disguise the taste of the rest of it," said Erin, adding, "I hope they finish before the traffic piles up too much. I have to be in Pasadena by four: my mother's still in the hospital."

"Oh, I'm sorry," said Cesily with feeling. "Is there anything I can do?"

"Short of pulling the plug, not a damn thing." They made their way back to their table and ate in silence.

Cesily was one hundred three days pregnant.

_____ *Irene Poulakis* _____

It was bad enough that the two galleries in town had turned her down, but Irene cursed herself that she had waited so long to have the clinic confirm what she knew already.

"We're sorry, but after the first three months, it's not as . . . simple a procedure, Missus Poulakis."

"Miss Poulakis," Irene corrected the receptionist. "I see. How far gone am I?"

"The report indicates that you are at least one hundred days pregnant." She did not lift her eyes from the page on her desk. "If there is some reason why it would be necessary to terminate now, there are risks you ought to consider."

"Great." Irene stood up. "Let me think about it, okay? I have to . . . think about it." She did not want to admit it, but she was more confused than she thought she would be. If only Tim hadn't taken that job in Phoenix, they might work something out, but as it was. . . . She shook herself. "Is there any place around here I could get lunch?" she asked.

"There's a deli in the next block. The sandwiches are pretty good." The receptionist looked at Irene with concern. "Are you all right, Miss Poulakis?"

"I will be. I . . . I'll be back. As soon as I've made up my mind." She wandered toward the door, castigating herself inwardly for her lack of decision. Usually she was the sort of woman who knew what had to be done and did it.

Over a bacon-lettuce-and-tomato sandwich, Irene came to the conclusion that she wanted the baby, no matter what else happened. She was an artist, she reasoned, and that gave her a bit more leeway than most women had. It was useless to wait for a possible husband, for that might never happen. She had always wanted to have children. "Might as well start now," she said to the air, and was given a refill of dreadful coffee.

She was one hundred nine days pregnant.

Much as she tried to, Hilda could not warm to her sister-in-law; Kirsten's religious fervor made her impossible to approach and difficult to speak with.

"God is showing you His blessing," exclaimed Kirsten when Hilda told her that she was carrying twins. "What favor!"

"I hope I think so when they both want a two A.M. feeding," said Hilda, smiling so that Kirsten would know she was making a joke.

But Kirsten's mouth became a straight line. "It isn't your place to make light of the gifts of the Lord," she reprimanded her guest sternly. "God has chosen you to be the vessel for two of His treasured souls, and you can think of nothing more than the . . . inconvenience. I'm ashamed of you, Hilda." She got up from the table and stalked into her kitchen, her spine rigid with suppressed outrage.

Hilda sighed. She had promised Sven that she would try to get along better with Kirsten—after all, Kirsten was the only family Sven had left—but she knew it was going to be more awkward than she had feared. As Kirsten came back with two plates, Hilda tried to show enthusiasm for the spartan brunch Kirsten offered: molded gelatin salad on a bed of lettuce.

Kirsten put the plates on the table, took her seat and bowed her head, waiting for Hilda to do the same. "Merciful God, we thank Thee for Thy bounty which Thou hast given us for the maintenance of our bodies, which are the temple of the soul. We thank Thee for the riches Thou hast bestowed on Thy handmaiden Hilda in the children Thou

9

hast seen fit to honor her in bearing. We dedicate ourselves and the unborn to doing Thy Will to Thy Glory and the Glory of Thy begotten Son Jesus. Amen."

"Amen," Hilda echoed, looking at the drab square of yellow gelatin and the slightly wilted lettuce beneath it.

She was ninety-eight days pregnant.

_____ *Catherine Grey* _____

Who would have thought that her life would turn out so perfectly? Catherine asked herself as she strolled down the deck of the cruise ship, watching the coast of Mexico slide by in the distance. After the hideous years with Gary, to find Jonathon at last.

At first she had been afraid that she would not be able to deal with his three children, or the occasional ordeals of sending them to stay with their mother; but in very little time her life had settled into a pattern that might have seemed routine if she weren't so completely happy. This five-day cruise was a second wedding anniversary gift, and she was thrilled with it, and more besotted with Jonathon than ever.

"I wondered where you'd got to," he said, coming up to her and putting his arm around her. "I was looking all over for you."

"Where could I go?" she asked, laughing. That was what she loved best about Jonathon—his innate capacity to make her laugh.

"Not overboard, I hope. Especially now." He leaned over and nuzzled her neck.

A quiver of apprehension went through her. "Are you really sure about this?"

"Of course I am," he said, shocked. "Aren't you?"

"I . . . yes. But the kids . . ." She put her hand to her abdomen, feeling the new tautness there.

"They're delighted. Really. And it will make us more a family, you'll see." He pointed out over the sea. "Look. There's porpoises, or dolphins, or whatever they are."

Obediently she tried to make out the rolling shapes in the glinting sea. "They're a long way off."

"We'll see more." He took her hand. "What say we go on in and get lunch? They've got a seafood salad with shrimp and crab and scallops that looks perfect."

"Good enough for *Jonathon's Table*?" she asked, referring to the best of his four restaurants.

"You bet," he said. "Besides, you don't want to starve the new kid on the block. Get him used to the best right away. Make a gourmet of him early."

"Him?" she demanded with false indignation.

"All right, him; her; whatever." He was drawing her toward the dining room. "You're going to love it."

She tagged after him, starting to think of names as she went.

She was one hundred twelve days pregnant.

Alexandra Porter

Frank was late again, and Alexa stared at the walls of the mobile home they shared while he was on the rodeo circuit. She wanted to be back home, in the small, familiar Oregon town where they leased a hundred-acre ranch, raised a few head of cattle and Frank broke horses to help make ends meet. But every year, from June to October, he made the rounds of the smaller rodeos, from Alberta to Texas, and after five years of it, Alexa was tired.

It was more than tired, she admitted: it was the baby.

And if Frank weren't so busy riding half-crazy horses, he might have noticed something by now. But no, he was out with his buddies, drinking and probably whoring as well. These last two years he'd spent more time with those eager, glittery ladies who wore jeans so tight and shiny that Alexa wondered how they ever sat down, let alone breathed.

She got up and went to the icebox. Nothing much in it but half a dozen slices of bread, a head of lettuce and some mustard. It wouldn't be much of a meal, she thought, but until Frank got back, it was all there was in the house except a six-pack of Bud. Sighing, she took the lettuce out of the icebox and began to eat it, pulling the leaves off, rolling them up, and eating down them as if it was asparagus.

She was one hundred seven days pregnant.

_____ *Susan Ross* _____

Susan was on her way to pick up Kevin at school—it was his first semester in kindergarten—and Grant from the preschool. She had packed a picnic when it became certain that the weather would stay clear through the afternoon. She was delighted that she would be able to tell her two sons that their father had got the post he wanted and that they would be moving to Seattle around Christmas.

Traffic was heavier than she had expected, and Susan was almost late to Kevin's school, which troubled her. She had been accused of being overprotective, but the constant reminders in the mail and on grocery bags and in the news of missing children made her vigilant, and she dreaded the thought of Kevin standing alone in front of his school, the potential target of any maniac who might come along.

"You're overreacting," she told herself aloud. "You get this way when you're pregnant, remember? It isn't good for the kids to see you like this. It isn't good for the baby. Relax." She started doing the anti-stress exercises her nurse had recommended the year before, and it helped some. At last she made the turn in front of the school and was relieved to see that Miss Brewer was standing beside Kevin and waving at her.

"Sorry I'm late," Susan called as she came to a stop and leaned over to open the door. "It's been—"

"It's fine, Missus Ross," said Miss Brewer. "We had a good talk, didn't we, Kevin."

"Yes, Miss Brewer," Kevin said in a subdued voice as he got into the car.

"What do you say to Miss Brewer for waiting with you?" Susan asked before she closed the door.

"Thank you, Miss Brewer," said Kevin without enthusiasm.

"You're welcome, Kevin," she said as if she were not aware of his disinterest. "Drive carefully, Missus Ross," she added, as she stepped back from the car.

"She smells like mothballs," Kevin remarked as they drove away.

"Kevin, that's not a nice thing to say," Susan protested.

"Well she does," Kevin insisted, then looked around. "You made liverwurst!"

"And tuna fish for your brother," she added, smiling at his obvious pleasure. And, she added to herself, a simple lettuce and cucumber salad for her since she had to watch her weight for the next six months.

She was one hundred one days pregnant.

PART I

September–December, 1995

_____ *Gail Harmmon* _____

When Eric met her after swim practice, Gail was pleased and puzzled at once. "Where's Dad?" she asked her older brother as she bounced out of the gym.

"Still in line for gas, I guess." Eric had four books under his arm and even though he had been wearing contact lenses for three years, he still looked as if he were wearing glasses. "Mom asked me to meet you."

"I can walk home on my own," declared Gail, with the defensive independence of her almost-thirteen years. "I'm not exactly a kid."

"You know what Mom's like," said Eric, as the only explanation for their situation.

"Sure; and she's been worse since she went back to work." They had fallen into step together, prepared to walk the mile and a half home, though pedestrians were not that common a sight in the San Fernando Valley, especially now that there were so many smog alerts.

"She's worried, that's all," said Eric, frowning. "She's a little guilty, too. You know what happened to Erin's kids —she thinks the same thing's going to happen to us."

"That's silly." They stopped at a crosswalk and waited for a break in the stream of cars to cross. "Jenny got into junior-crack because of that guy from Texas. I mean, it was legal, a look-alike, not the real thing, being manufactured and all." She tossed her head, her short brown hair shining in the ruddy afternoon haze. "Dad gave me this ghoully lecture about all the designer drugs. He's worse than the cops that come to the school."

Eric cleared his throat. "Well?"

"Well what?" she challenged. Until two years ago she

17

had idolized her brilliant older brother, but much of that glamor had faded as she began to shine in school sports.

"Is there any reason they should worry?" Eric asked in his usual oblique style.

"You mean do I mess with drugs? Of course not." Her scorn was tremendous and she increased her already long stride to emphasize her contempt for the idea. "I'm an athlete, for God's sake! You know what happens with those designer drugs? Well, I'm not taking any chances."

"Olympic gold in diving, right?" said Eric, repeating Gail's often-stated goal.

"For starters," she said, letting him off the hook.

"And then what?" He caught up to her, his breath coming too fast. There was a sheen of sweat on his forehead and the color had drained from his face.

"Oh, hey, I'm sorry," said Gail, slowing at once. "I keep forgetting. Are you sure we ought to be walking home at all?"

Eric gave her a crooked smile. "The doctors said that so long as I don't overdo, some exercise is probably good for me. I'm scheduled for another series of tests next week."

"Next week?" Gail was shocked. "But you just had a bunch two weeks ago."

"Which didn't turn up anything," he reminded her, pleased that she reduced the pace of their hike.

"But Eric . . ." She hesitated. "I mean, don't they know what's wrong? How can they not know? They've got all those machines and computers and all that. How can they not know?" They passed a service station with the usual twenty-car line for the pumps; neither Eric nor Gail paid any attention to the sight, which had become commonplace in the last two years.

"I guess because there's nothing . . . specific about what's the matter. It's a little bit like mono and a little bit like a lot of other things, but it isn't any of them." He sighed, giving way to the futility he had felt since he had his first tests last May, six months ago.

"Boy, what a ghoully thing!" Gail burst out. "I start my

crummy periods and then you get . . . what did they used to call it?"

"The vapors," he suggested, trying to make light of it again.

"Yeah, that's right. The vapors." She said it in an exaggerated way, her voice deep and what she hoped was spooky. "The vapors! It sounds like a third-rate monster mini-series, doesn't it?"

"Or a new video." He stopped briefly, smiling his apology at her. "Sorry. Can we talk about something else?"

"Sure," she said at once, switching to her own sports with ease. "I'm going to be in the freestyle as well as the diving next weekend. The coach asked me to fill in for Gretchen Wills—she's got something wrong with her, and Ms. Dennison wants to have a full team in all the events."

"Well, good for you," said Eric, doing his best to muster enthusiasm. He was never much good at sports, and recently he had been excused from the athletic program at his high school until his physician determined it was safe for him to resume such demanding activities. "I know Mom'll be happy to know that, too. She told Megan that she ought to practice more."

Gail shook her head over the lack of perception this showed. "Megan's no swimmer. She's okay, but that's all. Mom ought to get her those extra dancing lessons she wants, because that's what she's good at."

"How can you tell? She's only nine." Eric hated to admit it, but his youngest sister baffled him.

"Nine's almost too late for a dancer," Gail announced with authority. "You ask Meredith, and she'll tell you."

Eric shook his head. "Meredith doesn't talk to me that much anymore." She had almost been his girlfriend for more than a year, and then, as Eric's health changed, Meredith slipped away from him, as if she feared his unknown disease might touch her as well. "She's taking extra dance classes," he added, glad that there was a reasonable excuse for the change in their fading relationship.

"Well, see what I mean?" Gail asked, then paused. "Are you scared, Eric?"

"Yeah," he admitted. "Don't tell Mom and Dad, will you? They're pretty upset as it is." He cleared his throat and squinted across the next intersection. "They'd get me shrunk if they thought I was scared."

"So what? Getting shrunk isn't too bad," said Gail blithely.

"That's for the stringers on drugs and the weirdos with the tattoos and the tech-ers who won't let anyone touch them. I've got an odd disease is all." He coughed once, more to keep his voice from breaking than because he needed to.

"Whatever," said Gail, holding up an imperious hand to the approaching cars. They had four more long blocks to go before they were home. As they crossed the six-lane street, Gail watched her brother covertly, looking for signs of illness.

"Stop it," he said as they got to the curb.

"I didn't mean anything," said Gail, knowing it was useless to deny what she had done.

"Stop it anyway. I'm not going to drop dead in the middle of Victory Boulevard, for Chrissake." He studied her and then smiled. "I don't blame you for wondering."

"Well, you got to admit that it makes more sense for you to be wondering about college than a puke-o disease."

"It makes more sense," he said, knowing that if his doctors would allow it, he would start at Cal Irvine next fall. If. If. If. The word had put all of his life in suspension while a bunch of doctors looked over the printouts and pictures from their machines and tried to decide what was wrong with him. What puzzled him most was that the machines—for which he had more respect than he had for physicians—had not been able to pinpoint his disease and offer a solution to it.

"You ought to volunteer for some of those experimental groups, you know, the ones that try out all the new medical things. I bet they'd find out what was wrong in a couple of weeks." Gail favored him with an encouraging grin. "Those guys love to experiment, and they're into everything."

"Sure," he said, with a complete lack of confidence. He began to feel sick, and he touched Gail on the arm. "Can we just wait a minute?"

"You okay?" she asked, suddenly anxious for him.

"I think so. I'm just . . . a little short of breath." He stared toward the next cross street and glared at the traffic. "I guess the smog is getting to me. They issued a warning for this afternoon. I should have paid more attention."

"Yeah." Gail was more uncertain than ever. "Look, if you want to wait on the bus bench, I can run home and tell—"

"Tell who?" demanded Eric. "Mom and Dad are at work and they won't be home, either of them, for more than two hours." He hated the thought that his younger sister was in better shape than he was, though he knew it was true.

"Then we can wait a little while," Gail conceded at once. "You're right. Mom and Dad are still out. If I had my license, I'd drive you."

"You won't have your license for almost four years," said Eric, who had acquired his learner's permit only a month ago.

"I'd still drive for you if I could get away with it." She gave him a conspiratorial wink. "You could drive home, but I'd bring the car here."

They had reached one of the infrequent bus benches, and Eric gratefully sank down on it, chagrined at how much he needed the respite. "You're not supposed to know how to drive at all."

"That's silly," she declared. "And you know it as well as I do." She shaded her eyes and looked down the street. "We could try hitchhiking."

"Mom would have a fit."

"There's two of us. I wouldn't do it alone. I'm not that dumb. But you and me ought to be safe." She started to stick out her thumb, but Eric stopped her.

"All I need is a couple more minutes and that ought to be enough. If I didn't have this crap, whatever it is, I'd be fine."

"I know that," said Gail with more sympathy than before. "You can't help it that you've got something no one can figure out yet."

"That's so," said Eric, taking several deep breaths of the gasoline-tainted air. "But I got to tell you, Gail, I'm damned sick of being sick."

"I can imagine. It must be ghouly to feel bad all the time." She reached out and patted his arm. "You don't have to worry. They're going to find out what's wrong and fix you up in no time. Doctor Plaiting knows his job."

"He sure does," Eric agreed as he got to his feet. "What's the worst part is that I end up feeling out of it about half the time, and that means I can't think worth batshit."

"That'll change when you get well." They started walking once more, Gail slightly in the lead. "You'll see."

"Yeah," said Eric, striving to get more air into his lungs with each breath.

_____ Steven Channing _____

"There will be two more payments before the trust is exhausted," the insurance lawyer explained to Irene Channing, his old-fashioned glasses riding down his nose so that he could peer over them at her; he felt it made up for his receding chin and hairline. "And there is the matter of the two trusts for the children."

"Neil took very good care of us," said Irene, squinting out the window at the flat spread of Dallas. "Three years and I still miss him."

"You've already gone over the stock portfolio, I trust?" the attorney asked, knowing the answer.

"Yesterday, and Neil's personal attorney also." She was, she admitted to herself, growing very tired of attorneys and forms. In the three years since Neil died, she was sure she had spent more time attending to his estate than painting. On the other hand, she allowed as the insurance attorney droned on, Neil left her astonishingly wealthy and had provided for her son as well, and so she was the last woman on earth who had any reason to cry spoiled fish.

"If you'll sign this authorization," the attorney said at last, presenting her with a long, closely written document, "then I can make the necessary transfers through your banker."

"I'd appreciate that," said Irene, reaching over to take the pen he proffered. "Is signature enough?"

"Initials at the bottom of each page, please," said the attorney. He cleared his throat as Irene tended to the matter. "Have you decided which house you intend to use for the summer?"

"The boys like the little ranch," she said, scrawling her full name—Irene Dysis Poulakis Channing—on the space provided.

"When were you thinking of going there?"

"As soon as school is out. But that's months and months away. It's only November." She handed the pen back to him. "And frankly, I'm more concerned about my gallery opening in March than vacation in June."

"Oh, yes, the gallery opening," said the attorney in a strained tone of voice. "I read about it."

Irene made an effort to keep her temper. "I've had shows there before, but never a solo act. One-man—or one-woman—shows are hard to come by." She smoothed her skirt. "Is that all, Mister Parker?"

"For the time being. You must understand that when amounts of this size are involved, there are procedures that have to be undertaken for everyone's protection." He removed his glasses and tried to smile. "You might find this—"

"Difficult to grasp?" she finished for him, angry at his bland assumption that she, both as a woman and an artist, had no sense of business. "I supported myself and my son for five years before I met Neil Channing. At a gallery opening, incidentally. It's true that there wasn't much money to take care of, but most of the time I managed, Mister Parker. I know about contracts. Just as I know that you are employed by this insurance company to protect their interests, not mine." She reached for her suede jacket and pulled it on. "Thank you very much for your time."

His adam's apple bobbed under his collar. "Missus Channing, I hope you didn't take offence at anything . . . I didn't mean to say anything . . ."

She went to the door and let herself out, her mind on Steven and Brice. She reminded herself that she owed them the time it took her to deal with infuriating men like Parker. She remembered the many times Neil had taken her aside and told her that she would have to be careful of men like Parker, and not to let them frazzle her, because that was how they gained the advantage. She was out on the street before she was willing to concede the contest to Parker.

Driving home, she pulled off the Highland Park Expressway and stopped at Steven's school, taking a book from her purse and starting to read. She had four cars and a chauffeur at her disposal, but there were days when she liked taking her three-year-old Commadore and driving without fuss. Her mind wandered and she realized she had read the same sentence four times without any sense of what it meant.

"Hi, mom," said Steven as he got into the car.

Irene stared at him, startled and surprised to see him.

"You were dozing," he explained as he pulled his seat belt into position and secured it. "Dull book?"

"A silly book," she said, putting it aside and reaching to start the car.

"Oh." He narrowed his eyes as she pulled into traffic. "How was the insurance company?"

"Smarmy, as usual," she said, glancing quickly at him and seeing again the faint fuzz that grew on his cheeks and upper lip. He had already shaved once, and soon would have to again.

"Wasn't that what you were expecting?" he asked, frowning. "Mom, can we go by the Gradestons' place on the way home? Sean's still out sick and I want to . . . you know."

Sean Gradeston had been his best friend for more than four years; the two had played together and invented their own brand of raising hell. Now Sean was confined to the house, suffering from some unknown disease that sapped his strength and turned him from a tempestuous thirteen-year-old to a little old man in a kid suit.

"I sure do. We'll stop for as long as Ginny will let you stay," promised Irene. She carefully avoided asking how Sean was doing, since his continuing deterioration was a forbidden topic.

"Good." He scowled at the traffic wending its way out through Highland Park. "Are they going to give you the money?"

"They can't very well refuse," said Irene. "It's all in Neil's will and all the documents are on file. They're dragging their feet as much as the law permits. It's a great deal of money, after all, and no one thought that Neil wouldn't live past forty-six."

"Yeah," said Steven. "I liked him. He was a good jumper."

Irene was familiar enough with her son's jargon to know this was a compliment. "He sure was. I don't like to think where we'd be now without him."

"How about with my real Pa?" asked Steven.

"No way," Irene said, and the vehemence of her words surprised her.

"Was he that bad?" Steven said with less certainty.

Irene did her best to take the sting away. "Not that bad,

no. He just didn't want any kids. In fact, he thought he couldn't have any because of something that happened in Viet Nam. That was years and years ago. I heard," she went on, saying nothing about the private detective she had hired to do the work, "that he ended up with a family of his own, eventually." She knew that his wife was a teacher in a San Diego high school and that Tim Stevenson himself ran a gourmet market in La Jolla, the fourth business venture for him in ten years. Tim had three children and a hefty mortgage as well as two cars, a Dragon-class sail boat, a Schnauser, and an ulcer.

"Probably doing okay then," said Steven with that curious mixture of longing and indifference that marked all his observations and questions about his father. "Remember about stopping at Sean's."

"I will," said Irene, signaling early for the turn. "Sean will be glad you're coming for a visit."

"When he finds out about it, I guess he will," said Steven. "I wish he wasn't sick. Or maybe I wish I was sick along with him. It's weird—one of us fine and the other so wasted that he can't walk more than half a block without turning white and wheezing." He folded his arms and stared out the window at the houses.

"He'll get better. The doctors will find out what the matter is, and then they'll take care of it. After all, it wasn't so long ago that they couldn't cure any of the kinds of leukemia, and now most of them are cured or under control and the few that aren't can be slowed down." She said this to give her boy hope. "Is this Golden Orchard?"

"Next corner," said Steven. "I hope you're right. I don't want anything to happen to Sean."

"Neither do I," Irene said as she made the right turn onto the winding residential street. "When we get there, no matter how he looks, don't you say anything about it, okay? He's probably upset enough as it is." She warned him more for his parents than for Sean, who took Steven's ribbing with delight.

"Okay." He cleared his throat. "There's three more kids

out with something like what's wrong with Sean. One of the teachers said something about it at lunch. The Principal wants all of us to go to the nurse next week, in case there's a bug going around. You know what that's like."

"I haven't got a note about it," said Irene, feeling real alarm for the first time.

"They just sent them out yesterday. Mister Rosenblum, the biology teacher, you remember him? he said that there's been some of the environmental types around looking for toxic dumps and that kind of stuff." Steven straightened up as the Gradeston house came into view. "Wouldn't that be oxic? Yeah, oxic toxic." He indicated the open space in front of the Gradeston house, although Irene was already pulling into it.

"What's this 'oxic'?" Irene asked, hoping to get a little of her son's attention before he went in to visit his friend.

"It's . . . about armpits. You know how they stink." He had already unfastened his seatbelt and as the Commadore pulled to a halt, he pressed the latch. "Back in a bit," he said as soon as the car had stopped and the door released.

Irene watched him go, then locked the wheel and prepared to follow him.

_____ Adam and Axel Barenssen _____

"You are not down on your knees," Preacher Colney admonished the younger—by seventeen minutes—of the Barenssen twins.

"I . . . I'm sorry," muttered Axel as he obediently dropped to his knees and joined his hands in prayer.

"I've done my best," Kirsten, their aunt, declared fervently, her own hands knotted together and her lean, parched face set with unhappiness. "God laid His burden on me, and I have thanked Him for it." She stared at her two nephews. "But they're getting to be . . ." The words stuck in her throat and she looked away from the two boys, as if they were too bright for her eyes.

"They are of a certain age," Preacher Colney agreed, his expression ambivalent. "And you say that Satan is working in them."

"I have seen it."

From their place on the floor, Adam and Axel exchanged one quick look, a signal of outrage and frustration. "It's not Satan," said Adam, loud enough for the two adults to hear him. "It's just puberty. That's what they told me at school."

Kirsten's countenance became more severe. "That's part of it. That lying! Anything can be explained by glands or chemistry or . . . I can't think! I have begged my brother to remove his sons from that place. There are atheists and Jews and God-alone-knows-what there. I have pleaded with him to show his authority and forbid his sons to read what the teachers have given him."

Preacher Colney had every bit as rigid an attitude as Kirsten Barenssen, but he had learned enough of the law that he did not relish martyring himself to the statutes of education in the state of Oregon. He had been a minister long enough that most of his naivete had worn off and been replaced with a degree of tolerance for human frailty. "Patience, Sister, pray for patience and God will see you through."

"It's puberty," Adam said with more force. "It happens to everyone when they get to be our age." His knees were beginning to hurt and he shifted his place on the floor, watching his brother do the same.

"God sends His trials to all of us," intoned Preacher Colney. "And you are not the ones to judge what has been manifested through you. You are too young and if you are being used by Satan, you might not know it. Most of those who succumb to his wiles do not know they have fallen." He raised his well-worn Bible above the two boys and began to pray; his voice was harsh, more demanding than imploring, and he shuddered as if fighting against an invisible wind. "Hear us, your children, O God Who has made all things, and come to our aid in our time of tribulation and suffering. We call on You in our need and our weakness, for You will not give us more than we can carry, and we bow our heads to this."

"He's getting worked up again," Axel whispered to Adam. They were so alike that even those who knew them well often confused them. There was one marked difference between them, and that was the shade of their eyes: Adam's were dark blue, a smoldering shade between cobalt and prussian; Axel's were a soft, light green. Right now their dissimilar eyes were locked as if that contact alone would block out all unpleasantness, uniting them against the world.

"Lord, hear us and grant us Your mighty arm as our protection against the work of the Devil, who ravens like a lion among Your flock. Cast out the evil that has entered the bodies of Adam and Axel Barenssen. Save them from the fires of Hell and restore to them the cloak of perfect innocence and purity which is the greatest gift of Heaven." He directed his remarks to the old-fashioned light fixture on the ceiling, as if suggesting that God might find His work easier through electrical circuits.

"They're not right anymore," sighed Kirsten. "Things happen when they're around. I have seen it." She reached out and grudgingly supported herself on the back of an ugly, overstuffed chair.

Preacher Colney interrupted his harangue and stared at her, a new recognition coming to him. "Are you still ailing, Sister Barenssen?"

"It's them. It's their work," she told the pudgy minister. "They've brought this affliction on me as surely as they are the tools of Hell."

"You have been to the doctor since we talked? You told me two weeks ago that you wanted to break your appointment. You kept it, didn't you?" He could sense her stern resistance to his questions.

"I went, though it was a waste of time. They're worse than pagan witch doctors, those men, with their machines and tests, as if that had anything to do with healing." She raised her voice. "Where is the machine that can cast out the Devil?"

"What does your doctor say?" asked the Preacher, becoming concerned and wanting to keep the two of them on the matter of her health.

"He can say nothing. He does tests and he learns nothing. That's because it isn't a doctorable thing that's wrong with me, it's them." She pointed at her nephews kneeling on the worn carpet. "They're the cause. It's their doing."

Now Preacher Colney was distinctly uneasy. It was one thing to assume that the Devil might be getting into the bodies of teenaged boys—he had seen that often enough—but it was another to accuse them of causing illness. Little as he wanted to admit it, he knew that spinsters of Kirsten Barenssen's disposition and age often endured mysterious and unfathomable maladies that neither medicine nor faith could treat. He looked down at the twin boys, white-blond and fresh-faced; he came to a decision. "Adam, Axel, leave me alone with your aunt for a little while. I'll call you for informal prayers in a bit."

The boys got to their feet at once. "Thanks, Preacher," said Adam for them both, and they trudged out of the room, toward the kitchen.

"Don't go far," Colney admonished them, and then turned to Kirsten, seeing the shock he had expected to find in her eyes. "Before we go much further with this, Sister, I think we'd better have a talk."

"About the boys?" she said. "I've told you all about them, but you're not listening to me. You think I'm making it up."

"No, not that," he said, watching to be certain that the kitchen door was closed.

"I know what's happening to me. I know that my faith is being tested and that my soul and my body are besieged by the forces of Hell. Won't you help me? How can I fight them if you won't help me?"

"Sister Barenssen, think; it might be a snare, a deception of the Devil to lure you to waste your faith and your strength where it is not necessary so that you will not be able to resist the true enemy." He decided he would have to phone her physician and find out what the tests had revealed.

"You told me that I could call upon you, when I am tested. You gave me your word that you would help if—"

"Yes," he said mollifyingly. "And I'm pleased that you did. But I think that we'd better discuss your health for a while first. It might have a bearing on . . . how we handle the trouble here." He wanted to sound as neutral as possible, as removed from judgment as he could be without appearing to question anything that she had revealed to him.

"We handle the trouble by casting out the Devil. You've said that; Scripture says that." She touched the Bible he held. "All my life I've clung to the Word, and trusted in it above all else. Now it is my only defense."

"Of course," said Preacher Colney in a soothing tone as he drew up a slat-backed wooden chair so that he could face her as they talked. "Just as we were promised."

"Yes," she said with inward passion. "Ever since God took their mother, I've watched over them. Now I see the Devil in them as my strength fails. I'm . . . I'm frightened," she admitted, as if she were confessing to breaking all the Commandments at once.

Will Colney nodded, knowing that his reservations had been well-founded. "I want us to pray together for your health and strength before we try anything more with the twins. First things first, Sister Barenssen."

"But the Devil—" There was terror in her eyes now, and her face was paler.

"The Devil will be with us forever; we can take time to pray together for strength," he insisted, hoping that the repetition of the words would finally get through to her.

"I tell you that there is great danger in those twins. I knew it from the first." She tightened her hands and then met his eyes. "Even before God took their mother, I knew that there was something wrong with them. It was their fault that she died."

"She died in an automobile accident, along with thirty-four other people." Will Colney knew that he would have to proceed carefully with this distraught woman.

"It was a judgment on them, on all of them. For their wickedness." She wiped tears from her cheeks with the backs of her hands, and Preacher Colney was reminded of how an animal uses its paws. "And caring for her children was God's judgment on me."

"Why should taking care of your brother's motherless twins be a judgment on you? You offered your care, Sister Barenssen, it wasn't foisted on you. You gave your charity from the goodness of your heart. Didn't you?" This last question was deliberately phrased as an afterthought, a gentle prompting to Kirsten to explain.

"I . . ." She was weeping in earnest now. "She was a frivolous woman. She painted her face and she wore the sort of clothes that . . ."

"I know she was not part of our faith, but that doesn't mean that she was wholly without virtue," said Preacher Colney with great care. "God has admonished us to hate the sin and love the sinner."

"I know." She sobbed deeply. "I was punished for my error. I was made to watch my brother's children become the tools of the Devil because I could not learn to accept his wife. I know that now, and I repent my sins, I do. I have no words to tell you how great my remorse is." She locked her hands together and clapped them between her knees. "I ought to have known. I ought to have thought about it, but it didn't seem that important when I first came to care for them. I didn't notice the signs that the Devil was working to destroy me and them."

"How . . . what signs?" Will Colney knew he was out of

his depth with Kirsten Barenssen. He was not experienced enough to deal with this woman, but his calling demanded that he try. He took his handkerchief from his pocket and offered it to her.

She ignored him. "I saw at the first that Hilda was filled with vanity, and I did all that I knew to show her how wrong she was. I prayed for her and with her, and I spoke often with my brother, begging him to use a firmer hand with her."

"And the other boy?" asked Colney, thinking of the eight-year-old Robert.

"There is no Devil in him. He is only the poor victim of his mother's folly and my lack of vigilance." She was rigid and trembling. "Oh, God, God, how could I have failed so?"

"God will forgive you, whatever you have done," Preacher Colney assured her. "And His forgiveness will cast out the Devil to save those two boys." It was the inspiration of the moment and he hoped it would be successful, at least for a short time.

"I wanted my brother to find a better wife, to set aside that lighthearted harlot he married. May God pardon me for my sins, I wanted her gone. I know that divorce is as bad a sin as murder, for it countermands a sacrament, but in my heart I wanted my brother to put her away, to leave her to her sinful ways and take a wife who would honor him and his children. I prayed for that. Jesus, Jesus! I prayed for a sinful thing. And for that she was killed, and it is on my head, and the Devil has come for me through her boys." She collapsed forward, her forehead on her knees, and she cried wildly.

Perplexed and worried, Will Colney reached out and patted her shoulder. "God will forgive you, Sister Barenssen," he said, noticing that she felt hot through her shapeless woolen dress.

Under his hand she shuddered as she wept.

Laurie Grey

On the stage of the junior high school auditorium, Laurie Grey went through her last rehearsal of her solo before the recital. Her ballet teacher stood in the wings, gesturing with her hands as Laurie went through the most difficult part: tour jete, capriole front, tour jete, capriole back, tour jete, pas de chat and ending with eight coupe turns in a circle.

"And bow," said Miss Cuante as Laurie came to the end.

Obediently Laurie bowed, her mulberry-colored leotard showing sweat stains under the arms and down the back as she came toward Miss Cuante. "How was it? I thought I took the last turns a little too wide."

"You did very well. If you do as well in the recital to-morrow I will be delighted," said Miss Cuante as she reached for a towel. "You and Melanie will be the hits of the show."

"Melanie's so good," sighed Laurie as she accepted the towel and pulled it around her shoulders. "I wish I could do those leaps she does."

"You may, in time. Remember, she is two years older and seven inches taller than you are—it gives her an advantage." She looked at the wall clock over the rear back-stage door. "Your father will be waiting."

Laurie nodded. "He's taking me to his new restaurant tonight," she said, proud of the news.

"Ah, yes, his new restaurant. How many does he have, now?" She had picked up her tape recorder and was putting it into her worn canvas tote that was already filled with dance togs, tapes, notebooks and a heavy sweater. "Don't get cold," she added, reaching out to steady herself as she stood up.

"You all right, Miss Cuante?" asked Laurie, surprised at how pale her teacher had suddenly become.

"Just . . . tired, I guess. A dizzy spell." She laughed nervously and made a quick, dismissing gesture, something out of *Giselle* or perhaps *Firebird*, both of which she had danced more than twenty years ago.

Laurie said nothing but she watched her teacher with her enormous blue eyes wide, making her delicate face more fey than it already was. She found her own tote and took a lightweight jacket out of it. "Dad's going to be at the corner, I guess."

"I'll go with you," said Miss Cuante with extra briskness to show that her unsteadiness was well and truly over. "I don't think you should wait by yourself, if you have to wait."

"Thanks," said Laurie, who more than once had attracted unwanted attention; since she had started to grow breasts the problem had got worse.

Miss Cuante took time to put the single-bulb nightlight at center stage, then switched off all the others before joining Laurie at the rear door. As she fumbled in her tote for the keys, she said, "I want you here for warm-up at eleven, can you do that?"

"I'm supposed to go to the hospital with Mom first. It's my sister. She's . . ."

"Not any better, your mother mentioned," said Miss Cuante as gently as she could. Student and teacher walked together down the deserted hallway toward the glass doors.

"They don't know what's wrong with her. She just gets sicker and weaker and weaker and sicker." Laurie's elfin face was suddenly sad. "I hate to see her like this. It's terrible. She's always been nice to me, even when I was real little."

Miss Cuante pressed the crash bar to open the door for them. Outside, the sky was overcast and there was enough wind off the Pacific to make the cardigan and jacket they wore necessary. The teacher shaded her eyes. "Is that your father's BMW?"

"Yeah, the grey one," said Laurie. "All our cars are grey. You know." She shrugged elegantly. "The license plates are just as bad. Dad wants everyone to know what he does. He says that it's advertising, but it's also ego."

"Your father has a lot to be proud of, Laurie. You can't blame him for showing off." Miss Cuante thought of her own twelve-year-old Accord parked on the other side of the auditorium and could not entirely conceal her sigh. "It's a fine car."

"I guess." Laurie was slightly embarrassed and was doing her thirteen-year-old best to hide it. "Well, thanks. I'll see you in the morning. I'll do the stretching exercises tonight, the way you told me to, and I'll make sure I'm on time." She started away, lifting her hand to wave.

"Tell your sister I hope she feels better," said Miss Cuante, wishing the same thing for herself. As she walked toward the small lot where her car waited, she did her best to be sensible, recalling that she was approaching menopause and it was time to get a proper checkup. Her divorce two years ago had left some strange scars that still gave her emotional jolts at unexpected times—this dizziness was probably more of the same but there was no reason not to take precautions. As she unlocked her car door, she resolved to make an appointment for a checkup as soon as the recital was behind her.

Jonathon Grey beamed at Laurie as she got into the car and said, "Well, how'd it go, sugar?" In the last three years he had started to put on weight and although far from fat, he was becoming portly.

"Pretty well," Laurie allowed. "I think I'm ready. I miss having the mirrors like we do in the studio—on stage I can't see if I do anything wrong." She adjusted her tote between her feet. "How's Marilee?"

"We'll find out when we get to the hospital." He cleared his throat, a nervous habit which all his family recognized as a signal that he was not comfortable with what he had to say. "They're asking us all to come in for tests, the whole family."

"What?" Laurie was shocked. "Why?"

"Michaelson won't say right out, but I gather he's worried that this might be some kind of toxic waste reaction. He's been checking with other hospitals—you know that search service they have out of Atlanta?—to see if there are other cases like Marilee's out there." He waved to the front of *Jonathon's Table* which was still his favorite of his six restaurants, though his new one, *Moonraker*, was apt to displace it if it lived up to its promise.

"You mean they still don't know what the matter is?" Laurie demanded, shocked. "How can they not know what's wrong after all this time?"

"They can't because . . ." He faltered. "Maybe it's something new. You know, like all the problems they've had in treating AIDS."

"That's a special case," said Laurie. "Everyone knows that."

"Not everyone," said her father. "Otherwise it wouldn't still be around, even with the vaccine." He signaled for a left turn. "Your mother's waiting for us in Chula Vista."

"Oh?" She said it carefully, wary in how she spoke of her mother since her parents' reconciliation eight months ago. Everyone had held their breaths waiting to find out if Catherine and Jonathon would be able to make a go of it after all the threats her first husband had made. With Gary back in jail and the family no longer under siege, Laurie hoped that the worst was over and that they were all a family once more.

"Don't worry, sugar, everything's fine. We've straightened it out. You don't have to—" He interrupted himself to honk at a flashy pickup that cut in front of his car, swearing as the pickup driver responded with a wave of his raised middle finger. "Didn't mean to—"

"It's okay, Daddy," she said, reverting to her old pattern with him.

"It's been a rough couple years, I know it has. When

Catherine's first husband got out of jail—" He stopped, not finding a way to go on without distressing Laurie and himself.

"I know," said Laurie. "Everyone was scared." She did not like to admit that she was as frightened as anyone. "And now Marilee's sick."

"They're working on making her well. And we'll do everything we can to help Michaelson, won't we?" He nodded toward the road ahead. "Your mother already promised to stay with Marilee at the hospital if that would make things better. Jared and Shelley and you and I can manage on our own if Catherine spends a few days at the hospital." He cleared his throat. "According to Michaelson, there might be a pattern in this disease. If more cases come in, then they'll have a better idea what they're up against."

"I see," said Laurie in a soft voice.

"And you know how important it is to stop something like this early." He said it, repeating what Ben Michaelson had told him. "I wish I knew what was wrong."

"So do I, Dad," Laurie sighed, adding as she stared, unseeing, out the windows, "Do you know what kind of tests we'll have? Did they tell you?"

"No, not yet. Probably blood stuff. You know what that's like." When he had asked the same thing of the doctors, the answers had been vague and ill-defined, as if the physicians themselves did not know what they were looking for.

"How long will it take; did they say?"

"No. Not too long, though." He was determined to be confident, and he said the last with emphasis. "Whatever's wrong with Marilee is serious enough that they're taking precautions, that's all."

"Oh." She reached down and fiddled with the handles of her tote. "Is Marilee still in isolation?"

"Yes. Just in case she has something catching. That's one of the reasons for them to test us." He reached over and put his hand on her hair. "Don't borrow trouble, hon. There's no reason to assume they're being anything but careful."

"What if we have something catching? Will we all have to be isolated?" She was thinking of her dancing and her plans for the next year. If she had to be isolated because of something her half-sister had, she would lose precious, irreplaceable time. Guilt grabbed her by the scruff of the neck, shaming her for putting her ambitions ahead of Marilee's health, but the thought lingered and would not be denied.

"What's wrong, sugar?" asked her father when Laurie had been frowning in silence for the better part of a mile.

"Nothing, really. Worries."

"We all have 'em," Jonathon said quietly. "It's part of living."

"Yeah." She stared ahead, trying to find a way to make her own conflicting emotions more palatable. She never thought of herself as heartless, but perhaps she was, if she could be more apprehensive about a few lost months than that Marilee might have a fatal disease. She did her best to make her mind a blank and to concentrate on nothing but the people on the sidewalk. After a short while, she said, "There's Mom."

Jonathon signaled and pulled toward the curb. "You've got sharp eyes, Laurie," he said as he braked to a stop.

"Hi," said Catherine, opening the back door and pressing Laurie on the shoulder. "Don't mind me riding back here. I want to stretch out and it's easier in the back. You stay where you are, Laurie." As she pulled the door shut, she said, "I can't tell you how much trouble Dave is giving me about this second agency. He's convinced that we need three more people for the office, minimum, and there's no way we can afford them."

"Why all those people?" asked Jonathon, leaning back to exchange a twisted kiss with his wife.

"Because Dave can't stand the thought of having a small second office, that's why. He doesn't want to admit that all we need is three people and the computer and everything's fixed." She kicked off her shoes and lifted her legs onto the seat. "I don't know how to convince him."

"Far Venture Travel isn't exactly the biggest agency in the world," said Jonathon. "You don't need a huge staff, do you?"

"I don't think so," said Catherine. "Dave's trouble is he wants to be the boss, which means he wants someone to boss around, preferably a lot of someones. He hasn't said so yet, but I think he imagines himself as a travel mogul, booking two hundred tours a year for groups of seventy and eighty. Ever since we handled that cruise for that Del Mar company, Dave's got his eye on big package deals. He forgets that the bookings I handle—which he thinks are a waste of time—bring in more than sixty-five percent of our profit. Handling a European vacation for a family of three doesn't appeal to him." She put her hand to her well-cut greying hair. "Never mind that. I'm blowing off steam. I probably should have yelled at Dave, but that never gets me anywhere. How's Marilee? Have you talked to Ben yet today?"

"He still wants us to take those tests." Jonathon glanced at Laurie as if to reassure himself that it was correct to discuss this in front of his daughter.

"Well, if he thinks it's necessary, it probably is. We want Marilee to—"

"Get over the thing," Jonathon finished for her. He reached out and gave Laurie a pat on her arm. "One casualty in the family is enough, isn't it?"

"Um-hum," said Laurie, starting to feel scared again.

_____ Harold Porter _____

Finally the snow got so bad that Frank Porter pulled his camper off the road in the town of Mullan, a few miles over the Idaho border. He wrestled himself into his heavy shearling coat and then turned to his son. "You keep an eye out for company. I'm going to walk to that service station and find out if there's a motel open this time of night."

"Sure," said Harold, his voice cracking. "I'll do it."

"Good for you, son," Frank declared, taking the time to cuff the boy lightly on the jaw. "You're a good kid." Then he was gone into the blur of flakes swarming out of the night sky.

Harold pulled his knees up and sat huddled against the seat, trying to decide what was the best thing for him to do. His father rarely left him alone, and if he knew more about where they were, he might take a chance to find a phone and try to reach his mother. In the four years since his father had abducted him from his mother's home in Golden, Colorado, he had been able to call her nine times, so she would know he was still all right. Twice he had tried to get away and return to his mother, but both times his father had found him and beaten him so badly that now he was afraid to make the attempt again. He felt in his pocket for coins, in case he found a phone, and realized he had less than two dollars to his name: he would have to call collect. Little as he admitted it, he missed his mother, and the life they had had before his father returned. Alexa had found them a place on the outskirts of Golden where she raised ponies, specializing in a handsome Welsh Cob/Caspian cross which was starting to earn her a reputation and a growing income. Harold had liked tending to the ponies and being with his mother Alexa, who lavished affection on him as if to make up for the years they had followed Frank on the rodeo circuit. Now Harold was once again on that circuit, and Frank, aging unpredictably, had become increasingly suspicious and demanding of his son.

"You drifting?" Frank asked as he yanked open the door and pointed an accusing finger at his boy.

"A little. It's cold."

Frank grunted. "There's a motel about a mile up the road. They've got a room for us, and we can get sandwiches there." He wedged himself behind the wheel and twisted the key in the ignition. "Old fart better start," he muttered.

The engine turned over with a protesting roar, and Harold blinked to conceal his relief. "We going to stay here a day or two?"

"Have to, if the snow doesn't stop. Told me at the service station that most places around here are already snowed in. Shit, if I can't get going, I'll lose that job in Twin Falls. I said I'd be there next Tuesday." He tromped on the accelerator and the camper lurched onto the road, fish-tailing on the icy surface.

"Dad!" Harold said faintly, trying not to rouse his father's anger. Nothing made Frank Porter more upset than the fear that someone was criticizing his driving. Harold clung to the seatbelt and ground his teeth to keep from yelling.

"I can handle it," Frank growled as he fought with the wheel. "I can handle a lot worse'n this." He continued his battle for most of a minute until the camper steadied and began real progress down the road toward the motel.

"Hey, Dad, how long are you going to stay in Twin Falls?" It was a forlorn question; Frank had never remained in any one place as long as he intended to; someone would insult him, or he would get into a fight, or there would be accusations and Frank would take his boy and they would once again be on the road.

"Through May, in any case. I told Bowan that I'd help out with getting his horses in off the range and broke, if he'll guarantee my wages and a place to live for us both. He said there's two house trailers on his place and we can have our pick of 'em. Things are going our way, kid, if we can get there." This last was a dark reminder of Frank's belief that he had been the chosen target of a capricious and vengeful fate.

"We'll get there. You can phone from the motel, can't you, so he'll know where you are?" He made this suggestion carefully, so that it would not appear that he was in any way prodding his father to do anything. Frank hated any kind of manipulation unless he was doing it.

"I might," he allowed when he had thought about it. "Ah. There's the motel. Hang on, Harold." He swung the camper abruptly and it slithered across the road, sliding into the parking lot of the Riverbend Motel. "Wait here while I get us checked in. I'll be quick about it."

"Great." He watched his father stamp into the light over the office and pound on the door. For an instant he thought he might open the door and slip away, making his way toward the highway where he could hitch a ride back to Golden and his mother. But he had sense enough to know that the chances were he would freeze or his father would find him and take out after him with his fists again. Harold shuddered, and told himself that it was from cold.

"Okay," said Frank as soon as he came back. "We got Unit Number Eleven. Here's the key. I want you to get the duffles out and bring them in. We can get the rest in the morning. I'll be back in a little while. Don't let nobody in while I'm gone, you understand?"

"Yes, Dad," said Harold, knowing that his father would be going in search of drink, since he had run out of the cheap alcoholic liquid that called itself scotch earlier in the day. "Anything you say."

"You're a good boy, Harold," said Frank as he closed the door.

As soon as he had finished carrying the duffles into the motel room, Harold went back to the office and asked the manager if there was a pay phone around. "I . . . got some people to call, with the roads being closed."

"Sure, kid," said the manager. "There's one down the hall. Takes quarters only." He turned and started back to his sitting room behind the reception desk and then said, "You want a sandwich? Your father said you hadn't had supper yet."

"That would be nice," Harold said uncertainly. "But I don't have any money—he does."

"I'll put it on the bill," offered the manager, and once

again pointed down the hall. "Go ahead and make your calls. I'll have a couple sandwiches ready when you're through."

"Thanks," said Harold, perplexed by the kindness the manager was showing him. He quickly put that out of his mind as he went to the phone and punched in the familiar number and the code to make it collect. He felt a twinge of guilt at making his mother pay to hear from him, but it passed as he listened to the beeps and clicks.

"Who shall I say is calling?" asked the electronic voice of the computerized operator.

"Harold. Harold Porter." He felt his throat go dry as he waited, listening to the rings and counting them.

Alexa picked up her receiver on the ninth ring. "Hello?"

At the sound of his mother's voice, Harold had to swallow hard to keep from crying. Sternly he admonished himself to be more grown-up, but as Alexa took the call, he felt tears well in his eyes.

"Harold?" she pleaded. "Is that you? Really?"

"Hi, Mom," he said inanely. "Yeah. How are you?"

"I'm doing fine. What about you? Where are you? Are you all right? Oh, God, I've been so worried about you."

He knew that she was at the edge of her control and he tried to reassure her. "I'm doing okay. I miss you."

"Oh, baby, I miss you so much."

She was crying now; he could hear the sound of it in her words and her silences. "I miss you, too."

"Where are you?" she made herself ask.

"Somewhere in Idaho. It's snowing. We were in Montana last week, and then something happened and . . ." He choked.

"You don't have to tell me; I know." In her tears there was anger now. "He hasn't hurt you again, has he?"

"No, Mom, not really," he answered evasively. "Look, he said something about going to a Bowan place near Twin Falls. I don't know if there's anything you can do, but that's what he said, and maybe . . ."

"I'll try. I'll call the State Police again and see if they're willing to do anything. If he hadn't taken you out of Colorado, it would be a lot easier. It always takes time when there's another state involved." Determination drove the sound of weeping from her speech. "I'm going to bring you home, Harold. You'll see."

"I hope so, Mom." He tried to laugh and failed. "I keep hoping that . . . it's almost Christmas, you know? I wish I was spending it with you."

2"Me, too," Alexa said so softly that Harold barely heard her.

"Anyway, Mom, I got to go. I don't want to run up your bill and I don't want to . . ." He did not have to finish; they both knew what Frank would do if he even suspected that his son had called Alexa.

"You take care, Harold. I love you. I love you."

"I love you, too, Mom." Before he said anything more, he hung up.

There were sandwiches waiting, and the manager turned off his television so he could talk with Harold while the boy ate the two chicken sandwiches that the manager had made.

"This is real kindly of you," Harold said indistinctly through a full mouth.

"You looked half starved and miserable as a drowned puppy," said the manager, giving him a second glass of milk.

"Not real common, your hospitality," said Harold, this time with several questions implied in his tone of voice.

The man shook his head. "I'm waiting for my two kids to get back from rehearsal for their high school Christmas program. I can worry on my own, or I can worry with company. Thing is, I hope that if my kids ever showed up looking the way you did that someone would give them a sandwich or two." He indicated the television. "There's cable in the room sets, but no pay stations. I can get you a listing of what's on, if you want it."

"Thanks," said Harold, relaxing a bit.

"Think nothing of it. My name's Tucker, by the way. Norton Tucker." He held out his hand.

Harold took it. "I'm Harold Porter," he said feeling very grown-up for a change.

"Stick around, if you like, and meet my kids. They're a little older than you are, but you don't mind that, do you?" Tucker got up and took the nearly empty plate from Harold.

"I better get to the room. My Dad'll be back soon, and he wants me in the room." Saying the words made him uneasy.

"Whatever's right," said Tucker. "The kids'll be around tomorrow, if you change your mind. Maybe if I say something to your Dad, he might—"

Harold interrupted him. "No. Please. Don't say anything. He . . . he doesn't like me talking to strangers."

Tucker nodded. "All right." He watched as Harold started toward the door. "You let me know if you need anything."

"Sure. Thanks." He started toward the door, then turned back. "Don't say anything about the phone call, will you? Dad doesn't like me making calls."

If Tucker thought there was anything out of the ordinary in this request he did not reveal it. "You got it," he said with a wave that was almost a salute.

Harold made his way back to Unit 11, and took up his vigil.

Mason Ross

"We're so sorry about Kevin," said Joan Ellingham. "I wish there were something I could say—"

Susan nodded and tried not to cry again. "Thank you," she murmured as she reached out to take Harper's arm.

"Both of you," their neighbor Barry McPhee said as he held out his hands to them. "Caroline and I are going to miss him so much."

Harper said a few words as he tightened his hold around Susan's shoulder. He glanced at his other two children, so quiet in their dark mourning clothes, both of them grieving and awkward at their brother's funeral.

"Don't worry about the rest of the . . . the holidays," Harper's department head told him as he took his hand. "I'll put the grad students on your papers, so that you won't have to bother with them. I'm really . . . you know."

"Thanks, Phil," said Harper.

"You, too, Susan," Phillip Sanders said to her. "It's a real shock, and what a time for it to happen."

Susan had to stop herself from getting angry with Phil, to keep from screaming at him that there was no time that was good for a teenager to die. That it was Christmas made it no worse than it would have been at any other time of year. She nodded, not trusting herself to do anything more.

"I'll call you later, Phil," said Harper.

The line seemed endless, and by the time everyone who attended the memorial service had left the chapel, Susan was afraid she would not be able to walk as far as the car. She reached out for her two remaining sons, touching them blindly and with ill-concealed desperation. "We're going home."

"Okay, Mom," said Mason, reaching out to take her hand. Despite his youth, he was curiously mature and responsible, as if he had been born thirty years old and was growing ancient before he reached high school.

"You did a fine job, Susan," said Harper, his face closed and remote, as if he were lost in study rather than grieving for the loss of his child.

"How does anyone do a fine job with something like this?" she asked, but there was no heat in the words, only listlessness.

"We do the best we can," Harper said, starting down the steps of the chapel.

Seattle was swathed in cold; snow had fallen the day before and now there was a frigid mist that hung over the harbor and lakes and hid most of the city. The chapel, which was only two blocks from the University of Washington campus, seemed suspended in clouds; the massive buildings of the university, most of them perched on the hill, were all but invisible.

"I wish the doctors could tell us more," said Grant, who at sixteen was clearly the best-looking of the Ross boys. He had spent most of the fall in California, at a ranch near Santa Rosa in a program for drug abuse. His uncle, Susan's brother, had served as his guardian. Only Kevin's death had brought him back to Seattle.

"I wish they could, too, son," said Harper as he led them toward their Trooper III. "Hurry up; it's too cold to stay outside long."

"But what was it?" Grant asked, still bewildered and beginning to be angry. "Why don't they know yet?"

"Sometimes they . . . don't have enough to go on," said Harper in a distant way as he fumbled for his keys in his coat pocket. His heavy gloves made his fingers awkward.

"Isn't what they do like solving crimes?" Mason asked. "I mean, they're similar, aren't they?" It was a deliberate ploy; Harper Ross was a professor of criminology. As he got into the back seat, Mason added another thought to his inquiry. "Couldn't you help them out, Dad? You've got the experience to help them."

"They think it had something to do with toxic wastes," Susan said, so tired that she might as well have been up for three days without sleep.

"And you, Dad?" Mason prompted.

"It's possible," said Harper as he waited for the engine to warm up before putting the four-wheel-drive Trooper III in gear. "It fits with what we do know about it."

"It could be . . . anything," said Susan. "He died. That's the one thing we're all sure of." She put her hand to her eyes so that she would not have to explain her tears.

"But if it's something we can learn about," Mason

began, and saw that Grant was staring at him in unconcealed anger.

"It won't change anything," Grant said.

"It might mean that someone else won't die," Mason responded, meeting his brother's hostile stare. "That wouldn't bring Kevin back, but it could make a difference."

"Mason, for God's sake," said his mother.

"He's right," Harper agreed unexpectedly.

"Not you, too." Susan smeared her tears over her face, her mascara leaving wide, dark tracks.

"I don't think I could sit by and watch this happen to another family," said Harper as he concentrated on holding the car on the road. "It would be too much, if there was something I could do to prevent it."

"There's nothing anyone could have done," said Susan. "If there were, they would have. They ran out of ideas, you heard them say so."

"Susan," Harper warned sympathetically. "Think. Letting others die won't change Kevin's death, it will only make it worse; it would put other families through the same thing we're going through. Do you want that, Susan? Wouldn't you do something about it if you could?"

"Are you trying to convince yourself?" Susan asked softly. "Or do you want to make a gesture?"

"It's not a gesture, it's . . . the only contribution I can think of to give." Harper dared not take his eyes off the road to look at her, but the impulse was there in the angle of his head and the way he held the steering wheel.

"Yeah," said Mason, leaning forward in his seat. "I'd help, if I could. I don't know what I could do, but if there was anything . . . I owe it to Kevin, in a way." He fingered his dark tie. "If there are more cases of this stuff . . ."

"Shut up," Grant told him sharply. "Just shut up."

They drove in silence, each one alone in pain.

"I told Phil we wouldn't be there New Year's," Harper said to Susan as they neared the freeway entrance.

"He didn't think we would be, did he?" she asked, sufficiently shocked to respond with less lethargy than she had shown so far that day.

"No, but I wanted him to know. He means well, and it saves making a phone call later." He signaled to change lanes, maneuvering around a stalled van.

"All right." She put her hand to her eyes once more.

On the freeway the traffic moved at less than twenty miles an hour, progress toward the Bellevue exit slowed by the mist and the cold. The Rosses were quiet as the Trooper III moved along; only when they had reached the Medina exit did Susan speak again, her voice still thick with tears. "If you decide to do anything, to get involved —if there's anything to get involved with—then you do it on your own conscience. I've had all I can take. You do it on your own time, Harper."

He nodded slowly as he moved into the right-hand lane. "All right. If you want it that way, I'll do as you ask."

"Dad's being noble again," Grant said. "Always looking for something to help out."

"Stop it!" Mason yelled.

"Not another word, young man!" Susan commanded, turning in her seat to glare at Grant. "You get that chip off your shoulder and the smirk off your face and then maybe you can question what your father does where I can hear you, but not before." She was crying, but no longer in the helpless, depressed way she had since Kevin died. "I don't want to hear anything more out of either of you, is that understood?"

"Yes, Mom," said Mason, neither sullen nor chastened. "Shit."

"And none of that," Harper warned as they neared the Bellevue turn-off. "It's bad enough that we lost Kevin; I won't stand by and watch the family self-destruct." Since Harper was generally a soft-spoken man whose quiet, professorial manner gave away his occupation before he mentioned it, any outburst was regarded as important and significant, a thing to be respected. "Is that clear?"

"Yes, Dad," said Mason in the same accepting tone he had used with his mother.

This time Grant remained silent, though his face was flushed and his eyes sizzled.

They had almost reached Lake Washington when traffic came to a complete stop.

"What do you suppose it is?" Susan asked.

"Probably an accident, the weather the way it is." Harper sighed and studied the dials. "I wish I knew these methane engines better than I do. In the old Buick I would have known in a second, the way it sounded, if I ought to turn it off or not. But this thing . . ."

"You were the one who wanted to get it," Susan reminded him.

"I'm glad we did," he insisted, keeping his voice level and steady. "It was the only sensible thing to do; you agreed. Waiting in line for gas is—"

"Senseless," she finished for him. "I know, and wasteful and profligate. Methane engines are the wave of the future. As long as matter decays we have no lack of methane. Et cetera, et cetera," she recited, sounding like one of the more righteous of the advertisements for the new methane engines.

"It's true. I'm simply not used to it yet," Harper said in his most reasonable tone. "In weather like this . . ."

"It's okay, Dad. There's that special light on the thermometer, remember?" He pointed to the various dials, relieved to have something to talk about that was not connected with Kevin's death.

"Which one?" Harper asked, appearing more confused than he was.

"There. If it turns yellow, then you have to . . . you have to engage the supplemental coolant. I think that's how it goes. And if it turns red, then pull off the road and idle for two minutes, engage the supplemental coolant and then turn the engine off." He said the last with pride, amazed at himself for remembering what the mechanic had told them when they bought the car the year before.

"No yellow, no red." Harper leaned back in the driver's seat and adjusted the angle of the lower back. "So long as we're going to sit for a while, we might as well—"

He was interrupted by whooping sirens as two ambulances and a highway-rescue firetruck sped by on the shoulder of the road.

"Fuck a duck!" marveled Grant, watching the emergency vehicles fade into the mists.

"Oh, stop it," Susan said, more irritated than angry now.

"Must be pretty bad to bring all that sh . . . stuff out," said Grant. "Wonder where the cops are?"

"They're probably the ones who radioed for the ambulances and the firetruck," said Harper, lapsing into the same manner he adopted when lecturing in class. "It's the most sensible explanation, in any case."

"Someone with a CB might have done it," suggested Mason.

"Yes, that's true, but then the cops would have come along with the others." He had both a CB and police monitor in his car, and for a moment toyed with the idea of turning them on and listening in. Then he realized that more disasters could be more than any one of them was prepared to handle that day. He studied the instrument panel and let himself get lost in the information they offered.

"How long do you think we'll have to sit here?" Susan asked when almost five minutes had gone by.

"I don't know."

"You could turn on the radios and find out what's happened," she said sharply.

"I don't want to heat up the engine or put too much strain on the battery. We could be here quite a while and if we are, we'll have to use the supplemental interior heater; that thing eats up battery power like a hog eating hops." Harper hoped that his excuses were sufficient for Susan; he had no intention of turning on the radios.

She sighed. "All right. Why not? We might as well be stranded here as anywhere."

In the back, Grant started to fiddle with the zipper on his jacket, his face blank, his eyes drifting into the hypnotic stare that had been part of him for the last four years. He began to hum, first very softly and aimlessly, then slowly getting louder, until he was forcefully grunting out the same four notes in endless repetition.

"I wish you'd stop," said Mason, not expecting to get a response.

"Leave him alone, Mason," said Harper. "It's been a hard day for all of us." He paused. "I wish I could call Linda. I don't want her to think that we're not coming."

"Use the CB," said Susan, unconcerned.

"She probably knows about the accident. Restaurant people usually do," said Mason, doing his best to be neutral.

"If this lasts too much longer, I will call," said Harper, staring out into the mist. "It's terrible."

"They say it isn't going to clear up for a couple more days. Then we'll have rain," said Mason, repeating what they had all heard on the news that morning.

"I guess the McPhees are stuck in this, too," Harper said, in order to say something.

"They were going to the Ellinghams for a drink," Susan corrected him. "But who knows? it might go on long enough for them to sit here the way we're doing."

"They'll have it on the news. The cops will keep the traffic diverted," said Harper with more faith than certainty.

The air in the car was getting cooler, but no one wanted to mention it yet. Only Grant, locked away in his relentless mind, accommodated it to the extent that he stopped unzipping his jacket and instead ran his thumbnail down the interlocking bits of metal.

One of the ambulances hurried back the way it had come, all lights on and the siren on screech. A few of the other cars honked their horns at it, whether in derision or support was a matter of conjecture.

"When we get home, I'm going to call Jarvis and tell

him I'd like to help if they'll let me, if there's anything I can do." Harper's voice was distant, the words coming slowly. "I don't want to worry you or upset you, Susan, but I have to do it."

"You do what you have to do," said Susan in a constricted tone of voice. "I don't want to know about it."

Harper sighed, and let himself be distracted by the sudden return of the second ambulance, this time with a police escort. "I can't believe that Christmas was day before yesterday."

"Some Christmases aren't real Christmasy," said Mason, hoping he would not cry. He had wept for a week before Kevin died, so wasted and pale, with machines and tubes turning him into something as alien as a being from another planet. He had wept the night it had finally ended. Now he did not want to cry anymore.

"Next year we'll do something better," said Harper, pain and determination in his words. "Let's go to Hawaii, or to Florida, somewhere it's warm and Christmas looks like a midsummer fair."

"That's next year," said Susan, but with less criticism than before.

"We'll do something that won't remind us. That will be a start. Lots of people have holidays that have bad things associated with them," Harper said with deliberate simplicity. "That doesn't mean that the holidays were bad, or have to stay bad, but that something bad happened on one." He hesitated. "Remember that Phil's brother was killed in that plane crash the day before Thanksgiving five years ago. Phil still has Thanksgiving and . . ."

When no one said anything more, Susan regarded Grant with curiosity and worry. "Can you leave the zipper alone?" she asked, though she got no response and expected none.

PART II

January—February, 1996

Once in a while San Diego was visited by a major storm, a grey, vicious beating from wind and water that drove everyone indoors and made the streets unsafe, that drove the camp-dwelling Latin American detainees into the crowded Immigration Service Holding Station where frustration and despair often led to violence.

"How many of them are sick?" asked Sylvia, making sure that her California Board of Public Health and Environmental Services badge was clearly visible on her lapel.

"Old sick or new sick?" asked Clifford Gross, who had been working for the Immigration Service for thirty years, his medical oath long since abrogated in favor of bureaucratic survival.

"I mean sick, period. Public health sick," Sylvia declared, her patience already running thin.

"Well, you can figure that eighty percent of them are undernourished in some way, that seventy percent have some kind of parasites on them, that another seventy percent have some other chronic health problem, such as low-level allergies. Not long ago we ended up with a genuine, full-blown case of rabies. Tell me what you're looking for and we'll see if we've got any."

"I've been looking over your reports," Sylvia said, deliberately taking an indirect approach. "I've noticed that you have had an increase in toxic waste syndrome, at least that is what the printouts indicate. Obviously a machine can't tell us anything more than the information we give it, but if there is a contamination site we know nothing about, we must take action at once to protect—"

"I haven't noticed that there's been any real increase in

toxic waste reactions," said Gross. "Not that I've done much asking. Maybe there's more sickness around, Doctor."

"Why not?" Sylvia asked, doing her best to keep from challenging the man. "Why haven't you checked for toxic—"

"Because there isn't much of it around. Tetanus, TB, typhoid, you name it. Parasite infestations. Sure, those we find every day. It's because the country's so damned poor and most of the people are not educated, and those who are aren't doing much to help those who aren't. It doesn't matter whether we're talking about Mexico or Central America or South America, the problems are still pretty much the same." He opened his hands to show how futile it was. "Most of them have been slightly sick for so long that they think they're okay. They don't know what it means to be healthy, to have a body that really works properly. It's nothing we can change, not in a detention center like this one. Besides, what good would it do? Most of them are illegals, not refugees, and they're simply going home to more of the same."

Sylvia tapped the file of printouts she had on the edge of Gross' desk. "Make a few allowances, Doctor Gross. If you find anything that you suspect might be related to toxic wastes, I would appreciate it if you would flag it and send it directly to me. At once. Mark it urgent."

"It's not going to make a difference," warned Gross.

"It certainly won't if you aren't willing to make the effort." She made no apology for the pointedness of the remark.

"But a couple of aliens with suspect symptoms, come on, Doctor . . . uh . . ."

"Kostermeyer," she supplied.

"Yeah," he said. "You're asking a lot. Think about what the trouble is here, what we're up against." He waved in the direction of the door. "I've got over fifty more patients to see and that means I won't get out of here until seven-thirty at the earliest, assuming that nothing is seriously wrong with any of them and that no more fights break out." He folded his arms. "They said in Ninety-one that this new border policy would make things better, but you couldn't prove it by me."

"I realize you have difficulties here," said Sylvia with a patience she did not feel. "And I know that I'm asking a lot, but since December tenth, we have had seven deaths in the greater San Diego area from a condition that appears to be related to toxic contamination. There is debilitation, enervation, anemia, lethargy, a . . . an alteration of blood chemistry, followed by pulmonary distress and vascular collapse. We now have two more cases we're checking for the . . . blood condition." She was not anxious to go into the baffling and complex breakdown of connective tissue that was characteristic of the course of the syndrome.

"What if it's just another disease, a new version of, oh, say something like leukemia." Gross made an indulgent grimace. "Surely you've considered that, Doctor Kosterm—"

"It has some leukemia similarities," she allowed. "And it has others, like pernicious anemia and amoebic dysentery, for obvious examples. And death doesn't come from any specific agency of the condition, but from subsidiary breakdowns." She held out the printout file once more. "You might think that there are too few cases to worry about, but the thing that makes this so . . . upsetting is that so far we have yet to diagnose a patient with this condition and have them live. That's why we're looking for new cases, possibly early cases, and why we want to find out what toxic wastes are involved."

"But suppose it's not that?" Gross suggested. "Who says that it has to be toxic wastes, anyway?"

"What else fits the ticket so well?" she asked. "The only thing we haven't found so far—thank God—are incidents in infants and young children. Four of the victims so far have been teenagers."

"Have you thought about drugs? Especially the designer drugs?" He asked this with a faint, deprecatory smile, since the pervasive drug problem seemed to him far more obvious than toxic wastes.

"No trace of them in the blood."

"How can you know, if the blood chemistry changes?" Gross pursued. "If you haven't any gauge other than that?"

Sylvia stared at Gross before she answered. "It's what we have to go on, and right now. . . . Look, one of the patients did test positive for drugs, but that doesn't mean that drugs are the only explanation. We would have found traces in the others. They aren't that hard to identify."

"Unless one of the designer drugs is at fault. Have you considered that?" Gross rocked back on his heels.

"It's being checked out, but so far there's no indication that they're a factor." She sighed. "Will you help me out? I don't want to have more deaths if I can help it."

"Everyone dies," said Gross, more cynically than philosophically.

"Agreed, but—"

"Sure, why not? If I see anything suspicious, or if there are indications of toxic contamination of some kind I'll let you know. How's that?" He looked at the door. "And I have to get back to work."

"Of course. Thank you for giving me so much of your time," Sylvia said with automatic courtesy.

"Pleasure," said Gross, shaking her hand.

As she drove back through the rain, cursing the flooded streets and trying to keep from skidding in turns, Sylvia fought down her irrational desire to go back to the Immigration Station and remonstrate with Gross—his inadequacy as a physician, his conduct as a person, his total lack of manners—though she knew it would be useless. Instead she went over the cases of the puzzling condition she was investigating. Dead so far: Marilee Grey, aged sixteen; Jeanine Hatley, aged fourteen; Benton Smith, aged thirty-one; Paul Clancy, aged fourteen; Samuel Lincoln, aged fifteen; Elaine Bradley, aged twenty-seven; and Dwight Tracy, aged sixty-two. Ill so far: Isabeau Cuante, aged (about) forty-six or -seven; Lorraine Gomez, aged sixteen.

It was so disheartening that Sylvia almost missed her turn to the Public Health and Environmental Services building on Escondido, in the new complex built after the '93 quake.

"How'd it go?" asked her superior, Doctor Michael Wren, as Sylvia pulled off her coat and shook it.

"Don't ask." She ran her hand through her hair and shook out the drops from it.

"Problems?" Mike sat down, pulling up one of the two chairs so that he could face her over the corner of her desk.

"That man ought to be taken out and . . . and . . ."—she gave an unexpected smile—"and subjected to a lecture on manners from my Great-Aunt Lucy!"

Mike grinned, his large, white teeth appearing to be even larger against the blackness of his skin. "Sounds like a fate I wouldn't wish on anyone."

"Well, I sure as hell wouldn't," said Sylvia, settling down a bit. "I told him what we were looking for. That was after Rosenblum had his secretary ask me to leave a copy of the printouts so that he could look at them when he had time."

"Sounds like you've had a great afternoon," said Mike. "I don't blame you for being testy."

"Thanks. Oh, I think Steinmetz might get a fire lit under him if you'd give him a call and warn him that Environmental Services might have a mess on their hands. You know how good he is at covering his ass." She looked at the primrose message memos stacked in the center of her desk. "Three from hospitals?"

"It looks like we've got another two cases at least. All in the same general area with the exception of one man who works at a restaurant across from Coronado, a place called *The Galley*." He shook his head slowly. "I've put in a call to L.A. and another to Sacramento. One more case and we have to alert Environmental Diseases in Atlanta." This time he spoke with real concern. "God, I hope it doesn't come to that."

"Me, too," Sylvia admitted. "Timmons will have a fit."

"Humanity has always been his long suit," Mike said sarcastically.

Sylvia put the stack aside. "I'll take care of them in a bit. By the way, take care driving home. It's a mess out there and once the rush hour starts, it's going to snarl all the way to Mexico."

"Great." She glanced at her wall map, at the day-glo green labels indicating addresses of those with the new syndrome. "Most of them are within a two-mile radius still; that's something."

"And with the exception of the guy at the restaurant, they all work in the same general area, or go to school there." Mike stood up and went to the map. "Now, we have found toxic sites here"—he indicated an area ten miles north of the city—"and here"—this time his finger was east of San Diego near Spring Valley—"but nothing where these guys live."

"So that's no help, unless they all go out there for picnics." She stared at the map as if it was deliberately withholding information. "We're overlooking something. There's got to be a commonality somewhere."

"Well, Jeanine Hatley took ballet from Isabeau Cuante," said Mike.

"And the rest? Did they take ballet?" As soon as she spoke, she was sorry. "That was a bitchy thing to say. I beg your pardon."

"What would Great-Aunt Lucy think?" said Mike, rolling his eyes heavenward in simulated horror. "I don't blame you for snapping. It's shitty to be stymied this way."

"Agreed." She pursed her lips. "Do we have histories on the families of the victims? Have they been tested for signs of the syndrome?"

"A little hard to do when we're not sure what we're looking for," Mike reminded her gently.

"Well, have they been checked, period, just in case? Look for hangnails and dandruff if nothing else turns up." She folded her arms. "Complete histories, and neighborhood reviews, to find out if anyone else has had something like this that we might not have seen yet, and then . . . oh, hell." To her chagrin she had to stop because her mouth was quivering and her eyes were moist.

"Hey, Sylvia," Mike said, putting his hand on her arm. "We'll find out what it is and we'll stop it, right?"

"Sure," she said miserably. "Next week at the latest."

"That's my pal," Mike said, patting her arm. "Remember that and it'll be easier to get the job done." He touched the map, covering the area where the cases were. "At least it's contained, whatever it is."

"So far," she reminded him. "I guess since we've had teenaged victims we'd better contact the schools as well. I hate causing panic like that."

"I'm not too crazy about it myself. But you're right. It's probably necessary."

"If Timmons decides that we're being alarmist," Sylvia wondered aloud, "do you think he'll interfere?"

"Only if the sun rises," said Mike in a resigned tone. "I'm going to get back to my office, and I'll stop by before I head for home."

"Okay," she said, already reaching for the phone memos, her mind on the next stage of her investigation.

"If you need a hand . . ."

"Thanks," she said, waving vaguely as she punched in the number on the first memo.

_____ *Elihu Dover* _____

"I wish I knew what to tell you." Dover shoved his hands more deeply into the pockets of his tweed jacket. "Your sister is in failing health, and I don't know yet what the cause is."

Sven Barenssen swallowed hard. "Will she have to go to the hospital? We don't have insurance, you know."

Dover frowned ponderously. "I'm aware that hospitalization would be a hardship. There are funds for cases like yours, particularly where there is some question as to the cause." He added the last as delicately as he could, trying to diminish the worry Kirsten Barenssen's brother was feeling. "And her church has some money available for... special cases. With all she's done for them, I'm certain that if you speak to Will Colney, he would be more than willing to—"

"No. Kirsten wouldn't accept that." He stared up at the ceiling. "She's not one to take charity. Not even now."

"Well, you might have to make some arrangements, Mister Barenssen. I'm afraid that she may need quite a lot of care, and under the circumstances—"

"Under the circumstances, I can't afford it," Sven said flatly. "I know that. We both do." He took a deep breath. "How serious is it? I mean, is she going to get well?"

"I hope so," Dover hedged. "But since her condition is unfamiliar, I have no way of telling what might happen or what the... outcome might be. I suppose I ought to say that she is seriously ill now. Her blood..."—he lowered his head and tried to figure out how much he could tell Barenssen that he would understand—"is damaged in some way. She is anemic and there is a general breakdown of her bodily tissues. For some reason, she is having trouble keeping everything... connected." He laced his fingers together in futile illustration. Little as he wanted to admit it to Kirsten's brother, Dover knew he was out of his depth, and it troubled him.

"But why?"

The question was enormous, Elihu Dover knew, but he gave the simplest answer he could. "I wish I knew, Mister Barenssen."

"What if we took her home? Could we arrange for care? Isn't there someone who could come in and take care of her? Why does she have to go to the hospital? Is there a way you could arrange for a . . . nurse?" He looked at the doctor with desperate hope in his eyes.

"She needs more than that, Mister Barenssen," said Dover heavily, wishing now that he had had this conversation at the hospital rather than in his own offices: at the hospital there would be any number of excuses to end this uncomfortable discussion—here he was stuck with Sven Barenssen for at least another ten minutes. "You're fortunate that she's the only one in your family who has shown symptoms of this condition."

"What?" Sven asked, more dazed than before.

"The Standard Public School Blood Screen didn't turn up anything in your sons, and that's good news." He watched Sven, trying to see how much if any of what he was saying was getting through to the man.

"They're in a private school," Sven said, sounding more puzzled than anything.

"Oregon made it mandatory for all kids during the Tunis Flus Two and Three." He had thought at the time that it was a good idea—it had cut down not only on the Tunis Flu but venereal disease as well—but he agreed that it was probably on the borderline of constitutionality.

"Oh. That thing in September," said Sven. "Reverend Colney told the congregation not to protest. He said that it would only bring further problems." His large eyes, the color of faded denim, appeared not quite in focus. "The whole school did it, didn't they?"

"Yes," said Elihu, thinking that he might want to see the records from the district, just in case.

"Kirsten said that it wasn't godly to do that. It questioned Providence." He stood up and walked about the room. "She's real sick, isn't she?"

"Yes," Elihu said.

"How sick?" Sven was still baffled. "What kind of care does she have to have?"

"More than we can give in the hospital here. I want your permission to transfer her to the research hospital in Portland." He had already made a few phone calls and had been assured that there would be a place for Kirsten once the proper forms had been signed.

"Portland?" Sven repeated. "Why? Why so far?"

This was growing increasingly difficult, thought Dover. "You see, Mister Barenssen, your sister has . . . she has a number of things wrong with her. Any one of them alone and the local hospital would be able to treat her." This was a bit of a white lie, but one that Dover felt acceptable. "But because there are so many problems, she needs more monitoring and tests than we can provide here. Given the seriousness of her illness, I think it would be wisest to transfer her at once. Today, in fact."

"What? Today?" Sven's eyes had taken on the hard glaze of shock and he spoke mechanically, moving as if his joints were connected by loose wires and string.

"Yes. It is urgent. I wouldn't pressure you, but since these circumstances are so extraordinary, I think it would be best if you would agree to . . . permit me to make the appropriate arrangements." He knew how to bring the authority and dignity of his position into play, and he did it now as emphatically as he could. "You certainly can understand, can't you, why your sister deserves the best care possible."

"I can't afford it," Sven croaked.

"I'll do what I can to help you find the means," Dover said, speaking gently and evenly. "Will Colney can help out, if you like."

"Not with charity," warned Sven.

"With finding a way to pay for your sister's treatment," said Dover in the same calm drone. "You certainly want her to have the best treatment, don't you?"

"Sure." He was fidgeting, his fingers moving restlessly over his jacket, stopping at the zipper, then sneaking off to hide in the pockets. "But the cost."

Dover knew that if Sven ever learned how expensive the treatment would be, the enormity of the figure would terrify him. "That's why I want you to talk with Will Colney. He has excellent sources for community assistance, and surely all the years your sister has devoted to his congregation will guarantee that he will do his utmost for her." He took a pad of paper from the top drawer of his desk. Most of his notes and records were, in fact, kept on his personal computer in the next room, but he knew that most of his patients did not trust the thing, and so he still kept up the practice of written instructions and notes. "I'm going to give you the name of the assistant administrator at the hospital. I want you to go over and talk to her, and arrange for your sister to be transferred to Portland."

"I won't get to see her," said Sven, sounding lost.

"Until she gets well, she'll have to be kept in isolation, in any case. You see, we don't have enough information on what's wrong with her, and until we do, we must make sure that she does not spread her disease to anyone else." He knew that he ought to soften the blow somehow. "You know that Kirsten would not want to bring illness to anyone."

"Or any misfortune," said Sven automatically. "She's a good Christian woman. She wouldn't ever do anything to hurt anyone."

"Yes," said Dover. "Now, you go talk with Miss Bradshaw and she'll arrange everything." He had already spent ten minutes on the phone with Toni Bradshaw, and knew all that was needed now was Sven's signature on four different forms.

"I don't have time to take her to Portland," Sven began.

"It will be arranged. You don't have to do it, Mister Barenssen." Now Dover gave his very best sympathetic smile. "You're doing the right thing to help your sister. I know how difficult it must be, but it is the right thing." He resolved to call Will Colney after he straightened out the medical transfer. From the look of him, Sven would need the comfort his minister would offer.

"The assistant administrator at the hospital?" Sven asked as he stared at the piece of paper Dover had handed him.

"Yes; she'll be expecting you." He made a great show of

looking at his watch. "I have another patient, Mister Barenssen. I really must—"

"Sure." Sven got up and wandered to the door. "Thanks. I'll go right over to the hospital. Right now. Do you think they'll let me look in on Kirsten?"

"I'll see what I can do." As soon as he was alone, Dover picked up the phone and alerted Toni Bradshaw. "Call Medi-Copter and tell Eherman that it's urgent. And when Barenssen gets there, let him have five minutes with Kirsten. It might help him, and God knows it won't change her condition."

"All right; I'll call you as soon as I talk to Eherman."

Dover's next call was more complicated, since it required that he speak with three people in quick succession and the Center for the Study of Environmental Medicine was new enough and big enough to confuse everyone.

"Doctor Maximillian Klausen," Dover said to the automatic answerer. "This is Doctor Elihu Dover calling." He then waited for three minutes listening to a soft-rock rendition of the *Sleeping Beauty Waltz* until Max Klausen's familiar growl came on the line.

"Is this about the woman we discussed yesterday?" Klausen interrupted when Dover began to fill him in.

"Yes. I'm arranging to have her transferred to you now." He wanted to remind Klausen that there was such a thing as professional courtesy, and the least he could do was be permitted to finish his comments, but instead he added, "She's going to need some kind of financial aid. The family is poor."

"I'll get Sandy on it," said Klausen. "How's she coming?"

"I'm arranging transportation with our local Medi-Copter," said Dover severely. "They'll notify you of their time of arrival."

"Fine. What about the history and tests results?"

"I have a modem on the computer and so does the hospital. The records will arrive before the patient if your lines are clear." He was getting huffy and knew that he ought not to be so offended.

"Good. I'll give you a call after I've had a look at her. How late will you be available?"

"I take calls until ten-thirty, and after that my service screens them." He paused. "When you find out what the trouble is, I want to know about it."

"You got it. I'll switch you to admissions." Without any further comment the line went silent for almost a minute.

By the time the admissions clerk had switched Dover to the research lab, Elihu Dover had a headache and his face felt stiff, as if it had been covered in a thin layer of plaster. He repeated the basic information to a softspoken young man who sounded as if he belonged in high school.

"Condition of the patient?" asked the young man.

"It will all be sent," said Dover.

"Is the patient alert? Is the patient coherent?" The questions might have been about Dover's preference in toothpaste for all the interest they expressed.

"She is disoriented and frightened," Dover said with meticulous precision. "She is used to living in a small community, and she is strictly religious. If one of your ministers is available when she arrives, it would help her. Provided that the minister is Fundamentalist in his outlook."

"Fundamentalist? Here?" There was polite incredulity in the young man's voice.

"Then find one. Surely you have Fundamentalists in Portland." He cleared his throat. "Also, she is a spinster; she is easily upset if she has to take off her clothes in front of a man, even a physician. Arrange for a nurse to be present for all examinations. Otherwise you will upset her unnecessarily." He tried to imagine the young man—was he as smug as he sounded or had he merely been on the phone too long that day? was he a resident, an intern, a nurse, an orderly, or some kind of clerk?—so that he would be able to enlist his sympathy on Kirsten Barenssen's behalf.

"We'll take care of her," said the young man. "Will you want reports on her progress?"

"Yes. And all information about her condition. In case I happen upon another case." This last he said with heavy emphasis in the hope that it would have some impression on the young man.

"You got it," said the young man blithely and hung up.

Elihu Dover stared, fuming, at the receiver in his hand, and then shook his head. There was no dealing with the bureaucrats, he reminded himself, which was why he had remained in Sweet Home instead of finding work in a larger place. He got up and stretched, heading for the window where he could see the sleet that would make his drive home miserable.

On impulse he picked up the phone and dialed home. "Eunice," he said when he heard his wife's voice, "I think I'm going to come home a little early this evening. It's been a complicated day."

"El, are you all right?" she asked with a trace of humor in her words.

"I'm okay," he said slowly. "I've got two more appointments here and then I have to stop by the hospital, but I'll be as quick as I can." He smiled at the receiver as he pictured his wife's face. "Are you in the mood to have dinner out?"

"Now I'm certain you need help," Eunice said, actually laughing. "What have you been up to?"

"I'll tell you all about it when I see you," he promised, hoping that the familiar comfort of her presence would end the nagging sense of disaster that had haunted him all afternoon.

"Tell you what," Eunice said, "I'll call *The Embers* and ask them to reserve us a table for six-thirty. That way, even if you do take a little longer at the hospital, we'll be ready to have a pleasant evening."

"You're an angel," he said with feeling. "Wear that deep red outfit, will you?"

"Some angel," she scoffed affectionately. "All right. Anything else you'd like, El?"

He sighed. "Nothing you or I can do anything about," he said, gloom descending upon him once more. "I'll see you in a bit, darling."

"You take care of yourself, El," she said, her voice as near scolding as it ever got.

He held the receiver more tightly. "Anything for you."

"Flatterer," she said indulgently, and then added with the perspicacity of thirty-one years of marriage. "Over dinner you can tell me what's troubling you."

He knew better than to deny his concerns. "Thank you; I was depending on that."

"Depend away," she said, and hesitated once more. "Don't let it wear you down, El."

"I won't," he said, and then amended, "I'll try not to." There were so many things he rarely said to her that he wanted her to know: how much he valued her, how he appreciated her calm good sense, how important she was to him. Instead he made a kissing noise at the receiver. "See you in a while, Eunice."

"I'll be waiting," she said, and hung up.

_____ *Gerald Plaiting* _____

On one side of his desk Gerald Plaiting had a stack of article reprints and textbooks; on the other side he had the files for eight of his patients. It was almost ten-thirty and he was suffering from eyestrain that made it difficult for him to focus on the billboard opposite his windows, yet he was determined to get through the material in the hope it would shed some light on the cases he had been handling. He pinched the bridge of his prominent nose between thumb and forefinger, and considered having a sixth cup of coffee.

There was a knock on his office door and he looked up sharply as Muñoz, who was head of night security for the building, opened the door. "Just checking, Doctor," said the uniformed man.

"I'm glad you're here," said Plaiting. "Working late like this, I get scared sometimes." It was no more than the truth, and he said it with feeling, but he knew that Pablo Muñoz took it as a compliment and a sign of respect.

"You don't need to be with my staff and me around. We haven't had any trouble in more than three years." He took justifiable pride in this, for most medical buildings in the San Fernando Valley had some kind of theft or vandalism on an average of every fourteen months; Muñoz' record was excellent.

"Thank goodness."

"I'll tell my man in the parking lot to keep an eye on your car. It's that new methane Saab, isn't it?" This query was only for good manners—Muñoz had the make and license plate number for every person working in the Victory Plaza Medical Building.

"That's the one."

"What do you think of it? I don't like gas lines, but I don't know about the methane engines," said Muñoz, not moving from his place in the door.

"I like the car. It handles well and gets good mileage; you don't have to wait at the methane stations and there'll be more of them in a year or two." He sighed. "And we aren't going to run out of methane for a long, long time."

Muñoz nodded. "My wife is after me to get one of the methane vans. She keeps talking about the tax incentives, but I worry that they haven't got the bugs out of them yet." He nodded. "Well, thanks, Doctor Plaiting." He backed out of the door and closed it, leaving Gerald alone once more.

By midnight he was no closer to answering his steadily multiplying questions. He rose and turned off the desk light, stretching to get the worst of the stiffness out of his muscles. He thought ruefully of the time not so long ago when his knees and elbows never popped, and his muscles were springy as new rubber bands. "Hazards of age," he said, with his forty-third birthday facing him in a week. Then he winced inwardly, for there were six of his patients who would never see twenty, let alone forty-three. He stared at the eight folders and willed them to give up their secrets.

As he drove home to a cul-de-sac condo in Sherman Oaks, Gerald went over the cases once more. The first had been Eric Harmmon, who had died New Year's Day. The next had been Estrella Cincel, the star gymnast at her junior high school; she had died last week. Then George Layton, who had died on his sixteenth birthday, two days ago. There were three more kids with the baffling, lethal symptoms, and two adults, each growing more debilitated every day, until the body simply could not keep going. Technically whatever was wrong with them had not actually killed them, it had merely created a physical condition where death was inevitable. Death, he realized, was a side effect. Gerald ground his teeth as he turned off of Ventura Boulevard.

As he drove up to his condo, he felt the usual pang of loneliness that was the legacy of his divorce two years ago, but his fatigue was more demanding than the darkness of the town house. He parked his car in front of the garage and stumbled toward the front door, ignoring the mailbox and a UPS delivery tag on the security gate. As he fumbled with the light switches in the hall, he wondered again if he ought to get the kind of circuits that would unlock the door and turn on the lights at the sound of his voice, but the notion passed quickly as he went to the kitchen and opened the refrigerator, staring at its contents before deciding on a cup of comfrey tea and a hot bath.

By morning, some of Gerald's depression had lifted, but he had not yet come to any greater understanding of the disease that was claiming his patients. He coddled two eggs, adding sweet butter and a dash of paprika to the cup before sinking the coddler in hot water. While he made tea he made up his mind to send out a general inquiry to other physicians in the area to see if any of them had patients with similar symptoms. Perhaps he ought to be safe and include all of southern California; he was not eager to be branded an alarmist, but at the same time he could not bear to think that his negligence might add one more fatality to the list. He was still weighing these considerations when the phone rang.

"Plaiting," he said as he picked up the receiver.

"This is Joel Price at West Valley Medical," said his caller. "I'm with the Woodland Hills Clinic."

"I remember you," said Plaiting, frowning at the congealing mass of yolk at the bottom of the coddling cup.

"Look, I know that this is a little irregular, but I understand from Katherine Dial that you've had some cases recently that—"

"Anemia, lethargy, low fevers," Plaiting interrupted. "Is that the one?"

"Sounds like it," said Price. "I've had two admissions in the last week. I was wondering if you could spare me some time this evening. We're listing this as toxic reaction, but I'm not so sure it is."

"Okay; I was planning on calling Public Health and Environmental Services in any case. I'll hold off until we talk." He was relieved to find another doctor as troubled as he was, although the news that there were more cases did nothing to lessen his alarm. "How about eight?"

"Where?" asked Price. "I can come to you."

"Do that, will you?" Plaiting asked. "I have some test results that I'm expecting. It might help us."

"And it might not," said Price. "All right. I know where you are. I'll try to be there at eight, but if I'm going to be held up I'll give you a call."

"Great. Thanks." He started to hang up, then said, "Are your two still alive?"

"So far, but . . ." His words faded.

"Yeah, I know the feeling," said Plaiting. "Can you get more blood work done on your two today? We'll have current results to compare and that might tell us something." He reached for his cup. "If you have information on toxic waste dumps in your area, bring it along. We might be able to figure something out from that."

"I haven't got it, but I can try to get it by this evening," said Price. "Thank you for the help. I don't like to sound weird, but this one has a very bad feel about it."

"I know what you mean, and it doesn't sound weird to me," said Plaiting. "I hope we're both wrong."

"So do I," admitted Price. "Okay. I'll see you this evening. And maybe we can learn something."

As Gerald Plaiting made his way through the morning traffic, he decided that he would program the medical records of his dead patients once more in the hope that he might discover what they had in common. "Even a bad case of flu ten years ago," he said to the windshield. Terminal diseases had been triggered by stranger things, he knew, and he sensed that he could not afford to overlook anything in this instance. "There's a key, there's a key, there's got to be a key," he chanted in cadence with the tune on his radio. He turned off Ventura Boulevard and signaled to change lanes. Outside the sky was grey, some of it from winter cloud cover, some from the continuing battle with smog that was the bane of the greater Los Angeles area. "I wonder if it's nothing more than smog?"

Reynaldo Bata was on duty at the parking lot entrance, and saluted Gerald as he raised the barrier. "Morning, Doc," he called out. "How's it going?"

"Okay. And you?"

"One of my kids has a bug, but other than that everything's fine." He consulted his watch and made a note in his log. "You going out again this morning?"

"Over to the hospital." He drove to his parking space and pulled in. As he locked his car, he noticed that Cindy

Chung was getting out of her little British Lancer and he waved to her. "Cindy!"

"Gerry," she called out, returning his wave. "How are you?"

"Fine, fine," he said, and for the moment it was almost the truth. He joined her at the elevator doors. "How're things in the wonderful world of ophthalmology?"

"Optical," she said, grinning at him. "Are you busy this weekend?"

"I don't know," said Plaiting. "Am I?"

"Call me tomorrow; I'll know something then," she said as the elevator doors opened. "You look a little tired," she observed as they rode up.

"Probably. I've had a couple tough cases recently. You know what that can be like."

"Not the way you do," she corrected him. "It's not the kind of thing I deal with."

"Count your blessings," said Plaiting with more emotion than he realized. "Call me," he added as the doors opened at her floor.

"You, too." She left him with her remarkable smile to keep him company all the way to his office. As he looked over his schedule for the day, Plaiting permitted himself a brief fantasy: what would his good Protestant Irish family think if he showed up with a Chinese bride? His ex-wife had come from the same background he had, and their marriage had been a calamity from the first. Perhaps they would see Cindy Chung as a breath of fresh air, a new influence in a hidebound family. Then he laughed aloud once, and reminded himself that he had only been out with the woman once, had done nothing more than kiss her twice. And if his family didn't like it, then the hell with them.

"Doctor Plaiting, Helen Miller is in room two," said his nurse from the door, her tone slightly admonitory since Plaiting appeared to be dawdling.

"Tell her I'll be there in a minute. Have you got the—"

"Blood pressure, temperature, chest index all recorded," she said with brisk efficiency.

"Thank you, Missus Shepherd," he said. "I needn't have asked."

"She's got a low fever and some slight bronchial congestion," added Cynthia Shepherd. "She complains of loss of appetite and malaise; nothing specific." She paused. "Her color is pasty."

There was a sudden coldness in Plaiting's chest. "I'd better look at her," he said, all too certain of what he would find.

Samuel Jarvis

"Are you sure you want to do this?" Sam Jarvis asked Harper Ross. "You're still in shock about Kevin, and taking on more study right now . . ." He cocked his head and watched the other man with skeptical interest.

"I have to do something." Harper shook his head slowly. "I can't just let him die and do nothing. I can't leave it at that."

"Are you sure you aren't simply looking for an acceptable escape?" Sam asked gently. "Harper, I know how hard it is to lose a child—Lorna and I lost our boy fourteen years ago and it still hurts—but you can't let it weigh you down this way."

"That's what I mean," said Harper, his eyes sharpening. "I don't want to be weighted down, and for me, that means getting to the bottom of what killed him. I admit that I never thought I'd be doing something like this, but I do have some skills and they can be of some use to you, I know they can." He braced his elbows on the desk and leaned forward. "I know how to investigate crimes—that's what I teach and I'm fan-fucking-tastic at it—and Kevin's death *is* a crime. I'd be wasting my skills if I didn't help out in finding his killer."

Sam sucked his lower lip before he answered. "I won't say we can't use the help, because we can. I won't say you can't help us, because I've got a hunch you can. But I do want you to think about this for a while. Don't insist, not quite yet. Take a week to think about this, because once we get started, I don't want you pulling out. If you sign on, you've got to sign on for the whole schimoola."

"I've already thought about it, Sam," said Harper. "I've talked to Phil and he said he can arrange a leave of absence for me if I require it." He pushed his knuckles together. "I've told him that I want it, and with the option of an extension if it's necessary."

"Let's hope that it won't be," said Sam. "But I meant that about taking a week to consider," he cautioned his friend. "It isn't just for you, it's for Susan. Unless I miss my guess, this would be harder on her than on you—am I right?"

Harper closed his eyes briefly, and when he opened them, he looked toward the sleety window and the distant freeway down the hill. "She wants no part of this. She wants to forget about it. I've tried to explain, but—"

"You ought to talk to her, Harper. You know as well as I do that she's entitled to your support. If she'd be hurt by your working with us on this, you should think about what it might mean if you—" This time it was Sam who was cut short.

"She has my support, and she knows that. Shit, Sam, I did everything I could think of while Kevin got sicker and sicker. I've promised her that we'll get away next winter, and I intend to keep that promise, no matter what. But if I don't do something now, I don't think I could live with myself. That's got to be part of it. Doesn't it?" At last he looked at Sam again. "Doesn't it?"

"Sure," said Sam heavily. "Sure. Why not?"

Harper got up and paced down the room. "I've talked it over with her, and with Grant and Mason. Susan hasn't said much. Grant— well, who knows what Grant really thinks? Mason is very sympathetic. If he were a little bit older, he'd probably want to work with us."

"Mason's a very bright kid," said Sam carefully. "That's often a mixed blessing."

Harper nodded. He was standing by the tall bookcases that filled the far end of the room. "Where do I start?" he asked as he indicated all the texts.

"Next week, next week," Sam insisted. "I mean that. You need to think about this a little longer."

"Tell me something to read in the meantime, and I'll go along with your orders." Harper ran his hand over the spines of the books on the fourth shelf from the floor. "Which one should I start with?"

"I'd recommend waiting, Harper," warned Sam, although he knew it was useless. "You're not ready yet, not the way you think you are. You do need more time."

"If I don't get the books from you, I'll try the library. There must be some basic texts on the diagnostic techniques used in cases like Kevin's. Or what they've done with other mysterious diseases they could not identify. There must be something on how they found the vaccine for AIDS, at least." Harper's eyes were wet, but he went on as if everything were normal. "I think that it would be best for me to start with methodology, don't you? That way I can adapt my own field to yours. Do you think I should try virology as well, or—"

"Harper," said Sam in a quiet, penetrating way, "go home. That's what I think you ought to do. Go home. I want you to take one full week and think about this. Talk it over with Susan and with the boys. Determine if you want to get involved. I mean it, Harper. As your physician as well as your friend, I want you to know what you're getting into. Do I make myself clear?"

"You don't have to write out a prescription, if that's what you mean," said Harper, an undercurrent of defeat in his words. "All right, I'll do as you tell me, but it won't make any difference. A week from now I'll be back and I'll want something to do."

"If that's what you decide then, fine."

"How can you doubt it? Sam, I *owe* something to my son. I owe it to him to find his killer, and to do everything I can to be certain that killer claims no more victims." He stopped abruptly.

"You can't save them all, Harper," Sam said evenly. "No matter what you decide, you have to face up to that now; you will not be able to save them all no matter how diligent you are and how honorable your purpose."

"All right. I accept that. And I accept that murderers go scot-free and laws are circumvented every day. I can live with that reality. But I can't live with my own inaction. Can't you understand that?" He rounded on his friend, his face filled with pain.

Sam gave Harper a long, measuring look. "How much do you know about Kevin's illness? I don't mean what they told you at the hospital, I mean what you learned about it while he was . . . getting sicker."

Harper was about to snap back an answer, but then he stopped and gave the question genuine consideration. "I know," he said thoughtfully, "that there was some dysfunction of his blood, that he became weak and lethargic, that he ran a low temperature for several weeks, and then the temperature went up to one-oh-two and stayed there until just before he died. He had trouble eating, he developed respiratory problems, he became disoriented, he suffered severe pain and inflammation of his joints in the last four days of his life." He came back and sat down opposite Sam. "He was apathetic for the last two weeks, and by the time they put him on IV feeding, he had already lost more than twenty pounds, and he didn't need to take any weight off. He complained of cramping in his intestines, but that might have been from the lack of food as well as from the disease itself, whatever it is." Harper's face took on the distant look which indicated intense concentration. "For the six months before he was hospitalized, he had mild, flu-like symptoms from time to time, nothing very specific, but they hung on, and he never developed any stamina once the disease took hold. He had swollen glands in his neck and chest before he became really sick. That's when you ordered the extra tests in case it was leukemia. I remember how relieved we were when it turned out he didn't have leukemia."

"I remember, too," said Sam with difficulty.

"And I think that Kevin felt worse then than he let on, for whatever reason—"

"Pride," suggested Sam.

"Kids can have terrible pride," agreed Harper. "It might have been that, it might have been his own desire not to worry us. He kept telling us not to fret, not to be so concerned, that he would get well. I wonder if that was as much for himself as for us? Mason said it was."

"Mason's a smart kid, we're agreed on that." Sam folded his arms and watched his friend. "Anything else, Professor?"

"I don't know," Harper said after a slight hesitation. "I keep thinking that there ought to be something I could pinpoint, a detail that would show the way to the rest, but nothing comes to mind."

"You realize, I hope, that if you do decide to help us out with this that you might have to watch a lot of other kids die." Sam held up his hand to stop the objection Harper was beginning to voice. "I know I've said this before. You think you're prepared to deal with it. The trouble is, I'm not sure you are. Hell, I know I'm not. It isn't fun and there's no way to get used to it. Are you prepared to deal with that? Don't try to answer me now, but promise me you'll keep it in mind during the week."

"Sure," said Harper seriously.

"And I want you to accept that we might never find the cause, not in a way that would satisfy you. My personal belief is that it's connected to some kind of environmental contamination, a toxic waste dump or some other similar problem. I don't think you can decide in advance that you'll get the secret. These days, there are lots of conditions that come and go."

"All right, I'll do my best to remember that," said Harper. He was about to get up when something occurred to him. "Would my journal be any help? I kept a record of Kevin's condition once it became apparent that something wasn't right. Do you think you might be able to make use of it?"

"Could be," was Sam's cautious answer. "I think it would be worth looking at, no matter what. You probably saw aspects of his illness that the rest of us missed." He did not mention how slim a chance it was that this record would reveal anything of merit, but he knew better than to discard a document that might contain a clue to the cause of Kevin's death.

"How many other kids have you seen with the same symptoms?" Harper asked, the question sounding much louder than it was.

"Five so far, and two adults whose symptoms are similar. We don't know yet if this is the same thing, but we can't afford to take chances." Sam stood up. "Go home, Harper. Think this over. Don't decide until next Tuesday night, and if you still want to help out, I'll meet you here at nine on Wednesday morning. How's that?"

"I'd rather start right now," said Harper.

"That's what you think," said Sam, trying to make light of his warning. "Give it a week, a full week. If you don't, I know it will catch up with you later. Believe me."

"I believe you're trying to help," said Harper, taking Sam's proffered hand and shaking it. "I appreciate that. But I want you to understand that I will be back, and I want to stay with this all the way."

"All right, I'll keep that in mind," said Sam, his hands

braced on his hips as he watched Harper go to the door. "It wouldn't trouble me if you decided to change your mind."

"I won't," said Harper as he walked out.

Sam remained standing for a short while, his eyes fixed on the middle distance. Little as he wanted to admit it, he hoped that Harper would remain firm in his resolve. There was something about this damned disease that vexed Sam, and nothing that he had seen or heard from his colleagues had been able to dispel the deep sense of foreboding that had settled over him since he had admitted Kevin Ross to the hospital. Now he had more patients with the same ominous symptoms and he knew no more about what to do for them than he had when Kevin worsened and died.

He reached over and picked up the telephone and punched in the number of the hospital two blocks away. "I'd like to talk to the epidemiologist, please. Doctor Hal Shevis." He waited while the automated system transferred his call, playing him selections from *Laughter in the Dark* while he waited.

"Shevis here," said the man who answered the phone on the eighth ring.

"Hal, it's Sam Jarvis. Look, I need to get together with you. I need your advice." He was toying with a pencil, standing it on end, sliding his finger down it until the pencil tipped over and then starting the process again.

"The Ross boy again?" Shevis guessed.

"Indirectly," said Sam. "I think we have to talk. Really. There are other cases and even though there aren't enough to involve your department, technically, it seems to me that by the time there is, we'll all be in deep shit." He shivered as he said this, and blamed it on the light fall of snow drifting past his windows.

"I've been over your notes," said Shevis. "Little as I like to say it, I think you might be right. I've already ordered a review of toxic sites, as you suggested, and I've put out a request for the monitor records on contaminants. The regs on them are new enough that we're not going to get much, but it's worth a try."

Sam was pleasantly surprised. "You mean I don't have to come over there and throw a fit?"

"No," said Shevis. "We might be out of the mainstream of practice, but we're not stupid, you know."

"No," agreed Sam with a sudden rush of relief. He felt as if he had cleared an enormous hurdle with nothing more than a hop and a skip. "Thanks. I mean that."

"You're welcome," said Shevis. "And I would appreciate being kept abreast of anything you come up with. I'll do the same for you. When did you want to get together for this talk, by the way?"

"Tonight?" Sam said, wondering how Shevis would take such a suggestion.

"Fine," said Shevis at once. "I'm going to send out a few queries, just in case. I want to know if there are any other cases like the ones you have currently in the Pacific Northwest area, and if there are, how many and how advanced. I might have some news by five. If not, I will in the next day or so."

"Good. I'll check with the hospitals in the network, to find out if they have anything going." He started to make a note to himself, but Hal Shevis cut him short.

"I've already attended to that. And for what it's worth, there are another six possible cases at Harborview. Five of them are teenagers," he added.

"That fits," Sam sighed. "Why teenagers? What are they doing, where are they going, that it happens to them? Are they simply more susceptible, and if so, to what?"

"Thinking out loud?" Shevis asked. "Save it for tonight. Say eight, at the Moroccan restaurant?"

"Fine. I'll meet you there," said Sam, not sure he would have an appetite by the time he arrived.

"For what it's worth, I hope you're wrong," said Shevis.

"For what it's worth, so do I," said Sam.

Coach Jackson paced across the basketball court, his shoulders hunched and his scowl deepening with every step. "What do you mean, four of the boys can't play?" he demanded of the team physician.

"I mean that they're sick and they can't play, Jim; just what I said." Landholm hesitated. "They've got mono or something like it. I'm sorry, but that's the way it is."

"That's ridiculous!" Jackson insisted. "If we lose those four, we can kiss the season good-bye. Christ, they're—"

Landholm shrugged. "I'm sorry, Jim. More for them than for you. Those kids are sick. It's almost as bad as that fever that went around when those army storage tanks leaked, four years back. I've sent blood samples to Portland, just in case. I don't want any more surprises."

"There are medical labs in Twin Falls," said Coach Jackson, but with a reserve he had not shown before. "You mean that you have to check mono out with that new center in Portland?"

"It might not be mono," Landholm admitted. "It isn't typical, and I got worried. Four boys with the same thing, and that same thing isn't quite right—"

Jackson stopped in front of his friend. "Okay, Wil, what aren't you telling me?" His belligerence had faded and now he looked more concerned than annoyed.

"I wish I knew. That's no dodge: I wish I knew." He hooked one thumb in his pants pocket. "You remember that fever four years ago, how everyone said it was flu and ignored it for two weeks, until the rashes developed? And then everyone was scared shitless of even a cold for a year after that?"

"Yeah?" Jackson said.

"Well, at the time everyone wanted to blame someone for not finding out sooner that it was from those storage tanks. I don't want that to happen again, so I sent blood samples to Portland. I don't know if they'll find anything, but I don't want to take any more risks."

"It's bad enough that the Porter boy moved, now we have four more boys off the team," muttered Jackson, then stopped. "Sorry, Wil. You're probably right and I'm probably wrong about this." He stared at the steel beams crossing the ceiling. "I see your point. If there's any more hanky-panky going on, we'd better find out fast."

Landholm rocked back on his heels. "It might be nothing more than a new kind of flu, but—"

"Un-huh," said Jackson. "I guess you've told the administration?"

"I had to," Landholm said, making it an apology.

"I suppose so," said Jackson. "Does that mean tests for the rest of the team?" He did his best to be philosophical but it was clearly an effort.

"At least. If Portland finds anything strange, we might have to check the whole student body."

"All of Roger Brewer Middle School?" Jackson asked, shocked at the notion.

"We might have to," said Landholm cautiously.

"Jesus H. Christ," Jackson swore softly. "You really are worried about this, aren't you? Hey, Wil, it's only a fever. Kids get bugs all the time, you've said so yourself."

"Not like this bug," Landholm said somberly, and watched while Jim Jackson came to terms with what he said.

"You're on to something, aren't you?" Jackson asked at last.

"I don't know. Honestly, Jim. I hope I'm wrong, but I have to be careful." He looked up as the heater clicked on with the sound of an enormous yawn.

"You think it's another one of those viruses, don't you?" Jackson demanded, his face darkening again.

"I hope not." Landholm was hedging and both men knew it.

"But it's what you think," Jackson persisted.

"I hope I'm wrong." He glanced at the wall clock. "When does practice start?"

"Why?" Jackson asked.

"Because I want to find out if any of the team has sick brothers or sisters or parents at home, that's why," Landholm said bluntly. "And if they do, I want to find out what's wrong with them."

"You're kidding," said Jackson, and without waiting for a response, he shook his head. "No, you're not kidding, are you?"

Landholm shook his head. He wanted to deny the fear that was building in him, but he could not. "I have to find out, Jim."

"Oh, God." Jackson looked at the clock. "You have ten minutes yet. You want to get a cup of coffee while we wait? It's out of a machine, but it's hot."

"Sure," said Landholm, grateful that Jackson was not going to challenge him further. The two men walked out of the gymnasium and through the locker room to the faculty lounge; Jackson held the door for Landholm as they went into the small, drab room.

While Landholm fished for change in his pocket, Jackson got his coffee. "So are you going to tell me why you're going to all the trouble, or are you going to keep your ass covered until you hear from Portland?"

"Isn't four years ago reason enough?" Landholm asked as he counted his change and came up with the right combination for the coffee machine.

"For the administration, yes, for me, no," said Jackson. "What is it, Wil? What's got you so spooked?"

"Does it show that much?" Landholm inquired as he selected two-sugar-no-cream for his coffee.

"To me it does, but I've known you thirty years," Jackson said laconically. "You're not just being careful, you're frightened, and that isn't like you."

"Bob Turner is dying," Landholm said without preamble. "I don't know about the others, but I'm sure about Bob. He's fourteen and he isn't going to see fifteen." He sat down in one of the uncomfortable plastic chairs. "That's why I'm sending specimens to Portland and why I want to check out the school. That's what's got me frightened. I wish that the Porter boy was still around, too, so that I could check him out. I hate the idea of someone having a disease and not knowing it until it's . . ." He could not finish his thought.

"Are you sure?" Jackson asked. "About Bob?"

"Barring a miracle—and I mean miracle, Jim—there's nothing I can do for him." It was a difficult confession, and he could not look his friend in the eye as he said it.

"Bob. Shee-it." He drank down half his coffee. "What about Portland? Can they do anything?"

"I doubt it, but I hope they can tell me something that will help the others." Landholm stared down into the darkness of the coffee. "If I hear that anyone else but you and me knows about Bob, I'll know where it came from and—"

"I won't say anything; you know that," Jackson said, dismissing the implied warning. "What kind of bug do you think got away this time?"

"Whatever it is, you can be damned certain that the army won't tell us. Portland might, if they have any records on it. Ever since they opened, they've been assembling information on all those illegal stockpiles that are tucked into the mountains around here. If there's an ID on the bug, they might have it, and they might have something on record to tell me what to do about it. In any case, they ought to know that another one of the army's little biological toys has got loose." The bitterness that he usually sought to conceal was undisguised now.

"What if it's not that?" Jackson suggested. "What if it's something else?"

"You mean a real flu?" Landholm said. He let his breath out hard and fast. "If it is, it's brand-new, and that's troublesome in its own right."

"Well?" Jackson pursued.

"If it is . . . I'll hear soon enough from Portland, and then we'll have to get in contact with County Health Services. We'll probably have to do that in any event. Unless Portland takes over for the whole region." He lifted the styrofoam cup but did not drink from it. "I kind of hope they do take over. I don't like to think about handling a mess like this piecemeal. I'm not prepared for it, and neither is any other doctor in Idaho. Or Oregon. Or Washington. Or Utah. Or Wyoming. Or Montana. Or California. Or Colorado. Or anywhere else."

"You think it's bad, then?" Jackson prodded.

"I think whatever it is, it's bad." Landholm took a swig of the coffee, wishing it were bourbon, then looked at his watch. "Your team ought to be getting ready. Let's get to it."

Jackson nodded. "Whatever you say, Wil."

The team members answered Wilson Landholm's questions with a minimum of back talk and questions, thanks in large part to the strict orders that Coach Jackson gave them before the doctor was allowed to speak: "You've already heard that we've got four guys off the team because of illness, and Doc Landholm wants to be sure that's all we lose. You listen to his questions and you give him straight answers if you want to be part of the team for the County Play-Offs next May. If I catch any of you holding out or making things up, you'll be off before January's over. Understand me?"

Twelve boys nodded in agreement; they understood.

The report that Wilson Landholm sent to Portland listed a total of seventeen possible cases of the unknown disease, and promised specimens to follow.

Doctor Reed was always faintly disturbed by Irene Channing, and never more than when he had to give her bad news. She was so vital, so *present*, that he hated to say or do anything that might lessen that quality in her in the least. "Sit down, Irene," he said when he had finished the polite amenities that had become almost a ritual with them.

"You sound very serious, Dale," she said as she took the chair he offered.

"I'm afraid I am," he said. "I have the results from your family physicals, and I need to talk to you about them."

"Is something wrong?" She thought about Sean Gradeston, who had died the third day of January, and whose loss was still grating on her son Steven. "What's the matter?"

Dale Reed stared into her enormous, luminous eyes. He had often wanted to give her a gift, no matter how improper such a gesture would be. When he let himself, he considered giving her a necklace of Tiger's Eye beads, for they had the same eerie depths as her eyes, and were as mesmerizing. "I'm afraid . . . I'll have to run a few more tests."

"Tests?" she repeated. "For what?"

"There are some . . . anomalies," he said lamely. "I want to clear up the matter. You know what worrywarts doctors are."

Her laughter did not ring true. "Steven?" she asked.

"No," Reed said.

"Not Brice?" Her olive skin went a shade paler at her younger son's name.

"No, Irene." He stared down at his well-manicured hands. "I need to do the work on you. I'm . . . sorry."

"On me?" Irene said, baffled. "But why? What's the matter with me?"

"Nothing," Reed said hastily. "Nothing that we're sure of, but I want to be certain. You're in such a . . . a vulnerable position, a widow with two children. Oh, I know you were left comfortably well-off, but that doesn't change the fact that you're having to make your way alone." He reached for his pipe and tobacco pouch.

"I took care of myself long before Neil and I met," Irene said, more sternly than she had spoken at first.

"Yes, that's what I mean. I want to make sure that you're as well as you look." He tamped down the tobacco in his pipe and reached for his lighter. "All those years when you were struggling, living in Nevada and Arizona, it's about time you were free of that."

"But I am free of it," Irene said sharply. "Aren't I?"

"I . . . I hope so," Reed told her. "But if we check you over, we can be sure."

"Of what?" she insisted. "What are you tap-dancing about, Dale? What's wrong with me?"

"There's . . . there's some indication that you might have a blood dysfunction." He read shock in her eyes before it reached the rest of her face and he hurried on, "I doubt that it's anything very serious, but since you are past thirty-five, I thought it would be best that we make certain, in case there are problems later."

"Dale, menopause is not a disease, it's a natural phase of a woman's life, like puberty." She did her best to be patient with him, but this was precisely the kind of thing that irritated her. "If you're worried that I might be perimenopausal, why didn't you say so? I'll have the tests and you can prescribe whatever supplements you think will make the transition easier, and that will be that."

Reed stared down into the red glow of the pipe bowl. "There might be a little more to it than that," he said after a moment.

"Oh?" Now there was a catch in her breath. "How do you mean, more to it?"

"Well, there may be . . . a complication." He dared to look at her once more. "I wanted to warn you, in case you worried. Sometimes, you know, there are difficulties."

"What kind of difficulties?" she asked with care.

Reed sighed. "I don't want you to be upset because I want you to have more tests, but all those years you were living in Nevada and Arizona, you were in some areas that have recently been identified as toxic waste dumps, and in some cases—not all, but some—there have been side effects from exposure, some of them not showing up for years and years."

"And you think I might have been exposed to something like that? What about Steven?" Her voice was getting harsh.

"There doesn't seem to be any indication that . . . he's fine, Irene. We'll keep a close watch on him, of course, but right now, you're the one who has a . . . few irregularities in your blood test. I want to clear that up before . . . well, before it develops into something."

Irene leaned forward, her face set. "Develops into *what*, Dale?" she demanded. "Are you saying I might have cancer?"

"No, no," he assured her with a quick waving of his hands. "Good Lord, no. Nothing like that. Nothing. But since something isn't quite right, I want to find out more about it, so that it . . ."

When he did not go on, Irene slapped her hand on the desk. "What's this all about, Dale? What aren't you telling me?"

"I don't have anything to tell you, not yet. I don't know the extent of the problem. And I don't want you to get worried and anxious because there's a question about it. You see, you're already nervous, and that's exactly what I want you to avoid." He rose and held out his hand to her. "Irene, please. Don't do this to yourself."

"Do what to myself?" she snapped, pulling back from him. "Will you stop acting as if I'm made of antique porcelain? I'm able to take care of myself. I can deal with anything, so long as I know what it is. So, Dale, tell me what's wrong with me."

He lowered his hands to his sides, shaking his head to indicate his helplessness. "I don't know. I've tried to give you a sense of the parameters we might be dealing with, but so far I haven't enough to go on to tell you more than that there might be a . . ." He took his seat and came at it from another angle. "You see, when your test results came back they showed a minor anemia and a minor blood disorder. I don't know what sort yet, which is what I would like to determine, which is why I want you to have a few more tests. It would mean a day or two in the hospital, for convenience, and then we can determine what the extent and nature of the dysfunction is. I don't like to see you borrowing trouble before we know what we're up against."

"And how serious might this be?" she asked evenly.

"There's no way to tell, but judging from what I've seen so far, it shouldn't be anything we can't handle." He did his best to give her a reassuring smile. "Don't tell me you couldn't use a couple of days to rest."

"All right, I won't tell you," she said sharply. "But I remind you that I have a showing in March and I'm not prepared yet. If this is going to take time away from my work, I'd prefer to schedule the tests after the opening."

"I'm afraid," he said as gently as he could, "that it wouldn't be advisable to wait that long."

A silence settled between them, and then Irene broke it with one word: "Why?"

Reed put his pipe in the over-large ashtray at the corner of his desk. "In cases like yours, it's generally best to determine the condition as soon as possible, on the off-chance that there are complications."

"What sort of complications?" Irene asked him. "What are you talking about, Dale?"

"I don't know," he admitted heavily. "That's the problem. There was a flag on your blood work when it came back. I looked at the results." He stared at her in his helplessness. "I didn't recognize the anomaly, but I can't argue that it exists. It's there. I don't know what it is or how serious it might be, or what it could lead to. That's why I want to get to work on this at once, because the sooner I know what we're up against, the sooner you're over it." He did his best to smile, to show her his even, white teeth as a sign of confidence.

"This is new?" she asked. "Could it be because I had children later than most. I was thirty-eight when Brice was born, and thirty-one when Steven was. You warned me that there could be trouble. Is this what you meant?" She concealed the sudden fear that clutched her vitals, saying sarcastically, "I'm not that over the hill, Dale."

"No, you're not," he said at once. "As to when you had children, I have no idea if there's a connection. You told me that some of those years when Steven was young you got by on very little, and it could be that it triggered something that . . ." He stopped himself with a shrug. "The trouble is, I simply don't have enough to go on. That's why I want to do the tests as soon as possible, and have you in the hospital, in case—and it's a long shot, Irene, I promise you—we find something that needs prompt attention."

"Cancer," she said.

"Possibly, or any one of a number of other diseases. It might be that you're developing anemia at the start of menopause. It isn't usual, but it does happen. Do you know if your mother or any of her sisters did?" He was trying to keep the tone of their conversation as calm and normal as possible, but he sensed that she was nearing the edge.

"My mother died when I was twelve. I don't know anything about her side of the family. She never spoke about them and once she was dead, my father . . . well, he wrote to her family to tell them she died, but so far as I know that was their only contact. I gather they were very strictly religious and didn't approve of her marriage to a Greek Orthodox man. I have a brother in Philadelphia; that's all. My father died two years ago." In her lap, her hands were locked in combat. "I suppose I could hire someone to find her family, if you think it's wise. That is, if you think this could be hereditary. Or is that a very long shot?"

"It could be a factor, but since you'd have to go to some effort, we can hold off for a while." He wanted to say that he was horrified that any family could be so callous as to shut out as gifted and wonderful a woman as Irene, but that would not be proper or acceptable, especially now. "If it comes down to that, I can recommend a good firm to locate them. They're very discreet."

"I know of a good firm, too." She recalled the detective firm that had traced Tim Stevenson to San Diego for her, and kept her informed of his life. They could be employed to locate her mother's family, she guessed.

"Let's do the tests first; no sense getting worked up over a little anemia." He leaned forward and touched her arm. "Listen to me, Irene. I won't let anything happen to you. I give you my word."

"As a southern gentleman and a Texan?" she chided him. "Don't tell me that yet, okay?" With an effort she disengaged her hands and smoothed her skirt. "How soon would you want me to do this? I'll have to arrange with the housekeeper . . . Steven and Brice don't need any more upsets. Especially Steven, since Sean Gradeston . . ." She looked at him. "They said he had an unknown blood disease."

"There are all sorts of blood diseases, Irene; all sorts, and there are new conditions we're identifying every day." Reed shook his head, proud of the leonine mass of russet hair that was only slightly frosted with white. He was a good-looking man and knew it; often he took advantage of his attractiveness to distract his patients, but now he could not bring himself to use that. He was too worried about Irene Channing to charm her into false hopes. "That's one of the reasons I want to do these tests, to eliminate any possibility that you might have come in contact with the same . . . oh, virus or contamination, whatever caused Sean's death. Or any of the other factors that could enter into your problem. Don't let it get to you, though: it's a long shot, but I want to make sure you didn't pick up a case of it."

"Whatever it is?" she suggested.

"Whatever it is," he concurred.

She watched him, perusing his features as if searching for a flaw in a painting. "You've almost convinced me," she said finally. "Almost."

"All right, almost is the operative word until you tell me otherwise," he said with some of his gallantry returning. "I'll do everything I can to show you—"

"Don't start," she interrupted him. "Please." A little of her control was shaken and she brought one trembling hand to her face. "I . . ."

Impulsively, Reed came around his desk, his hands extended to her. "Irene. Don't." He pulled her to her feet and into his arms before he could remind himself that he never intended to reveal his feelings to her, not this way, not any way, not ever.

"Some bedside manner," she said, swallowing hard against the panic in her chest. "Dale, I . . ."

He did not release her. "It's not bedside manner, dammit."

"I should hope not," she rallied. "Half the husbands in Dallas would be after you with shotguns."

"Stop it, Irene." Now that he had gone this far, he let himself be lost. "This has nothing to do with doctor and patient. It has to do with you being my oldest friend's widow. If you weren't, I . . ."

"Dale, don't be ridiculous." She tried to push away from him, but changed her mind, finding absurd solace in being held.

"I'm forty-nine; no one's ridiculous at forty-nine," he said, his face against her shining hair.

"And the tests? Are they a ploy?" She knew better, but it was the one hope that she could seize upon. "An outflanking maneuver?"

"No. A post-opening private dinner would be an outflanking maneuver," he said bluntly. "I've been thinking about trying it."

She nodded. "And if I were, oh, Missus Jack Smith from El Paso, would you still order the tests?"

"Yes," he said, no banter left.

"Because something's wrong?"

"I'm concerned, I admit it. If you were a different patient, I might not be quite so worried, but I'd still want the tests done."

"Oh." This was hardly audible; Irene sought for strength to deny her dread, but could find nothing but the sting of anger and apprehension.

"It's a little late now," he said, finally moving a step back from her. "But suppose, Irene, suppose I had asked you to a post-opening private dinner. Would you come?"

"I'm counting on it," she said, with more emotion than she realized.

"That makes two of us," said Reed, feeling shaken and lightheaded. He had taken shameful advantage of her vulnerability and his position, he reminded himself sternly, and all he could do was repress the urge to grin.

"But tests first?" she said, sounding weary.

"It's the most sensible way," he told her, deliberately trying to minimize her apprehension. "That way, you won't have unanswered questions hanging over you and you can get on with your work." He wondered if he sounded too glib.

"And if I have answers I don't like, what then?" She looked at him with her direct, unnerving stare. "What if you have every reason to be concerned, what if there is something seriously wrong?"

"There won't be," he said at once. "But on the off-chance that you might have something chronic, that will give you a little time to learn how to deal with it. You'll be able to pace yourself better and be more on top of things." He let his hands rest on her shoulders. "Irene, I shouldn't have done this, and I won't take any of it back. I would have said something later on. If I hadn't been worried, it might never have come up." This last was a lie, but he said it as much for himself as for her.

"Really? Do men cherish unrequited passion in this day and age?" She had meant it to sound teasing but it came out wistfully.

"This man was prepared to." He meant it, and his manner told her that he would not modify his statement to suit her whim.

"That's a little daunting, Doctor Reed," she told him, her face turned toward his.

"Does it frighten you?"

"I don't think so," she said. "I'm too busy being scared of the tests to be frightened of you. Once I know if something's wrong with me, then I'll have a chance to be afraid of you." Her mouth curved into a smile. "In the meantime, I plan to take full advantage of your involvement."

"How tactfully you put that," he said, moving away from her with reluctance. "Call me tonight, when you've spoken with the housekeeper, and I'll make arrangements for you at the hospital."

"All right." She picked up her marten-fur coat and pulled it around her shoulders before he could help her with it. "I'll do what I can to get everything settled. Will you visit me while I'm having the tests done?"

"Twice a day at least. More if I have the time and you want to see me." There was a question hidden in his last few words and he waited for her response.

"Hospitals bore me when they don't terrify me. I'll monopolize you if I have the chance." She started toward the door, then looked back at him. "Why did Margaret leave you?"

"She fell in love with someone. I wish I could say someone *else*, but she was never really in love with me. I don't know if she thought she was. When she met Daniel Spears, it was as if a light went on in her that had never shone before. She would have mopped the floor with her hair for him." Reed looked down at the top of his desk. "I understand they're very happy together."

"I'm sorry, Dale," Irene said simply.

"I used to be. But that was some time ago." There was no mistaking the intent of the look he gave her. "I'll talk to you later, Irene."

"Fine," she said.

_____ *Edgar Haliburton* _____

"Laurie's fine," said Doctor Haliburton to the Greys as Jonathon and Catherine faced him over the counter in the medical lab. "That's the good news."

"The only good news?" Catherine asked, shock making her face appear stark and old.

"It's not that bad," Haliburton assured her at once. "I want to do a few more tests, in case we've overlooked something obvious. If Marilee hadn't . . ."

"Died," Jonathon said bluntly. "She died."

"Yes," Haliburton agreed slowly. "If she hadn't, I might not be so cautious, but under the circumstances, I believe that it is wisest, psychologically as well as medically, to check as carefully and as thoroughly as possible. Do you understand my purpose?"

"Yes," said Catherine for Jonathon as well as herself.

"I realize that you have had a terrible loss," Haliburton went on, determined to say something encouraging to these grieving parents. "I wish I knew what to say. If I had been on the case sooner, I might have been able to spare you this now, but since it's only been six weeks, there's a lot of ground to cover." He knew that everything he said was dismaying to the couple, and he tried to minimize the impact of his words once more. "If I were in your place, I might end up deciding not to help out; there's no reason you should. But there are others coming down with the same thing Marilee had, and . . . we want to find a way to treat it."

"You mean Miss Cuante?" said Catherine, remembering the illness of Laurie's ballet teacher. "Have there been other deaths?"

"Nine that we're sure of, another four questionable, and we're seeing more cases of it all the time. Most of them are teenagers, and we still don't know why." Haliburton did not know the way his face had changed, the hardness that had come over his features, sharpening his mild expression to one of honed determination.

"I'm . . . so sorry," said Jonathon. "One of my employees got the disease. In a way I feel responsible."

"You're not," said Haliburton promptly. "Whatever is spreading this bug, it isn't your food, or all of San Diego would be sick by now, just because the people that eat in your restaurants have friends and family. And it would be spreading much faster than it is. We think that it has something to do with an unidentified toxin, and an unregistered toxic waste dump. We want to identify it." He stared toward the banks of machines along the wall, as if by will alone the computers would bring forth answers and solutions.

"And these tests help?" asked Jonathon.

"We hope they will. They can give us needed information. They might show us where to look for the cause, for the specific toxin that is behind the condition." He put his hand out in an unconscious bid for aid. "We don't want to see any more of this if we can."

Catherine shook her head. "I don't know. I don't understand this."

"Neither do we, Missus Grey." Haliburton met her eyes. "I hope we do before we lose any more."

"Suppose we agree to help out—what would that entail?" asked Jonathon in a quick, decided way.

Haliburton concealed his relief; he knew that the Greys would be willing to cooperate if he did not press them too hard, and he did have access to their health records and the

Standard Public School Blood Screens. "For one thing, we'd need to do a regular monitoring of your family. As I've said, Laurie is all right, but there are a few indications that I want to keep an eye on."

"What indications?"

"There's an odd reading—nothing dangerous in itself, you understand—on Adrenocorticotrophic Hormone and Corticotrophin Releasing Factor. These are chemicals found in the brain, and it's true that there are subtle changes in this balance at puberty. The ACTH and CRF levels might tell us more about what—"

"Do you mean that she—and all of us—might have what Marilee . . . had?" Catherine asked, her voice becoming faint and her face paling.

"I doubt it," Haliburton said quickly and mendaciously. "This has all the earmarks of something in the environment, and in cases like this where there may be contamination involved, I want to make sure that any change in you and people in your general area be noted and tracked. That means Laurie as well as everyone else," he added for emphasis. "Just because no one else in the family has shown symptoms, it does not follow that there has been no further contamination. We have to be careful, not only for your family, but for all those who might be in the contamination range."

"I can't stand this," Catherine said softly. "I don't think I can take any more right now."

"Catherine, honey," Jonathon said, putting his hand on her arm, "we've got to listen."

"But monitoring and tests . . ." She put her hand to her mouth and shook her head vigorously. "Please."

"Missus Grey," Doctor Haliburton said, "I remember you were one of the parents who supported the Standard Public School Blood Screens. You know what a difference it made and continues to make. Without it, Tunis Flu Two and Three would have been far worse than they were, and we might not yet have stopped AIDS. This isn't much different than the SPSBS." He looked to Jonathon. "You can understand the problem, can't you?"

"I . . . think so," Jonathon said slowly. "I think I see what you're getting at." He turned to Catherine. "We ought to do it, honey. We owe it to Marilee. If there's anything that could go wrong because of what she had and we don't do our part, we . . . we . . ." He put his arms around her. "Doctor Michaelson has been telling us all along that it will take time to work out what . . . what Marilee died of. You said you wanted to help, and now you can."

She swallowed hard; her eyes were wet. "I keep wanting to put this behind us, the way we put Gary behind us."

"It's not the same thing," said Jonathon to her, his words so sad that Haliburton felt a pang deep within himself in response.

"I know, and I know that we said we'd consider the tests and all the rest of it, but Jonathon, I don't know . . . It's been so hard already. What's the point of dwelling on it?" Her eyes were reddening with her effort not to cry. "It's bad enough that Marilee died, but if we're constantly reminded, what then?"

"We have to . . . keep going." Jonathon pressed his lips together, enforcing his self-control with determination. "And that might mean we have to help. There may be more to go through before it's really behind us."

Catherine nodded several times. "What about Jared and Shelley? Is there any reason to think that they might . . . have the same thing?"

"I don't know yet, Missus Grey," said Haliburton. "Between Ben Michaelson and this office, we hope to avoid that possibility." He had great difficulty dealing with such naked pain, and was honest enough with himself to know that some of his passion for research sprang from his reluctance to deal with the helplessness and anguish of others. He sensed that he had come to a point where he might lose that precious insulation, which was briefly more distressing to him than the prospect of continuing deaths. At once he rebuked himself for his own cowardice.

"But constant tests... why?" Catherine asked. "Why more than one?"

"We don't know what this is," Haliburton repeated patiently. "Until we have an identification, we won't know what we're up against or what has to be done about it. I don't mean to frighten you, or to cause you trouble, but your family has been touched by this trouble already and it won't go away."

"And once you know what it is, what then?" Jonathon was curious as much as worried.

"That will depend on a great many things," Haliburton admitted. "I believe that whatever has caused this problem is related to a certain group of toxins, and there are methods for minimizing the damage they do. I won't promise you that we can eliminate the effect from everyone totally, because, unfortunately, that simply is not possible. These conditions are very complex and often the reactions cover a wide range of symptoms and recovery curves." He paused, weighing his next words. "I wish I could tell you that all we had to do was identify the toxin and that would be that. I can't. But if you agree to help us, we might speed up the identification, and that means that fewer people will be harmed by the contamination."

"You're certain that you're dealing with contamination?" Catherine challenged.

"What else could it be?" Haliburton countered. "If it's a matter of infection or contagion, I don't understand..." He shook his head. "We aren't ruling anything out, not yet. But I have to tell you that it isn't likely that it is any disease. It might be that there is a disease factor, but without more tests, there is no way to—"

"What if it is a disease? What if it's like the thing that killed all those sheep back in the Seventies? I remember Dad saying that there was lots more where that came from." The words poured out of Catherine, and she was powerless to stop them. "What would all those tests be worth if it's that kind of disease?"

Haliburton held her eyes with his own. "I don't know. Which is all the more reason to do the tests."

She looked from Haliburton to Jonathon. "I want to talk to Ben Michaelson. I'll cooperate, but I want Ben to tell me what's going on, every step of the way."

"All right," said Haliburton evenly. "That's not an unreasonable condition." He waited a moment. "I want to schedule tests for your family next week, and every month thereafter, at least for the next four months. It might be necessary to have more, but until we know more, this will provide basic comparisons. It's for your own safety as much as the public safety, Missus Grey." The last was more apology than warning.

She made a complicated gesture of acceptance. "Can we arrange this with Ben?"

"Of course," said Haliburton at once. "That's fine with me, with this department."

"All right," said Jonathon, his arm still around Catherine's shoulder. "We'll call and make the arrangements. Do you have the results you wanted to show us, or . . ."

"I have more than that," said Haliburton, indicating the door into the hallway. "I have someone who wants to talk with you, who's been interviewing everyone who has been exposed to the toxin. She is working up studies on the syndrome so that we can narrow in on where it comes from." He came around the counter and started for the door. "She'll be here in about ten minutes. In the meantime, I'll show you what information we do have and what we're doing with it."

"Conclusions?" Jonathon asked.

"We haven't reached any yet, except for tentative ones. Which is why your cooperation is so important to us." He frowned. "There are more cases being found every day, and that means that we're all at risk."

"Oh?" Catherine said sharply.

"Yes, Missus Grey. Every one of us might be carrying the toxins in our bodies right now, and whatever triggers the active syndrome . . ." He stepped into the hallway, waiting for the Greys to come after him. "Doctor Kostermeyer is gathering the necessary material to make an assessment."

"Why?" Catherine demanded as she followed after Haliburton.

"Doctor Kostermeyer works for the Department of Public Health and Environmental Services; many physicians do." He ushered them into a small conference room near the elevator bank.

"What kind of assessment are we talking about?" Jonathon asked as he pulled the door closed behind them and stood near the smaller of two tables, one in each arm of the L-shaped room.

"A PHES assessment," said Haliburton as he opened the draperies to reveal a stand of eucalyptus trees against an overcast sky. "They're used to determine the hazard potential to public health in the State of California. Sacramento requires it when more than a certain number of people are stricken. Where toxic factors may be present, the epidemiologists have certain discretionary powers. Doctor Kostermeyer has been actively investigating this syndrome since it began."

"Investigating how?" Jonathon asked, intrigued and puzzled at once.

"Gathering statistics on who has shown symptoms and getting as much of a history, medical and standard, as she can. She wants to find the pattern, such as living in the same area, or attending the same school, or going to the same shopping center. Any of those commonalities might give an indication of the kind of toxin we're looking for, and when we know that, then we're on the path to doing something about it." Haliburton hoped ardently that his last assertion was more than wishful thinking. He stared out the window. "It's important that we act quickly, in case—"

"In case what?" Catherine asked sharply when Haliburton did not go on.

"Oh, many things," he responded vaguely. "If we could anticipate the whole thing, it wouldn't be so fucking scarey." He was as astonished as the Greys were to hear this admission, and it took him a few seconds to recover. "That was out of line."

"But was it accurate?" Catherine prodded.

Haliburton sighed. "Yeah. Yeah, it's accurate. Most of us aren't admitting it yet, but there're indications—Doctor Kostermeyer will be able to tell you more about them than I can—that this might be one of those long-fuse things, and it could be that no one's really safe. Maybe every one of us will end up . . . tainted with it." He cleared his throat. "My Uncle Paul died of AIDS, and I remember how much panic there was about it before the vaccine. And that was a disease that was hard to get. But a syndrome that is the result of environmental contamination—how do you deal with something like that? How do you find a way to stop it when it—"

He was stopped by the opening of the door as Sylvia Kostermeyer stepped into the room. Her face was lined, her eyes were bright in shadows like bruises, and there was a trace of grey in her hair that had not been there two months before. "Hello," she said to the three people in the conference room. "I'm sorry I'm late."

"Are you?" Haliburton asked with surprise. "I thought . . . you . . ." He looked at his watch and realized that she was almost ten minutes late. "It's okay."

"Apparently," she said, with a flicker of a smile that was gone before it had a chance to form. "Is there any coffee?"

"I'll get you some," Haliburton volunteered, eager to have a few minutes to himself. "I'll get a pot and bring it back here; how's that?"

"Thanks," said Sylvia, tossing her large leather case onto the larger of the two tables. "I could use coffee. Or twelve hours of uninterrupted sleep." She looked at the Greys as Haliburton left the room. "Forgive the delay. I know it's hard on you, and all these tests and questions are inconvenient and troublesome, but I assure you that it's in a good cause."

"We know," said Jonathon.

"I'm sorry about your daughter," Sylvia said wearily.

"I'm sorry about all of them. And that's the trouble." She hesitated and then said, "We have confirmation of another sixteen cases."

"Sixteen cases?" Catherine repeated.

"Bringing the total of verified cases to a grand total of forty-seven."

"Is that—" Jonathon began, only to be cut off by Sylvia's next words.

"With thirty-four fatalities."

PART III

February—March, 1996

Maximillian Klausen and
————— Elihu Dover —————

Betty Radston was suffering from the first of her long series of spring allergies, but she smiled gamely as she brought in the morning reports to Max Klausen's office and set them along with a cup of fresh-brewed herbal tea on his desk. "Morning, Doctor. Are you officially awake and in yet?"

Max put his long, thick fingers over his eyes. "I wish I weren't," he muttered.

"Why?" Betty asked, aware that he was more than usually upset. "Bad news?"

"Eherman brought Eunice Dover in last night—thing that Barenssen woman had, it looks like. I had to call Elihu and tell him this morning before I left the house. Cassie gave me a lecture on being surly." He looked at the tea as if it might be a lab specimen. "How do you tell someone you've known most of your life that the woman he's been happily married to for over thirty years appears to have come down with some kind of syndrome that—" He dropped his hands to the desk, narrowly missing the tea-cup.

"If you've known him that long, perhaps it wouldn't be necessary to . . ." Betty ventured, not entirely sure herself what she was attempting to say.

"It would be necessary, no matter what. Elihu's been practicing medicine longer than almost any human being I've ever met and if it weren't for him, I might not have gone into medicine, and not into environmental medicine. Hell, what did I know, or care? I was twelve years old and my mother had moved my sister and me to Sweet Home to get away from the pressure of the city; she was in pretty bad shape back then. I got a kick out of taking care of chickens and sheep and goats—most of the time, anyway. Elihu Dover was our GP, and he kept encouraging me to look beyond where I was and to think about . . . oh, all kinds of things. Even if I didn't like him, I'd owe him." He lifted his teacup as if it weighed more than ten pounds.

Betty took a handkerchief from her pocket and blew her nose. "Allergy," she reminded Max. "How bad do you think it is?"

"You mean Eunice? Bad enough: the Barenssen woman died." He looked up at his assistant. "Elihu said he'd seen a couple other similar cases, but they're all part of that religious school there outside of Sweet Home, and getting any of them to go to the doctor isn't easy. They don't believe in it, think that it's contrary to Biblical order because it's an attempt to thwart God's will. They're Fundamentalists, the back-to-the-old-ways and back-to-the-land-and-simple-life stripe. I think the only reason we saw Kirsten Barenssen is because her brother isn't part of that sect, and he brought her to Elihu." He shook his head slowly. "I gather Eunice has been looking after the Barenssen kids until something can be arranged. I'm babbling, aren't I?"

"Nothing unusual in that," said Betty. "What information do you have on"—she could not remember if she knew the woman's name—". . . on Elihu's wife's condition?"

"Not enough, I can tell you that." Max stood up abruptly. "And I'd better do something about that. I want to see Eunice first and find out what the monitors have got on her since last night. If there's a chance, I'd like to talk to her. She's a steady woman and you can bet she's aware of the potentials of her condition. Then I have to go to that meeting that Watt has called and find out what he's tearing his hair about. And then I think I'm going to arrange for the afternoon off."

"Doctor Klausen!" Betty was genuinely shocked. She had rarely known Max Klausen to do anything impulsive or so irresponsible.

"I want to go out to Sweet Home and have a talk with Elihu. I might even try to get into that sub-community, the religious group, to find out how many other potential cases they have, and how serious they are. I've got a very bad hunch about this, and if I don't do something, it'll drive me out the window." He picked up the papers she had left for him. "I'll go over these as soon as I've seen Eunice."

"When do I schedule appointments, then?" Betty wondered.

"Tomorrow. I have one meeting this afternoon; I'd like for you to move it to tomorrow or the next day, if you can. If not, tell me before I leave and I'll see who can take it. It's nothing drastic—a report on the fluorescent light/computer screen readings at Vehicle Registration. They aren't going to like it much; neither total is acceptable." He looked for his overcoat. "See if Garland can take it. She's more involved in that than I am in any case."

Betty sneezed again. "I'll attend to it, Doctor." She was very careful to call him Max only on social occasions and when they were speaking privately in his office. "Anything else?"

Max was pulling on his overcoat, fussing with the collar and trying to button it at the same time. "Later," he said. His voice was naturally gruff and often those who did not know him thought him brusque because of it, but Betty smiled.

"I hope your friend Eunice turns out to be a false alarm."

"So do I," said Max as he headed for the door, annoyed that the shortest way to the hospital wing of the complex was across the large U-shaped courtyard; in April it would be a pleasant diversion, but today there was a sleety rain falling. Only the pines and low-growing cypress were green, and the walkways were slick and treacherous.

By the time he reached the hospital wing, his hair was wet and his shoes were soaked. He strode through the lobby and to the elevator bank, trying to ignore the squitch of each step. As he rode upward, smelling wet clothing and one or two lingering unidentifiable perfumes, he thought over the last few days of Kirsten Barenssen: the woman had faded away, losing strength and that sense of being present. She did not resist her disease, and what little time she was truly conscious she devoted to prayers that were a mixture of self-recrimination and ecstatic anticipation. The head nurse had said that Kirsten Barenssen had lost the will to live.

Eunice was in an isolation room, everything about her monitored and controlled. Even the sheets on her bed were the use-once-and-throw-away variety. Seeing Max come through the door, she smiled warmly. "You and El are too overprotective," she greeted him.

Max came and stood beside her bed, his overcoat left at the nurses' station and his body covered by a full-length disposable garment like a caftan. "They tell me I'm not supposed to kiss you."

"Probably a sensible precaution," she said. "We won't shake hands, either."

For a moment they looked at each other, each feeling awkward at being denied these basic courtesies, then Max drew up a chair and sat down beside her bed. "How are you feeling?"

"Not as well as I'd like," she said calmly. "I haven't got any stamina and I feel almost . . . shaky. El insisted that you check me out. He's convinced that there's some kind of epidemic breaking out in Sweet Home. I can't change his mind. And," she said more seriously, "if this is what's going around, I don't blame him for his concern."

"Is it going around?" Max asked with exaggerated nonchalance.

"That's your department, Maximillian," she said, taking her tone from him. As she leaned back on the pillows she gave an aggravated sigh. "I wish I could keep up. I haven't any strength, and that . . . irks me." Her fingers moved on the edge of the sheet. "I was exhausted all of Thursday because on Wednesday I did the shopping and put all my groceries away. For a while I thought I had something wrong with my stomach—I felt as if I was about to throw up, but I never did. Which nerve does that?" Before he could answer, she waved the question away. "It's not important. I really don't care which nerve it is; I'd simply like it to stop."

"So would I, Eunice," said Max with rising emotion. "I promise you that if there is a way to stop it, I will, just as soon as possible."

"You're hedging, Max. You aren't positive that you have enough information to treat this, are you?"

Max looked down at Eunice, at the greying hair that framed her face and the gentle, tired curve of her mouth. "Not yet, but we're working on it."

"Good." She nodded twice. "How long is it going to take?" She looked at him, then away. "No, it isn't fair to ask that, is it? How can you know yet how long this or anything is going to take? I know better; El's shown me a lot in thirty-one years, and I do know that it isn't reasonable to make such demands. But, Max, it is so tempting."

"I know." He reached down and put his hand over hers, annoyed at the sterile mittens that covered his fingers. "It's the most frustrating job in the world at times like this. I keep thinking that there ought to be a sensible way, an easy way, to figure out what's going on, for this or any other disease, but there never is." He studied her face, aware that she was pale—that was the effect of the anemia. There was also a lack of animation that came from bone-deep fatigue; the latter concerned him far more than the former. "It might be a bit of a fight," he said, offering her the warning as consolation.

"I've had some experience with that," she said, remembering back to her twenties when she had been a social worker in Eureka. "I won't expect miracles and I won't squander what resources I have left."

Max nodded. "I'm counting on it, Eunice." He cocked his head to the side. "Are you afraid?"

"Of course I'm afraid," she said curtly. "In my position, you would be, too."

"Don't let that get in the way, if you can manage it," said Max with strain coming into his words. "There are times the fear is a thousand times more deadly than the condition, whatever it is."

"I know; I learned that from El." She coughed gently, her expression becoming apologetic.

"Well, if you can, keep it in mind while we're running our tests and all the rest of it, okay?" He wished he had something cheering to tell her, but the glib assurances stuck in his throat.

"Remind me, Max," she said, doing her best to be playful. "But keep in mind that I don't like being in the dark. Tell me what you do or don't discover, and what changes are happening. I know I'll be less worried if I know what's going on. If I don't, I'll start imagining, and that will be worse than anything." She looked at him with the pert intensity of a bird. "You will do that, won't you?"

"Yes, Eunice. I'll do that." He made a mental note to himself to instruct the nursing staff not to waffle. He recognized the slight hesitation in her voice, the trace of breathiness as she spoke that told him more than any chart or tracing that the condition was taking its toll on her. Now that he looked, he saw that her skin was not only pale but waxy as well, and that her hair was without lustre, falling in lank tendrils around her face. "We're going to take good care of you, Eunice," he said with determination, as if his promise would drive away what he had seen.

"I should hope so," she responded with a cough that was meant to be laughter.

Max made himself go on. "I'm planning to visit Elihu this afternoon, to find out how many other cases have cropped up in Sweet Home, and to see if there are others in the immediate area."

"There isn't much but Sweet Home in the immediate area," said Eunice. "You remember what it's like? It hasn't changed a lot in the last twenty years." She turned her head on the pillow. "It's strange, but I have these moments of dizziness. I never know when to expect them. They pass, but for a short while it's almost as if I were seasick."

It took Max a little time to think of the right comment. "When were you ever seasick, Eunice?"

"Well, actually, I was once," she said, grateful for the chance to speak of something other than the mysterious disease that had brought her to this hospital, this room, this bed. "It was years and years ago, and I was going out with my father and brother, on a small party boat out of Coos Bay. It was cold, and I'd eaten extra pancakes with lots of everything." Her face softened with her memory. "That lots-of-everything was my undoing, of course. It was a rough day, with an eight-foot swell. I was so dreadfully embarrassed." She was able to smile briefly. "What other tests are you going to run?"

Max took a deep breath. "We're going to run a PAST scan on you. It's one of our newest toys, the PAST scanner. You'll like it—it looks like something out of a bad science fiction movie. It's very low radiation and it measures temperature fluctuations, mineral concentrations, nerve reactions and oxygen levels, along with the usual things. It's very good at showing toxins in bone and tissue; that's what it was developed to do." He held up his hands. "What we do next depends on your PAST."

It was a feeble joke, but Eunice obliged with the ghost of a chuckle. "Isn't that always the case?"

"Yes," said Max, and turned as a nurse in full protection came in the door. "What now?"

"Sorry, Doctor. We're taking her downstairs in half an hour and there are certain—"

"I know," Max cut her off, then turned back to Eunice. "I'll give Elihu your love and try to get him not to worry."

"I haven't been able to do that in all the years we've been married, but you're welcome to try," she said, sounding tired.

"I'll try to get by your room this evening, but if I don't, I'll see you tomorrow," said Max, ignoring the ferocious scowl of the nurse. "You take care. We're going to lick this thing, Eunice. We are."

"Good," said Eunice flatly, her attention now on the nurse.

Max shed his throwaway garments and sought out his overcoat once more.

By the time he reached Sweet Home it was almost three o'clock, and he was tense from the long drive in the heavy rain. Max debated stopping for a late lunch, but could not bring himself to delay his meeting with Elihu. As he drove through Sweet Home, he was surprised to see how few buildings had changed in the last twenty years. On the west side of town there was one stand of small townhouses, and what had been a six-acre field when Max was a teenager now held a seven-shop mini-mall. Two of the main street stores were a bit larger and had modernized their front, but for the most part, nothing was different. Max turned on his lights and took the right turn that would bring him to the Dover house.

Elihu Dover was waiting for him. "I canceled two afternoon appointments," he said when perfunctory greetings had been exchanged. "One's Ned Cherny—owns the hardware store, you remember?—for his ulcers; it's not urgent. The other is old Missus FitzSimmons. The worst thing wrong with her is loneliness, and there isn't much I can do about that. Poor woman. She really hasn't anyone since Jerry was killed in Morocco." As he spoke he led the way into the living room and indicated the chair nearest the fireplace. "Sit down and get warm. If you'll let me have your coat I'll hang it up to dry. Is there anything I can get you to drink?"

"Elihu," said Max quietly, stopping the evasions of his host, "I'm sorry. We still haven't isolated the toxin. We're doing everything we can: you can bet on that."

"I know," said Elihu, standing near the living room entrance with Max's coat still in his hands. "I know."

"When I told you I needed your help, I meant it. With Eunice, you know I'll do everything I can to . . ." He sat down and stared into the fire, noticing that it had just been started and that the two split logs were not yet burning.

"I'll do anything I can." Elihu stopped, unable to speak until he brought his emotions under more control. "Out here, who would have thought that there would be something like—"

"That's part of the trouble," Max said, pleased that there was a bit of explanation he could offer to Elihu. "Twenty years ago, thirty years, there were companies that looked for places like Sweet Home because of their isolation as a dumping site for all kinds of wastes. The laws weren't as strict and enforcing them was much more difficult."

"I remember," said Elihu. "That case in '88."

"For example," said Max. "The State lost its case."

Elihu shook his head, bewildered and angry. "And now this?"

"Possibly," said Max carefully. "It might be some other toxin we have yet to identify." He looked back into the fire. "I want to check out anyone in town that's known to be sick. Including those people in the religious community. I want to get a better idea of how widespread this thing is."

"I'll call Barenssen. His kids are staying out there, and since Kirsten died of the stuff, he might be able to persuade them to see you. I can't be sure—they're pretty stiff-necked."

"I don't need guarantees, but a good try might save lives. Tell them that, will you?"

"All right," said Elihu dubiously, and went to hang up

Max's coat before he made his phone call. As he lifted the receiver, he said, "What about Eunice?"

"I don't know yet, Elihu," Max said.

"I mean, if we can find the toxin and isolate it," he enlarged. "What do you think her chances are?"

"It depends," said Max as he listened to Elihu use his old-fashioned dial phone. "Principally on time, but to some degree on the toxin itself. What kind of poison has got into her, and what has it done. Until we can answer those questions, there's nothing we can do but try to alleviate the worst of her symptoms." He was aware that this was not news to Elihu, that his old friend only wanted to hear something that would give him hope. "There are times when we've seen dramatic recoveries if we reach the source in time." It was a concession, but sincerely felt.

"Suppose you can't isolate the toxin? Suppose it's not natural or—" He might have gone on, but he interrupted his words to Max to speak into the phone. "Hello, Sven? This is Doctor Dover calling." There was a little silence. "I have a colleague visiting from Portland, the man who's treating Eunice, in fact, and we were wondering if it might be possible to visit you and the boys. And Reverend Colney as well." Once again there was silence. "I see; unhuh." More silence. "My friend has only the afternoon, and it's important that—" Pause. "I understand the difficulty." An impatient silence. "It's not just your sister or my wife who could be involved, Sven, it's your children and the people of this community. I realize that there's some . . . opposition to medical treatment, but in this case, since the possible cause is man-made, wouldn't it seem that it was man's responsibility to take care of it?"

Max could tell that Elihu was on the verge of anger, and so he rose and moved toward the entry hall where the phone was. "Tell him for me that others could be affected. Innocent men, women and children."

"I'll let you tell him yourself," said Elihu testily as he handed the receiver to Max.

Thrust into this awkward situation with no preparation, Max found himself at a loss. "Mister Barenssen?" he said, cutting into the long argument Sven Barenssen was offering, "This is Doctor Klausen, from Portland. I specialize in environmental disease and I was the one who looked after your sister. I'm very sorry that there was nothing we could do to save her."

"God had other plans," said Sven Barenssen with nervous conviction, reciting the words like a frightened child.

"Possibly," Max said, going carefully. "What worries me is that in this case, it may have had more to do with human error than the will of God."

"Human error *is* the will of God," said Sven.

"But surely we're allowed, even expected, to improve?" Max asked, hoping it was the right question, hoping that he would not lose contact with this terrified man.

"That is why we are subjected to trials," declared Sven.

Max mentally crossed his fingers and plunged ahead. "And this is apt to be one of them. I know you're aware of it. I know that you've been through a lot these last years, and I hope that there may be ways we can lessen your burdens."

"God will lessen them in His time," Sven said.

"Yes, and possibly with a little human help, we can all avert a very real disaster," Max said, pleased that Sven had not yet hung up on him. "I have reason to believe that your sister and Doctor Dover's wife were damaged by the same . . . the same factors. We haven't isolated the cause of death yet, but every indication is that the cause is environmental, possibly even worse than that, such as leakage from a toxic material storage dump, or—"

"Were they radioactive?" Sven cut in.

"Not exactly," said Max, tempted to lie and say yes. "But the problem of toxic contamination is not unlike being hurt by radioactivity." He sensed paranoia in Sven Barenssen, and decided to use it if he could. "It has many of the same results."

"Really?" Sven asked, for the first time not sounding like he was speaking imperfectly learned lines.

"Yes. I know how hard this is, and how much courage it takes to speak out, but in this case, you could save lives, lives that might otherwise be lost to this poison that has touched the lives of your family already." Max decided that he sounded like a bad political campaigner and was trying to find a way to modify his bombastic statements when Sven spoke to him.

"I don't know what Preacher Colney will say, but I'll talk to him right away. He's a good Christian and he knows his duty to succor those in need. If he gives his permission, we'll arrange for you to speak to the congregation before prayer meeting tonight. All I ask is that you don't frighten my boys too much—they've been through so many trials already..."

"You have my word that I will not distress your boys if I can help it," said Max with the beginning of relief. "I appreciate this, Mister Barenssen."

"Thank the Lord, not me. And if Preacher Colney says no, that's the end to it."

"Fine, fine," said Max, preparing to hang up.

"We'll pray for you, and for the souls of those afflicted, whatever else we do," promised Sven. "I'll call you back in half an hour. Thank you, Jesus." This appeared to be his way of saying good-bye, for he hung up without waiting for a response from Max.

"Well?" asked Elihu as he closed the door to the hall closet where coats were hung.

"He'll try to arrange for us to talk to the congregation before prayer meeting," said Max as he went back toward the living room.

"Well, that's a start," said Elihu, who was picking up the phone.

"Who're you calling now?" asked Max.

"I just thought of her: Annie Melton, the midwife. There's lots of remote farms and ranches out in the mountains, and the only person they see who might know something about disease is Annie."

Max leaned back, trying not to count the minutes, trying not to think about what he would do if the congregation refused to let him speak to them. He hated the bleakness of spirit that threatened to overcome him. "Elihu, when you're through, I better phone home and tell them not to wait dinner for me."

"Okay," said Elihu, and resumed his conversation with the midwife's answering machine.

Dale Reed and
_____ Wendell Picknor _____

Irene Channing's room was on the isolation floor and was as close to a penthouse as a hospital could boast; it was large enough to accommodate twenty people in comfort if they didn't mind standing up, or sitting on the massive isolation bed where Irene now lay, her features pale and drawn, her luminous eyes sunken.

"We're making progress," Dale Reed was telling her, leaning over the bed. "We've been doing another series of tests on the blood samples we took, and we're reasonably sure that this is a toxic reaction of some sort. Are you sure the only thing you're allergic to is aspirin?" For a joke it was feeble, but Irene was willing to smile for him.

"Just aspirin, and anything else coming from willow trees," said Irene, sounding more exhausted than Reed had ever heard before.

"There are allergies that might account for the trouble, even as serious as yours appears to be." He stopped and looked at her closely. "You have the most beautiful eyes."

To his surprise she made a dismissing gesture. "Christ, don't say that; it's almost as bad as saying that I have pretty hair or good skin."

"But you do," protested Reed, bewildered by her reaction.

"Sure. And every plain girl that ever lived has been told those things, over and over and over again. Just like the pep talks that say if you work to bring out your good points, the bad ones won't matter. Or the worst of all— that if a guy really cares for you it won't matter what you look like. I heard every one of 'em when I was growing up." She stopped abruptly, her face slightly flushed, the shadows around her eyes deepening. Her nearest hand extended toward his, but the protective clothing and bed covering hampered them and she let her hand drop.

"We've found another fifteen cases, all in the same general area—Highland Park, unfortunately—and we're trying now to find out what the cause is."

She did not want to be distracted. "I'm sorry to hear that. But what does that have to do with my miserable youth, I want to know?"

"Was it really a miserable youth?" Reed asked, hardly believing it.

"It wasn't very happy," she amended. "There I was, all elbows and knees and graceless as a pelican on the beach. The only thing I could do was draw, and my mother, a very sensible woman in her own way, wanted me to learn something worthwhile, such as how to be a legal secretary so I could land a good catch. That last was her phrase."

"And you got a man worth millions," said Reed, "because of your drawing."

"Painting," she corrected, then took a deep, uneven breath. "Highland Park, hum?"

"Yes. There's a lot of pressure being put on the State Health Bureau to investigate for toxic wastes. Of course, no one in Highland Park is anxious to open that can of worms, either—millionaires are like that—and so there's a delicate little ballet going on. We'll see what comes of it in the next couple weeks." He hesitated. "The boys are doing well. I'm trying to get the hospital to bend the rules a little so they can visit you, but I'm not making much headway." It was not easy to admit this; still he felt she had to know that she was not forgotten.

"So long as they're okay," said Irene. "Do either of them have anything . . . you know, *wrong*?"

"You mean symptoms like yours? No, neither Steven nor Brice have shown any sign of your condition. All the same, I do think it's just as well that they stay with their cousins in Austin."

"How do the Hills feel about it?" Irene asked, her manner a bit arch. "Don't tell me they're thrilled, because I won't believe it. Having cousins dropped on them in an emergency like this is nothing to be happy about." She looked toward the window, at the drawn blinds. "Is it still snowing?"

"It stopped about an hour ago," said Reed. "Irene, if there's anything I can do, *anything*, all you have to do is name it and you can bet it's done." He smiled, hoping she would see it in his eyes since his mouth was hidden. "Your mail is being taken in, and the arrangements for the show are going on as planned."

"But I didn't finish all the paintings I wanted," she protested, nearly whining.

"There were nine more in the house, and that's enough. You'll have over forty works on display, and that's—"

"Almost enough to cover my medical bills?" she quipped.

"Your insurance covers everything but the first five hundred dollars," he reminded her, not amused at her observation. "Not that it matters, under the circumstances."

"You mean I could sell the farm and the house and some of the trinkets and I'd be okay?" Her lightness was fading as fast as it had come. "I suppose that would do it, if I have to pay. If the mortuary has to be paid, someone else can make that choice."

"Don't say that," Reed ordered sharply. "I don't want to hear that from you, Irene."

"Don't you?" She turned her head away from him. "But I have to face facts. I don't have the luxury of ignorance, and if I pretend I do, I'll only leave a greater mess for the boys, and that isn't fair. I've been trying to put my affairs in—"

"You tell me what you want done and I'll attend to it," said Reed, leaning as close to her as all the protection permitted. "You have instructions for your attorneys, you let me know what they are and I'll handle it. You're not to do anything that's tiring or distressing, and that is not negotiable."

"You men, you always think you can shape the world the way you want it if you only can be strict enough and boss enough with it." She looked at him again. "Don't you understand that you can't make those sorts of changes?"

"You do as I tell you," Reed insisted, paying little heed to what she had said. "If I find out that you're running yourself down and working yourself into a depression because of wills and bequests, then you'll be in real trouble."

"I'm worried about my children. I'm worried about my work. I'm scared shitless that I'm going to die before I've taken care of it all. If I don't work on these things, Dale," she said more emphatically, speaking slowly for added impact, "then I will fret and get depressed. If I know that I've settled as much as I can, then I'll be more relaxed." Her eyes met his directly. "If you stop me from doing this, you are not helping me."

Reed smacked his hands together, and though the protective garments he wore muffled the sound, he spoke as if the clap had been loud. "I'll tell you what: I'll arrange for your attorney to visit, and you can talk over your predicaments with him and then—"

"Her," corrected Irene.

Caught in mid-thought, Reed was thrown. "What?"

"My attorney, my personal attorney is a woman. Her

name is Edith Kentish." Irene watched Reed digest this information.

"All right; Edith Kentish can visit and you can tell her what you need her to do. The trouble with illness is that it is debilitating all by itself, and that doesn't leave much room for handling other things. I don't want to argue with you about this. I'm stretching rules for you already, and frankly it doesn't always sit well with me." He smiled as he said this, as if the smile would mitigate his twinges. "It's not just you, Irene, but everyone else around you, since we don't know what your disease is, only that several people have it and so far it has shown a pretty high fatality rate."

"How high?" Irene asked, and when Reed hesitated, she said, "Dale, tell me. I'll hear the hospital scuttlebut in any case, and this way the information has a chance of being right."

"We haven't had anyone come in with it so far who has . . . recovered." He knew that this was more than she could handle and he did what he could to soften the blow. "That doesn't mean quite what you think. So far we haven't been able to isolate what we're treating. That's really the crux of the problem, that we aren't sure what is disease and what is side effect. Once we do, then there are many methods of treatment open to us. We're being cautious so that we don't inadvertently fuel the fire." That, at least, was accurate.

"I see," she said, her face turning from him again. "Will you leave me for a couple hours, Dale? I have to think about this. I have to steady myself."

"Sure," he said reluctantly. He reached out and patted her arm through all the gear between them. "I'll be back. You're going to get well, Irene. I'm set on it."

"Thanks," she said in a voice that quivered.

"Nothing to thank me for yet," he said, damning himself for the truth of his words. He was at the door when she spoke again.

"I know that my hair looks awful, and that I'm chalky-pale and that I don't smell very good. Half the time I want to sit and cry. I'm glad you want to cheer me up, and I know that when you say I look good, you mean that you care about me. But don't flatter me, okay, Dale?" She had propped herself on her elbows and was watching him closely. "It makes me doubt everything you say when you do that."

"I'll try to remember," he promised her.

"See you."

Once he had shed the protective clothing and passed through the double partition that separated the quarantined rooms from the rest of the hospital, Dale Reed headed at once for epidemiology on the second floor. He went at a brisk pace, his eyes fixed forward so that it was not likely he would be stopped by one of the nurses or his patients he might encounter on the way. He kept thinking about what Irene had said to him, and about the doubts it caused. It was not possible or sensible, yet he wanted to go back and argue with her, to straighten it out with her so that she would know for him it made no difference if her hair wasn't perfect, or her make-up was on, or any of the rest of it: to him she was beautiful. That was for later, he vowed, when he had some hope to offer her as well.

Wendell Picknor's office had a view of the freeway interchange and the parking lot, but it was large and had access to the computer room. Wendell himself looked more like an overgrown farmboy than a highly qualified physician with an additional Ph.D. in public health and a genius IQ. He wore a lab coat over his plaid flannel sport shirt and his tawny hair needed cutting. "Hi, Dale," he said as Reed came into his office. "Just the man I wanted to see."

"Convenient," said Reed, making sure the door was closed. "How's it going?"

"We're comparing test results for all the patients with the same condition Missus Channing has. I've got the first printout right here"—he indicated a stack of paper atop other stacks of paper on his desk—"and they're running the second batch right now."

"And?"

"Nothing so far," Picknor admitted. "We're drawing blank after blank. I'm getting all of this ready for Atlanta. The Environmental Disease branch has more statistics and information than we have in Dallas. They might have records from other parts of the country where this has cropped up. I think we might be looking at a condition with a long fuse—possibly years of incubation—and that complicates the problem. Atlanta's better able to develop information than we are, if that's the case." He looked up at the ceiling, as if reading dim runes there. "They also have access to some of the information on secret government dumping sites, in case this is one of those little goodies the feds cooked up and threw away." He raised his head so that his lantern jaw stood out. "They might even have enough records there to show us where to look for what's wrecking the collagen on all these patients. After the fever starts, their blood comes apart, almost. It can't hold on to anything." He sighed abruptly and looked at Reed. "Which is why I wanted to talk to you."

Reed had been listening with increasing apprehension. "What does that have to do with Missus Channing? Are you telling me her condition is deteriorating?"

"It's what I'm trying to find an obtuse way to suggest. I don't want to tell you anything, because I don't know enough, not really."

"When you consider her case, how optimistic can you be?" Reed asked, trying not to be too sarcastic. "Are we talking about weeks, or what?"

"I don't know. She's alive, and though she's very weak, she isn't going downhill as fast as some of the others. She's as close to holding her own as any patient I've seen, and that is encouraging, simply because it isn't bad news. I don't know how she's fighting it, or if she has some kind of resistance to it built into her genes, but if there's anyone in there I think could pull through it's your Missus Channing." He patted the printouts again. "There isn't much else to report, not yet. I've sent word to most of the major hospitals in the Southwest, in case they're seeing any of this stuff. So far, there's only been one possible case in Flagstaff, which is all the more reason to think that we're dealing with environmental contamination."

Reed nodded. "Suppose other parts of the country have something like this spreading—how would you know about it, and what difference would it make?"

"Well, any doc worth his salt would run the standard tests, and given the peculiarities of the disease, would have to reach the same conclusion: environmental contamination of some sort. It's the only diagnosis that fits." He crossed his arms and grabbed his elbows as if to restrain them. "I hope Atlanta comes through for us. I hope that someone, somewhere, has a line on this shit."

"Where do I come in? What about Missus Channing?" Reed smoothed his tie nervously. "Isn't there a way to get her more help than she's getting now?"

"There would be, if we knew what we were up against; you're sensible enough to know that." Picknor looked out the window at the winter afternoon and the traffic snarl on the freeway. "How many other cases are out there, that's what I want to know. Who else is walking around with this crap in him, waiting to shred his blood?"

"What about an alert or a screening?" Reed suggested.

"I asked Public Health to start a screening program, the same kind we used for the Tunis Flu Two in Ninety-one, but they're not willing to do it yet. They've agreed to send around a bulletin to all physicians, hospitals and clinics in the state—it duplicates some of what I've done, but what the hell—and to follow up any leads."

"That's a start," said Reed cautiously. In the distance he could hear the whoop of an ambulance siren. "I'm willing to do a blood workup on all my patients as standard for as long as you say it's a good idea."

"Fine," was Picknor's absent response. "What bothers me is the number of teenagers who've come down with the stuff. It's way out of proportion, almost three teenagers to one adult, and that doesn't make sense."

"Maybe the contamination, whatever it is, was dumped, or released, or started while they were younger and that's tended to make the condition show up sooner." Reed frowned. "Mono is pretty much a teenagers' condition."

"But what about younger kids? Why aren't any *little* kids coming down with it?" Picknor asked angrily.

"Long fuse, like you said," Reed answered, dissatisfied with it as Picknor.

"That's a fucking weird long fuse," Picknor said. "I'm going to get a cup of coffee. You want one?"

"Sure; thanks," said Reed, his mind still on the puzzle of the strange disease.

"I hope that Atlanta can give us a hand on this one. If they can't, I haven't a clue about what to do next. I want to get to the bottom of this, but I don't have enough to go on yet." He went toward the door to the computer room where the coffee machine was. "Cream or sugar?"

"Black, with a dash of cinnamon," said Reed, endorsing the latest coffee fad. "What if Atlanta can't give you a hand on this?"

"Then we're up the proverbial creek," came Picknor's voice from the next room. "And I don't want to think about that yet."

Reed nodded slowly. He began to think over his patients and to consider the complaints he had had from them during the last six months. One of them, a principal at a local high school, had come in suffering from mild anemia and fatigue. There had been nothing more wrong, and Reed had not been very concerned since the woman had a history of heavy menses. Now he wondered if he ought to call her back and run more thorough tests on her. It would alarm her, of course, but surely he owed it to her to make certain she was not suffering from the same disease that was devastating Irene Channing. He reached for the phone on Picknor's desk and dialed his own office. "Marge?" he said when his receptionist came on the line with his name and the name of his partners.

"Doctor Reed?" said Marge.

"Look, I want you to call Jenny Wentworth and schedule a full blood workup for her."

"What?" Marge said, then, before Reed could speak, she said, "Missus Wentworth called an hour ago. She wants to see you as soon as possible."

"Why?" Reed asked, though he was already certain he knew the reason. "Did she tell you?"

"Only that her condition was worse and that she was starting to run a fever. She's pretty upset, Doctor Reed. I told her I'd let her know how soon you can see her."

It took Reed a few seconds to gather his thoughts, and then he had to school himself to speak in his usual brisk fashion instead of with the worry that was at him. "Ask her if she can come to the office this evening at say, six. Tell her that I may want her to check into the hospital for a few days. If she can't manage this, call me back at once. I'm in Picknor's office and will be for another half hour." He held the receiver away from his ear, knowing that Marge would tend to it in her usual efficient way. "Thanks," he said before he hung up.

"You look rotten, if you don't mind my mentioning it," said Picknor as he came back into the room with two cups in his hand. "Had bad news, or what?"

"I think I might have turned up another case of the same thing Missus Channing has," said Reed heavily.

"You might as well get used to it," said Picknor, handing one of the two cups to him. "If I'm right, you'll be seeing more of it in the next several months."

"You sure know how to make a guy feel good," said Reed. He tasted the coffee but the savor did not register. "I'm having her come to the office this evening. Is there room for her?"

"I'll call admissions and see what I can arrange," said Picknor. "Give me the name and I'll take care of it."

Reed scribbled Mrs. Wentworth's name on a memo and handed it to Picknor. "She's forty-nine, married, three children and one grandchild. She's a high school principal. You'll like her."

"Highland Park high school?" asked Picknor with false casualness.

"No. But not far from there, come to think of it. It's a private school, specializing in problem kids—not behavioral problems; learning problems, dyslexia, that sort of thing—and kids with minor handicaps. They do a lot of sports there; in fact, their track team walloped the competition all through last semester."

"Interschool competition, then?" Picknor said.

"What are you getting at? Do you think that might be connected?"

"I don't know what to think. I don't know what's connected, and damn it all to perdition, I don't know where to start. I only pray that I don't make a wrong choice and lose valuable time chasing down false leads." Picknor slapped his thigh in disgust. "I hate this. I fucking hate it."

"Yeah," Reed said. He drank most of the rest of his coffee, then said, "Look, after you talk to Atlanta, will you let me know what you've found out, if anything."

"Sure. Where can I reach you?" Picknor did not let Reed answer, but held up the memo. "Call me once Missus Wentworth's admitted. Maybe we can compare notes then. I ought to have the first response by then. If not, I'll try to catch you on rounds tomorrow."

"Okay," said Reed. He let his thoughts wander briefly, and then he said, "Do you mind if I look over those printouts? I don't know if I can help any, but sometimes two heads are better than one."

Picknor shrugged and handed a stack to Reed. "Help yourself. If you see anything you can make heads or tails of, tell me about it, won't you."

Reed was almost halfway through the printouts when his office called back saying that Mrs. Wentworth would meet him at his office or the hospital, whichever he preferred, at six-thirty. "Tell her to make it the hospital, then, the out-patient entrance—that'll save time. Thanks, Marge."

"Sure thing, Doctor Reed," she said.

Reed went back to the printouts with a growing sense of defeat.

Corwen Blair and Wilson Landholm

"There are more than twenty kids in the school out with that stuff, and that's in addition to the dead ones," Wil Landholm shouted into the telephone. "I want someone from your department to move ass down here right now and start checking this out before we have a full-scale epidemic on our hands."

"Doctor Landhold, I'm sure that—"

"Land*holm*," he corrected. "Doctor Wilson Justice Landholm. Your office must have my credentials on file somewhere." His temper was not helping him, he knew, but he was not willing to play the endless games that the bureaucrats demanded. "Don't give me any shit, Blair. I know about you and the trouble you got into during the Tunis Flu. We could have saved two thousand more people if you hadn't held us up with paperwork forever. Your office was so busy making sure you were protected that you left everyone else out in the cold." Before he could compound his offense, Landholm took a deep breath and deliberately let it out on a slow count of eight.

"Doctor Landholm," said Blair in a condescending tone, "I don't want to upset you any more than you obviously are already, but you have to understand that one of the purposes of our office is to assuage the general public's fears so that we will not have any panic. If there is some sort of communicable disease with a high fatality rate, than it behooves us to do everything possible to calm the citizens. If they are permitted to panic, they might leave the area, and then we would have trouble, because the disease could not be contained."

"Did you actually say 'behooves'?" Landholm wondered aloud.

"It is the correct word, Doctor Landholm," said Blair. "Not that it would matter to you. You specialize in athletic medicine, don't you? Sports injuries, tennis elbow, football knee, that sort of thing?"

Landholm bit back two equally contemptuous retorts, then said evenly, "I want to understand why it is that you are permitting this to go uninvestigated. I want it on record that I believe you are exceeding your authority in this matter, that you are abusing the public trust, that you are not acting in the best interests of the people of this state. And furthermore, I am going to contact the Environmental Authority in Washington to find out what might be causing this outbreak." He wanted the satisfaction of slamming down the receiver, but was stopped by the cold, imposing tones of Corwen Blair.

"You're free to do that, of course. But if it turns out that you have made a mountain of a molehill, Doctor Landholm, I want you to know that I will do everything in my power to see that you lose your license and I will sue you for slander and defamation of character. Win or lose, I will tie up your life in litigation for the next decade."

"See you in court, Doctor Blair," Landholm muttered as he hung up.

Blair glowered at his telephone, furious that he was deprived of the satisfaction of hanging up first. When at last he put the phone down, he had brought his breathing almost back to normal and the flush had receded from his fair skin. He stared at the notepad on his desk and tried to decipher what he had said to himself.

"Doctor Blair?" said one of his underlings from the door, a fresh-faced young woman recently out of internship. She was an exotic in this office, a talented internist of Mexican-Vietnamese parentage who had placed fifth in her class but had not yet found a specialty that attracted her.

"Miss Paniagua," he said, forgetting her proper title as usual.

"You sent for me? It's eleven o'clock." She looked at her watch as if there might be some doubt.

"Oh, I hadn't realized it was so late. That last call took longer than I had anticipated." He moved away from the desk, then said as if he had a passing thought, "Have we had any change in the incidence of mononucleosis recently? Any increase or more severe cases?"

"I don't know," said Dien Paniagua. "Would you like me to look up the records?"

"If you would. There's no rush, of course, but I gather that there might be a slight increase and it would be sensible to keep an eye on the stats, in case we need to issue schoolwide recommendations and physicians' advisories." He squared up the stack of envelopes at the corner of his desk. "Also, if there are any indications that we ought to be on the alert for some kind of toxic reaction in the general public, something that has to do with an old dump or maybe delayed fallout reaction from the old testing grounds, keep me informed, will you?"

"Of course," said Dien Paniagua, curious to know who had brought this on. In the sixteen months she had worked for Blair her respect for him had eroded steadily, so that now she thought of him only as an incompetent physician interested in protecting his place in the power structure, and willing to do whatever seemed expedient to maintain it. As she followed him down the hall, she decided that she would take the time to review the various reports that came into their office to try to find out what was behind this atypical interest.

The conference room was larger than necessary, and the chair at the head of the long table was taller than the others, and had two massive padded arms to enhance its throne-like image. Though there were only going to be four people at the meeting, Blair predictably took the head chair and indicated that Doctor Paniagua should sit four places down from him. Neither of the other two persons attending the meeting was permitted any nearer their boss.

"I have called this meeting in order to inform you that we will be up for federal review again in six months, and the matching funds from the federal government will be reassessed. If we are to keep up our current duties, we will need to convince both the federal and state authorities that we are in need of more money and more help. You will all agree that the work load is too great for the number of men and women we have on the job here. Therefore, I want each of you to take the time to outline the upcoming projects you plan to pursue and to specify the amount of money and personnel you will need in order to complete those projects with the greatest dispatch. I do not want you to cut corners, nor to be sparing of budget. Remember, we always have ways to spend the money we have, but we do not always have ways to get more." He spread his hands face down on the table. "So far each of your departments has shown a tendency not to meet deadlines, and for that reason, I think it best that you consider your projects both at current manpower and with increased employment."

"But it isn't a manpower problem, it's a time problem," said Tracy Bell unwisely. "We simply don't have time enough to gather all the data we need. If we could extend our deadlines we could manage with our current work force very easily."

Blair's face darkened. "I don't believe what I am hearing, Doctor Bell. You do not appreciate our position within the State Department of Health, and if you do not, it is time you did."

All three of his underlings concealed sighs with varying degrees of success.

"Doctor Blair," said Daniel Vitale, "we all share that same problem, and there's no use saying that it isn't important, or that more manpower is the answer: it isn't, that's all there is. You may want to think so, and that's up to you, but I have to warn you that the reports we are sending out of my section are inadequate and misleading because we do not have enough time to compile our material and get useful comparative curves. We handle disability in my division, and that is a tricky area. In limiting us to six-month units, we have little opportunity to show either recovery rates, or seasonal fluctuations in the various accidents and injuries we have to process." He stood up, one hand on his hip. "Recently there's been a slight increase in short-term claims, but unless we're given longer units of time, we can't know if this is part of a normal cycle, or something else."

"I'll consider what you say. It might be worth while to consider establishing a long-term statistical analysis branch to overview all the departments. That way we'll be able to interrelate all our data." Blair's close-set eyes shone at the very thought. "We'll need to think about that."

Vitale shook his head with frustration. "If you'll forgive my saying so, Doctor Blair, we do not need another layer of paperwork and muddle to weight us down, we need, if anything, a simplification of our current system, not the addition of another cumbersome department." He looked at Tracy Bell and Dien Paniagua. "What do you say? Can we get together and come up with a plan for simplification? Would you be willing to spend a couple extra evenings a week for the next month or so working out a way to streamline our departments?"

"Fine with me," said Bell.

"I can make arrangements," said Paniagua, who had a three-year-old son at home.

"You see, Doctor Blair? We're willing. It won't cut into your time and there's no reason for you to—"

"This is ridiculous!" thundered Blair. "Good God, man, do you realize what you're suggesting?"

"I'm suggesting we find a way to deliver health information to the people of this state," said Vitale with asperity. "We aren't doing a very good job of that now, and if we muck it up with more bureaucracy, we'll deliver even less."

"Your behavior is inexcusable," said Blair with a frown that had frightened lesser men than Dan Vitale.

"I'm trying to do the work I was hired to do, sir. No disrespect intended, Doctor Blair, but this department has not been very successful in that department. After the way we screwed up on the Tunis Flu, I think we ought to try to clean up our act."

That was twice in one day that the Tunis Flu had come up and by now Corwen Blair wanted to hear no more of it. He rose to his feet and leaned forward on the table so that he loomed over the others. "I have heard quite enough out of you, young man. When you have dried off behind the ears, you might be prepared to offer your criticism on the performance of this department, and the rest of the state bureaucracy, for that matter. But until you have a track record that consists of more than your medical degree, I suggest—I very strongly suggest—that you comply with my order. Is that clear?"

"You bet," said Vitale angrily. "Yes sir, sir."

"I am going to dismiss you all and I will expect to hear from you tomorrow with the plans I have already outlined to you. If you have some reason to question the advisability of these plans, we may discuss them in private then. Otherwise I will regard these last remarks as an unfortunate lapse, the result of zeal. If they are renewed in any way, I will have to change my mind. And that might have repercussions, Doctor Vitale. Is that clear?"

"It's clear," said Vitale. "I got you." He turned on his heel and left the room.

In the abrupt silence that followed Vitale's departure, Tracy Bell and Dien Paniagua exchanged covert and uneasy glances, though neither gave any sign of noticing the gravity of the insult Vitale had given Blair.

"I will expect both of you to be in my office before noon tomorrow," Blair announced, his voice loud and forceful.

"All right," said Tracy Bell, rising and gathering up her attaché case. "Tomorrow morning."

"Tomorrow morning," echoed Dien Paniagua, wishing she had the courage to do what Dan had done. If only she did not have a child to support, if only she did not fear being unable to work. If worse came to worse, there were clinics where she might practice, but the pay was often poor and the locations unsafe. The reason she had taken this job was that the money was good and the hours predictable, so that she would not have to leave her child with sitters all the time. These considerations and apprehensions ran in endless repetition as she went back to her office.

At last, in desperation, she went to the main computer room and asked to see the reported incidents of mononucleosis for the last four months. She needed something to take her mind off the conflicts that seethed in her. Long ago she had learned the anodyne use of study and now she sought it as eagerly as an addict.

Two hours later, looking at the improvised graph she had prepared, she knew she had not escaped from anything, that the unpleasantness in the office was nothing more than a minor irritation. What she had found in her reading and figuring was more than an outbreak of mononucleosis, it was a potential epidemic of an unknown and deadly disease that appeared to have the greatest incidence in teenagers. She leaned back in her chair, pondering the best way to convince Corwen Blair that his greatest success might lie in bringing this to the attention of the medical professionals in the state as soon as possible, a prospect that chilled her almost as much as the thought of the possible outcome if he did not, for she knew without doubt that unwatched and unchecked the disease would increase and spread quickly, geometrically. She put the graph in her leather file envelope, determined to study the figures further in order to strengthen her argument. She was not looking forward to trying to convince Corwen Blair that they had a potential epidemic on their hands.

Sam Jarvis and
———— Maximillian Klausen ————

"We've got an inquiry I thought you might be interested in," Sam told Harper Ross on the phone.

"Oh?" Harper sounded more fatigued than the week before, but his determination had not slackened. "What about?"

"About the syndrome," said Sam, knowing that those words would get Harper's full attention.

"What does it say?" Harper asked sharply.

"It's from Portland, from the new complex there, the one that specializes in environmental conditions. It seems that there's a small town in Oregon that's been hit with the same thing we're seeing in Seattle, or something very like it."

"That is interesting," said Harper after a moment. "How much information do you have?"

"Not as much as I'd like," said Sam. "Which is why I'm going to call them and ask a few questions of my own, before I jump to too many conclusions, in case they're facing something different than we are. Would you like to be in on this?"

"Damn right," said Harper at once. "When are you going to make this call?"

"Say an hour? Can you be here by three?" Sam looked at the clock on the wall and weighed up the various alternatives available to him. "I think I'll call now and set up a phone appointment. That way, if this Doctor Maximillian Klausen isn't going to be free, you and I won't waste part of the afternoon." He picked up his pencil and started to doodle.

"Fine. I'll be waiting for your call-back. How's that?" Harper paused. "I have to be here at four; I can arrange to be a little late, but. . . ."

"We can do a conference call from your office and mine to Doctor Klausen in Portland, if that would be easier." Sam frowned and drew several emphatic lines on his doodle. Much as he appreciated Harper's aid, he preferred it when the criminologist was with him. Sam did not doubt Harper's dedication to their project, but he did question his expertise where medicine was concerned.

"How many cases have we had to date?" Harper asked.

"Over sixty. Thirty-nine fatalities." He crumpled his doodle and dropped the paper in the waste basket. "I've been asking around, to see if other hospitals have unreported cases."

"And do they?" Harper asked.

"There are a few I think might have patients with the syndrome. There's reason to be suspicious about the illnesses in any case. I'll wait until I see the blood work to be sure, but the profile is right—most of them are young, and those that aren't are showing the same symptoms we've seen so far." He cleared his throat. "Most of them are still in your area, but I think it is spreading. How're your analyses coming?"

"Nothing specific yet. I haven't been able to isolate any specific poison spectrographically; I've also asked for any indication of radioactive particles and gas levels, both on the skin and the internal tissues. It ought to show something. I've called the medical examiner's office and asked that they do a full poison workup on the bodies they get to autopsy." Harper stared at the wall, his eyes on the calendar though he did not focus on the figures there. "I'm hoping to get a full chemical analysis on the samples I have in the next twenty-four hours."

"Um. Keep me posted." Sam hesitated. "How about Susan? How is she doing?"

"Same as before. She wants nothing to do with this, and she has refused to discuss it with me. She's planning to go to California, to visit Grant and her brother. I haven't the heart to argue with her." He did not quite sigh, but his breath came a little harder and slower than before. "I hope in time that she'll decide that this investigation is a good memorial to Kevin."

"I hope so," said Sam, privately not holding much hope. Over the years he had seen families pulled apart by lesser things than this; he wanted to believe that the Rosses would survive their disagreement about Harper's investigation but he dared not rely on it too much. "When does she leave?"

"Next week; Tuesday." Harper cleared his throat, changing the subject. "I've got some extra lab time if I want it on Friday. If you have anything you want checked here, let me know and I'll schedule it."

"Thanks," said Sam. "Let me call Portland; I'll get back to you." He decided it would be important to have as much information before he and Harper talked to Doctor Klausen as it was possible to get. That way, if they were following the wrong trail, it would not take much of their time or attention. Sam wanted to be convinced that the disease they were seeing in Seattle was isolated, that no other areas had been touched by it.

"Fine," said Harper. "Talk to you later." With that he hung up.

Sam referred to the letterhead number and the extension indicated beneath Klausen's all-but-illegible signature. He placed the call and waited first for the switchboard and then for the extension to be answered.

"Doctor Klausen's office," said a woman's voice made heavy with sinus congestion.

"Hello, this is Doctor Samuel Jarvis in Seattle at Harborview. I have a general letter from Doctor Klausen about a disease that he found in the town of Sweet Home in Oregon. He was requesting information about similar conditions . . ."

"Oh, yes, Doctor Jarvis. I have your name here on the

list. I can reach Doctor Klausen for you, if you like. Do you have patients with similar symptoms?"

"Unfortunately, yes," said Sam.

"Oh, dear," said the woman with a deep sniff. "I'll put you on hold; do you mind?" Before Sam could answer, she had done it.

For the next few minutes Sam was treated to a rock version of the *Acceleration Waltz* with four electric guitars, rhythm and synthesizer.

"Doctor Jarvis, is it?" a deep, gravelly voice said. "This is Doctor Klausen. I understand you have seen symptoms like the ones I've found in Sweet Home."

"Yes," Sam said. "What we have here fits the profile, including the age distribution. Almost seventy percent of the patients are teenagers."

"I'm sorry to hear that," Max said with feeling. "I've now seen more than ninety patients with the symptoms, about sixty-five percent of them teenagers." There was a brief pause. "I'll send along the statistics and diagnostic printouts through your modem, if you like."

"We can trade," Sam said, feeling almost overwhelmed with pessimism. "Have any of your patients survived?"

"Not once the fever has gone up," Max admitted unhappily.

"Have you heard of any other incidents of the disease?"

"I had a call this morning from a doctor in Idaho, named Landholm. He's been treating several high school athletes with the symptoms you're seeing. Most of his practice is with athletes, and therefore he didn't have much information about other cases, although he mentioned that there were other patients at the hospital where he practices with what might be the same thing."

"Great," said Sam, lowering his voice. "I want to get back to you after I've had a chance to go over your printouts. Do you have anything from Landholm you can send?"

"Not yet, but I will by tomorrow. As soon as I've got the

material, I'll see that it's forwarded to you." Max paused. "When did you see your first case of it?"

"November," Sam said at once. "The son of close friends, in fact." This last was an awkward admission.

"I'm sorry." Max swallowed. "An old friend, a colleague of mine; the man who alerted me to the disease in the first place—he and his wife have both died from the disease."

Sam tried to think of an appropriate response and could not. "That must be hard on you," he said at last.

"On all of us, I'm afraid. My wife hasn't forgiven me yet for their deaths." He wanted to make light of this but could not; Cassie's ire was too real, too alive and present for him to dismiss it. "How soon can you get your material to me?"

"Most of it by nine this evening," said Sam, adding, "I'm working with the father of the patient I mentioned. He's a professor here, of criminology, and he's treating his son's death as an unsolved crime. He's running some tests and I doubt I'll have the results before tomorrow. Do you want to have them as well?" He had started another page of doodles, this one more scattered than what he had done before.

"That might be useful," said Max. "Sure, send them along. His data can't be any more confusing than the material we already have." He cleared his throat, trying to rid himself of the tightness that was there. "Do you have any indication of what's causing the trouble?"

"Not so far. We're assuming some kind of toxic waste— it fits the symptoms and the pattern."

"Yeah," Max said. "We've been checking out toxic waste dumps. We haven't turned up anything so far."

Sam glared at his doodle before wadding the paper into a ball and tossing it across the room. "Neither have we. I thought it might have a connection to some of the reforestation chemicals, but no luck so far."

"Reforestation?" Max said. "No, we haven't got anything on that, but it might be a lead we can use. There were all sorts of fertilizers used as part of the reforestation, five, ten years ago. Maybe there was a toxic combination resulting from that."

"Nothing specifically wrong with any one element, but cumulatively dangerous?" Sam said, taking up the idea. "I hadn't thought of that; I hate to admit it. I'll put Harper onto it. Still you'd think something would turn up spectrographically if that was the case."

"Not necessarily," Max said. "What about comparative levels? Have you tested for that?" He had already decided that would be his next area of testing. "You might have to do slices of all major organs to get a comprehensive picture. Also bone marrow."

"You'd think the computers would pick up on it," said Sam, his scowl growing deeper.

"Not if they weren't programmed to look for it," Max reminded him.

"Right," said Sam, scribbling a note to himself before he began another doodle beneath it. "I'll see what I can come up with, and I'll put Ross on it as well."

"Good," said Max. "Will you be free tomorrow evening? I think we ought to wait until then to compare notes."

"Yes," said Sam. "I'll want to go over your material with my criminologist friend as well as set up comparisons with what we have on file here. Then we might be able to get somewhere."

"What about Atlanta?" said Max with less certainty than before. "Have you been in contact with them?"

"Not yet. I don't want to cry wolf. They're not very forgiving of that." Sam had written *Atlanta* in the middle of his doodle and surrounded it with several versions of a question mark.

"Amen," said Max. "But I'm getting worried about this stuff. It's here in Oregon, it looks as if it's in Idaho and Washington as well. Where else has it cropped up?"

"Atlanta's a warehouse," Sam said bluntly. "If we can't get anyone there interested in this disease, whatever it is, it's worse than useless to talk to them. You know how they are, how much bureaucracy they have."

"The Environmental Division is less hampered," Max said, though his words were more of a question than a statement. "We might have a chance there."

"I hope so," said Sam, as dubiously as Max. "It might be necessary, but I'm not looking forward to it."

"No, nor I," said Max. The two men were silent for several seconds, and then Max went on. "I'll call you tomorrow."

Sam looked at his daybook. "I probably won't be back in the office until almost seven. Is that acceptable to you?"

"Let's make it seven-thirty then, just in case you get held up."

"All right. And I'll make sure Harper Ross is here as well, in case he turns up something we haven't spotted. That is one thing he's shown me—that his perspective is different, and in a case like this, it's damned useful."

"A professor of criminology," said Klausen, not believing what he was being told.

"You'll see what I mean when you talk with him," said Sam, and prepared to hang up. "We'll talk later."

"Good."

Harper's response was more enthusiastic. "That's terrific. Now we're starting to get somewhere. What's this about Atlanta? What can we do to hurry that up? It sounds to me as if we should have been talking to them before now."

"You're wrong there, Harper," said Sam. "Atlanta is constantly getting material from all over the country, especially in the Environmental Disease branch, and unless you have something major to show them, it just goes into the files and stays there. The fact that we might have proof that this outbreak is not limited to one area gives us a reason to have more attention than we might have otherwise, which is why we've got to be damned sure of what we tell them." He had no more paper left on his notepad for doodles and so began to make random lines on the cardboard backing.

"You mean to tell me that they're so inefficient?" Harper demanded indignantly.

"I mean that they are overworked, understaffed, and that the whole area of Environmental Disease is so clumsily defined and understood right now that half the time they're in no position to give data a real evaluation." He saw that he had broken the point off his pencil and reached for another one.

"This is outrageous," said Harper, his tone more subdued but as intense as before. "What if there are dozens of cases of this stuff all over the country, but there hasn't been enough checking? You mean in Atlanta they would not do a cross-check, just in case there were other reports?"

"If they had time and someone was willing to do it, they might," Sam answered carefully. "But no, it isn't part of the routine."

"It bloody well ought to be," Harper said. "What's this about Idaho?"

"I wasn't sure you noticed," said Sam. "There might be some cases in Idaho. Klausen's going to find out more before we talk. We need a conference. Three locations will demand attention." He let out his breath slowly.

"What's the matter?"

"Oh, I was thinking about the spread of the disease. We still haven't isolated what causes it, and how long it takes to develop. What if it takes a couple of years, and there are people who lived here two years back and have moved, who might still get the disease? Since we don't know how long an exposure is needed, what about travelers or students who have been here for a time but have moved on? How much of a risk are they? How do we locate them? How do we warn them?"

"I've considered that," Harper said softly. "I worry about what it tells me."

Sam tore the cardboard sheet in half and dropped it on the floor. "Yeah."

"Keep in touch," said Harper quietly.

"I will. We'll talk this evening, probably." He scratched

his head reflectively. "Don't talk to anyone about this unless it's absolutely necessary, and don't reveal any more than you must, will you, Harper? If we had a panic now, I don't know what we'd do."

"I know," said Harper. "But what about the poor bastards who might have the stuff, been exposed and not know it? What about them?"

"Wait for a couple more days. It won't make that much difference." He got up and paced as far as his telephone cord would let him. In a remote part of his mind he longed for his cordless telephone at home which gave him the luxury of rambling and pacing; such phones could disrupt some of the more sensitive medical instruments in this building and so he was bound by the telephone cord which tethered him to the desk.

"Except to someone who's been exposed," Harper reminded him grimly. "All right. I'll call you from the lab tonight after we run the tests for you."

"Thanks. I'll be waiting for that." He said good afternoon and hung up, futility and foreboding competing for supremacy in his thoughts.

Sylvia Kostermeyer and Gerald Plaiting

Though it was only the first week of February, the day was sunny and warm; thanks to a short-lived rainstorm the day before the air was clear; and from his hospital bed Plaiting could see the distant Santa Lucia mountains wearing a light topping of snow. He could hear the steady beep of the cardiac monitor over his bed and the hiss of the purifier that cleaned the air he breathed in his isolation tent. A book lay open and facedown where he had abandoned it an hour ago.

"Your visitor is here," said a nurse as she came in the doorway, her protective quarantine garments making a sack of her.

"Thank you," said Plaiting with feeling. He did not like to admit he was so bored and frightened that he had lost his desire to concentrate on anything but his (rare) human company.

Sylvia Kostermeyer, fourteen pounds thinner than she had been at Christmas, came into the room, her quarantine gear obscuring everything about her but her exhausted features and the new touch of grey in her dark hair. "Doctor Plaiting?" She held out her mittened hand toward the plastic surface of his isolation tent.

"You're Doctor Kostermeyer," he said, lifting his hand a few inches and waving once with his fingers. "Sorry we have to meet this way."

"Believe me, so am I," she said, pulling up one of the formed plastic chairs—there were two of them in the room and both would be destroyed when the patient left—toward the bed. "I've got a recorder; do you mind if I tape our conversation?"

"Please," he said quietly. "And I hope it does some good."

"Thank you—so do I," she said as she produced the little machine already protected by a double-layer quarantine box.

"You're from San Diego, they told me." He said this to make conversation, in the hope that some sense of medical camaraderie could be established between them; he hated feeling like a victim.

"Yes, that's right. I work in the San Diego County division of Public Health and Environmental Services." She did her best to smile with muscles that had lost the knack of it.

"And you're checking up on what you think I've got," he said.

"We're seeing increasing amounts of it, but nothing as far north as your case." She had flipped on the machine and was doing her best to maintain eye contact with him as she spoke.

"Well, if that's the case, I hate to the bearer of bad tidings, but I'm not the only one around here. The first case of this I treated showed up last fall—a boy by the name of Eric Harmmon. You can get the records from my office; I've already authorized their release to you." He was already starting to feel tired and he cursed himself.

"How many cases have you treated?" she asked.

"Up till I got sick, I saw probably two dozen cases. From what I've heard, there are more now. About seventy percent of them are teenagers, but—again—from what I've heard, that's starting to change, getting closer to a basic cross section." He had to stop and take several slow, deep breaths. He was dimly aware that his cardiac monitor had speeded up and become slightly irregular in its beeps.

Sylvia nodded once, as if reluctant to admit that much. "I've taken the liberty of contacting PHES and the hospitals in the Greater L.A. area, looking for more cases. I admit I'm troubled that the condition wasn't noticed or reported sooner."

"Four counties, and 'seventy-nine villages in search of a city'," he reminded her, quoting one of the more accurate summaries of the problems of Greater Los Angeles. "In the last five years, communication's got much worse. Talk to the cops if you don't believe me."

"I believe you," she said, recalling many other times she had run into the bottleneck of Los Angeles. "But from what I can tell, fewer than ten cases were reported to PHES. That concerns me."

"You mean it scares the shit out of you," Plaiting corrected her with a trace of humor. "Too-fucking-right."

"Precisely." She frowned at her tape recorder as if she was not sure it was working. "When did you develop symptoms?"

"That I noticed? Not quite a month ago. I probably had

them before then, but I feel tired enough that I don't pay much attention to it. I did some blood work when I noticed that my stamina was shot." He leaned back. "I think if I hadn't seen this stuff before I would have assumed I had some kind of anemia. That's what I thought the first case was."

"And now what do you think?" Sylvia asked.

"Probably something very like what you're thinking," he told her, the words crisp and deliberate. "I'm assuming that there's a new kind of poison out there that's good at killing people. It sure as hell looks that way."

"Yes it does," she said. "And that makes it very difficult. We're starting to look for synergistic patterns now, in case what we have is two or more substances interacting." She tried to pinch the bridge of her nose but her protective clothing made this impossible.

"What do you think? Is it two substances?" He discovered that her answer would not particularly interest him; now that he had the disease—whatever it was—he was far more interested in its treatment than its causes.

"I think we haven't got enough evidence yet, but from what little we do have, my best guess would be that we're dealing with two substances, things that probably are well within the acceptable toxicity levels by themselves, but together . . ." She could not find a way to finish.

"How many cases in San Diego?" he asked when most of a minute had gone by in silence.

"That we know of? over three hundred now, and climbing. I've sent two reports to Atlanta, but so far we haven't got a response from them," she said, not quite resigned.

"Unhuh. Figures. It took them nine months to get into gear with that Great Lakes Dysentery three years ago. There were over four million people affected before Atlanta went to work. What's eight or nine hundred in Southern California compared to that?"

"You're bitter," she said, not surprised but curious.

"My dad's family is from Cleveland," he said. He could hear the cardiac monitor beep still faster.

"I didn't mean to upset you," Sylvia said, her eyes on the display he could not see. "Take a couple of minutes and calm down. I can wait. Do you want your nurse?"

"No; they'd probably want to sedate me—that's about all they can do for me—and I wouldn't be able to say anything useful then. If it gets worse, I'll ring." This last was more for her benefit than his.

"Okay." She watched the monitor as she went on. "Tell me what patterns, if any, you've noticed, especially in terms of locale: is there a connection between place and outbreak of the disease?"

"I think so," said Plaiting. "But that could be because so many of my patients come from the same general area. You can check that out with other hospitals, though. If there is a relation, you'll probably be able to pinpoint it for a while. If the stuff starts spreading, you'll have a lot harder job on your hands."

"I know," she said, with such tremendous fatigue that he was convinced that she did. "The first patient again. Tell me about him."

"Eric Harmmon. Bright kid. I thought he had mono, or that mono-sub-one stuff that's been cropping up in the last six years. I ran the usual tests, saw that he was anemic and tried to find out what viruses he had or had had recently. I hate those things!" he burst out in sudden vehemence. "Time bombs, all of them."

"A lot of them," she agreed.

"Anyway, about Eric. Two sisters, younger, neither of them showing any symptoms. I've kept an eye on them, and about the only one who worried me is their father, who's one of those workaholics and spends most of his time in harness." He reached up and rubbed the faint stubble on his chin. "I'd be careful talking to the family; they're very touchy. You'd think that Eric did something socially gauche by dying the way he did. The kid who'll tell you the most is Gail. She's thirteen and a real jock; gymnastics, swimming, diving, the whole works. She's held up through her brother's death better than anyone else in the family, if you want my opinion. The youngest girl is more fragile. She doesn't talk about Eric, she just . . . goes away. The mother's been taking the brunt of all this, and defending her husband's lack of involvement as the demands of his work. Cesily works twice as hard as Brandon, but neither of them know it or are willing to admit it." He fell silent, doing his best to gather up what little energy he had left.

"I ought to talk with them. And the others." Sylvia turned away. "I'm getting tired of this—talking to families after they've lost someone, or more than one someone."

"Have you seen much of that?"

"Not at first," Sylvia said, thumbing off the tape recorder. "In the last month or so, there seems to be a change going on. One family in Chula Vista has lost the mother and two kids to it. We're intensifying our investigation in that area, doing soil analysis and water testing and all the rest of it. It's a real pity—the second kid, their daughter, was a very promising dancer. I think her name was Melanie. Her dance teacher also died of the disease, whatever it is."

"Another geographic clue?" Plaiting suggested, intrigued in spite of himself.

"Possibly. I was hoping we'd find one site, one location with a crucial drainage pattern, or seepage into a local reservoir, or a position in relation to prevailing winds, but so far, nothing. Some of the illegals coming in seem to get it, but we don't know why or how." She reached out and turned the tape recorder back on. "I'll want to go over your records—are they on disk, or can you arrange to transfer them to the PHES computer in San Diego?"

"I'll call my receptionist and have her put the records on a disk for you. We've got compatibles for PHES systems." He was starting to feel lightheaded, something that usually happened only after he tried to walk any distance. "Will you call me, to let me know what you find out?"

"It might not be very revealing," she warned as gently as she could.

"Look, Doctor Kostermeyer, I'm assuming this shit's going to kill me. I know the progress of the disease, and even if you came up with the cause tomorrow and a treatment the day after, I've sustained a lot of damage, and I don't think my blood's ever going to be the same again, even if you find a way to arrest the disease. But I'd like to know what's killing me, if that's possible. I want to know what's doing it and how." He felt his face go hot, but was reasonably certain that he had not managed to change color. The beep of the cardiac monitor was shrilling and he could read the alarm in his visitor's eyes.

"Doctor Plaiting . . ." Sylvia said, getting to her feet and reaching for the buzzer.

"Dammit, Doctor: *listen to me!*" He had straightened up in bed, putting his pain and the intrusive reminder from the monitor out of his mind. "I haven't lost my mind. I have nothing to do but lie here, dying. I can be *useful*, for Chrissake! I can help out! I want to fight back. If it has to be from the grave, so be it. But if there's anything—*any-thing*—I can do that might change the course of the epidemic we've got on our hands, I"—he saw the shift in her eyes—"Oh, yes," he said, more calmly and more certainly than before, as if the admission itself gave him strength and purpose. "I know we're beginning an epidemic, just as much as you do. I know that what you've seen, what I've seen, what other baffled docs have seen is that proverbial tip of the iceberg. Whatever is coming from this disease, it's much bigger, much worse than anything we're imagining now. Tunis Flu was bad enough, and AIDS was tragic, but this is going to be worse. That's why I want to work as much as I can, as long as I can. Don't you see?" To his intense shame, his voice broke.

Sylvia came and stood by the side of the bed looking down at him with more direct compassion than he had seen in a human face since his mother's death. "I'll see what I can do."

"Hey, I didn't mean to—" He hoped she would not think

less of him for the weakness he had betrayed, though he thought less of himself.

"You're right; we're going to need help and you know more than anyone else I've come in contact with. I'm . . . grateful."

"Thanks," Plaiting said, falling back on his pillow.

"I can't promise that—"

"I know. Thanks anyway." Plaiting wanted to smile and achieved nothing more than a twitch at the corner of his mouth. "You're a good sport, Sylvia."

"Takes one to know one, Gerry," she countered.

A month ago, he would have had half a dozen quick responses. But, he reminded himself as he closed his eyes, a month ago he was not in the hospital dying of a pernicious, unidentified disease, and the conversation would not be taking place. He was half asleep by the time Sylvia Kostermeyer let herself out of his quarantine room.

Jeff Taji

Atlanta was chilly and there had been an incredulous warning on the news that temperatures might drop below freezing during the night. Now, at a few minutes before seven A.M., the thermometer hovered around forty degrees. People on the street bustled toward their destinations in the heaviest clothing they owned and most of the drivers became so uncharacteristically cautious that there were more accidents than usual. Pedestrians rushed into buildings and hesitated when leaving them. As Jeff Taji drove his new black Honda Sturgeon—license plate CAVIAR—into the parking lot, he narrowly avoided colliding with the neon-red Pontiac Sunbird driven by Susannah no-relation-to-the-Vice-President Ling. Earlier in the morning he might have cursed, but now he shook his head and laughed, and waved her on.

"Sorry about that," Susannah said as she joined him at the elevator. "There was a heavy frost out by my house; I skidded twice backing out of the driveway. Made me twitchy. You'd think I was a kid with a learner's permit."

"I know how it is," said Jeff, whose accent was so faint he was often mistaken for Italian or Greek instead of Persian. He had lived in America for sixteen years and only his aunt called him Jamshid instead of Jeff.

"You know, it's times like this that I really miss being married. That does *not* mean that I miss Daryl; I miss having someone around who wants to help me out of sticky situations, and that would not have described Daryl at the best of times." She entered the elevator ahead of him and pushed buttons for both of them. "How're you doing these days? The environment keeping you busy?"

"So far. We're about to have the two-week report collation." No one in the Environmental Division of the National Center for Disease Control liked the collation.

"It's a good idea, Jeff," said Susannah. "I know you agree; it's realistic and you're a realist." She was about his age, from a family that traced its line back to French Huguenots who came to Georgia in the seventeenth century. She was bright, well educated, articulate, ambitious and divorced. "It's what comes of being a stepchild."

"A stepchild?" Jeff repeated, not understanding what she meant. "How am I a stepchild?"

"You *qua* you are not; the Environmental Disease Division is. The whole area of environmental health is somewhere between medicine and witchcraft in the view of the more conservative members of our profession, the ones who still can't believe that fluorescent lights can cause hyperactivity in some children." Most of her work was concerned with environmental health hazards in schools and she took her responsibilities very seriously.

Jeff laughed. "Let's face it, the rest of the Center would be happy if we were on the other side of the country instead of the other side of town from them." They reached his floor and the doors opened. "Nice to see you."

"Same here," said Susannah as the doors closed on her.

Jeff's office was at the end of the hall, overlooking a small park that was a part of the NCDC Annex. At the far side of the park, squatting at the base of a small grove of half-grown Italian stone pines, was another building, this one as formidable as a World War II bunker, where the laboratory facilities were located. As he usually did in the early morning, Jeff started out by making himself a cup of very strong coffee, which he drank while gazing out at the sky. He had done this for more than twenty years and he insisted that it cleared his mind. This morning the stack of printouts waiting on his desk intruded on his reverie, and finally he reached out and picked up the top file about an outbreak of what appeared to be toxic reactions of some sort in the Pacific Northwest. The information covered several cases, more than he might have expected, and claimed that the symptoms were present in patients in three states. He pursed his lips as he read, noting the high fatality rate and the disproportionate incidence of the disease in teenagers. From what he could surmise, the blood and brain were the most affected by the disease, while the bronchial complications were minimal unless the patient developed pneumonia. "That's a bit redundant," Jeff said to the air. "Either blood or brain going would do it."

There was a noise in the hall and Jeff looked up to see the first arrival of the morning, Dr. Weyman Muggridge, a rangy fellow from South Carolina in his mid-thirties. "Morning," he called out.

"Morning, Jeff," Weyman answered, poking his head in the door. "Found anything juicy?" Like the other doctors working in the Environmental Disease Division, Weyman Muggridge was trying to find an area of expertise.

"I found something puzzling," Jeff said, continuing to read the report from Oregon. "It's three hours earlier on the West Coast, isn't it?"

"I think so—if it isn't three hours later," said Weyman.

He was pulling off his overcoat all anyhow, having trouble freeing its sleeves from the sleeves of his tweed jacket.

"The sun still goes east to west, I believe," Jeff said, faintly amused.

"If you say so," Weyman agreed, tossing his overcoat aside as if he had won a battle with it. "Has Drucker got here yet?"

"I haven't seen him," said Jeff carefully, not wanting his poor opinion of his colleague at the other end of the hall to be too apparent.

"Then he isn't here." Weyman stepped back into his office and pulled the door closed.

Jeff went on reading, half-listening for the arrival of the rest of the staff. What he found especially perplexing about the report from Seattle was the constant reference to unusual levels of Adrenocorticotrophic Hormone and Corticotrophin Releasing Factor. He had not encountered environmental toxins in the past that produced those patterns of abnormalities. There was also an indication that several of the patients who had died from the disease had elevated endogenous triglycerides, as evidenced by the presence of xanthomata tuberosum. Jeff shook his head and stared out the window again, letting the last of his coffee go cold.

A little before nine, most of the staff had arrived and the noise level had gone up. Noise from the street carried up the side of the building and occasionally penetrated the sealed, double-thickness windows, signaling the beginning of the working day. Jeff took his place at his desk and pulled the stack of reports toward him, thumbing through them so that he would not be wholly unprepared for any questions that might arise during collation. That was, he added to himself, assuming he got onto the agenda and was permitted to speak.

Weyman stuck his touseled head in Jeff's door. "Ten minutes to go. Want some coffee?"

"I think I'll make another cup for myself," said Jeff,

knowing that Weyman hated the very strong coffee he brewed. "But come in. Sit down. What's on your mind?"

"The usual. It looks like we've got another minor outbreak of good old Tunis Flu in St. Louis. I know it's supposed to be all gone, thanks to the vaccines and drug Smithson and Faber came up with, but there are some questions about what's causing it, so we're authorizing the Clinic for Environmental Medicine there to take a hand. Just in case." He selected the most comfortable chair and dropped into it, raising his crossed legs so that he could rest his heels on the edge of Jeff's desk.

"Tunis Flu isn't our concern," said Jeff as he measured out his coffee. "That's a standard medical problem, according to the central office."

"It is our concern if there's an environmental factor."

"There's an environmental factor to every disease, if you ask me. A body is an environment." He said this without force because he had said it so many times before.

"You know what the definitions are," Weyman reminded him. "Say," he went on, changing the subject a bit, "did you hear that Sally Martin's dad died?"

"No; when?" He started his coffee machine and came back to look directly at Weyman. "He's in Dallas, isn't he?"

"That's right, just retired from teaching, I forget where. Sally flew out last night." He cocked his head to the side. "I wonder if good old Drucker will make a motion to send flowers to the funeral? He did when Baxter's mother died. Of course, she had Great Lakes Dysentery, so that might make a difference. I haven't heard what Sally's dad died of." He sniffed the air lavishly. "Too bad coffee never tastes the way it smells. I tell you, if I had a machine like that, I'd just brew the stuff and inhale all day."

"Keep your door open," suggested Jeff as he came back to his desk with a little cup and saucer in his hand. "Have you come across anything you want to bring up this afternoon? We both have to tell Claire for the agenda, in"—he consulted his watch—"six minutes."

"Stupid way to run things," groused Weyman. "It only mucks up the works. It's like making an appointment to make an appointment."

"The trouble with you, Weyman, is that you are not a bureaucrat," Jeff said.

"Neither are you," Weyman said with a grin.

"True." He took a sip of his coffee, then set it aside.

"So tell me, how do all those reports look? I didn't have as many as you do this time, but so far nothing grabs me." He motioned toward the printouts. "The joy of being the head of this section."

"I'd just as soon have nothing to do because there were no more toxic dumps or hazardous wastes or dangerous chemicals in the work place or any of the rest of it," said Jeff slowly. "It's appalling how many risks a person runs in this world."

"That's what we're here for," said Weyman.

"That assumes we know a risk when we see one, that we can recognize a legitimate environmental disease when it happens." He reached out and put his hand on the stack of reports. "In this."

"But is there something you think might deserve our attention?"

He answered with care. "Possibly. Something on the West Coast."

"Like AIDS, or all the other loony things that come from there? What was that stuff called that you found before I got here? What did they call it?"

"Silicon Measles," said Jeff with distaste. "It wasn't measles and it wasn't caused by silicon, but electronic workers were its main victims and it did cause a severe rash, high fever and a certain percentage of optic damage." He shook his head. "And Drucker has never forgotten that he overlooked it."

"Well, it does show something about his judgment," said Weyman with a broad wink.

"One could look at it that way," said Jeff.

"One does," Weyman told him. "All right, you put your

find on the agenda and I will take one last futile look through my stack." He lowered his feet and stood up. "I'll wish you luck and you can take it any way you wish."

"Thanks," said Jeff, and picked up the report from Oregon. "And excuse me while I go try to find a slot in the schedule." He convinced the secretary to place the Oregon file on the agenda by threatening to call Portland and requesting a full, formal application for investigation. This worked better than Jeff had hoped, and he hurried back to his office, determined to look through the other files before outlining his position for the collation.

He was on the eighth report, this one from Southern California, when he recognized the same pattern he had noticed in the Portland file, the same abnormal readings in ACTH and CRF that were present in the patients who had died. He sat back, reading the figures with care. The woman who authorized the report was a Sylvia Kostermeyer working out of the San Diego Office of the California State Department of Public Health and Environmental Services, and her list of cases included ones from the Mexican border to the northern flank of Los Angeles. Jeff laid the two reports side by side and began to read, his brow darkening.

When the collation meeting began, Jeff was annoyed to learn he had been put fifth on the list. It was Drucker's way of minimizing the time Jeff would have to speak. So while the possibility of toxic chemicals in wrapping papers was debated, Jeff excused himself long enough to arrange for copies of the Portland and San Diego files to be made and full sets of printouts to be ready in the next hour. Then he returned to the conference room and waited for his chance.

"I see you have something you want to bring to our attention, Doctor Taji," Drucker said shortly after four-thirty. "Considering the hour, do you think it might be better to postpone your presentation?"

"No," said Jeff baldly. "And in the interests of brevity, I have already arranged for each of you to be given copies of the two reports that have caught my attention," he said, getting up and signaling one of the two secretaries in the room to get the printouts.

"Why did you authorize making these copies before we had a chance to discuss the cases?" Drucker demanded, his jaw muscles standing out.

"Because I know how little time we have, and in this instance, I fear that we have no time to spare." He smiled as the printouts were distributed. "As you see," he went on, not allowing Drucker to shift the subject, "the reports come from two different parts of the West Coast. Apparently the two physicians in question—a Doctor Kostermeyer and a Doctor Klausen—are unaware of what each is doing, which gives me more grounds for worry than if they had been in contact." He paused as the fourteen other men and women in the room shuffled and rustled the pages. "The age curves are very similar, the course of the disease from first reported symptoms to death follow a very similar course, the ACTH and CRF readings are abnormal in the same way. Whatever is wrong, it is wrong in more than one part of the country."

"Either that, or the disease spread quickly," pointed out the oldest person in the room.

"I might agree, but reports of the disease are recorded at roughly the same time. This does not rule out a rapid spread, but since we do not know if this is the result of toxicity, and we have no idea if there is an incubation period and if so, how long, we cannot rule out the possibility that there is more than one infection area." He held up the Portland data. "Doctor Klausen has cases not only from Oregon, but from Washington and Idaho. He suggests that there may be some leakage from military storage or illegal stockpiles that are involved here. His report has asked us to find out from the Pentagon if there are any more cannisters like the ones that killed the sheep in Idaho. I haven't had a chance to look up the specifics, but I think that at the least we ought to attempt to get that information for them."

"There may be illegal dumping by foreign powers in the Pacific," said Drucker.

"And the influence is felt as far away as Idaho?" Weyman protested. "Hell, Pat, if that were the case, we'd have reports from San Francisco and Honolulu. Probably even from Canada, or Alaska. The Pacific's a big dumping ground. And there are no reports," he added as an afterthought, "of dying whales spotted off the West Coast. Let's keep it simple if we can."

"Even if it is something in the ocean," Jeff said, doing his best to be as reasonable as he could, "that comes under our purview. We have an obligation to check it out."

There were several nods of assent around the table; Drucker's face hardened still more.

"How long have the cases been showing up?" asked Amy Wilde, who specialized in agricultural chemicals and health hazards.

"Apparently since last November," said Jeff. "If there were others, we can't find anything specific about them. And so far as I know, there has been no victim under the age of fourteen nor over the age of sixty-eight, for whatever good that information may do us." He looked around the room. "And it may indicate that we have a disease of long incubation, something that is cumulative and required prolonged exposure in order to become active. In which case, we could have a very serious problem on our hands."

There were more nods now, and Robert diCerni pulled his calculator out of his breast pocket and set to work with it. "I don't suppose we have any idea about the total number of cases that have occurred since November? No, I thought not. Still, assuming that we have a cumulative disease that requires prolonged exposure to become active, there could be several thousand people running around the West Coast who stand to develop the disease in the next year." He punched a few more keys. "That's a conservative estimate, and it assumes we have all the pertinent information about every case diagnosed so far. And that isn't very likely, even if it is the result of toxic wastes."

Drucker stared at the far wall, his eyes fixed on a spot

about ten feet beyond it. "Do I gather that it is the consensus to mount an investigation on this condition?"

There was a show of hands in favor, and Jeff felt a surge of relief when he realized that his support was almost unanimous.

"We better get out to the West Coast and find out if the two diseases are the same thing," Weyman said promptly. "First things first. And I hope it is the same thing—two brand-new toxic diseases is a little more than I want to handle." He was one of three people who chuckled at his remark.

Drucker frowned and looked around the room with suspicion. "Is that really necessary? Wouldn't it make more sense to send queries to other parts of the country, to find out if there are other reports of the disease, and then coordinate the search for the cause from here?" It was part of Drucker's personality that he disliked having to leave Atlanta and his office, where he was secure in his power.

"I'll go," said Weyman. "Jeff and I will be on the next plane west. We can work as a team, or split up." He smiled as he made the offer. "And we'll report in, so that the rest of the group can add what we learn to what you find out from the other parts of the country."

"That sounds like an excellent idea," said Jeff at once. He held up the printouts. "Given the two geographical areas, we might as well decide now who goes where."

"What about your family, Taji?" Drucker interrupted.

"My aunt has been running the household for years. The kids are old enough to take care of themselves." He was determined not to let Drucker goad him. "If you're really concerned, I can arrange for all of them to stay with my brother in Florida for the time I'm gone, but that seems a bit extreme, doesn't it?"

"My neighbor will take care of my dogs and bring in the mail," Weyman chimed in at his most laconic. "I'll give them the milk in the fridge so that it won't go bad while I'm gone."

"That's enough, Muggridge," Drucker said, his chin coming up. "It's not decided."

DiCerni raised his hand. "I think we'd better act on this. If it turns out to be a general hazard, the sooner we get moving on it, the better. It's a case of better safe than sorry."

"I agree," said Donna Howell, who spent her spare time working with the Committee for Public Utilities Responsibility. "There are more than enough victims in either location to justify our investigation; if we don't act soon, we may have to justify our failure to do so later on."

The tacit threat of governmental review was not lost on Drucker. He was silent; the others at the table remained still until he cleared his throat. "Perhaps I think it might be a good precaution. We will authorize one week's travel pay. That will enable you to conduct a basic investigation. At the end of that time, we'll have a review of your findings and relate them to anything that we discover in other parts of the country." He patted the table with the flat of his hand, as if using a gavel to dismiss a session of court.

"When do we leave?" Weyman asked. "So I can arrange for the dogs?"

"Would tomorrow be all right?" Jeff asked. "I think that the sooner we act on this, the better."

"You're an alarmist, Taji. You don't grasp the size and complexity of this country." Drucker stood a little straighter, as if he were defending the United States from foreign corruption. "It's not uncommon for physicians from smaller countries to see the U.S. on the same scale as what they're used to."

"Drucker," said Jeff with as little irritation as he was able to achieve, "I've worked for the World Health Organization, as you are well aware. Are you telling me that your problems in the U.S.A. are more complex than those of the entire continent of Africa?" He did not wait for an answer. "I will agree that you have one complexity that is a particularly significant factor in a disease of this sort—mobility. Who knows how many persons have been exposed to the toxins and have traveled away from the area? If there is a long incubation period, while that cuts down the number of persons likely to have sufficient levels of toxicity to bring on the disease, it also complicates the search, in that those who could potentially become ill might have left the Pacific Northwest or Southern California two, three, four or even five years ago and gone—who knows where?"

"That's rather an extreme view," Drucker said stiffly.

"Do we dare risk having a less extreme one?" asked Jeff, taking in everyone in the room with his question. "I'm prepared to leave tomorrow. I think it's necessary that we do something at once."

"All right," said Drucker, knowing that if he continued to refuse it would not look well on his record. "Tomorrow. I am sorry for this inconvenience, Muggridge."

"Fine with me," said Weyman blithely as he got to his feet. "Can we talk before we go home to pack?" he asked Jeff as the meeting began to break up.

"Sure," said Jeff. "Do you know where you'd like to go?"

"Given a choice, San Diego. I've never been to Seattle when it hasn't been raining, and the two times I've been in San Diego it was sunny and warm." He smiled. "If I've got to go looking for a deadly substance that's killing something, I don't want to be depressed every time I look out the window." His smile had become a grin.

"All right," said Jeff, shrugging. "I'll take the Northwest. But I think I'll start in Portland and go to Seattle afterward. Damn," he added as he considered it. "I wonder if there's a direct flight or if I'll have to change planes?"

"Probably in Denver, or Salt Lake," said Donna, who had crossed the country nine times last year. "Take Denver, if there's any choice."

"Why?" Jeff asked, surprised to hear her express an opinion.

"Denver's a little nicer if you get stranded there, and there are more ways to get out of it, if you have to make plans." She had gathered up the copy of the printouts she had been given. "Do you really think this is going to be bad?"

"Yes. I think it is possible that there are five thousand people out there who have been sufficiently exposed to the toxin, whatever it is, to contract the disease."

"That sounds pretty high," she said. "If that's the case, why are we starting to see it only now, and only in those places?"

"We don't know it's only those places," said Jeff, holding up his hand and ticking his points off on his fingers. "We don't know if there are milder versions of the disease than the one we're seeing, we don't know why it has cropped up so suddenly, but it may indicate that this is a two-stage toxicity, in which case, it could develop spontaneously wherever both toxins are present."

"Okay; okay," she said, holding up her hand. "I don't dispute the possibilities."

"I hope I'm wrong," Jeff added.

Weyman tapped Jeff on the shoulder. "Come on; we got to get a few plans made."

"Excuse me," said Jeff to Donna as he picked up his printouts and his attaché case.

"I didn't want to give Drucker a chance to buttonhole you," said Weyman as he held the door open for Jeff. "He's itching to pull some kind of stunt; he hates it when he's put at a disadvantage. He wants everything this group does to be his idea or an idea he can take credit for."

"If that means we can get the job done, it doesn't matter," said Jeff, almost meaning it.

"Stop being so altru-fucking-istic," said Weyman as he yanked open the door to his office. "And for God's sake, think up something I can tell Jennie when I break our date for tomorrow night."

"Tell her the truth," Jeff recommended.

"What good would that do?" Weyman asked in mock distress. "She thinks that all we bother about here is smog levels and the occasional PCP leak. You know what that means. Medical emergencies don't happen to doctors like us, not according to Jennie."

Jeff shrugged. "Is she so important to you that you are concerned with her good opinion? Really?" There was a humorous and ironic note to the question; he knew Weyman's history with women and sensed that Jennie was not much different than the other very pretty, very venal women he attracted.

"Not the way you mean, no," said Weyman. "I wish you didn't see through me quite so easily. Probably just as well that we have a trip like this. If we didn't, God alone knows how difficult things might get with Jennie."

Jeff studied his colleague. "Are you seriously involved with her?"

"No," he admitted bluntly. "But it's getting to be a little bit boring, all this independence and no-strings fun."

"It doesn't hurt so much when you lose it," Jeff pointed out as gently as he could; his wife had died along with sixty-five others in a train wreck caused by terrorists, and though it was more than four years since it happened, his grief was still strong in him. He had stopped blaming himself for not being with her, and had almost forgiven her for being in Greece on her way to Bulgaria, and therefore in danger. "I beg your pardon?" he said, realizing that Weyman had spoken to him.

"I said I'm calling upstairs to get plane reservations. How early is too early for you?" Weyman held his receiver tucked between his ear and shoulder while he reached for one of his memo sheets.

"I wouldn't like to have to leave before six; anytime after that would be all right." He wanted to get back to his office and telephone Doctor Maximillian Klausen in Portland, to inform him of his plans, and to find out what more he could about the disease in Klausen's report.

"Okay." Weyman spoke rapidly to the coordinator, and promised to hang on while arrangements were made. "That's one to San Diego and one to Portland, Oregon, honey," he said, speaking with great care. "San Diego's in

California." Whatever the coordinator said in reply made him grin.

"I'll be in my office," said Jeff. "Let me know what the schedule is as soon as you know." He rose and left the room, his things slung under his arm in a haphazard way.

It took three different tries, but Jeff finally reached Klausen at the pathology laboratory of the Portland Center for the Study of Environmental Medicine. "Doctor Klausen?" he began tentatively, "this is Doctor Taji with the Environmental Division of the National Center for Disease Control in Atlanta."

"Oh: hello, Doctor . . ."

"Taji," he repeated. "We have your reports and we're very concerned. I was hoping you might be willing to tell me anything more you've learned since you filed your report. If your first indications are typical of the disease, there may be some very real trouble coming."

"I can't help agreeing with you," said Klausen with an edge to his words. "I'm helping in an autopsy of the most recent victim—female, aged seventeen. And it appears that her cousin also has the disease."

"I'm very sorry to hear that," said Jeff, so quietly that Klausen held back any sharp rejoinder he might have offered if Jeff's response had been glib.

"So am I," said Klausen. "The prognosis is pretty grim."

"I gathered that from your report," said Jeff. "And that's one of the reasons I'm going to be flying out to Portland tomorrow. I don't know what time I'll arrive, but I hope to be there before noon, since I will have the time advantage with me. Perhaps you'd be willing to spare me some of your time around one in the afternoon?" He did not want to push Klausen, for he sensed the strain the Oregon doctor was under, but at the same time he knew that if he did not press, more crucial time could be lost. "I want to spend time in Seattle as well, but since the reports originated with you, I'm hoping—"

"Fine; one o'clock will be fine. And I'll be happy to

make time to go with you to Seattle. I want to see what they've got firsthand."

"Then we're in accord, Doctor Klausen?" Jeff said, looking up as Weyman came in the door and handed him a memo. "Doctor Klausen? I'll arrive tomorrow at eleven-seventeen on Western Canadian from Denver."

"I'll have someone meet you, Doctor Taji," said Klausen at once. "Hell, I'll come myself."

"You needn't, but I'd be most grateful if you would," said Jeff, fighting the vertigo that threatened to overwhelm him; whatever was ahead, it terrified him already.

"I'll be there," said Klausen with more force. "We can talk on our way here."

"Excellent," said Jeff. "I'm looking forward to it." That was just short of a lie, but he consoled himself with the reflection that it was not Dr. Maximillian Klausen that sent a grue slithering up his spine, but the thought of that new and malign disease.

"Thank you for calling, Doctor Taji. To be frank, I didn't expect Atlanta to do much about this."

Jeff closed his eyes and nodded. "Unfortunately there are times your doubt is justified. I hope that in this case I can vindicate the NCDC."

"I'll see you tomorrow, Western Canadian from Denver, eleven-seventeen," said Klausen, not bothering to comment on what Jeff had said.

"Tomorrow," Jeff agreed with the dead line.

PART IV

April, 1996

Jeff Taji, Sam Jarvis and
———————— Harper Ross ————————

For Seattle it was warm; from their vantage point, they could watch the ferry pull away from Mercer Island, churning toward the pier at the foot of the hill.

"Why don't they simply build a bridge?" Jeff asked. It was a question that had puzzled him the day before, when he had arrived at SeaTac early enough to be caught in traffic.

"All kinds of reasons," said Harper, "mainly that Seattle doesn't want one." He was holding the printouts Jeff had given him yesterday. "I went over these last night. They're not very encouraging."

"No, they're not," said Jeff. His first trip to the Pacific Northwest, only two weeks ago, had filled him with an abiding dread. "We've had confirmation on over a thousand cases now, and the number is climbing."

"And the fatality rate is still as high as it was?" Harper asked, the image of his dead son still fresh in his mind.

"Yes. There may be those with resistance or immunity, but so far we haven't been able to locate them." He turned away from the window and went back to the head of the conference table. "How are your other children?" he asked, with the uncanny knack of reading Harper's face.

"Grant's still in the rehab program in California. Susan's there with him." This last statement did not come easily, and he shifted in his chair as he spoke, his hazel-green eyes moving away from Jeff's face. "Other than the drug thing, he seems to be fine."

"And your youngest?" Jeff did not want to prod, but he

175

had a deep sense that he needed every bit of information he could garner from this man. "Is he all right?"

"He's fine. Sam checked him out last week, and there's no sign of anything wrong with him." He sighed, not quite in defeat but a long way from hope and acceptance. "It helps, you know."

"But there are more cases of the disease in Seattle, aren't there, most of them concentrated in the north, in your end of the city."

"Strictly speaking, Bellevue is a separate city from Seattle proper," said Harper.

"So I understand," Jeff said. "But it's a little like other large centers, isn't it? everything gets lumped together." He looked at his watch. "Jarvis isn't due for another ten minutes."

"I'm sorry he had to be late." Harper fiddled with the edge of the printouts. "Barry McPhee is in the hospital with this shit."

"I'm sorry to hear that," said Jeff, automatically and sincerely. "Who is Barry McPhee?"

"Our next-door neighbor. He and his wife Caroline have been friends of ours ever since we moved here, before Mason was born." He shook his head slowly. "I went to the hospital before I came here. He looks just like Kevin did —pale and listless and so enervated that anything can be too much to deal with. He's in quarantine, of course."

"Does that bother you?" Jeff hoped that Harper would talk about it, clearing out the complex emotions that were draining him of purpose.

"Of *course* it bothers me." He shoved the printouts across the table, watching the paper slide out, wave-like, toward Jeff. "Everything about this disease bothers me, especially that we haven't found out diddly about it, and it keeps getting worse and worse and worse." He jammed his knuckles together and glared up at the clock. "This is supposed to be one of the four best medical facilities on the West Coast. It cost over a billion dollars to build and they aren't finished yet. You'd think with everything top of the line and state of the art that there'd be *some* headway by now."

"It would be wonderful," said Jeff. "It would be better if it never happened, or if the agents that cause it—whatever they are—had never been created. But that is out of our hands now. We have to accept the fact that we're caught up in a crisis that is very close to becoming an epidemic. There've been eight news items about it already, none of them featured stories as yet, but the day is coming."

"Sam said that you've confirmed several centers of infection," Harper said, making an obvious effort to put their conversation on a less personal footing.

"Yes: Southern California, Wyoming, Montana, Utah, Texas, along with the Oregon sites you already know about." He pulled out his old-fashioned agenda book. "I have colleagues in Southern California, in Montana, in Twin Falls, and in Dallas. We're doing everything we can to speed this investigation." No thanks to Drucker, he added mentally. "We have filed fourteen requests with the Pentagon for information on military toxic stockpiles—"

"They were supposed to have been destroyed," Harper reminded him.

"Yes. That is what makes it difficult," Jeff agreed. "No one wants to admit that the orders were not carried out, or were only partially carried out. We have to be diplomatic about our dealings, and that slows us down." His voice dropped with the last and he made a gesture of frustration.

"Do you think it will do any good?"

"Well, the National Security Agency and the Executive Security Department are both breathing down the necks of the coordinator in Atlanta. She can handle them, but from what she tells me, the ESD is being very touchy. According to her, even the FBI has been more helpful."

"That's a strange state of affairs," said Harper.

"Yes, it is," said Jeff. "By the way, don't be surprised if someone from the ESD shows up here and starts checking up on the patients you have here." He put his agenda back in his pocket. "I know it isn't easy, but if you can accom-

modate them, it might be best if you try. They can make
things go smoothly or put all kinds of barriers in our
way, and we've got enough to handle with the disease
without—"

"Sorry," said Sam Jarvis as he came through the door. "I
got tied up with that new admit. She's only fifteen and
she's going to die, that's how she put it." He was thinner
than two weeks ago, and the lines of his face were more
deeply scored than before. There was fatigue in every line
of his body; when he sat down he slumped and it was a
short while before he picked up his copy of the printout.

"When did you go home last night?" Harper asked with
concern.

"I didn't," Sam confessed. "I ended up sleeping in the
surgeon's lounge. The two beds in there are filled with
boulders." He worked his shoulder, as if trying to relieve
its stiffness. "And I'm not as young as I was once."

"Who else is coming?" Jeff inquired while Sam went
over the material in the printouts.

"This ACTH reading is what gets me. It doesn't make
any sense at all." Sam stopped. "Most of the quarantine
staff will be here in half an hour—that's the time when the
shifts change. We only keep them on for three hours, then
they have two off and another three on. It's awkward at
times, but we've found that the concentration is better and
in most cases there are fewer mistakes, and fewer of the
staff become ill." He watched Jeff as he said this, as if
measuring his response for approval or disapproval.

"I wish more hospitals would be as careful," Jeff told
him, knowing that a response was required from him. "I
think we lose more patients to carelessness than to infection."

"You were saying something about the ESD when I
came in," Sam said, making another of his abrupt changes
of subject. "What was that all about?"

"They're checking out this investigation, because of the
possible involvement of the government. We've requested
all information on strategic substance storage areas, just in

case." Jeff regarded Sam through narrowed eyes. "We have to go along with them or we won't get much help."

"Great. Okay. I'll brief everyone on the floor, I guess. You can tell the quarantine staff." Sam stifled a yawn. "And I'd appreciate it if you talked with the administration."

"Yes, if you like." Jeff very nearly smiled. "Have they been giving you much trouble?"

"They have their procedures, but those procedures aren't designed to handle something like this outbreak." This time the yawn would not be stopped. "Sorry about that."

"You need rest," said Jeff.

Harper was openly curious. "What you said earlier, about the carelessness—do you mind if we talk about that some more, Doctor Taji?"

"Jeff; please, Jeff," he said, wanting as few barriers between them as possible. "Yes, I'd be very happy to talk to you or anyone else working on this investigation about the issue of carelessness." In his mind, he heard the groans of his colleagues back in Atlanta, who were heartily sick of his pet theories about carelessness.

"By the way, we have found one person on the staff who was exposed to the syndrome and has no sign of contracting it," Sam went on, mastering his exhaustion for the moment. "It's probably too early to tell, but . . ."

"Keep an eye on . . . him? her?"

"Her," said Sam. "She's already volunteered." He looked over at Harper. "If it turns out that she doesn't have the disease, then we'll try a few tests on her. We've done a blood workup already, but I want a full series of scans."

"How do you know she was exposed?"

"First, she lives in Medina and her roommate has come down with the disease. Second"—Sam had started to play with a pencil, turning it end to end with each number— "she works in the lab, and she accidentally got splashed with blood serum from one of the patients who has it."

"It might not be transmitted that way. If it's a case of environmental toxins, she can't be considered exposed."

Jeff delivered his warning in as neutral a tone as he could achieve, for he knew how much this investigation meant to Sam and Harper. He shared their feelings, but not in the terribly personal way of someone who has lost family and friends to the disease.

"You can't rule out secondary transmission, either," said Sam.

"No; we can't rule out anything," Jeff concurred at once. "All right. She's probably the best source of information we have at the moment. Go ahead and do as you think best where she's concerned, but don't expect too much, and, if you can, resist the urge to look in only this one place for the solution."

"I'm not precisely an amateur," Sam bristled.

"No. I don't mean that." He braced his arms on the table and leaned forward, his eyes fixed on Sam's. "I know from experience how tempting it is to come up with the solution you want, and the explanation you want, and to start selecting your evidence to support that theory."

Surprisingly, Harper seconded him. "That's what we always warn the students about in criminology—the tendency to want the facts to fit the theory rather than the other way around. It's easy to do." His tone changed slightly, and he sounded more like a professor again. "You find a victim who has all the outward indications of strangulation and so you don't look for poison, just in case. Or you find a crime scene where the evidence of a struggle suggests that the assailant came through the window, and so you aren't as careful as you ought to be about how much broken glass has fallen on which side of the window." He looked squarely at Jeff. "You think the families of all the victims are at risk, don't you?"

"Yes; but I think everyone in the area is at risk, to a greater or lesser degree. For what little impact this might have, that's the consensus of my colleagues." He stopped, then went on, "We're starting to issue warnings for all hospitals west of the Rockies and south of Denver. I think we ought to be sending warnings everywhere, but—"

"And then what?" Harper demanded.

"We have to pinpoint the cause of the syndrome, the key to the disease, and then, if it is at all possible, isolate it and get rid of it. Barring that, we have to find a treatment for the disease." Jeff looked at Sam. "Have you had a chance to go over the material I left you before?"

"Not closely, no," Sam admitted. "It's been too hectic. But I think that I'm going to go over all of it this evening, and the hell with everything else." He set his pencil aside. "Have you talked to Max Klausen yet?"

"No, not yet," said Jeff, sensing tension in the question.

"He called last night. His wife, Cassie; she's a remedial reading teacher. She's come down with the symptoms." Sam touched the tips of his fingers together. "They're very close. It's a good marriage."

Harper looked shocked. "Poor bastard," he said with intense sympathy. "God, after losing his friends, to have this happen."

"And how is Max? How is he handling it?" Jeff wanted to know.

"He's beside himself. He blames himself. He says that he must have carried something to her. I told him that doesn't make any sense, but he's . . . he's taking it hard." Sam changed the subject once more. "I've asked Hal Shevis to join us here, along with the quarantine staff. He's—"

"I know Doctor Shevis," Jeff interrupted. "We've dealt with him before, and he's already supplied us with corroboration for the material sent by Klausen. I'm very glad you thought to include him. I ought to have done so myself."

"His niece is in the hospital with the disease," Sam warned. "It's been very hard on the family. Her father's a disabled vet, and he doesn't have any other kids."

Harper looked down at his hands, not trusting himself to speak; Jeff cleared his throat. "Do you know if he would rather not work with us? I could certainly understand if he decided to stay away from our work."

"It's going to be okay," Sam said. "He needs something to do, and this is probably the best answer for him right now. Just like it is for Harper." He did his best to sound optimistic, but could not sustain it.

"Doubtless," said Jeff enigmatically. "Then I hope you're willing to give me a little extra time after the meeting. I want to know the current status of everyone working on the quarantine staff in regard to this disease. Who's been through the most, who's in the middle of . . . loss. Who's getting frightened, who's getting angry about the disease." He thought of what it had already been dubbed back in Atlanta: Taji's Syndrome, TS for short. He hoped the nickname would not catch on here.

"Almost everyone on the staff knows or knows of someone who has it. The number of cases has gone up sharply in the last week," said Sam. "Either that, or we're seeing more of it and identifying it."

"Both are likely," said Jeff. "All right. We'll deal with this as we must. But I'm going to need your assistance. I think that it would be useful if you'd take the time to get twice-daily updates from the labs. Who besides Shevis could help us?"

"I'll get the names for you," said Sam, "but Hal Shevis is the boss here. We've got one other problem: the press. The disease has made the papers and the evening news and we're getting pressure. I don't want to see a love of sensationalism taking over the investigation."

"No; no one does," said Jeff, recalling how the reporters had flocked to cover the terrorist attack that had killed his wife. "We'll have to give them something that can buy us some time, that much is plain." He looked at Harper again. "How are you with the press?"

"I don't know," said Harper. "Are they anything like grad students?"

Jeff did his best to smile. He appreciated all that Harper was doing. "I don't know what grad students in criminology are like. It wouldn't hurt to treat it like a class." He looked back at Sam. "Would Shevis handle this for us, do you think?"

"Oh, I guess so. Ask him." Sam had slumped back in his chair and was staring at the window in an abstracted way. "I like these days when the mountains are out. Sometimes you can't see them. They disappear in fog or clouds or rain or snow. I had a patient once, very old and a little out of touch, who was afraid that the day would come when the fog would lift and the mountains would still be gone."

Jeff and Harper exchanged one quick, questioning glance. "It's almost time for the meeting," said Harper, getting up. "I want to be sure the coffee and tea are available."

"Good idea," said Sam. "Make mine a double."

While Harper was out of the room, Jeff took out his two notebooks and opened them on the table; all the while he kept covert watch over Sam Jarvis, trying to determine how much more strain the man could bear before he would not be able to take any more.

Sylvia Kostermeyer and Weyman Muggridge

Sylvia folded her arms and glared at Weyman. "What kind of remark is that?"

"Just a simple question," Weyman responded with a maddening lack of concern. "I'm curious about private hospitals, religious hospitals. They don't all have to report to PHES the same way that community and state institutions do. I wanted to know who's covering them and what you've found out. What's upsetting about that?" He had a slow, winning smile that served only to infuriate her more.

"I don't know," she admitted sullenly, furious that she had overlooked something so obvious. "Do you want me to call and find out?"

"Or I will," he volunteered, and fell silent as she glared at him. "I didn't mean that badly, Doctor Kostermeyer."

"Of course not," she snapped and reached for the phone. Half a dozen folders slipped off her desk and onto the floor, their contents scattering. "Oh, *shit!*" she burst out, slamming the receiver back into the cradle and putting her hand to her head. She started to pick up the folders and was gently stopped by Weyman.

"You sit. I'll take care of it. And I'll make the call. I won't make you look bad, I promise. I'll make me look bad." He was already at his self-appointed chores, and from where he hunkered down to get the printouts that had slipped under her desk, he asked, "How much sleep have you been getting, Doctor Kostermeyer?"

"Not enough," she admitted, one hand over her eyes. "There's so much to do. Two docs in this office have symptoms of the disease, and—"

"TS," said Weyman.

"It sure is," Sylvia agreed.

He looked up at her, his lopsided smile broadening. "No, I didn't mean it that way. TS is what we're calling the disease in Atlanta. Jeff Taji was the one who started the investigation. He's in Seattle or Portland right now. Anyway, since it's his disease, we're calling it Taji's Syndrome. TS."

"Medical humor?" Sylvia asked as Weyman stacked the files on her desk.

"I don't know that everything's in the right order, but it's all there." He reached for the phone. "What extension do I want?"

"Dial eighty-one and then...uh...seven-three-three. That's Doris' line. She'll know what to do." Sylvia rubbed her face, unaware that she had smeared her mascara, which along with lipstick was her only make-up.

Weyman did as she told him, and after little more than a

minute, he said, "Hello, this is Doctor Muggridge? Am I speaking to"—he looked at Sylvia for help and read her lips—"Doris Lytton? . . . Yes, Doctor Kostermeyer told me how I could reach you. . . . Look, Ms. Lytton, I seem to have made an oversight. I should have asked for this before I left Atlanta, and I'm sorry to cause you extra work, but Doctor Kostermeyer's right; I really do need to get the stats on this disease we're investigating from the various private hospitals in the greater Southern California area. I know that it's a lot of work but she's absolutely right, and I must have been woolgathering before I took the plane. . . . All the private hospitals, yes . . . and the religious, yes . . . As soon as possible . . . I know it's a lot to ask . . . I'm certain that you're shorthanded, but . . . It could make a difference, Ms. Lytton. Call Doctor Kostermeyer and ask her. She's the one who . . . She does deserve credit, I agree."

"You're the most shameless—" Sylvia whispered, only to be stopped by his warning finger held to his lips.

"All right. If she approves, yes . . . Thank you . . . Yes, it was foolish. . . . I'll wait for her to contact me, then. . . . Yes . . . Yes . . . I won't forget, no . . . Thank you, Ms. Lytton. Good-bye." He hung up. "She's going to call you to find out if you'll authorize the inquiries."

"What do I have to do with it? You're NCDC, you've got more authority than I do."

"Not with Ms. Doris Lytton, I don't. And don't let her know I'm here. This is all news to you." He drew up one of the old, straightbacked chairs. "She's insisting you get the credit for remembering to check private institutions. Fine with me."

"But you thought of it," she protested.

"You tell Ms. Lytton that and she won't believe you, and she might not help you. And you would have thought of it." He snatched the phone as it rang and handed it to Sylvia, listening with amusement as she gave her unnecessary permission for the inquiries. "See?" he said when she hung up. "That wasn't as hard as you thought it would be."

"You're incorrigible."

"So they tell me," he said. "Come on. I want to get over to the medical complex before the traffic piles up too much."

"All right." She rose as she looked around for her jacket and was surprised to see he was holding it for her. "Thank you," she said doubtfully as she slipped her arms into the sleeves.

"Where I come from, we still do this sort of thing." He held the door for her as they left her office and insisted on opening her car door for her, although she said it was silly since she was driving.

"Well," she said as they drove down Chula Vista Parkway toward La Mesa, "it's . . . a treat," she said, not sure that she intended to be so candid.

"You know," he said, as if he had not heard her, "I remember the hoopla when they opened this road, when was it? five years back? Supposed to be the most beautiful stretch of road in Southern California."

"That's what they say," she told him. "It's a lot more fun than I-5, and it beats the city streets." Slowly she began to relax. "We're meeting with Doctor Gross from Immigration and my immediate superior, Mike Wren. They've got some men from Miramar and Pendleton coming; the military's getting worried. We're hoping to get some cooperation and time."

"Is that why you wanted me to bring all the material we have with me?" He was expecting worse, but did not want to alarm her.

"In part, yes, but actually, I wanted to see it for myself. I'm worried about this. And I'm afraid that it's partially a problem with the government or the military, and that scares the living shit out of me." She tried to laugh and botched it. "Back in the Sixties, my parents were real activists. They went on the marches and rioted in Chicago and demonstrated against Viet Nam. They weren't famous, but they weren't unknowns, either. And it's followed them ever since. They're paying for all the time and care they put into this country, and . . . I get frightened. I don't want to fight with the military or the government, especially if they're to blame for this."

"Hey girl, that's the wrong attitude," Weyman chided gently. "You're a doctor with a big, scary M.D. after your name. That's worth a couple of pips on the shoulderboards any old day. You and Wren and Gross can stand up to them on the strength of the M.D., and you can win. This is your bailiwick, and there's no reason you should be intimidated. If anything, the military ought to be intimidated, especially if they had anything to do with this, anything at all. If they even suspected that they were endangering the lives of American citizens. Ever since the Supreme Court upheld the suit of those six families in Utah for wrongful deaths because of the bomb test fallout, the military's been treading on eggs. All you have to do is remind them of it."

"But that has nothing to do with this," Sylvia said, turning into the right lane, getting ready to exit. Overhead large warning signs announced there were stoplights in half a mile.

"You don't know that for sure, and neither do they." He tugged on his seatbelt. "I wish these things were adjustable for height."

"Amen," said Sylvia, then signaled to leave the parkway.

"Is it my imagination, or are there a lot of new buildings in this town?" Weyman asked.

"We had a mild quake six years ago. There's been rebuilding and upgrading since then." She turned east on El Cajon Boulevard. "Do you think we're looking at an epidemic, a real epidemic, Weyman?" It was difficult to breathe as she waited for his answer.

"Yes, and so do you, or you wouldn't be asking me." He shifted in his seat so that he could look at her face. "What has me worried more than anything is that we can't get a handle on how the stuff is transmitted, or how long it takes to develop. We still haven't seen anyone with the disease under the age of twelve, and that's one of the most puzzling aspects of the syndrome."

"TS," she said with faint amusement.

"You bet," he responded. "Who else is going to be with us?"

"There's a Doctor Azada down from Sacramento. That's why we're using the State Regional Administration Building for the meeting. Azada wants it that way, that's the way it is." She signaled for a left-hand turn, and drew into the parking lot beside a block of angled metal and glass. It looked like an exotic and overgrown crystal set out on the hillside with a newly planted park around it.

There were three Marine, one Air Force and two Naval officers waiting for Sylvia and Weyman in the fifty-person auditorium on the fourth floor. They all made nervous, overly polite introductions and agreed that it was unfortunate that the others were running late.

"I realize that this is a difficult time for all of us," said Commander Tolliver, meeting Sylvia's eyes with a diplomatic smile.

"You mean," she said crisply, "that there are people sick and dying and we have yet to establish a cause."

"That is part of it, certainly," said the Commander with an awkward chuckle.

"And it isn't funny," Sylvia reminded him.

Whatever rejoinder he might have made was lost when Michael Wren came into the room. He looked worn out and there was a shine on his black skin that Weyman noticed with alarm. "I got held up," he said as he closed the door.

"Gross and Azada aren't here yet," said Sylvia before any of the men in uniform could speak.

"Gross isn't going to be here," said Mike. "He was admitted last night. Looks like he's got the stuff."

"They're calling it TS in Atlanta," Sylvia said to Mike, waiting for some sign of amusement.

"They got it right for once," said Mike as he stumbled down toward the speakers' platform. "TS. Yeah, that's it."

"Doctor Wren?" Commander Tolliver said, coming forward with his hand extended. "We're very anxious to do everything we can to assist your investigation in any way we can. If you can make use of our facilities, we would be very pleased to arrange it."

"What about finding out if one of your biological toys is causing it?" Mike said, his voice uneven.

"Certainly. It's our understanding that the Joint Chiefs have issued a directive to all personnel that a complete search of all records is to be made at once."

"Great. And then you slap a top secret on it and none of us ever finds out . . ." He did not go on. "I'm sorry," he said after a moment. "I've been up all night, and I've been losing patients at a terrible rate. I didn't mean to take it out on you."

"We're all under stress just now," said Tolliver, trying not to look as self-contained and smug as the other officers did.

The rear door opened and Victor Azada came into the auditorium, his hands laden with two attaché cases and a number of rolled-up papers. Dark hair, olive skin, he was either Mexican or Japanese, but not clearly one or the other. "It's been a difficult morning; I hope you'll forgive me for delaying the start of the meeting." He was as smooth as the most adept politician, making a point of underplaying his authority without relinquishing it to anyone. "I was sorry to hear that Fred Timmons passed away," he said to Sylvia and Mike Wren. "He was a good man."

"He got this disease, this TS, and it killed him," Mike said, his head coming up sharply.

"TS?" said Azada.

"What they're calling this shit in Atlanta. Can't think of a better word for it, myself," said Mike, doing his best to stand straight and look Azada in the eye.

"We'll miss him. He's contributed a lot to PHES, and it isn't often that regional heads are so conscientious. We'll miss him." He had reached the speakers' platform and started to spread out the things he carried. "We have much to go over, and time is crucial, isn't it? I want to be back in Sacramento before six, if we can manage that."

Three of the officers grew serious at once. "Doctor Azada, we believe that there are a number of things to cover, and for that reason, it might be best if we agree to a greater flexibility."

"Oh, I have no reason to stop you from carrying on when I leave. I want you to be as direct as you can and that will save us misunderstanding later. You gentlemen and Doctors Kostermeyer, Wren and Muggridge will have plenty of opportunity to work out your testing program as well as a screening method before you finish up this evening." He favored them with another expert smile. "Shall we get down to it?"

The officers gave Azada their attention at once; Sylvia and Weyman exchanged glances and Mike Wren put his hand to his forehead.

Tolliver, who was watching Azada prepare his materials, remarked, "I wonder if it might be better to assume that this is a preliminary discussion. From what we've been told, this is a very delicate and complex investigation and the disease in question is a deadly one. It would probably be in our best interests to plan to meet again—all of us— before the week is out, so that we can determine how best to proceed."

Azada stopped spreading out the graphs and reports. "I'm not sure I follow you, Commander."

"What have I said that confuses you?" His manner was respectful; he had not raised his voice, but the authority of his presence was indisputable. "You apparently aren't aware, Doctor Azada, that there are ramifications here that could turn this investigation very unpleasant for all of us— civilians and military alike."

Victor Azada had not moved. He regarded Tolliver carefully, reassessing the soft-spoken Commander in the swift, canny way of politicians. "What do you recommend?"

"We don't know yet, and, with no offense intended, nei- ther do you. If anyone can tell us what our predicament is and how we might deal with it, it's these physicians, especially Doctor Muggridge, since his department in Atlanta has been developing protocols for situations like this one."

"That may be so, but I don't see why it's necessary that I remain once we—" Azada stopped abruptly as Mike Wren collapsed to the floor.

"My God," said Tolliver, and to the surprise of most of the others in the small auditorium, he crossed himself.

Sylvia was on her knees beside Mike less than five seconds before Weyman joined her. "He's running a fever. Feel his face. I'm having trouble finding his pulse."

"Someone call an ambulance," said Azada nervously.

One of the officers left the room quickly, and the others gathered around, trying not to ask too many questions. Captain Rockell, his Marine uniform so perfect it was hard to imagine that he had sat down in it, leaned forward. "Do you know if this is . . ."

"It's TS," said Weyman as he did his best to get a reading on Mike's pulse. "Faint, irregular, fluttery. It fits the pattern, Sylvia."

"You mean we might all be exposed?" Azada demanded, stepping back three paces.

"If you can get this stuff being around someone who has it, then, yes, you've been exposed, we all have," said Sylvia as she wiped the sweat from Mike's forehead. "But we have no reason to believe that you can get this through exposure to someone who already has it. If this is an environmental toxin, it doesn't matter what you do to or with someone who has it—you're exposed to the disease because you've been breathing the air, or drinking the water, or walking on the pavement, or any number of other things." She took Mike's hand in hers. "Hang on, pal. The ambulance is on its way, and we'll get you to the hospital as fast as we can. Okay?"

Mike mumbled something that might have been assent, or merely a reaction to hearing a voice.

Weyman had removed his jacket and folded it into a pillow. "Here," he said, offering it to Sylvia. "Put it under his head. He might as well be as comfortable as possible."

"Too bad this isn't the good old days, like you see in the movies," said Azada, keeping his distance. "One of the doctors here would be carrying his medical bag. Or her medical bag." This time his mouth would not supply the required smile for Sylvia. "It would have been nothing more than a couple of minutes, and he'd be back on his feet."

"It doesn't work like that," said Sylvia. "Or have you forgotten, Doctor Azada?"

"It's too bad that it . . ." Victor Azada moved to the far corner of the platform and began to fold his graphs and displays once again.

"How's he doing?" Tolliver asked. "Is there anything you want us to do?"

"He's doing badly. He's having trouble breathing. Look at his skin—it's grey." She smoothed Mike's hand. "God, I should have noticed his skin before now. His being black doesn't excuse me."

"You both being exhausted might," said Weyman. "You had no indication that he was ill." He gestured so that the military men would move back. "When the ambulance attendants get here, they're going to need all the space we can give them."

Sylvia once again smoothed his brow. "Don't fade on me now, Mike. Keep fighting a little longer."

There was the whoop of an ambulance at a distance, and all those gathered in the little auditorium listened for it with a relief that they dared not express.

"I'm . . . sorry," Mike said, doing his best to focus on Sylvia's face. "I . . . I . . ."

"It's okay, Mike," she said, hoping that it was, that there would be no reason to regret her concern and care for him. "It's going to take a couple more minutes, and then you'll be on your way."

"I think we ought to move this meeting to another room," Azada announced. "I'm going to arrange it right now." He had found the excuse he wanted and he bolted from the room.

Commander Tolliver said nothing, but his expression of condemnation and disbelief made words unnecessary.

"We're going to have them run all the tests they can on you in the ambulance," Weyman told Mike, speaking slowly and distinctly. "We'll also make sure you get quarantine space. As soon as we know which hospital can take you, we'll be out to see you."

Sylvia moved back, suddenly shaking all over. "Oh, God."

"What is it?" Weyman asked, startled. He saw how pale she had become, and that her mouth was not steady. "Sylvia?"

"It's like Gerry Plaiting all over again," she murmured, shivering now as if the room were frigid.

Weyman could not place the name, but he said, "No, it's not like that at all."

"The ambulance is here," announced Commander Tolliver, his manner firm. "Gentlemen," he went on to the two attendants with the gurney held, legs folded up, between them, "hurry, if you will."

The older attendant signaled his companion and they came down to the speakers' platform. "Excuse me, Miss," said the older, trying to push Sylvia aside.

"Doctor," she corrected sharply. "Handle this man with great care. He's running a fever and by the look of him he'll need saline before you give him anything else."

Neither attendant paid much attention as they busied themselves loading Mike onto the gurney and strapping him down.

"The Doctor gave you instructions, fellas," said Weyman at his most laconic as he held up his identification from NCDC. "I suggest you do what she says."

The younger attendant peered at the credentials and nodded twice. "Okay, Doctor." He looked around at Sylvia. "Saline first, Doctor. Is that right?"

"Yes; what hospital is he going to?" Sylvia demanded.

"They've got room at La Valle," said the older, as if unaware of how far away that hospital was.

"Isn't there something closer?" Sylvia asked in quiet horror.

"Not with an open quarantine bed, there isn't," said the older. "You're lucky we didn't have to go all the way to Long Beach."

"You mean to say that there are no quarantine beds in San Diego left?" Sylvia insisted. "What about the private hospitals? We can arrange something. He works for PHES, for God's sake. Can't one of the private hospitals—"

"They're full, too," said the older driver. "They're all full. Get it?"

The men in uniform said nothing, but their eyes moved restlessly.

"La Valle," said Sylvia. "That's Del Mar, isn't it? Out off of San Andreas Drive?"

"That's the one," said the younger attendant. He looked at his associate. "Ready?"

"Let's go." The two men carried Mike out of the auditorium, leaving Sylvia staring after them.

Captain Lorrimer, who had said nothing so far, finally broke his silence. "We might be able to make arrangements at Pendleton and Miramar. My Air Force colleague might be able to help out, even though he's not a Navy flyer."

"I think there might be something we can do," said Colonel Packard. "I'm here on tolerance, but I can see what can be arranged. We do have medical facilities in Southern California that could be turned over, in part, to the civilian population, if that becomes necessary."

For the first time, Sylvia wondered what Colonel Packard did for the Air Force, and who he answered to.

Victor Azada appeared in the rear door. "We can move to the conference hall on the floor above us. It's all arranged. They'll send up two secretaries to take notes."

For almost a minute no one moved, and then Commander Tolliver said urbanely, "We're quite satisfied where we are. Why go to all that bother? The secretaries might be handy, but there's no reason to move."

"But that man . . . Doctor Wren . . . he collapsed. If it's

TS and . . ." He made himself be quiet. "I think it would be wiser if we changed rooms."

"We'd prefer to stay here," said Colonel Packard, and this statement was supported by nods from the other military men.

"It might not hurt for us to remember why time is so important, staying here," said Weyman. He had slipped his hand under Sylvia's elbow and was helping her stand straighter than before.

"Yes," she said. "What happened to Mike Wren could happen to any of us, at any time. Until we know what the cause of this disease is and do something to stop it, none of us is going to be safe." Her face was set as she looked at Azada. "Why don't you set your graphs out again?"

With a sigh of nervous acquiescence, Azada put his materials back on the table. "All right," he said, and strove to take control of the meeting once more. "The way I see it is that we have been able to isolate the disease in the southern fourth of the state, and if we're careful, it can probably remain that way."

"Except for the men on the ships and in the planes posted to other bases," Commander Tolliver reminded him.

"And the tourists coming to see the zoo and the wild animal park, and Sea World, and just passing through to Ensenada and Tiajuana. And the families visiting relatives, and the truckers and suppliers who come here on the roads, and the businessmen in cars and planes . . ." She let Azada think about what she was implying.

"To say nothing of the usual transients and the students and those who simply get transferred or move away," added Captain Lorrimer. "I appreciate the implications, Doctor Kostermeyer."

"We don't know how long an exposure is necessary, nor do we know what elements must be present, but for the time being, we have to assume that anyone who has been in this area has had some degree of exposure to the disease." Weyman addressed this primarily to Doctor Azada.

"And we have to take precautions based on that assumption."

"The Governor has said that he wants the outbreak contained as much as possible and the outbreak itself not given any sensationalistic coverage." Azada tapped one of the charts he had opened. "According to the figures at PHES, there is no reason to think that this will be more widespread than it is; it's possible that the disease cycle has already peaked and that we'll see a reduction of cases over the next month."

"Wishful thinking, Vicky," said Weyman with a sweet, insincere smile. "Very wishful thinking."

"The Governor has a very large state to consider," began Captain Lorrimer. "That means that he might not appreciate how serious the situation is here."

"He has an excellent staff and PHES has some of the best epidemiologists in the field," Azada reminded them defensively.

"Yes," said Weyman. "Like Doctor Kostermeyer, here, and of course, Doctor Wren." He waited a bit to give everyone in the auditorium an opportunity to consider what he had said. "The epidemiologists in Sacramento are very good, we all know that, but the operative word there is Sacramento. They haven't been here, they are basing their evaluation on reports only. That can cause inadvertent misunderstandings, which is why there are four of us in the field now from Atlanta, working to determine what areas of investigation are the most crucial."

Azada glared at Weyman. "You've got a much larger staff than we do at PHES. You're dealing with other states, as well."

"Which is what PHES better start doing pretty damned quick," said Weyman mildly. "Or there is likely to be hell to pay."

"I think," said Commander Tolliver, "that it's time we make some of our hospitals available for your use. It will take about twenty-four hours to process the paperwork, since this is an emergency. After that, you will have another eight hundred quarantine beds at your disposal. I hope you're willing to put them to use."

"I can't think why we wouldn't be," said Sylvia. "What about your personnel on base? Does that leave enough space for them, if the disease spreads there?"

"Oh, yes. We're reserving a comparable number for our men and their families. We have already seen about twenty cases of—did you call it TS?—TS, and we're prepared for more. I hope that we're being too cautious, but . . ."

Colonel Packard cleared his throat. "The Marine base is making similar plans."

"I don't believe it," Azada protested. "You guys are acting like this is the Black Plague or something. This isn't the Middle Ages, you know. We've got vaccines for everything from flu to AIDS. This is just another one of those leaking cannisters, and once we find out what it is and where the whole thing will be under control. You're overreacting."

"You might try to explain that to the families who have lost members to TS," Weyman countered. "You're afraid that the Chamber of Commerce is going to be upset over an epidemic, that it won't be good for tourists. Well, I should fucking hope so. I'd like to think that most people have the good sense to know to stay out of an epidemic zone. But you can't bet on that. Knowing how people are, you might have to pay them to stay away from San Diego."

"You're out of line, Mister!" Azada burst out.

"Doctor," said Weyman. "And I'm not. I'm trying to talk sense."

"Listen to him," said Sylvia. "Please listen. He's telling the truth; this place is already a high-risk area, and until we know more, we can't rule out any possibility."

"If it's a toxin, it isn't contagious," Azada reminded them huffily.

"But what if it's triggered by a toxin, what then?" said Weyman. "What if the combining element is a virus, which is mild when the toxin isn't present, but deadly when it is?" This was his own pet theory, but so far he was the only person who thought it was a possibility.

"It's safer to be careful," said Tolliver, attempting to mollify the outraged doctor from Sacramento.

"And what am I supposed to tell the Governor?" Azada asked sarcastically. "Oh, Governor Derelli, there's some kind of toxin in San Diego and we have to close the state for repairs? Come on!"

"I've heard of worse ideas," said Weyman.

"What is *wrong* with you?" Azada shrieked at Weyman. "Are you Lord-High-Mucki-Mucks from Atlanta completely unaware of how much this state depends on tourism, and how much of it is devoted to agriculture? We've got commitments for produce and dairy products that have to be met. We can't hold up trucks and drivers and the rest of the commercial shipping on a whim."

"This isn't a whim," said Sylvia. "When the nearest bed in a quarantine wing is half an hour away, there is something wrong. Don't you understand that?" She was shaking again, this time from anger. "If you haven't the guts to tell Governor Derelli what's going on down here, I will; and if that means you throw me out of PHES, so be it."

"They won't throw you out," said Weyman, looking Azada in the eye. "Will they?"

"No," said Azada.

Once again Tolliver intervened. "I hope that you will talk to Governor Derelli, Doctor Azada. Because all of us"—he indicated his fellow officers—"have to make official reports about this meeting, and it would appear strange if you did not give the Governor the same information that we will report."

Azada gave a low, angry gasp. "All right, all right. I'll recommend a provisional quarantine and a . . . a six-month testing period. Will that do, or is there more?"

"That will do for a start. It's close enough to what we plan at Miramar." Commander Tolliver gave his attention to Weyman. "And you? What will you tell them in Atlanta?"

"My recommendations might be more stringent, but that's because I'm used to having them made less so. For the time being, I think the program could provide some containment until we have enough information to change what we believe to be risks. And for all our sakes, I hope we find out quickly. We're on the edge of a real mess." Weyman looked around the room, wanting to convince every person there of the danger he saw. "If this is contagious, and if it has a long incubation period, then we are all likely to catch it, sometime down the line."

"Because of a toxin?" Azada mocked, but without any support from the others.

"It could be," said Sylvia. "It would be foolish to pretend that it couldn't."

"And if you're wrong, and we have a panic, what then?" Azada persisted.

Sylvia answered for all of them. "Then we'll be very, very lucky."

Dale Reed, Wendell Picknor and Donna Howell

"What's so unusual about Irene Channing's case," said Donna Howell to Dale Reed as they faced each other over the small cafeteria table, "is that she's still alive."

"She's a very strong woman," said Dale, his face changing color subtly.

"It could be more than that. So far, we know of only one other patient who has run a temperature of more than one-oh-two and survived more than five weeks beyond. She's had a fever, and it's done something quite unprecedented with TS: it's come down. That makes her a curiosity, if nothing else."

Dale lifted his chin. "But you've already said that we've had far fewer cases in Dallas than they have in Southern California and the Pacific Northwest. Perhaps the outbreak here isn't as severe."

"Perhaps, but that doesn't change the death statistics, does it?" Donna took a forkful of what was fairly tasteless salad. "Have you seen any patients other than Irene Channing who have run a high fever with this disease and lived?"

Slowly Dale shook his head. "No."

"Then I reiterate—there's something quite remarkable about her. I wish I knew more." She had some of the lukewarm tea and continued on with the salad. "I'm puzzled about this small outbreak now in Arkansas. You said that you have reports of a couple dozen cases."

"Yes. We've been doing some investigating on our own, and it appears that there are at least twenty-five cases in the Ben Lomond-Hope area, and that's troubling. I can't stop thinking that there's a relation to the cases in Dallas."

"Well, there are many families in the Dallas area that have recreation homes in that part of Arkansas, just as some of them do down toward Shreveport. It gets them away from the city." He had a barbecued chicken sandwich which he had not touched, but now he bought himself a little time with a large bite.

"What are your contacts in that area like? I'd rather use yours if we can. If I mention Atlanta, everyone gets defensive." She saw that he was more at his ease and this relieved her. "Is there someone I can talk to?"

"I can give you the name of four docs in Texarkana and one in Hope. If you're eager to talk to them, they can probably help you contact more." He paused to chew on the sandwich.

"Do you think you can persuade them to take the necessary specimens for our analysis? There are times that docs can get pretty territorial about their patients, especially when we're involved." She did her best to make it apparent that she did not include him in that number. "We're hoping to find out what toxin is causing the disease, or what combination of toxins. Every sample we get, every analysis we can complete, brings us closer to finding a solution."

"You don't have to give me the pep talk," said Dale as he wiped barbecue sauce from his mouth. "I agree with you. I want to see this disease stamped out as soon as possible."

"And we do want to run a few more tests on Missus Channing." She hoped that he would not balk at the request.

"Why?" he inquired, suddenly reserved.

"To learn, of course. It may be that she has something in her blood that resists the breakdown we see in others. You know how the blood looks before they die—it's all to bits. But so far as we can determine, that hasn't happened yet with Missus Channing. You said yourself that no other patient you've seen has lasted so long." This gentle reminder did not have the effect Donna was hoping for.

"She's not a guinea pig for you to experiment with!" He slapped his sandwich back onto its plastic plate. "She's already lost her husband, she's separated from her children, and now you're proposing to . . . to make a lab animal out of her. Not a chance, lady."

"But—"

"She's my patient. And I say she's been through enough and you ought to leave her alone. I don't want her to have to endure anything more. As soon as she can leave, I want her out of the hospital and off with her kids, taking a rest." There were spots of color in his face.

"What if she isn't safe to leave?" Donna suggested as diplomatically as she could. "What if there is—"

"She isn't a carrier. All the work we've done indicates that she's had the disease and she's recovering. She has two sons who need her, who've been kept away from her. She wants to be with them, to get back to her painting again and to put this behind her." His insistence was so emphatic that Donna decided not to push it.

"Tell me about her kids." What she wanted most to know was if either of them had shown any sign of TS, but she was afraid to ask directly, given Dale's current frame of mind.

"They're fine, both of them. There's Steven—he's thirteen, and Brice—he's almost seven. Neil Channing adopted Steven, but . . . he was Irene's by a . . ."

"Previous marriage," supplied Donna, not understanding the reluctance that Dale showed in talking about it.

"No. She lived with a man for two years, when she was younger. Steven's his boy." He swallowed awkwardly. "I know that this isn't supposed to be important anymore, but there are parts of the country, and this is one of them, where an illegitimate child is a . . . hindrance. Some of the people who knew Neil thought he'd made a mistake marrying Irene because of Steven."

"Where are the boys now?"

"With the housekeeper, away. It seemed the sensible thing to do." He gave her a hard, challenging look. "Or do you want to do tests on them, too?"

"We might, eventually," said Donna, as if she were unaware of the hostility in his question.

Dale rose from his place. "I don't think there's much more we can say to each other just now, Doctor Howell."

"As you wish. I was hoping you'd come with me to Doctor Picknor's office, but if you'd rather not . . ." Donna left the suggestion open-ended.

"I have rounds to make," he explained. "When I've finished, then I'll see if you're still with Doctor Picknor. It might be useful to hear what he has to say." This last was a concession, grudgingly given and spoken in a low, aggravated tone.

"Good. I look forward to it," said Donna, determined to ignore his bad manners.

"Are you going to see Irene?" He had started away from

the table, leaving his sandwich unfinished, but he turned back again.

"Yes."

"Don't upset her." He said it softly, without any of his earlier harshness.

"I'll try not to," said Donna.

"All right."

She watched him leave, and spent the next ten minutes going over everything that Dale Reed had said. By the time she had got up from the table, she was convinced that she would need to talk to the doctors in Arkansas Dale had said he would put her in touch with. It seemed like the only reasonable thing to do. How did Irene Channing feel, she wondered, knowing that at least one of her children was at risk? She could not imagine what it would be like to have one of her three children in their teen years. All hers were under ten, and for once in her life, she was deeply grateful because of it. As distressing as this investigation was to her, she knew it was worse for those who faced losing children as well as spouses, family and friends.

"Glad to see you," said Wendell Picknor when Donna entered his office. "Dale's not with you?"

"He's going to join us later, perhaps," said Donna carefully.

"Still hot under the collar about Missus Channing, is he?" Picknor asked. "Not surprising. He's so stuck on her that he doesn't know which way is up."

Donna was curious, but asked no direct questions. "How is she doing?"

"Well, she's weak," said Picknor, "but she's still alive, and that puts her ahead of anyone else I can think of. Her temperature is still normal—in fact, a little sub-normal— and she's able to eat and keep it down. We're officially guardedly optimistic about her." He cocked his head to the side. "What's your opinion?"

"My opinion is that we have a two-stage toxin. That's becoming our consensus. And that makes it especially difficult to trace." Donna reached into the case she carried and took out the latest stack of printouts. "You'll have a copy sent you this afternoon as well, but I thought you'd like a chance to see it before we see Missus Channing."

Picknor took the sheets and looked over them. "These ACTH readings are the ones that get me. Whatever else this disease does, it sure changes things in the brain."

"In Missus Channing's case," Donna ventured, "have those readings changed since she started to improve?"

"Somewhat, yes. But they're a long way from normal. That's the one thing that really concerns me about her," he went on in a more confidential tone. "I don't know what that will mean in terms of recovery. It could be that she's going to be left with a permanent brain dysfunction, and that has ramifications that are, well . . ."

Donna waited for him to end his thought, and when he did not, she folded her arms over her chest as if to protect herself from the implications of Picknor's worry. "Have you talked to her about this?"

"No, not yet. I don't want to cause her any stress if I can avoid it. She's been through so much." He tapped the printouts. "What about the docs on the West Coast? Are they getting similar reports?"

"I haven't gone over yesterday's printouts yet, but as far as I can tell, yes. They're seeing far more cases, but we don't know the reason for that yet." She studied Picknor. "Is there anything you want to tell me about before we go see Missus Channing?"

"Not really," he said as he picked up his clipboard. "I don't want to bias your opinions or reactions any more than I have to. You've seen so many cases of this—you're calling it TS in Atlanta, aren't you?—TS, you'll know what to look for." He left his office ahead of her, content to have her trail after him like a student.

Irene Channing was painfully thin and her eyes now seemed much too large for her face. When she spoke her voice was low and rusty, and her movements were as slow and painful as those of a victim of a beating."Wendell," she said when he came through the door.

"How's it going, Irene." He came to the side of her bed, his quarantine gear making static-like noises as he walked.

"You tell me. I'm alive." She put one hand to her forehead. "Today I feel as if I had an allergy at the back of my eyes."

"How's that." He made room for Donna beside him while he studied the monitors over Irene's head.

"You know that I can read the monitors backward in the TV screen?" Irene asked as she watched Picknor make a few notes.

"Really?" His calm was not as convincing as before.

"Yes. These long afternoons, I've been watching them when they won't let me have the TV on. The patterns are very pretty sometimes." She looked at Donna. "Did you visit me yesterday?"

"You were asleep," said Donna.

"Half asleep," Irene corrected her. "I do remember someone being here. I know all the nurses. I didn't recognize you."

"Donna Howell. I'm with the National Center for Disease Control in Atlanta, the Environmental Division." They could not shake hands; she compromised with a wave.

"I've been talking with Doctor Howell," said Picknor stiffly. "We're reviewing all the cases that involve your disease."

"Do you know why I'm not dead yet?" Irene asked, doing her best to make the question a joke.

"No; you're our second greatest mystery," said Donna. "The first mystery is what's causing the disease in the first place."

"I don't know," said Irene. "I've been thinking about it a lot, lying here with the monitor patterns on the dark TV screen." She paused to catch her breath. "When Sean Gradeston died, that was bad enough. Sean was my son Steven's best friend. They'd been almost inseparable for years. That, coming after Neil's death, really knocked Steven to pieces. And there were the kids in his school who got it. He told me he wished he'd get it so he wouldn't have to watch them all die." Tears ran from the corners of her eyes but she did not sob. "When I got sick, he tried to blame himself. He said I wouldn't have got it if he didn't have so many sick friends."

Donna listened in silence. "Steven's okay, isn't he?" she asked when Irene did not continue.

"He's fine. I guess he's resistant to it, the way I am."

"That's a possibility," said Donna, not at all convinced of it. "I understand you sent him and his brother away?"

"The housekeeper's with them, and I arranged for a home tutor. They're at our summer farm." She tried to push herself up on her elbows, but was too weak.

"Don't exert yourself," warned Picknor as the tracings on the monitors jumped in ragged lines of light.

"Sorry," she said, lying back and panting.

Donna saw that the monitors were returning to normal and she gave Irene the thumbs-up sign. "I've been told you're willing to have more tests done."

"Anything if it will help end this disease," said Irene.

"We're very grateful," said Donna. "Until now, we haven't had a chance to study someone who's getting over Taji's Syndrome."

"Is that what it is?" Irene asked, as if the name reduced its mystery.

"That's what we're calling it," Donna said with a half-smile. "Would you mind if we studied your sons as well? I know it's a risk, and I know you have every reason to refuse, but I hope you'll consent."

"What would studying them entail?" asked Irene, her sudden apprehension reflected in the movements on the monitors' displays.

"We're not sure yet. Blood work and probably a complete series of scans. If your family is resistant to Taji's Syndrome, we want to know why. It could save many lives, Missus Channing." She did not want to make her picture too optimistic, but at the same time she was determined to make as strong as case as possible. As she watched Irene's face, she knew that it would take a more convincing argument to win her over.

"I don't want my kids turned into freaks," said Irene, her voice betraying her fatigue. "I won't have it. It was bad enough when I had Steven. I don't want it to be worse for him. Do you understand?"

"Of course," said Donna at once, her sympathy genuine.

"Irene," Picknor interjected, "don't reject the idea out of hand because you're afraid of what people might think of your kids. The way things are going, no one will have time to think much about your kids—they'll be too worried about their own. And if it turns out that your kids could spare others getting TS, how do you think they'll be regarded if you don't let them help? How do you think they'll feel themselves if they learn they might have made a difference and you said no?"

"Aren't you being a little heavyhanded?" Donna asked in an undervoice. "Look at the monitors."

There were urgent, jagged points of light moving over the screen graphs. "Don't put that on me, and don't you dare put it on my children!" Irene told them, the breath coming quickly in her throat. "I won't have it!"

"She's right," Donna said, her gloved hand on Picknor's sleeve. "Doctor Picknor, leave it alone."

"We need their help. We're looking at thousands dying and all you can think about is two kids!" He slapped his clipboard down hard on the side of the bed, then turned away from her. "Jesus Christ, woman! don't you get it? This TS is deadly, deadly, deadly! As far as we know you're its only survivor to date. You have a responsibility, goddammit. If you're a human being, you owe it to the rest of us to give us a chance." He rounded on her. "How can you refuse!"

Donna tugged on his shoulder. "Doctor Picknor, you are out of line," she warned him. "Stop it. Right now."

One of the monitors began an urgent, high beeping and two bright lights went on.

Irene's breathing was too quick and very shallow. Her

eyes had taken on a glazed look and her skin had gone two shades paler. "I . . . I . . . no . . ."

The door burst open and three residents in quarantine gear burst in dragging a rescue cart with them. The one in the lead shoved Donna aside and reached to lift the quarantine tent that covered the bed. "Out of the way."

"She needs something to ease her breathing and calm her," Donna said in a steadying, measured way.

"It's not . . ." Irene panted. She was sweating profusely now and her eyes had lost focus entirely.

On the far side of the room, a bedpan rose slowly into the air and wobbled toward Wendell Picknor. The residents with the rescue cart did not notice it until it clanged into the side of Picknor's head.

"Christ on a crutch," he swore as he rocked from the blow.

The bedpan dropped abruptly, clattering as it landed.

Donna stood stupefied, unable to believe what she had seen but equally unable to deny it.

Maximillian Klausen and Jeff Taji

As Jeff ran from the taxi to the entrance of the hospital wing, he pulled his overcoat collar up to protect him from the slow, persistent rain that had been falling for the last two days. At the desk he showed his identification to the night guard. "Doctor Klausen's expecting me."

"That's quarantine floor," said the night guard.

"Yes, I know," Jeff responded as he took the tag and

clipper handed to him. "Will you let them know I'm on the way so they can have a quarantine suit ready for me?"

"Sure, Doc," said the night guard, lifting the phone as Jeff started toward the bank of elevators.

Two nurses were at the station, one of them holding the throwaway sterile garments he had requested.

"Thanks," he said as he took them and headed for the alcove to put them on. "How is Missus Klausen?"

"Not too good," said one of the nurses. "Her fever's been spiking at one-oh-five."

Jeff stopped in his dressing. "For how long?"

"The last six hours. For a little while it dropped, but now it's right back where it was. She's not really conscious anymore."

"Just as well," Jeff said to himself, then, to the nurses, "How long has Doctor Klausen been here?"

"A little over three hours. We didn't notify him until ten-thirty."

"Why did you wait so long?" That was two hours after her temperature went up.

"We thought she was responding. The quarantine docs said she was showing improvement." The nurse hesitated. "We should have called him, no matter what the docs said, but you know what can happen if you try to get around one of them." She helped Jeff fasten the gloves around his wrists. "He's waiting for you. We told him you were here."

"I appreciate that," said Jeff, no longer aggravated at being wakened. "Will you release the door for me?"

"Of course," said the nurse, and in a moment the green light went on over the first of the two doors that protected the quarantine beds.

Max was slumped in a chair in Cassie's room. Even in the engulfing quarantine gear, his despair was apparent. He looked up as Jeff came through the door. "Morning," he said.

"That's one way to put it," said Jeff as he came to look

at Cassie, lying beneath the quarantine tent. "What's the outlook?"

"Another hour or two if she's like the rest," Max said, not meeting Jeff's eyes. "Not much longer." He lifted his gloved hands. "I can't even touch her. I can't hold her hand. I can't wipe her face, I can't kiss her, I can't do anything for her."

Jeff shook his head. "I'm sorry."

"She's my wife." He stared down at his shoes. "It was bad enough with Elihu and Eunice and all the kids, but Cassie . . ." His moan was that of a man whose grief was beyond tears.

There was nothing Jeff could say. He stood at the foot of the bed, watching Cassie Klausen slip beyond their reach, her pulse fluttering and fading until, shortly before dawn, it vanished completely.

While the hospital quarantine staff dealt with the body, Jeff took Max off to the doctor's lounge with orders to the senior orderly to bring two stiff brandies to them.

"We're not supposed to do that," said the orderly, for form's sake.

"You're acting on my authority," said Jeff. "If there's any question, refer it to me and I'll handle it. You won't get in trouble."

Max, dazed by shock and exhaustion, permitted himself to be handled like a three-year-old. He sat on the couch where Jeff placed him, and when the brandy arrived, he took his glass in his hand obediently, moving as automatically as a machine.

"To your wife," said Jeff, touching the rim of his glass with Max's.

"Yeah," said Max, and took half the brandy in a single swallow, drinking it down as if it were warm milk.

"Is there anyone at home?" Jeff asked a little later.

"Home?" repeated Max as if the word were in an unknown language.

"Your home. Is anyone there?" Jeff had seen this dreadful neutrality before; he had felt it himself. "Or is there someone I should call?"

"Megan's at school," said Max, frowning distantly.

"Your daughter."

"Stepdaughter. I ought to phone her, I guess." He sounded far away and puzzled.

"Let me deal with it," said Jeff. "Is there anyone else you want me to call?"

"Sam?" suggested Max.

"Right after I call your stepdaughter," Jeff promised. "Who else?"

"Cassie's mother." At that he broke, sobbing so deeply that his whole body shuddered with it. He had to put his glass aside for he could no longer hold it.

Jeff rose and crossed the lounge. He put his hand on Max's shoulder and left it there while Max mourned.

When the worst was over, Max rubbed his reddened eyes and looked at Jeff. "I'm okay."

"No you're not," said Jeff steadily. "You're rocked to the foundations, which is to be expected. If you weren't, there'd be something wrong with you."

"Yeah," said Max unsteadily. "What time is it?"

"Nine-eighteen," said Jeff, reading the clock on the wall.

"I ought to be in my office. I've got a call coming in from Idaho. I should take it."

"I'll handle it," said Jeff. "I want you to lie down and get some sleep."

"I can't sleep." Max moved back as if the word itself were repugnant.

"Try it and see." He knew from his own experience that Max needed the lost, anodyne hours to help him through the ordeal that the next several days was bound to be. "I'll tell them not to disturb you."

"Fat chance," said Max even as he stretched out. "I'll rest my eyes. They're bloodshot."

"Yes," said Jeff, turning out all but one of the lights in the lounge. "I'll be back in a few minutes."

For the next hour, Jeff was on the phone, first to the associates in Portland Max regarded as friends, then to Sam.

"Too bad," Sam said when he heard the news. "I didn't think it would happen so fast."

"About average," Jeff said, trying to maintain clinical detachment.

"But she was Max's wife—I was hoping that would give her some kind of edge."

"I don't know what to tell you about Max. He was worn out before this happened; now, I doubt he'll be in any shape to stay with the investigation." He did not like admitting this, but as he expressed his misgivings, he sensed that Sam was relieved.

"We're all on the edge," said Sam. "I had a full-scale anxiety attack day before yesterday. I was afraid I was going to have to check into the hospital myself, for tachycardia. It passed, thank goodness. But I know the signs."

Jeff rubbed the stubble on his cheek. "Anything more from Idaho?"

"They're slow to part with information, but I've got some figures. About what you'd expect. Also the report of another case in Montana and one in Alberta." He paused. "I don't think we can assume it will stop at one."

"How the devil did it get into Canada?" Jeff asked.

"Diseases don't recognize borders," Sam reminded him. "What I want to know is why that strange pattern is showing up in that part of the country and nowhere else."

"Yeah," said Jeff slowly. "Yeah. It doesn't figure."

Sam made a harsh sound that might have been a chuckle. "Nothing about TS figures."

"I wish you wouldn't call it that," Jeff objected, though he was already resigned to the name and initials.

"Too bad; it fits and you're stuck," said Sam. "I'll call

Harper and let him know about Max's wife. He said he's onto something over at his lab."

"Then let me call him. What's his extension at the University?" Jeff asked, thinking that perhaps there would be an opportunity for him to discuss his growing doubts with someone whose perspective would add to his insights.

"4753 or 4788, the first is the lab, the second his office. He'll be at one or the other." He cleared his throat. "When's the funeral, do you know?"

"No; I'll make sure you're told." He was about to hang up when something more occurred to him. "Have you been doing serum cultures from the victims?"

"Some, yes, why."

"I'm curious about susceptibility. If we can establish who is more likely to get the disease, we'll know where to put our greatest efforts."

"I'll tell my staff," said Sam. "Anything else?"

"Not right now, thanks. I'll talk to you tomorrow." He hung up and dialed Harper Ross' lab number, and was rewarded by a grad student who gave the phone to Harper at once.

"Jeff!" Harper said. "Any progress on your front?"

"No, and that's what I want to talk to you about," said Jeff. "It's pure speculation at this stage, and three of my colleagues think I'm crackers, but..." He broke off. "I ought to tell you some bad news first, I suppose."

"The world's full of bad news," said Harper. "Go on. Then get back to what you called me about." He sounded patient, but as he listened to Jeff, his eyes grew cold. "I don't think thanks is the right word, but I appreciate your telling me. God, what a rotten thing to have happen."

"And it will happen more and more until we track this thing down," said Jeff. He knew he could not take every death personally, but the urge was there and it took more will than he wanted to admit to resist it. "About this other thing."

"Go on," said Harper.

"I think it's time we did some real detective work, some backtracking. You've lost a son to . . . TS, but the rest of your family appears to be okay for the time being. I want to have them checked out, complete workups, scans, the lot of it. I want to get as much material on this as we can. I want to find out who can get this stuff and why, and who can't. I want as many comparisons as possible, as complete medical histories as possible. Is there any way we can do this?"

"Hell, I don't know," said Harper, his voice thoughtful.

"I want this thing backtracked to the first cases we saw of it, and I want all similarities, no matter how obscure, noted and cross-checked. I want any fact, no matter how trivial or unrelated, to be supported and documented. Damn it, there is something we are overlooking, something basic that we haven't seen. If we can get material on every family where there has been a death, we might begin to make some headway."

"You came to the right place." Harper was more energetic now, his words were clipped and eager. "What we don't know about medicine, we do know about criminology and learning to identify and trace clues and facts. I'll put my grad students on it, if you'll give us access to your records."

"Certainly," said Jeff. "I'll need about an hour to set it up, but by then it should be possible for you to tap into the system. Drucker will object, but I'll make sure that won't stop us."

"How?" asked Harper, fascinated by the machinations that went into this investigation.

"I'll go over his head. He won't like it, but that doesn't bother me at present." He made a note to himself. "The person you're to talk to in Atlanta is Susannah Ling. She'll arrange everything." As he said her name he was surprised to discover that he was missing her.

"Ling? Any relation?" Harper asked.

"No relation." He wondered if the Vice-President had ever been asked if he were related to Susannah Ling of

Atlanta and the National Center for Disease Control? Probably not, he conceded.

"I'll call in ninety minutes, just in case," said Harper. "I'm glad you're finally giving me something useful to do. I've felt as if my wheels were spinning for the last two weeks."

"Okay. I'll want daily reports while you work on this," he continued. "Collate everything, cross-reference and flag."

"You bet. Just as soon as we get information." Harper had lost his distracted tone entirely.

By the time they hung up, Jeff was half-convinced that he might be on to something. As he placed his call to Susannah, he hoped she would agree.

"How's Portland?" she asked after the first exchange of greeting.

"Damp. Listen, Susannah, I need a favor." Saying this made his mouth dry.

"What is it?"

"I'd like to get all the information we have on the victims and their families transferred to Seattle. I know there might be difficulty with the Privacy Act, but there are provisions for waiving that in cases of emergency." He was pleading and they both knew it.

"I think I can justify invoking emergency medical privilege. What are you looking for?" She did not sound harried or pressured, though Jeff knew that she was both.

"I wish I knew. That's why I want all the material. I hope there's a key in all the facts that . . ." He did not know how to go on.

"Is this for Doctor Klausen?"

"No, for Doctor Ross in Seattle, at the University of Washington." He realized he was not being entirely accurate, for Harper's degree was a Ph.D., not a medical degree.

"Research lab?" guessed Susannah.

"Yeah, and willing grad students," said Jeff.

"Always useful," she agreed. "I'll start the paperwork

right away. The ESD might want a statement from you as to the necessity of the information; get one off to me sometime today."

"I will," he promised. "What's it like in Atlanta?"

"Warm," she said. "Lots of flowers. Three blocks of Peachtree were tied up last night—there's a movie company in town. Are you going to buy me dinner when you get back?"

It took Jeff a moment to realize what she had said. "Dinner? I—"

"Say yes before I lose my nerve," she insisted.

"Yes," he said at once. "Tell me where you want to go. I'd be happy to see you. One warning," he added as an afterthought.

"What?"

"I might not be very good company." He tapped the receiver twice. "I want you to know that."

"Two glasses of pinot grigio should take care of that. Do Persians drink?" A giggle sputtered.

"This Persian does. My family isn't Muslim, it's Orthodox."

"I didn't realize you were Jewish," she said, clearly confused.

"Not Jewish Orthodox, Armenian Christian Orthodox. It's a long story." He hesitated. "I'll tell you all about it over dinner, if you like."

"Good—I don't want to talk shop any more." It was her first actual concession to the strain of her work. "I'll make sure your Doctor Ross can get his material. And I'll look for your statement."

"Fine." He was beginning to hope that there might be a way to avert the worst of the epidemic he could see emerging. "And thanks."

"You're welcome. Call me when you know something." She was about to hang up. "Take care of yourself, Jeff."

"You, too," he said quietly, and hung up before she said

good-bye; a farewell was too final for him now.

When Max Klausen woke up, night had fallen and there had been eight more admissions to the hospital for TS, three of them nurses. These patients were put in the critical-care wing instead of the quarantine wing because there were no more beds available in quarantine, in this or the other sixteen major hospitals in Portland.

"You talked to Sam?" asked Max when he had showered, shaved and got into the change of clothes he kept at his office.

"Yes," said Jeff. "And Harper. They send condolences."

"Uh-huh," said Max, averting his face. "That's good of them."

"I've put Harper to work on a new project. I'm having him collate information for us."

"What kind of information?" Max adjusted the knot of his tie.

"Every kind of information we have about all the victims and their families. I'm hoping we'll discover a pattern." Hearing himself talk, Jeff felt that his position was weak, his goal so vague and ill-defined that there was no way he could learn anything of use.

"What kind of pattern?" Max asked reasonably.

"Damned if I know." Jeff sat on the corner of the desk. "I've been thinking that it could be that we have not a toxin, or even a couple of toxins, but a bacterium or virus that uses the toxin as a springboard, or the other way around."

"You mean that the disease is contagious?" Max asked.

"Or infectious," said Jeff somberly.

"I don't like the sound of this," Max told him after a brief silence.

"Nor do I," Jeff said.

"Either the disease lowers the resistance to the toxin," Max said, thinking aloud, "or the toxin eliminates resistance to the disease. Either way—"

"Either way it's risky."

Max looked at him with desolate eyes. "Risky? You mean deadly."

Dien Paniagua, Wilson Landholm and Jeff Taji

It was unseasonably warm in Twin Falls and the windows of the local office of the State Board of Health and Environment were open; the chill that pervaded the meeting had nothing to do with the glorious weather.

"So in the Idaho, Wyoming, and Montana areas, we can now assume more than a thousand cases," said Dien Paniagua. "We're looking for more cases, perhaps ones that haven't yet been reported."

"I know the feeling," said Wil Landholm. "We've stopped all sports programs in the state for the time being —I wish we could persuade the others to do the same." He looked over at the secretary who was recording their conversation, since it was official and would be entered in formal records.

"Our department has tried to find a way to determine how great the risks are, but so far we haven't been very successful." Dien looked at her watch. "The doc from Atlanta should have been here fifteen minutes ago."

"Maybe his plane was late," Wil suggested, resisting the urge to add his complaints to hers.

"He ought to call," she insisted, then shook her head. "I didn't mean that the way it sounded. I'm very tired. I'm worried about Dan Vitale."

"Someone special?" Wil asked, trying awkwardly to make conversation until Dr. Taji arrived.

"We work together. He went to the hospital two days

ago. They think it's TS. Two members of his family have it already." She took out her handkerchief and blew her nose. "He's the third person in our office to get it."

"Makes you wonder, doesn't it?" said Wil, then went on, "This disease is supposed to be toxic in origin, but I wonder. I agreed with that at first, but I don't anymore. Now I think that it's communicable beyond the toxins." He got up and walked down the length of the large office they had been provided for the conference with Dr. Taji. "You think you know how you'll handle something like this. You think you've got the perspective. Then it happens and you don't have any perspective at all after a while, and you don't have the foggiest notion how to handle it. I remember watching a boxing match when I was in the Navy. This guy was getting beaten, but he couldn't fall down. He stood there, and took blow after blow after blow. I'm starting to feel like him, and that's nothing compared to what the victims go through."

"I am afraid," Dien admitted simply. "All the time now."

"So am I," said Wil, doing his best to ignore the secretary. "Look, when this is over, let's you and me go get a cup of coffee. I have to talk to someone and I guess you do, too."

"Yes," said Dien. "I'd like that." She blew her nose again, saying, "It must be allergies."

"Un-huh," Wil said.

"With the weather so warm." Her face was composed but her hands shook as she opened her purse and took out a small vial of pills. "I really do have allergies," she said.

"Lots of people do," Wil told her.

She poured herself a glass of water from the carafe provided for the meeting, and as she swallowed the pill, she heard brisk footsteps in the hall.

"Finally," said Wil, looking at his watch again.

Jeff Taji was carefully dressed as always, but his face was haggard and there were thumbprint-sized smudges under his eyes. He handed his attaché case to the secretary and said, "Forgive my late arrival. There was fog in Portland and it delayed our takeoff by half an hour." He looked from Wil to Dien. "Doctor Paniagua, Doctor Landholm." Each shook hands with him. "I'm grateful you're willing to meet with me this way. It seemed there was no other means to get around Doctor Blair. Who *is* that fellow, anyway?"

Both Wil and Dien became guarded, and Dien said, "He's my superior," without inflection.

"I hope I won't offend you if I say that he's an irresponsible physician," Jeff told them both. "I don't mean to tread on toes, but Doctor Corwen Blair is a menace."

Both Wil and Dien relaxed visibly. "He's difficult," Dien agreed.

"He's a self-serving hack," Wil said at the same time.

Jeff drew up a chair, looking at the secretary. "You may delete that, if you wish."

The woman, her features rigid with disapproval, said, "I can't do that, Doctor Tahi."

"That's zhe, not heh. I'm Persian, not Spanish." He opened his case and took out a stack of printouts. "You've already got the most recent material from Portland, at least you ought to have."

"It got here this morning. There's an awful lot of it," Dien said.

"Yes. And now I'm going to give you some more." He handed each of them a stack of papers. "I'm afraid that we're off on the wrong foot with this disease, and I'm hoping you can help me prove it. I realize these questionnaires can't be completely filled out by every patient you see, and certainly some of the information isn't available, but I hope you'll be willing to make an attempt at getting the information I'm looking for."

Wil was going through the forms, brow furrowed. "There's an awful lot of questions here, and they cover—"

"Some rather strange ground?" Jeff finished for him. "Yes. I'm toying with the theory that there is a communicable disease that is triggered by an environmental toxin— that seems to be the best bet so far. There may also be a genetic factor, but at this time that still looks like a long shot."

"Why didn't you just send these to us? Why are you visiting us personally?" Wil moved closer to Dien and regarded Jeff with a measuring look.

"For a number of reasons, actually," said Jeff. "One of them is psychological expediency. If you have me here face-to-face and can ask questions directly there is a much greater chance that you'll cooperate with me in my secondary investigation. Frankly, I need all the help I can get. Another reason is that I want to make a few direct observations myself, not only of you, but of the circumstances here, which is why I want to see the quarantine wings of the three community hospitals before I fly back to Portland tonight."

"We could send you a videotape and you could have spared yourself the trips to the hospital." Wil was not going to let Jeff off the hook easily.

"That's true, but you and I know videotape isn't the same thing as a room with a human being in it. I can get a very good impression from the videotape, but it will only be an impression." He paused. "I trust what I feel far more than I trust images on a videotape and two miles of print-outs."

"You may run into Doctor Blair at one of the hospitals," said Dien, her attitude less challenging than Wil's.

"I won't say I want to meet him, but it might give me a chance to find out why he's so reluctant to assist this investigation."

"I'll tell you why: he wants his slate kept clean," said Wil. "He's a politician and what he cares about is keeping his ass covered and gathering favors owed him. An epidemic looks bad on his record."

"Not cooperating with the NCDC doesn't look terrific on a record," Jeff pointed out.

"You're there and he's here," Wil said. "Never mind all this. Let me have a little time to go over this new stuff."

"Also," said Jeff hesitantly, expressing something that

had occurred to him on the plane, "if you can, I'd appreciate any tracing back you can do to the first cases of ... TS you saw. What's been puzzling me is how it occurred in such divergent places within such a short length of time."

Dien shrugged. "That might be hard. You know that the outbreaks we've had have come from several locations."

"About the first case I know of was a motel owner, name of Tucker, in the town of Mullen. The next cases were in Twin Falls." Wil braced his hands on his hips. "That's what brought me in on this."

"A sports team," Jeff said. "I remember. And there were also some ranch hands, weren't there?"

"From the Gowan ranch, yes," said Dien. "Only one of them survived, but in the last month they've reported only two new cases. The Twin Falls high schools aren't so lucky." She glanced once at the window, at the lavish start of spring, and felt despair for those who would never see summer.

"Any military or civilian dumps on the Gowan ranch that you know of?" Jeff asked.

"Not that we know of," Dien answered carefully.

"And no record of new dump sites near this city or ... Mullen, was it?"

"Not that we can find a record of," Dien said.

"What about incidence of the disease in anyone under age twelve?" Jeff remembered the discussion he had had on the phone with Weyman the night before. "No case of this disease striking any patient who has not reached puberty."

"No," said Wil, looking uncomfortable.

"No," Dien concurred.

Jeff slapped his hands together and pressed his steepled fingers against his jaw. "I *know* we're on the wrong track. I can feel it. We've got a communicable disease that does strange things to the blood and the brain and for some reason is triggered by the hormonal changes of puberty. I don't *care* if it looks like a dozen other kinds of environmental toxic reactions, it's not. It's not."

"Doctor Taji?" Dien ventured, unsure of herself in the face of Jeff's outburst.

Jeff looked around at her and his attitude softened. "I didn't mean to do that. It's been nagging me, and the more I learn, the more convinced I become. I know we're seeing a pattern like toxin disease, but I know in my bones that it's not. I've seen too much toxin reaction not to know it when it's under my nose."

Wil had listened carefully. "That's the reason for all the questions and whole family histories, isn't it?"

"Yes," Jeff said. "I don't know what I'm looking for, but I pray I'll know it when I see it." He laid one hand on the printouts. "I'm a minority of one on this. Everyone else in my division believes that this is a double-toxin reaction. For what it's worth, I thought so too."

"But you've changed your mind?" Wil prompted. "Why?"

"Because it's the only thing that makes sense," said Jeff slowly, as if the admission weighted him down. "Everything else leaves unanswered questions. The trouble is, we got so spooked by the Tunis Flu that we're locked into seeing every new disease as an extension of the Tunis Flu; we think we've got to find two or three strains of everything and if we don't then the disease isn't as dangerous or as real as those three strains were. It can't be avoided, I guess, seeing all new forms of disease this way. And this . . . TS, it acts like environmental disease. The incidents of it are in limited geographical areas, those affected are from a narrow slice of the population, at least for the time being, and we haven't a clue to the resistance pattern, if any."

"And you haven't encountered unanswered questions before?" Wil was not quite mocking him, but was dangerously near it. "How lucky for you, Doctor Taji."

"I've ended up with long lists of unanswered questions," said Jeff, refusing to be baited. "But not like this. The thing is, if it turns out that there is a biological trigger to this disease, if it is communicable, or communicates a susceptibility to toxins, then there are fewer unanswered questions, and the questions all make sense. That's what convinces me to pursue this line of inquiry." He met Wil's gaze directly. "Can you help me? Will you help me?"

Wil puffed out a sigh. "I suppose I've already said yes."

"Doctor Paniagua?" Jeff said.

"Certainly." She pulled the material she had been given toward her. "I'll set to work on it this evening; if Blair will permit it, I'll start sooner. But don't assume he will cooperate. I'm planning to work around him."

"Thank you," Jeff said.

The three remained silent a short while, then Wil said, "If you're right, Doctor Taji, then there may be an explanation for the pockets of TS we've been seeing. The trigger might be quite common but localized. The other alternative is that someone out there is a carrier."

"That's what worries me," Jeff admitted. "If carriers are involved, who are we looking for, and what is it going to take to find them." He looked at his watch. "I'm due at the Twin Falls Community Hospital in fifteen minutes."

"I'll drive you," offered Wil, who was reluctantly starting to agree with Jeff's theory. "We can talk on the way."

"I want to come along," said Dien decisively.

"I'll still drive," said Wil, and might have reminded her of his invitation, but was uneasy about Jeff's presence.

"Excellent," said Jeff. He busied himself with gathering up the three stacks of printouts that he had taken from his attaché case. "You can brief me on what I have to expect at the hospital."

"You've probably seen it all before," said Dien. "The lab work has backed up, there's too much red tape to change that. The hospitals' staffs are not up to handling this heavy a case load this long. There's pressure coming from the local paper and newscasters and that's causing trouble. Some of the local physicians are not answering our inquiries for a variety of reasons. And we're running short of beds in critical care and we have almost nothing left in quarantine."

"Damn damn damn," said Jeff softly. "Damn it all to hell and perdition."

"Sounds about right," said Wil as he took out his car keys and indicated the door. "I'm in lot A."

Sylvia Kostermeyer and
Weyman Muggridge

At midnight Sylvia realized that neither she nor Weyman had eaten dinner. On reviewing the day, she was surprised to recall that their last meal—if that was the word for it—had been tuna sandwiches more than thirteen hours ago. The low ache in her head began to make more sense and she pushed back from the charts and printouts spread across the table. "We've got to take a break."

Weyman, his eyes slightly bloodshot, met her gaze. "How much more is there to do?"

"Enough that we can't get it done in the next hour. I'm worn out, Weyman. I need something to eat and a hot bath and two or three glasses of wine. Ten hours of uninterrupted slumber would also be nice." She made herself stretch and heard the protesting snap of her joints.

"Ten pounds of prime-quality uncut diamonds would also be nice, but you're no more likely to get that than you are to have that much sleep." He yawned suddenly and widely. "You're right. We're both worn out."

His yawn was contagious, and brought moisture to her eyes. "Let's find a place that's open and buy the food, okay?"

"That place down by Ocean Beach Park is open all night. We could go there; it's out of the way, I know, but there isn't much open around here. Unless you want hamburgers." This afterthought was so lacking in enthusiasm that Weyman laughed.

"Heaven forfend," he said as he began stacking their material in a single heap at the end of the table. "It won't take too long to get there at this time of night, will it?"

"Twenty, twenty-five minutes, probably." She leaned back in her chair and rubbed her eyes. "We can take the Expressway."

"You direct me," said Weyman, though he was reasonably certain he could find the restaurant on his own.

"Too bad the *Moonraker* isn't open this late. They've got great food there." She got slowly to her feet, thinking as she did that it was a good idea to wear her athletic tights instead of panty hose—if she had the panty hose on her ankles would be the size of grapefruits by now.

"Another time," Weyman said with a worn-out grin.

"You're on." Her coat was hanging in the closet down the hall, but her jacket was draped over the back of her chair. She started to pull it on and was stopped as Weyman took over for her. "Thanks."

"I'm just an old-fashioned boy, Sylvia. My mama brought me up to do for ladies." He shrugged into his own tweed jacket and then fished in his pocket for the keys to the door. "How soon will this floor be open in the morning?"

"Probably about seven-thirty, maybe earlier." She swallowed another yawn and wondered if she would be able to stay awake through supper. "Makes sense to lock the door if we're not going to be in until later."

"Okay." He found the key, and as they left the room took the time to lock up. A freshening wind met them as they went to her car on the far side of the parking lot. "I thought San Diego was supposed to be warm all year round."

"It depends on what you compare it to," said Sylvia as she clutched her coat more tightly around her.

"It's frigid compared to Bangkok. Great. But I'm getting cold." He chattered his teeth as demonstration.

"Weyman, it's after midnight and we're only a few miles from the ocean."

"The way this wind feels, the Pacific is filled with icebergs," he said, undaunted by her practicality. He made a show of holding the door for her and then went around to the passenger side of the car.

"One of these days, I'll hold *your* door for *you*," warned Sylvia as she turned the key in the ignition.

There was little traffic on the streets at this hour of the night. For two blocks they were flanked by Jeep Suburvans filled with sailors in uniform who were bawling out the words to the All Electric Kitchen's latest hit, but that was the only incident in their drive. When they reached the restaurant, they found a dozen cars in the lot and lights blazing.

"It looks inviting but garish," said Weyman as they started up the walk to the door.

"That about sums it up," Sylvia agreed. Weyman had taken her arm and she was not certain how she felt about this courtesy. "The food's good and the service is pretty fast," she added, in the hope that it would make their meal seem more ordinary.

"Fine."

They were seated in a booth, windows at their backs, and a seven-foot television screen off to the right. "I haven't seen the news in days," Sylvia said, mildly chagrined.

"You've had things on your mind," Weyman reminded her. "What's the country up to?" He glanced at the screen. "Reruns."

"The sea bass is fresh," their waitress announced as she walked up to the table. "So's the trout. The rest were flash-frozen. We're out of swordfish."

They ordered, and when the waitress was gone fell into an uneasy silence. From time to time they glanced at the screen where images flickered.

"Commercials," said Sylvia unnecessarily as the face of a local realtor praised his new "quake-resistant" condos.

Then the face of one of the regional newscasters appeared, her face elegant and serious. "This is Nan Kinny in Sacramento with headlines of the stories we'll feature at our six A.M. newscast: Governor Guy Derelli has declared an environmental emergency in nine southern California counties. At a special news conference yesterday evening, the Governor said that all necessary measures were being taken to control the toxic factors. On the national front, the National Center for Disease Control in Atlanta has issued a general advisory regarding Taji's Syndrome to all western states and President Hunter has said that he might extend the advisory to the entire country if circumstances warrant it. In Los Angeles, Horace McReddy said that the Screen Actor's Guild would support the ASCAP strike if the—"

"Oh, my God," whispered Sylvia.

"That's—" Weyman began but was interrupted.

"I can't believe it. What's been going on?" She had started to rise, hands flat on the table.

"Hey, Sylvia," Weyman said gently, putting a restraining hand on her arm. "We can't ask the set. We'll pick up a paper on the way out, and I'll get on the phone to Jeff first thing in the morning."

"There can't be that many cases, can there?" she pleaded with him, facing him as she took her seat again. "I mean, I can understand about Southern California, but the rest of it . . . You said that there were cases in Portland and Seattle, but this sounds a lot worse, doesn't it?"

"It doesn't sound good," said Weyman. "But you've seen the printouts. Something had to be done; you said so yourself."

"But my God . . ." She looked back at the television as if it could provide more information on request.

"Jeff'll straighten it out," Weyman said, hoping it was so. "I'll try to find out how much of it is his decision and how much is pragmatics and politics."

"Like the Tunis Flu," she sighed. "What a mess."

"Except that so far as we know, we have a single form of

TS, if only we knew what it was." He looked up as the waitress returned with their food. "Smells great."

Sylvia stared at the plate as it was set in front of her; her tongue felt like terry cloth and the fragrant steam that rose from the broiled albacore made her slightly nauseated. She blinked. "I don't know if I can eat," she admitted. "I . . . I'm shocked. Food doesn't . . . well—"

"Take a taste," Weyman advised. "If you don't want it after two bites, no big thing, but give it a chance, okay?" He had already reached for the bread and was tearing a slice in half. "It's been a long day and tomorrow ain't gonna be no shorter." He made his Southern accent much stronger and got a half-smile.

"Did you really talk like that when you were young?"

"According to my family, I surely did, honey," he continued in the same vein. "Most of 'em still talk this way. Me, I took on airs when I got my medical degree, as they always remind me." He grinned at her and went on in his usual speech, "Try the rice, too. It's good."

"All right," she said, and obediently picked up her fork. To her surprise, she was ravenous. Each bite was more delicious than the last and she could not bring herself to stop, even though she was afraid that she was being impossibly rude to eat so voraciously.

"See?" Weyman said between mouthfuls, "it isn't so bad after all."

"How did you know?" she asked.

"Because I did it myself a couple of times while we were working on the Silicon Measles investigation. I let myself get worn out and then not eat." He spread butter over his bread and handed it to her. "Jeff forced food into me then. I'm just passing on the lesson."

"Say thanks to him for me sometime," she said, her embarrassment passing.

When they were through with supper, Weyman insisted that they order dessert and a glass of port. "There's not enough alcohol to fuddle your wits but it will take the edge off. You need it more than coffee."

She was skeptical enough to order a pot of tea as well, and sipped nervously at the dark, heavy wine. "My mother used to make a drink for us when we were kids and got all wound up. Warm milk with a little port and honey in it."

"Makes sense," said Weyman, watching her. "Let's figure to get to work at nine tomorr— this morning. I don't think that we need to push any harder than that."

"What?" She was so startled she almost dropped her glass.

"Work. Morning. We don't need to start before nine." His lips did not move but his eyes smiled. "What did you think I meant?"

Her face reddened. "Nothing."

"This isn't the right time or place to proposition you, if that's what you were thinking," he said lightly.

Her blush deepened. "Of course not," she lied.

"For one thing, I'm too tired." He lifted his glass to her. "I won't say it hasn't occurred to me, but there'll be a better time."

Her face grew somber again. "Will there?"

PART V

April–May, 1996

Jeff Taji and
Susan Ross

There was no attempt made to conceal the hostility Susan felt at Jeff's intrusion. She sat on the sofa in the living room of her brother's house and glared at her unwelcome visitor. "I don't know anything that could help you," she told him without apology. "You came a long way for nothing."

"But perhaps you do," Jeff said, apparently unaware of her attitude. "That's the thing that comes to light in complex investigations like this one: so often there are those who know something and are not aware of it. If you're willing to answer a few questions, I'll make this as brief as possible."

"What questions?" Her hands became fists in the drape of her skirt. "I have to pick Grant up in forty minutes."

"I hope this won't take that long; I'll do my best to be as brief as possible." Jeff referred to a leather-bound notebook, although he had no reason to do so—he knew all the questions since he had written them. "You see," he went on after closing the notebook, "we're drawing a blank. So we're going back to the first reported cases of TS and we're trying to find out what those cases had in common, if anything."

"The people who got the disease are dead, that's what they have in common," Susan reminded him bluntly.

"Yes. And most of them were young. Before the summer of last year, as far as we can determine, no one had ever contracted this disease. And as of last autumn, only a few had."

"You mean Kevin?" she asked tightly. "That's what you mean, isn't it?"

"Yes. He was one of the first to . . . to die of it. We're hoping that we might discover how the disease got started by learning as much as possible about the first victims."

"Harper said you'd already got the family health history. Why do you have to talk to me? Isn't that enough?" Her voice got harsher with each challenging word.

"It might be, but you know as well as I do that there are a great many things that never get into such records."

"If you mean the trouble we've had with Grant, ever since we found out about it, there's been no attempt to—" Her features grew more stark.

"No, no; nothing like that. I hope you won't mind if I assume that you're willing to tell me how your children have been in the last two years. You certainly know more than Sam Jarvis does about them and you've got a different perspective than Harper." He smiled and wished he wore glasses; he knew how useful they could be in changing the "feel" of a question.

"We could have done this over the phone," she said resentfully. "There's no reason for you to be here."

"Well, with the blood work and PAST scans we have ordered, I thought we might just as well do it all at once." He watched her stiffen with disapproval. "What's troubling you, Missus Ross?"

"It's bad enough that Kevin's dead, but you refuse to leave it alone. You're bringing it all back. You're making a case for it. You won't let it be. How are we supposed to get over it if you keep it under our noses all the time?" She got up and paced down the room. "Grant's started to make a little progress here and you don't understand how disruptive your presence here can be. You come in here, ordering tests and scans and all the rest of it. It was bad enough to have all the kids put through the Standard Public School Blood Screens."

Jeff did not attempt to argue with her. "It's never been an easy thing to know where the right to privacy stops and public safety begins. The SPSBS is up for review in two years—who knows? Now that we've got the AIDS vaccine, it might be reversed."

"You wouldn't like that, would you? If the Supreme Court decided that you weren't entitled to so much intrusion, you'd have to find some other way to do your work." Her chin came up. "I wish you'd find some other way now."

"Missus Ross, your husband has authorized the tests; I hope you'll be willing to permit them." He watched her as she picked up a magazine, then set it back down. "Your son Kevin was a tragic loss for you. I hope that we can spare your family and other families further grief."

"Naturally," she said dryly. "What does it matter, anyway? You've got your permission already, from Harper. You don't need anything from me. All you have to do is take your document along to the hospital and get the court to order Grant and me to appear."

"Is there anything I can say that might convince you I don't mean to impose on you, that my only purpose is an attempt to stop a dangerous and deadly disease?" He had risen but did not move either toward her or away from her.

"I doubt it," she said. "And I don't think it matters one way or another if you have 'noble' motives. You're here because you want your ass covered and you're using my family to do it. So get it over with and go back to Atlanta and file your reports. And leave us alone."

"Thank you." He said it without sarcasm but also without any vestige of patience. "I'll notify the hospital to be ready for tests first thing tomorrow morning. And it might interest you to know that there are four cases of TS in the Santa Rosa Community Hospital right now."

"Then we're probably too late. That's what Sam told us after Kevin died—that by the time he got to the hospital it was already too late." Her eyes glittered with tears but she refused to weep.

"Missus Ross," said Jeff mildly, "do you watch the news?"

"Yes," she said guardedly, unprepared for this change of direction in his questioning.

"And you will agree that there has been some mention of TS, but that it hasn't been emphasized," he went on, as if discussing the weather.

"Probably the Public Health Exemption at work again," she said nastily.

Jeff neither confirmed nor denied, though it was true. "Who do you watch most of the time? Which newsman?"

Now Susan was truly puzzled. "John Post," she answered as if it were a trick question.

"John Post's youngest son—a fourteen-year-old named Aaron—is in the hospital in Shreveport with TS and has been for the last two weeks. Post suggested that the feature his network is preparing not hide that fact, but that he would prefer a balanced presentation so that he would—"

"You're making this up!" Susan shouted at him.

"I wish I were," Jeff said. "My colleague, Doctor Howell, sent me confirmation of this last week."

"I don't believe you," she said directly.

"It's the truth, whether you believe it or not," said Jeff. "And by Saturday night, the whole country will know it. Yesterday Elizabeth Harkness taped an interview with Aaron in his quarantine room. They'll show it on *Final Edition.*"

"I don't believe you," she repeated.

Jeff went on as if he had not heard her. "I'm telling you this in the hope you will stop thinking that my request for all this extra information is capricious or intended to shore up my position with the government. I want to stop TS. I wanted to stop it as soon as I learned about it."

Slowly and sarcastically Susan clapped a derisive smile on her lips. "I haven't heard such medical integrity since *Urgent Care* was canceled."

"Then you haven't been talking with your husband or Sam Jarvis, have you?" he shot back, ashamed of himself for this behavior but too irritated to resist the urge.

She stood very still. "I talked to Mason last night."

"Ah, yes; Mason," said Jeff, glad for a change of focus. "He's been helpful and cooperative. He volunteered to any tests we might need. So far he shows no symptoms of TS. I pray there's no change, but I don't want to rely simply on prayer."

"Next you'll try Apple Pie," said Susan. "I really don't want to talk to you anymore, Doctor Taji."

Jeff made one last attempt. "The Governor of California has declared nine Southern California counties disaster areas because of TS."

"A lot of Californians consider Southern California a disaster area even without your disease," she said sharply, and laughed without amusement.

"Please help us, Missus Ross. If nothing else, let us run a Standard Public School Blood Screen on you and your son." It would not be much, but it was better than nothing.

"I'd like you to leave now," Susan informed him.

"All right." At the door he stopped. "If you reconsider, I'll be at the Sonoma Hilton until tomorrow morning. I'd welcome a call from you."

"And the permission from Harper? You mean you aren't going to wave that around?"

"I'm going to leave it with the local office of PHES and let them tend to it. Your husband is in Washington State and this is California. They'll have to make up their minds how or if they want to enforce it," he said, feeling defeated.

Susan gave a tight smile. "I'll call an attorney if I have to. I don't want any more disruptions for Grant, not with what he's already been through."

Against his better judgment, Jeff made one more try. "Missus Ross, you're not protecting Grant if he's got TS, you're only increasing the likelihood that he'll die from it."

"Everyone dies from it," Susan countered.

"We don't know that for sure. It's got a very high death rate, but there is at least one woman in Texas who has survived it. I read the report two days ago. And if there is one, statistically there ought to be more. We're looking for others now, in the hope that through them we can save more." To his own ears he sounded pompous, but he noticed that Susan was staring at him with skeptical interest rather than outright hostility.

"Who survived?" Susan demanded.

Jeff took a deep breath. "Her name is Irene Channing. She's an artist, a widow, with two children. Boys, I think. She lives in Dallas. Her fever broke more than a week ago and it hasn't returned. Blood tests and PAST scans aren't normal yet, but they're . . . improving."

"One woman in Dallas," said Susan. "What about the kids?"

"No sign of TS in either of them," said Jeff, mentally adding the ominous word *yet*.

"And what does that have to do with Grant or me?" This was blatantly a challenge.

"I don't know yet. I won't know if you don't have the tests. But Harper will be doing a complete battery tomorrow and Mason will the day after. If you were willing, you might have the key. Someone has the key."

She looked away from him, out across the street where a large truck emblazoned with the name and logo of a local nursery was drawing up. "The Doniers are getting roses. It's a little late for planting them."

"Missus Ross, please reconsider. It's very, very important. To all of us."

"They don't understand about gardens," said Susan. "They expect them to be ready in a minute, like microwave dinners."

"Missus Ross." He waited until she grudgingly gave him her attention. "Help us."

She made a gesture in front of her eyes and said nothing.

"TS is out of hand. We don't know how it's triggered, but we know that in pockets where it has been reported, it's spreading." He tried to read her expression and failed. "If only you'd take the tests. It takes three hours, Missus Ross. That's all."

"No, it's not all. There are the tests and the waiting and

the reports and everything that happens afterward. You're asking me to turn my boy—and he already has serious problems—into an all-out freak. There are kids in his school who won't speak to him, won't sit near him, because his brother died of TS. Do you know what that's like for him?"

"I have some idea," said Jeff quietly. "I'm truly sorry, but it doesn't alter anything. In fact, if we can give Grant a clean bill of health, it could improve things for him."

"And if you can't?" Susan braced her hands on her hips again. "That doesn't matter to you, does it? Not really. No, not really. You're determined to have those tests done, and one way or another you'll find a way to get them. I don't want them done, but you can win, and you can let PHES sanitize it for you." She looked out the window, once more entranced by the nursery truck. "My brother thinks we should go to the ACLU."

Jeff lowered his head. "If that's what you want. But if you're concerned about Grant feeling . . . out of place, then you might reconsider." He opened the door. "I didn't mean to take up so much of your time, Missus Ross. I'm sorry—"

"Don't you ever get tired of saying that?"

"Yes: I get tired that it's necessary, not of the sentiment." He let himself out, taking care to close the door. As he walked to his rented Nissan Comet, he shook his head, defeat blackening his thoughts. He ought to have found a way to make her understand how urgently her help was needed. He upbraided himself for botching the interview, and then he opened the door of the car and got in.

Susan watched Jeff drive away, anger rising volcanically in her. She turned on her heel so abruptly that she almost tripped on the carpet as she crossed the living room toward the family room, which opened onto an enormous covered patio filled with large tropical plants. Since she had come to her brother's house she had spent a lot of time on the patio; the huge plants seemed to restore her perspective and calm.

This time she realized it would not work. Frustrated, feeling betrayed, she rushed to the phone and dialed Harper's lab number. It irked her to have to ask the department switchboard to find Harper, and she was outraged when she was given a number at the medical center to call. She slammed down the receiver and paced through the kitchen twice before trusting herself to dial again.

"Just a moment, Missus Ross," said the operator at the medical center when Susan had identified herself.

"This is long distance!" Susan barked.

"Just a moment," the operator reiterated.

By the time Harper picked up the phone three minutes later, Susan had worked herself into a thunderous rage.

"Susan? Is anything wro—"

"What the fuck do you think you're doing, sending that two-faced bugger down here?" She was shocked by her scream and she made herself speak more evenly. "If this is your idea of being a good father, then you have real problems, Harper."

"Jeff Taji was there?" Harper said.

"You signed the papers for him: you know damn well he was here. What are you playing at, Harper? Isn't it enough that we've lost one son? You're like one of those neurotics who pick open a wound as soon as it scabs over, and make it bigger and bigger and bigger each time. Let Kevin rest in peace and let us get on with our lives. Keep out of that cesspool."

"Is that how you see it?" Harper asked, pain in his voice.

"That's what it is," she corrected him sternly.

"Susan, I know you don't believe this, but there is nothing I want more than for us to be able to put Kevin's death behind us, and for the family to get on. I swear to God that's what I want."

"Liar."

He paused, making himself ignore her accusation. "We can't get on with our lives with this hanging over us. We need to get questions answered or they'll haunt us forever."

"You're not convincing me, Professor," she said with deliberate malice. "You're playing Sherlock-Holmes-meets-Jonas-Salk. You're exploiting Kevin and the rest of us."

"I don't mean to do that," said Harper, afraid that out-right denial would close the door. "I don't want TS to claim any more victims. It's had too many already. I have to do something to help stop it, or I'll never forgive my-self. I wish you could believe that, Susan."

"It's a touching justification," she said sarcastically. "I thought for years that I knew you. I used to think how lucky I was to have a husband I could understand. But it wasn't so. You're a stranger, Harper. You're some for-eigner who wandered into my life in my husband's skin and I don't know what to do about it."

Harper remembered how he had felt in the one serious accident he had had in college, when his motorcycle car-eened off a center divider and flung him into a lightpole. The anguish in him now was more inescapable, more in-tense than the broken femur and three broken ribs had been. "Susan; please."

"They tell me you're going to do a test series again. Don't you get tired of it?" She hung up before he could say anything more, but the surge of victory eluded her, and she wandered back to the living room to watch the gardeners wrestle with the roses.

Corwen Blair and
Maximillian Klausen

Whenever Corwen Blair sensed he was at a loss, he would stand in front of the wall where his autographed photographs and sealed testimonials were displayed. He stood there now, his shoulders squared and his jaw firm as he faced his unwelcome visitor. "You don't know how impossible that is."

"No, I don't," said Max, coughing once. "I only give up on impossible things. I'm not giving up on this."

"We can't possibly issue such an order."

"You saw Aaron Post last night. You heard what half the country heard. You know that we're"—he interrupted himself—"Do you mind if I sit down? I'm running on five hours' sleep for the last thirty-six and I'm tired."

"Of course, of course," said Corwen unctuously. "The chair by the window is the most comfortable."

"Thanks." Max slumped into it. "Aaron Post has about six weeks left, assuming he follows the usual curve. You say that you don't want a panic in your schools, and that there is no guarantee of cooperation from other states." He cleared his throat. "There's no guarantee of non-cooperation, either."

"Doctor Klausen, you're behaving as if I were the enemy, not the disease. I am only trying to discharge my responsibilities to the best of my ability and with the greatest good served." He rocked back on his heels. "I have to answer to Governor Cooper as I am sure you are aware. The Governor has always put public safety as his highest concern. I can't help but think that I would be remiss if I contributed to the sense of panic that has already begun. I think it would be best if we took a moderate course during this time."

"Which says a shitload of nothing," Max responded in his most polite tone of voice.

"That's offensive," said Blair.

"It was meant to be. *You're* offensive. You stink, Doctor Blair. We're in the middle of a disease outbreak that might well be potentially damaging as AIDS, and you're thinking politics as usual. Well, it won't fadge, Blair. You have work to do and whether or not you want to do it, you will." He broke off, his hand over his mouth. When he spoke again, his voice was low. "My wife died of TS. Died of it, Doctor Blair. One of my oldest friends and his wife died of it. You have less than six quarantine beds left in the State of Idaho, and you don't want to contribute to panic." He laced his hands together. "Oh. One more thing. I have TS. It isn't at the critical state yet, but I have it, and unless we achieve a major breakthrough, I'll be dead before August."

"A-a-a-hg," went Blair.

"You're one who has said that since the disease is triggered by the environment, it isn't communicable in the accepted sense and therefore there is nothing to worry about. I have that right, don't I?"

Blair had taken a step back and smacked his shoulders into the wall. "Don't you think you're being unwise?" he asked in an effort to regain his position with Max.

"How do you mean?" Max inquired innocently.

"In your condition, you ought to be under care, not running around, possibly increasing the risk of others." He put his hand to his throat, a curiously feminine gesture.

"I'm doing this because it's all I can do. There aren't any more quarantine beds in Oregon, even if I wanted one. We're asking the military to let us use two of their hospitals, but so far no luck." He stared calmly at Blair. "So what is it going to be? Are you going to help me? Are you going to contact the Departments of Health in Utah, Wyoming, Nevada and Montana, or are you going to sit on your ass?"

"I haven't the authority . . . I—"

"But you've said you have authority. Or is it that you have it when you refuse to use it, but don't when you do use it?" He let his smile widen. "Do you enjoy your impotence?"

Blair straightened up once more. "I refuse to become embroiled in a multi-state dispute. If you are truly as concerned as you imply—"

"I'm as concerned as I can be and still be alive," interjected Max.

"—then you'll bend your efforts toward a change in national policy instead of this . . . this piecemeal approach to the problem." He had the satisfaction of feeling indignant.

"We're working on a national change," said Max evenly. "But that takes time. We haven't got that. So we're working on our own as well. By the way, did you know that there have been over one hundred new cases of TS reported in Idaho in the last seven days?"

". . . I . . . over one hundred?"

"I think it's one hundred eight, but I could be mistaken." He leaned back, his gaze directed now to the patterned ceiling. "We're asking the Canadians to help us. They're pretty upset about the cases in Alberta and Saskatchewan. I don't blame them."

"But surely there's no link . . . This is an environmental disease. The SPSBS show that. It makes no sense that the . . . that anyone would think that—"

"We've assumed all along that the disease was environmental, either cumulative or having an environmental/biological trigger. In either case, it fell under the environmental division. But it doesn't change the fact that something is transmitting the disease and that the vast majority of the cases are in the western half of the United States, and that more than sixty percent of those cases are on the West Coast." He paused and then reminded Blair: "Neither Alberta nor Saskatchewan are in the United States, nor are they on the West Coast. That might be called indicative. Given the pattern we've seen."

"Given the pattern we've seen," Blair said with ponderous emphasis to make his point, "this is an almost classic outbreak of environmental toxic disease. The areas of outbreak are specific and limited, the spread beyond the area of contamination is slow and the disease is more properly a syndrome, in this case one that disrupts blood and brain chemistry. Now you say that you have doubts and you think there might be other factors."

"Yes," Max said, determined not to be distracted from his purpose by Blair's condescending attitude.

"You mean that the trigger is communicative," said Blair at his surliest.

"That seems likely," said Max. "The ironic thing is," he

went on in a distant, amused tone, "that from the first we've quarantined the patients with TS, not for our safety, but for *their* safety. We didn't want to introduce anything that might make the disease worse. Could be that the precaution was as much for us as for them."

"You're looking for explanations for your own disease. Why is it impossible that you have reached the level of toxin necessary to trigger the disease?" Blair folded his arms and watched Max without sympathy. "I am sorry for your misfortune, but I will not be party to the kind of deception you propose."

Max turned on Blair, no longer willing to keep his temper. "That is the most self-serving, the *shittiest* thing I've heard all week! Jesus H. Christ! You don't get it, do you? You won't let yourself see it."

"If you mean that I refuse to box with shadows, then I agree. I don't like your attitude or your choice of words and I am not going to give in to either." His voice had got louder.

"You're irresponsible and dangerous, and I am going to stop that. I can't permit you to continue this way, Doctor Blair. You're indulging your ego at the cost of human lives: that's going to end." He strode to the door, his big, knobby hands seizing the knob as if to crush the brass. "You are placing the people of your state at risk, and I won't allow that."

Blair stared at him. "You're overreacting."

"The hell I am!" Max shouted as he flung out of the room and crashed the door closed behind him. He hastened down the hall toward the office occupied by Dien Paniagua. He was breathing hard; his ears rang and he felt lightheaded. For an instant he fought down the dread that TS was catching up with him sooner than he had thought it would. He put out his hand and braced himself in the open doorway, forcing himself to calm down, to breathe normally, to put Corwen Blair out of his thoughts.

"Doctor Klausen," said Dien as she came out of her office. She sounded hoarse and her eyes showed fatigue and worry but she did her best to make him welcome. "I wasn't sure you were here."

"Until tomorrow, then on to Boise." He disguised his panting with a breathless laugh. "When I was in college there was a foreign student—from Belgium—who wanted to have a look at the U.S. So he got one of those bus tickets and rode around for two weeks. He said the strangest place he found was Boise, which he pronounced *bwahs*, as if it were French."

Dien dutifully joined his laughter, but it did not reach her wary eyes. "You've had a call from a Doctor Picknor in Dallas. It has to do with the TS investigation. He asked that you return his call as soon as possible."

"Picknor?" Max repeated, trying to place the name. He was more in control of himself now and he indicated her office. "Did he say what he wants?"

"He said he's working with one of the survivors of TS. He wanted to get some information on your investigation from you. He mentioned he has already spoken with Doctor Taji." She stood aside so that he could enter the office. "If you want to be private, I have some work to do in the lab downstairs. I'll be back in the next hour."

"Thank you," Max said, gratefully sinking into her chair and steadying himself with his arms on her desk. He let the shivering pass through him before he attempted to concentrate. They were becoming more frequent, he realized, those moments of sudden weakness and chill, like the onset of the flu. A week ago it had happened only twice; now it occurred at least four times daily. He thrust these depressing thoughts from his mind. "Note, note, note," he whispered as he examined the various stacks of paper on Dien's desk, while trying not to pry.

The note was on the top of a stack of printouts, and he read it as if deciphering code. "Doctor Paniagua?" he called, but received no answer. He picked up the note and reached for the telephone, dialing the 214 area code as soon as he got the tone for an outside line.

Ten minutes later, Wendell Picknor was talking to him.

"Well, yes," he said when Max introduced himself. "I've been hoping you'd reach me before suppertime, Klausen. I see from the records transmitted from there that a Coach James Jackson appears to have survived TS. What do you know about him?"

"I haven't checked," said Max honestly.

"Well, I would appreciate anything you can tell me. So far, my only patient to survive is Missus Channing, and there are some rather...surprising developments in her case." His voice had taken on a note of caution.

"How do you mean, surprising developments?" Max had heard the rumors that TS could cure anything from warts to heart disease if you survived it; he had expected something of the sort and so was not annoyed at these myths.

"I mean that Missus Channing is... How secure is that line?"

"About average, I would say," Max said, intrigued and irritated at the secrecy that Picknor showed.

"Not safe enough," Picknor muttered. "All right, hang up and go to the sixth floor of that building and request to use Doctor Dawson's office. I'll arrange it. Sybil owes me one." With this cryptic comment, he hung up.

Max sighed as he put the phone down. Slowly he stood and made his way to the elevators. He wanted to get some sleep, he wanted to feel some strength in his body again. As he rode to the sixth floor, he tried to decide what Doctor Wendell Picknor wanted of him that required some kind of increased security.

Lydia Dawson was waiting for him, a small compact woman with a precise haircut and no-nonsense glasses. "Good afternoon, Doctor Klausen," she said, accompanying her words with a direct and firm handshake. "Doctor Picknor is on the line. When you've finished your conversation, I hope you'll save some time for me. Health and Environment has a few questions that need answers." She smiled as she spoke but there was no attempt to disguise the fact that she had issued an order, no matter how politely expressed.

Ms. Dawson's office was large and neat. There were photographs on her wall, just as there were on Blair's, but Lydia Dawson preferred to display pictures of her family and headlines from papers that dealt with environmental legislation. One picture showed Lydia Dawson standing in a creek trying to land a medium-sized brown trout. As Max picked up the phone, he sat so that he could study the photographs at leisure.

"Doctor Klausen?" Picknor said sharply.

"Yes; I'm here." He saw that there was a notebook and pen set out for him, and he hastened to grab for them. "What is all this secrecy about?"

"It's because I'm worried—worried about Missus Channing first of all, but about this whole TS project." His voice dropped, as if having a secure line did not console him.

"What are you talking about? What's going on in Texas?"

"Let me tell it my way, okay?" Picknor asked in his best crusty style.

"Go ahead, Doctor Picknor," Max offered, determined to keep his mouth shut as much as possible. His head was aching now, along with his back and arms.

"Well, the thing of it is, we thought Irene Channing was as good as dead when we brought her into the hospital. We made all kinds of arrangements for her kids and got her lawyer to handle things like household accounts and the like. Missus Channing is a woman of some means. She's also an artist. One of the galleries has a show of hers going on right now. Anyway, we were all pretty set for her dying, her included. But it didn't happen. She got the high fever, her blood—well, you know what her blood looked like— and the ACTH readings were what you'd expect with TS. And then, just when we thought that was that, the fever broke and she started to recover."

"By recover, what do you mean?" Max warned himself that he had no reason to expect things to work out so well for himself, and that he did not know what recovery from

TS might entail. There were diseases that left their survivors little more than human flotsam.

"We're not quite sure yet. There hasn't been a long time to observe her, and ... and we don't know if it really is over." Picknor sounded unsure of himself and as he went on, his uncertainty increased. "Her temperature has been normal and most of her tests look okay. She's starting to take exercise again, and that's been coming along. Her blood isn't normal, and her ACTH and CRF levels are ... abnormal."

"How, abnormal?" Max went cold again, but this time he did not blame his disease.

"They're higher and ... the cycles are unfamiliar." He cleared his throat. "There's something else."

"What is it?" He prepared himself for the worst.

"Well, I don't know how to say it." He faltered, then went on without prompting. "The thing is, she seems to have acquired a new talent."

"What kind of talent?" Max smiled at a photograph of Lydia Dawson, her husband and two children as they chased two half-grown Samoyed puppies over a wide lawn. From the shadow at the base of the picture, it had been taken by one of the neighbors.

"It's something to do with the mind. We can determine that much through the ACTH levels. Her fever goes up, too, and comes back down almost at once." Picknor was decidedly uncomfortable now and he hesitated. "She says she can't do it often, and when she does, it wears her out. She says that it makes her feel dizzy and that she has to sleep a long time after she does it."

Max's patience was almost exhausted. "What is it she does?"

"She ... uh, moves things." Picknor fell silent.

When there was no more information coming, Max let his attention stray from the photographs. "What's remarkable about that? Or are these very large or heavy things?"

"It doesn't matter. She moves them." Picknor coughed.

"I've seen her do it. The nurses here have seen her do it. There's no trick to it. She's really doing it."

"Moving things?" Max asked dubiously.

"Yes," Picknor snapped. "Even if she had the ability before, it was latent. If it is the result of the disease, then who knows what the ramifications might be."

"You mean that she's recovered enough to handle normal work?" Max did not want to sound incredulous.

"You aren't listening to me," Picknor argued. "You aren't paying attention."

Guiltily Max turned away from the photos. "I am," he said.

"She *moves* things; she doesn't *handle* them." He waited and went on. "She lies in bed, and the sweat pours out of her like a cutting horse at work on an August afternoon. And something—the TV or a chair or a nurse or a vase of flowers—rises into the air. The last time she kept something up for about half an hour. Then she slept fourteen hours."

Max could say nothing for the better part of a minute, and then he asked, "Are you serious?" He was tempted to laugh, but was afraid that he might be making a mistake if he did.

"Serious as I can be," Picknor said somberly. "I have signed and witnessed statements from several members of the hospital staff. I have photographs. And it scares me, Doctor Klausen. We already know she's one in several million because she's alive, but what if . . . what if she's not the only one? What if TS can do this?"

"You mean cause spontaneous psychokinesis?" Max asked as if he were talking about a picnic lunch.

"Either in its fatalities or its survivors. You think we're not up to handling it the way it is, can you imagine what it would be like to have—" He could not go on.

It took Max several seconds to collect and organize his thoughts. "Doctor Picknor, how much documentation do you have on this?"

"Not as much as I'd like."

"Un-huh," Max said, doing his best to sound neutral. "Could you prepare it all and see that copies are sent to the Environmental Division of the NCDC in Atlanta? Give us as much information as you can, with all the backup material you can find. You're making some very . . . unusual claims, and we'd better check them out for all our sakes." He wanted to talk with Jeff and with Sam Jarvis. He did not care that the others might laugh. "If you can spare a copy for us in Portland, I'd really appreciate it."

"If you insist," said Picknor. "I don't mind telling you, I'm scared for Missus Channing. If it gets out that she's survived TS and ended up able to use her mind that way, who knows who might want to get their hands on her?"

Max privately thought that this was the least of Mrs. Channing's concerns, but he kept his opinion to himself. "I don't know what to tell you until I go over your figures. I'll talk with Doctor Taji and get back to you."

"Be careful," warned Picknor. "You could be watched."

"Oh, I doubt that," Max said unwisely.

"Still, be careful," said Picknor. "Call me on a secure line when you've gone over the things I send you."

"All right; thanks," he said and was trying to think of a suitable phrase to end the conversation when Picknor hung up.

Max went back to Blair's office in a thoughtful frame of mind. Supposing that Picknor had been right and that in some unknown way TS had triggered psychokinetic powers in Mrs. Irene Channing, what could that mean to him, or to anyone else for that matter? Who would bother themselves with the few who actually lived through TS when so many were contracting the disease and dying of it? He decided he would have to find this Coach James Jackson if he wanted to learn for himself.

It was well after eight that evening when Max finally found a reference in the patient records to James Joseph Jackson. It referred to the man as being in critical condition, temperature spiking at close to one hundred five, breathing labored, blood disastrous, ACTH levels incomprehensible. Max admitted that if he had seen these readings, he would assume the patient would not last another forty-eight hours. But he found no death entry for Jackson in any of the records for that day or the day after or the day after that. Then, strangely, there was an authorization for a transfer to a Veterans Administration hospital dated nine days later, well after Max would have thought the man dead.

"Dien?" he said when he reached her at home. "I don't mean to disturb you, but I have something here that puzzles me."

There was a child crying somewhere near the phone and Dien's response was distracted. "What is it?"

"I've got a few questions about a TS patient."

"Oh." The phone clattered, there was a brief struggle and then Dien said, breathlessly, "Sorry. We're having a little jurisdictional dispute here."

"Your kid?"

"He's growing. The terrible twos." She paused, then went on more calmly. "What patient is it? Anyone we've discussed?"

"No, not directly. He was transferred to a VA hospital last month. He had TS but apparently his condition . . ." He could not find a word to describe what might have become of Coach Jackson.

"They're trying to get some of the vets into VA hospitals," Dien said at her most sensible. "We need as many beds as we can find these days."

Max hesitated. "That's not quite what I mean," he said. "I mean that he was still alive after going critical. Has that happened before?"

She did not answer at once, and when she did, her voice was thoughtful. "No. Of course not."

"Judging from the records, it did in this case." He thumbed through the printouts again. "There's one notation here that almost looks like he was listed as dead. Understandable, but a little premature, I think, because the transfer was authorized almost three weeks after that."

"I'll give Wil Landholm a call. He knew...knows Jackson." She was more determined now. "He told me Jackson was dead."

"Good guess, if he had TS," Max said ironically but without bitterness. Since the death of Cassie, his wife, he was less attached to life. "Tell me what you find out. I leave at ten in the morning. I don't mean to put pressure on you, but if you can have something for me before then?"

"If I can reach Wil, you'll hear from me." She made it a promise. "Where was the VA hospital, can you tell me? Is in on the records?"

Max shuffled through the stack. "It says it's in Coeur d'Alene."

"Coeur d'Alene? I didn't think the VA had a facility there," Dien said. "It can't be very big."

"No record," Max said, frowning as he tried to recall what Veterans Administration hospital it might be. "I'll call Atlanta before I go." He added a few more notes to his already extensive list, trying all the while to hold back the insidious weakness that sapped his will as well as his strength.

Jeff Taji and
Susannah Ling

Stapleton Airport in Denver was almost deserted. Few travelers waited in the lounge areas, and the ticket counters were inactive. When Jeff found Susannah in the baggage claim area, she gave him a rueful smile.

"This is worse than during the Tunis Flu Two and Three," he said, indicating the empty terminal.

"Everyone got scared. They're afraid to travel, afraid of

what they could catch or carry, or what they might sit next to. You remember all the dire warnings during the Tunis Flu. Other people remember them, too. Ever since that story on Aaron Post, half the country's convinced that TS will get them no matter what they do. The other half are preparing for siege." She had two bags—a carry-on and a large Pulman—and a two-wheeled hand trolley to move them.

"I'll do that," Jeff offered, taking the handle as she secured her bags to it.

"If you like," Susannah said, faintly amused. She leaned over and kissed Jeff on the cheek. "I missed you."

He gave her a startled look. "I missed you, too," he said, returning the kiss.

As she fell into step beside him, she said, "I warned you at that first dinner that I don't know how to flirt. I'm not kidding."

"I don't know how, either," he said, letting her precede him through the doors. "It's chilly."

"It's bloody *cold*," she corrected him as she pulled her coat more tightly around her. "It's almost May, for Lord's sake."

He indicated his government car parked near at hand in an illegal zone. "Privilege of physicians," he said as he opened the door for her.

"Very convenient." She got in and waited while he put her things in the trunk. "I brought most of the information you wanted. I still don't understand why you wouldn't let me send it by phone."

"Because," he said as he started the car, "I don't want the information leaking out too soon. There are too many people who can tap in on that."

"You have a point," she said, leaning back as he headed for the freeway. "There are cases cropping up all over the country now, you know, and the Canadians are furious."

"You can't blame them," said Jeff.

"No." She lapsed into silence. "Jamshid," she said a

little later as they headed through Denver toward Golden. "It's a nice name. I like it."

"So do I," said Jeff. "My aunt still calls me that. My kids use Jeff. It's Jeff on my passport. I list Jamshid as a middle name."

"Jeffrey Jamshid Taji?" Susannah inquired, faintly amused. "Sort of exotic."

"Pragmatic," said Jeff seriously. "As long as I'm Jamshid, I'm a Persian in exile. Jeff is someone who has come home." He glanced at his watch. "This woman we're going to see—she's not very cooperative. She's had more grief than help from government agencies in the past, but it appears that she might have a clue to the problem."

"And she might be a nut case. You did say that, too." She rubbed her eyes. "Is Patrick Drucker always a pompous ass, or does he do that trick just for me?"

"He does it for all of us. He knows his stuff, but he doesn't know or trust his people." It was so relaxing to be able to speak candidly, and for the first time in days Jeff began to let down his formality and guard. "Get Weyman Muggridge to talk to you about it sometime. Drucker doesn't like Weyman."

"And you?" Susannah asked acutely.

"He tolerates me, but he never lets me forget I'm a foreigner. He has a very low opinion of the World Health Organization, and he would love to get transferred across town, to the *real* Disease Control Center. He is very keenly aware that we're poor relations, and it galls him, I think." He passed a huge truck pulling two tankers with enormous warnings of radioactivity plastered all over them. "I wish we could get those things off the highways, or restrict the times they can be on the road."

"Um," she agreed.

"Some day there's going to be a twenty-car pile-up with one of those things smack in the middle of it, and we'll have a contamination problem that no one is ready to handle." He took a deep breath. "Preaching to the converted; I won't waste my time."

She turned her head and looked at him. "Yeah, you're preaching to the converted, but it's nice to know you care." Her face softened. "How much longer?"

"Not too long. And we can have dinner before we head back to Denver. There's a meeting in the morning at nine, and another one at eleven-thirty. One of the local TV stations wants to do an interview at two—I haven't said yes or no yet—and there's another meeting at four. I'm sorry they got stacked up but . . ."

"Don't apologize. It works out that way sometimes." She opened her purse and rummaged in it, finally drew out a lipstick wand and reddened her mouth. "I look hagged," she said, addressing her reflection in the pocket mirror.

"You look fine."

"My hair needs a trim, my nails are a mess and even jersey pantsuits don't really survive airplane trips." She checked her purse once more and put her cosmetics away. "Tell me more about this woman we're going to see?"

"Her name is Alexandra Porter. She goes by Alexa. She's got a small ranch a few miles outside of town. She raises ponies and shows them in harness; apparently she's got an enviable reputation. Her son was kidnapped by his father several years ago, after the parents divorced. From time to time the boy calls her when he gets the chance. What is interesting is that all the areas the boy has called from have had outbreaks of TS."

"What's the connection?" Susannah asked.

"Damned if I know," Jeff admitted, "but you know and I know that we have to run every bit of this to earth. Ms. Porter sent a number of letters to the Colorado Bureau of Health and Environment, and it took a while before anyone paid any attention to her. One of the statisticians there— you'll meet him tomorrow: a bright kid named Wakefield —did an analysis and checked Ms. Porter's claim with phone company records. Lo and behold, there was a strong correspondence. There is also no hospital admission on this kid. Harold Porter would appear to be in good health, from what we can tell. And, incidentally, the last time he called his mother, he was in Edmonton."

"The Canadians!" Susannah clapped her hands together.

"Well, it is one explanation, no matter how unpalatable." He signaled to change lanes in order to pass a slow-moving recreation vehicle that looked like a motel room on wheels. "I ought to have cleared it with you first, but under the circumstances, I thought that—"

"You're right. We don't have time for all that going-through-channels nonsense. And I trust you, Jamshid Taji." When Jeff said nothing, she asked, "Do I embarrass you?"

"No: I . . . embarrass myself." He changed lanes again. "I'm in the middle of an emergency and I have fantasies about my superior. It's a strange problem for me." When he went on, his voice was more reflective. "Ever since the Silicon Measles thing, there have been people in our division who have been waiting for me to make a big, big mistake. They want to have me make an ass of myself, so that I don't have the—"

"The enviable reputation you have," she supplied for him. "We all know you're the best we have at environmental disease, no matter what anyone says."

He shook his head. "This TS is a lot more important; it isn't a matter of assembly workers, it's much bigger than that."

"And what are you thinking now that you're afraid will be wrong?" She touched his arm. "You can tell me. I'm talking to you as Susannah, not Division Coordinator Ling; okay?"

"You can't turn off part of yourself, Susannah. It's one of the things I like about you. You *are* my Division Coordinator as well as my friend." He considered his position for another mile, then shrugged. "What the hell. When TS first showed up, everyone was convinced it was environmental. It fit the pattern. The outbreaks were regional, the victims fit a nonstandard curve, and it didn't appear to spread. The SPSBS eliminated drugs and sexually transmitted diseases right at the start and the HEW bi-annual surveys seemed to rule out viruses. So we were all convinced that we had a strictly environmental disease going, and we acted accordingly."

"What's wrong with that?" Susannah asked without accusation.

"Nothing. Only I'm pretty sure we were wrong."

"You mean the cumulative or synergetic theories?" she prompted. "They make sense, and they explain a lot of what we're seeing."

"But not enough, and they're too complicated. The more complicated a disease, the fewer people can catch it, that's the general rule. But that's not the way this stuff is working out, is it?"

"I don't follow you," she prompted.

"Look," he said as he turned up the heater, "suppose that this thing isn't really environmental at all—suppose it's straight medical?"

"Then it belongs across town," she said, referring to the main complex of the National Center for Disease Control in Atlanta.

"Not quite. I have a hunch—"

"Silicon Measles was a hunch, as I recall," she interjected.

"This is a stronger hunch." He slowed down and moved back into the right-hand lane. "I think we're dealing with something coming from eroded cannisters, or other broken-down storage. I think there's one of those manufactured bugs out there, something that the feds ordered thrown out years ago. And now the storage containers are starting to leak. Think about it. There are military bases in and around most places where TS has shown up. With the exception of those in Idaho, Montana, Wyoming and Canada, and if Ms. Porter is right, we have an answer to that."

"You're reaching pretty far, Jeff," she warned him.

"Yes. I know that." He indicated the highway sign. "We exit in three miles."

"Fine," she said. "Go on about this theory of yours."

"Even after biological research was officially stopped, it went on in the form of gene research and DNA experiments. Now that all those projects are under annual review, things are better. That's now. We have to look back to when experimentation wasn't so carefully monitored."

"You mean before the Great Lakes Dysentery?" Susannah suggested, to agree on a time.

"More or less." He signaled to leave the freeway. "I've been toying with the idea that something being developed wasn't working out as planned; something to do with ACTH, to alter the brain in some way, and so it was discontinued and put into storage. And now it's coming back to haunt us."

"You know, Jeff, even if that's true, there's almost no way to prove it at this late date." She was sitting straighter in her seat, her face showing the tension of anticipation.

"I realize that," he said. "And I accept the fact that I might be completely wrong. But we're getting nowhere the way we're going now."

"And you think that talking to Ms. Porter will give you a lead?" Susannah said. "Well, it's worth a shot, I suppose. And we had to be in Colorado anyway."

"True enough," he said as he turned toward a tall white gate set back about a quarter mile from the road. "That's Ms. Porter's place," he explained. "I assume the herd is hers."

"They don't look much like ponies, not the way I remember them," said Susannah, looking at the dark bay and black animals grazing in the pasture.

"I gather that's part of the idea," said Jeff as they drove through the gate.

Alexandra Porter had been a pretty, girlish young woman fifteen years ago; now her body was square and muscular, her shoulders broader than was fashionable and she was not slim, though the fifteen extra pounds she carried did not show as flab. She was dressed for hard ranch work, and from her muddy boots to her knit cap, she was all utility. "Hello there," she called out as Jeff stepped out of his government car. "You're the doctors?"

"Yes," said Jeff as he went around to open the door for Susannah. "I'm Jeff Taji and this is the Coordinator of the Environmental Division of the National Center for Disease Control, Susannah Ling."

"Any relation to—" began Alexa as she offered her hand.

"—the Vice President, no. Arthur Ling isn't one of us." She smiled. "Thank you for taking the time to speak with us."

"No trouble," said Alexa, then she yelled, "Hey! Emilio, take care of Penny-Girl! She's got a cut over her offside rear pastern!" She managed a half-grin. "Sorry about that. We've had trouble with this mare before and I'm not anxious to spend another five hundred bucks on vet bills."

"I can't say I blame you," Susannah told her. "How many horses do you have here?"

"Forty-six right now. I'm small but exclusive as breeders go. We've got three proven studs, fifteen mares, eight geldings and the rest are under two." She indicated her house. "Come on in. Elvira's supposed to have coffee ready." As she led the way, she went on, "I know most people would think I'm crazy, and maybe I am. This trouble with Frank over Harold, it gets to me from time to time, and then I'm not real sensible about it, you know how it is?"

"Yes," said Jeff for both of them.

The kitchen was large and cozy at once, with two walls of distressed brick and an oak-beamed ceiling. At the far end of the room near the restaurant-style stove, a massive white-haired woman was pondering the contents of a large kettle of soup.

"Take a seat at the table. I'll be back in five minutes. In the meantime—Elvira! Coffee and pastry for my guests. *Pronto, por favor.*"

"*¿Quienes son?*" asked Elvira, giving them a slow, disinterested glance over her shoulder.

"They're doctors, very important. *Muy importante*, God damn it. You treat 'em well." With that order, Alexa tromped off down the hall. By the time she reappeared—good to her word, in less than five minutes—Elvira had condescended to pour two large white mugs of strong coffee and to bring out a plate of custard-filled tarts.

"We don't want to cut into your time," said Jeff as Alexa, showered and changed, sat down opposite her guests.

"Go right ahead. If it can help find my boy, it's great. If it gives you a hand with this TS stuff, even better." She smiled as Elvira put a full mug down at her elbow. "*Gracias, amiga mia.*"

"*De nada*," Elvira said as she went back to her stove.

"Don't think badly of Elvira. She's a little like a cat—she's afraid that if she's too nice to you, you'll take advantage of her. But she's stuck it out here through some rough times and her nephews are the best workers I've ever had." She took a large swig of coffee. "That doesn't interest you, does it? You want to know about Harold."

"A man in Denver—a Doctor Wakefield—went over your letter with the records of calls from your son," said Jeff, in order to make his position clear at once. "There is a very high correlation between the times and places of his calls and the outbreaks of TS during the last six months."

"Ah," said Alexa, as if putting down an unwelcome burden. "So I'm not entirely crazy."

"I don't think so," said Jeff cautiously. "But there are some things we have to know. And if you're willing to help us, we'll do everything we can for you."

"A horsetrade?" Alexa suggested with more despair than cynicism. "You've come to the right place."

Susannah opened her portfolio and brought out a notebook and a small tape recorder. "Do you mind if I tape our conversation?"

Alexa blinked. "Tape? Sure. Why not."

Jeff kept his papers in his attaché case, afraid that too much interest might frighten Alexa Porter. He had seen that happen before and he was anxious that it not occur now. "I understand that your boy has been missing since May of 1989."

"May fourteenth," said Alexa. "Frank went to the school and said he'd come to pick up his boy early, because he had some rodeo he had to ride in. The school knew he had Harold on weekends, and so they let him go. That was the last I ever saw of him." She hesitated. "Ever since then, Harold calls when he can. Harold Porter is a good boy, or he was while he was with me. There are times I want to kill Frank for doing this." The tears which had been standing in her eyes spilled at last. "Damn. Dammit. I'm sorry. Shit, what a stupid thing to do."

"It's all right," Susannah said gently. "We understand. We don't mind."

"Well, *I* mind," said Alexa brusquely. "Damn." She paused to wipe her eyes. "I *hate* it when I do that. It doesn't do anybody any good."

"If it gives you some relief, it does you some good," Susannah told her.

"But it doesn't. It only gives me a headache and a stuffy nose," she muttered. It took her a couple of minutes to stop crying and cursing, and during that time Susannah turned off the tape recorder. "Sorry," she said finally. "I won't do that again. Let me tell you about Harold, okay?"

"According to our information, he was born in Spokane, Washington, on September twenty-ninth, nineteen eighty-two. Is that correct?"

"Yeah. We'd been there three weeks." She took a deep, uneven breath. "Frank was working for a rancher there, a guy running Quarter horses. He had a couple hundred head and most of 'em were green-broke. Frank and two other guys were hired on to put a little polish on them before spring sales. We were there until January of Eighty-three, and then we went to Montana."

"You traveled a great deal while you were pregnant?" asked Jeff.

"We traveled all the time we were married. Hell, Frank's *still* traveling."

"Where were you in Eighty-two?" asked Susannah, taking up Jeff's line of inquiry.

"You mean all the time before Harold was born?" She sighed and stared up at the ceiling. "Oh, we started the year in New Mexico, I recall. Then came through Arizona, went up to the Salinas area. We stayed there about four months. Then we went on to Reno, then over into Oregon, and from there to Spokane. Those last three months, it was hell to move. It was hot and I felt like an overbuilt house on a cliff. Frank was mad at me all the time, and I didn't know what to do about it. He threatened to leave me once, and another time he disappeared for a week. I got damned scared then, because it was August and I didn't have any more money and I was so pregnant I could hardly walk."

"Quite a fellow," said Jeff dryly.

"Well, I came to my senses, didn't I?" She gulped down the rest of her coffee and shouted for more. "After Harold was born, we spent almost a year in Wyoming, and then we came down into Colorado. That's when I decided that I'd find a way to leave Frank and stay here. It took me three years, but by the time Hal was old enough to go to school, I'd scraped together enough to put a down payment on this place. Not that it was anything like it is now. All I had was an old cow barn to use for a stable and a two-room shack for a house." She folded her arms on the table. "You know, Harold was about three weeks premature. I don't know if that means anything."

"Neither do we," said Susannah, "but it might have some bearing."

"Anyway, the school has all the blood screen records on Harold. You can get 'em with my blessing. That's the only way I've been able to try to keep track of him—through the Standard Public School Blood Screen. Every time he transfers he has to get one, and there are times I can find them even though they're out of state. I had a lawyer working on it, but it got too expensive and I wasn't getting any closer to Harold." She picked up one of the pastries and bit into it.

"If we get a full set of SPSBS results on Harold, that would help us collate the information you and the phone company provide," said Jeff, "and we could release the information to you once we have it."

For an instant Alexa's face brightened. "Would you do that for me?" Then she deliberately grew somber. "I'm not going to get my hopes up. I tried for years and years and years, and I'm not going to do that again. If you get me those records, I'll do what I can with them, but I don't . . ."

Susannah reached out and put her hand on Alexa's wrist. "I know this is very hard on you. You're being very generous to help us out. We want to do everything we can to find Harold, because we have to learn a little bit more about him. He might have a clue to the disease we're looking for."

"I know that." She stared down at the custard tarts as Jeff outlined what was known about Taji's Syndrome and what his own theories were.

Alexa listened closely and when he was through, she shook her head. "My son isn't like that. He was never sick as a child and he wouldn't have that kind of disease in him, Doctor Taji."

"It wouldn't necessarily be obvious. We have no way of knowing what he is carrying, if anything, and how it triggers the disease, if it does. It's all suppostion at this time."

"It's all bullshit," Alexa said conversationally. "But I'll have to go along with it for now. I got too much to gain from helping you out, don't I?"

It was almost dark when Jeff and Susannah left Alexa. They had come to a distrustful understanding that troubled all three of them.

"Well, what do you think?" Jeff asked as they drove into the town of Golden.

"I think you'd better be right or she'll kill you." Susannah opened her purse and checked the three filled tapes.

"And I hope we can mine a few nuggets from all this. She sure had a rough time of it."

"It isn't over yet," Jeff reminded her sadly.

Sylvia Kostermeyer and
———— Weyman Muggridge ————

When the alarm went off at six-thirty, Weyman found it and flung it across the room without raising his head from the pillow.

"Hey," Sylvia protested as she heard the clock break. "I like that clock."

"I'll get you another," he mumbled. "But promise not to set it for earlier than eight." He was lying facedown; he rolled onto his side as he reached out his arm to pull her closer. "How much time have we got?"

"Depends on whether you want breakfast." She smiled faintly and kissed the corner of his mouth.

"What if we get coffee and rolls at the office?" He nuzzled her neck.

"What about shower and shave?" she asked, this time grinning.

"Probably a wise idea. If I have my wicked way with you right now, you'll look like you've been sandpapered." To demonstrate he rubbed his chin over her shoulder.

"They wouldn't see most of it, would they?" She was pleased and shocked with herself for how she was acting. Last night she had been astonished to realize how intense her desire for him was, and how wholly unselfconscious she felt with him. Was that what being abandoned meant? She had never done or said such things.

"They'd know. But who cares?" He tussled with her playfully, kissing her between growls.

"Weyman?" she asked seriously a bit later.

"What?" He had caught her tone; he braced himself on his elbows, his face only inches from hers, and looked her directly in her eyes. "Something the matter?"

"Did I . . . shock you?" She could not meet his gaze.

"You sure did," he said, grinning lazily.

"I . . . I didn't . . ."

"You shocked me the best possible way, by giving me exactly who and what you are, no lies, no deception, no frills, no bells and whistles, just whole, real you. It's the best possible shock in the world, you know that?" He kissed her nose.

"It didn't bother you?" She was starting to feel better, as if she might not have wrecked it after all.

"You mean worried or troubled me? no. Not in the least." He took her face in his hands. "What does bother me, Sylvia Ingrid Kostermeyer, is that you seem to think you've done something that might offend me. What makes you think that?" He watched her closely, with warmth in his eyes.

"Oh, nothing." She had to suppress a giggle and did not entirely succeed.

"Tell me, Sylvia. Please. I want to know." He rolled onto his back and pulled her across his chest. "God, you feel good."

"So do you," she said, growing a little bolder.

"Go on; tell me." He held her close without restraining her. "Sylvia."

"Oh, I don't know," she said.

"Now you are giving me ribbons and bow and bells and whistles. I like you better just as you are. If you don't want to talk about it, say so. But you can tell me anything. I mean that." Suddenly he broadened his accent. "Hell, chile, I growed up in the mountains an' there ain't nothing I ain't seen or heard of." He watched her smile and felt some of the tension go out of her. When he spoke again, his voice was low and gentle. "Sylvia dear Sylvia dear Sylvia, nothing you could say would change my feeling about you, for you. No matter what you have done or might do." He pulled her tumbled hair back. "You can trust me, Sylvia. Truly."

"I wish . . . I wish I could believe you," she said, and bit her lip to stop herself from crying.

"No more than I do, Sylvia," Weyman said.

"Why can't you simply take this for what it is," she began only to have him interrupt her. "Enjoy the moment."

"That's what I'm doing. But there's more than a moment. This isn't a fling." His hands were still and his eyes grew solemn. "Word of honor."

"What makes you think it's not? We're thrown together for a short time during a crisis. Everything is tense and frightening. We're working against time and an invisible enemy; we've got so much at stake. It's perfect for a fling, for trying to find something positive and fun in the ruins." She was astonished to hear how angry she was, to feel the tightness in her shoulders and arms as if she wanted to lash out at him. "If we weren't investigating TS, this never would have happened."

"That's true. We met because of a horrible disease. TS might be our matchmaker, but I refuse to feel guilty about it." He waited, holding her, and after four long minutes had passed, he asked, "Are you trying to drive me away, is that it? Are you hoping to get rid of me?"

She brought her head up so quickly that she clipped his chin. "What?"

"Well, that is what you're trying to do, isn't it? I'm getting too close. You're scared to death that you might want me to stay, and so you'll drive me away to keep from having me leave." His hands moved slowly, languidly over her back. "Since I'm not going, it's kinda dumb, don't you think?"

"I'm not . . . Weyman, it's not that." She lowered her head so that she would not have to look into his face. His lean, craggy features held no secrets from her and she saw no deception there.

"Appears pretty much like it to me." He continued to hold her. "Better listen up, Sylvia, because I'm putting you on notice right now. I am not leaving. I am not walking out. I am going to stay with you until one or the other of us is six feet under. That isn't wartime panic talking, it's the way we are together: work, sex, dinner, all of it."

"That might be pretty soon—the six feet under, I mean," she said, and swallowed hard against the cold tightness that had not left her throat. "With TS all over the place, who knows how long any of us is—"

"Who knows anyway? You might have another quake any day now, and it might be a really big one that will do more than wreck a few old buildings and roads. You might eat something that's contaminated. You might be stricken with any number of illnesses. You could choke on a chicken bone. You might get run over by a car or shot by a burglar or—"

"Stop it," she said, not quite able to laugh. "Stop it, Weyman."

"You can't spend your whole life wondering when it's all going to fall apart, Sylvia. It isn't that it's going to end that matters, but what you do in the meantime. The meantime is what it's all about, not the end. You can't let that keep you in a box. Boxes are for when you're dead, not when you're alive." He wrapped his long arms more tightly around her. "Who walked out on you? Who made you so afraid? Can you tell me?"

She rested her head on his shoulder, her face away from his. "Nothing's ever certain."

Gently he stroked her hair. "No, it's not."

"And if you depend on it, you'll be disappointed or hurt." She started to cry, and did not know how to make herself stop.

"Hey, hey." Lying beneath her, he rocked her slowly. "It's okay. It's okay, Sylvia. Go on."

"What's the point?" she asked, but her tears continued.

"It doesn't need a point. It's okay."

Quite suddenly she turned her head and kissed him, her mouth open and insistent.

"Hey," he said when she broke away from him. "Sylvia, if that's what you want, I'll do it. If you want a hard, fast, deep fuck, you can have it. I won't object. But there's more, if you want it; more than you or I ever dreamed of. And God, God, I hope you want it. I hope you won't be scared away." This last was a plea, and it reached a part of her she had tried to hold inviolate.

She collapsed on him, her sobs deep and anguished. She caught the sheet in her hands and held it so tightly that it tore. She did not know what brought about this overwhelming emotion, but she could not stop it now. "I can't I can't I can't," she chanted as she wept.

"Yes, you can," Weyman said, feeling an echo of her pain in him. "For me." He held her until it was over. "That's better," he said, kissing her forehead and her eyelids. "Good for you."

"Shit, I'm ashamed of myself. I shouldn't have—"

"Stop that," he said with stern kindness. "Don't say that."

"Say what?" She wanted to get up now, but could not get out of the circle of his arms. It was the strangest thing, she thought with a still, remote part of her mind. He did not seem to be holding her tightly, but she could not break free of him.

"Say you're ashamed of yourself. You have no reason to be. None whatever." He kissed her slowly, thoroughly. "No reason."

"Weyman . . ."

Very quietly he whispered "Shut up," before he gave her a longer, more complex kiss, one that left both of them slightly breathless. "How much time have we got?"

"An hour, tops, and that means a short shower," she said as she peered at her watch on the nightstand. "Just a wash, nothing more."

"Terrific," he said, his smile widening. "I'll hurry."

"Hurry?" she asked incredulously. "An hour?"

"Haven't you heard that us country boys like to take our time?" he teased, his hand sliding over her hip, fingers sensitive and playful at once.

"I heard quite the opposite, but never mind." She was doing her best to match his bantering tone, but her attention was increasingly on the subtle and marvelous things he was doing to her, and doing so casually, so . . . laconically. It was so wonderful not to be rushed, she thought, and resolutely turned away from her watch.

"I'm going to shift you over a little," Weyman said from beneath her. "I can't reach everything unless I do." He wiggled his hand to show her what he meant and she inhaled sharply.

"Go ahead." If anyone had asked her the day before, Sylvia would have said it was impossible for her to forget the catastrophe that had struck San Diego, even for a moment: she found out now this was not so. For an undetermined length of time there was only Weyman, his hands, his mouth, the smell and taste and texture and weight of him, the way they moved together in the bars of morning sunlight across the bed. All the rest of it faded. Even while they rushed through the shower and he shaved while she tried to salvage her hair, TS hardly crossed her mind. It returned as they raced to the car, and started toward the Expressway.

They walked into their morning meeting five minutes late and were confronted by the five men in uniform they had seen not long ago.

"I'm sorry," Weyman said while Sylvia was still trying to think up a plausible excuse for their tardiness. "My fault. I took a wrong turn on the Expressway. Serves me right for insisting on driving in a city I don't know. God knows how much later I'd be if Doctor Kostermeyer hadn't been with me." He had put his attaché case on the conference table and had pulled out a chair for Sylvia as he spoke.

"We could arrange for a driver for you," offered Captain Jacob Lorrimer.

"A good map would do," Weyman told him. "Provided I have the sense to use it."

"One of my assistants could prepare an orientation for you, Doctor Muggridge," offered Commander Tolliver. "I have a staff that will be happy to assist you if you like."

"Doctor Kostermeyer does a fine job, as well as providing an opportunity to discuss the investigation, which I doubt your staff could do, or would be allowed to do," said Weyman as he pulled papers from the case. "And five minutes isn't that crucial, is it?"

The men in uniform exchanged glances but said nothing.

"Doctor Muggridge has updated figures on TS, most of them are . . . are not optimistic." Sylvia took her place beside Weyman and started going through a few of the printouts. "We've been instructed to go back to the first reported cases of TS and to determine as much as possible about those who first died of it."

"We received the formal requests for assistance," said Tolliver. "We have also agreed to provide fifteen quarantine beds in the Naval Hospital and the Naval Air Hospital, as well as twenty quarantine beds at the Marine Hospital." He looked at Weyman as if expecting gratitude.

"Good to hear it," said Weyman when he realized what was required. "I have another request, if you can help me."

"Of course," said Tolliver smoothly.

"My colleague, Doctor Klausen, in Portland, has been trying to learn about the present location of a James Joseph Jackson of Twin Falls, Idaho. He's a high school athletic coach and he contracted TS in January. He was moved to a VA hospital and we can't get any more information on him. I'd appreciate it if you could unsnarl the red tape." He looked from Tolliver to Colonel Packard. "I don't know what service he was in."

"We'll take care of it. In a situation like this, it's probably a simple question of misfiling." Captain Lorrimer nodded and the officers sat down. "We have a request that I understand has encountered some resistance from your Atlanta organization, Doctor Muggridge."

"Oh?" Weyman said innocently, trying to figure out what the military might want in return for their help with Coach Jackson.

"Yes," Commander Tolliver said, taking over from Lorrimer. "We can't understand why the National Center for Disease Control would refuse to answer the Executive Security Agency's requests for information about TS and its victims, especially in matters of public health risk where the few survivors are concerned."

"Probably because we don't know what kind of risk the survivors are," Weyman suggested with every appearance of bonhomie.

Packard and Tolliver exchanged looks; Lorrimer said, "It could be a matter of national security."

"Yeah, it could," said Weyman, not quite concealing the sharpness of his response. "But so far there is no reason we know of to think that it is. We have possibly five survivors to assess with a disease we do not yet understand. It is impossible to determine the extent and nature of the hazard they present, if any. We are not yet in a position to appreciate the long-term effects of TS. And until that's the case, we'd be remiss in turning over what are confidential files under the Right to Privacy Act. I guess the NCDC doesn't want to be sued."

"Possibly not," said Packard. "But there are others who might bring suit if the request isn't honored." He held up his hands in a placating gesture. "Not that we'd want anything like that to happen."

"I bet," Weyman said, catching Sylvia's hand in his under the table. "We have a responsibility to protect the public and to guard the health of the nation. Just as those in the ESA are obligated to protect the personal safety of the President and his cabinet. Occasionally the immediate goals of our work would seem to clash, but that's rarely the case, when you examine the question more objectively."

"We are satisfied that there is a high degree of risk," Commander Tolliver insisted.

"No argument," Weyman said at his blandest. "But what kind and to whom. That's the part we can't answer yet."

Colonel Packard stared at Weyman, the weight of his gaze intended to intimidate. "You realize that President Hunter is considering establishing martial law in this part of the country because of TS."

"And I know he has decided against it," said Weyman, his affability gone. "It looks to me, gentlemen, as if you are after something and you will not say what. That troubles me. Because as a civilian I outrank you, in case you had forgotten. I am not inclined to be bullied into providing you with information you have obviously been unable to obtain through usual channels." He gathered up his materials and squeezed Sylvia's hand again. "Until I have a better understanding of what my superiors have decided, I think it would be best if we postpone this meeting. Another can be arranged in two days." As he put the last of the printouts into his attaché case, he added, "I hope you will not withdraw the offer of quarantine beds. All the rest of what we've said this morning was jockeying, but that could mean the difference between life and death for someone with TS, and that is what matters, isn't it?" He stood up, letting go of Sylvia's hand. "You know, gentlemen, it's a mistake to ignore Doctor Kostermeyer because she is merely an epidemiologist for the state. She probably knows more about TS than anyone from Atlanta does." With that, he opened the door for her and followed her out of the room.

"I wanted to kill them," she muttered as they waited for the elevator.

"Me first," said Weyman, and as the doors of the elevator closed and they rode down, he said, "We've got to hurry. Whatever they're fishing for, we've got to find before they do or we'll lose what little edge we have."

She looked at him in astonishment. "You mean they scared you? You didn't show it, if they did."

"Why give them an advantage?" he asked, and as the door opened, he added, "Sylvia my darling, I've been terrified for the last two months."

Jeff Taji and
Dale Reed

"I'm sorry about Doctor Picknor," said Jeff to Dale Reed as they left the enormous new University Medical Center.

"I feel I'm responsible," said Dale, his head lowered and his eyes wetter than usual. "He got involved in this because of me and now look at him. Did you see the ACTH readings? Even if we could bring his blood under control, what would we do about that?"

"I can't answer you," Jeff said. "But I hope your Missus Channing will give us a clue." He made his way between the parked cars to his rented Comet. "How far is the private hospital?"

"It's on the west of town, out toward the airport. I called ahead. They're expecting us." He frowned as he got into the car. "What worries me is that I haven't seen signs of it myself. I've been working with it, and so many of the medical staff have got it, I wake up at night, afraid that I've got it, too."

Jeff started out of the parking lot. "I know the feeling," he said directly.

"I've had patients with AIDS and it didn't frighten me. I knew what was required to get it. But what scares me is that whatever gave Irene TS is still around, and we don't know what it is. I have times when I'm afraid to breathe or eat or bathe because I might be getting something that will kill me." He gave a shaky little laugh. "Left at the next light."

"Thanks." He remembered what Donna Howell had told him about Dale Reed: the man was in love with his patient and it was increasingly difficult for him. "How is she—Missus Channing—doing? Is there more improvement?"

"She's stronger and she's doing some sketching—she's an artist, you know—and her muscle tone is improving. It's the other. That's what troubles me."

"What about it?" This was what Jeff wanted to know the most about, the thing that caused him almost as much alarm as the rising fatalities from TS.

"She's . . . getting stronger that way, too. It wears her out. If she moves something, she goes to bed for the rest of the day, and just naps. She says it exhausts her and makes her unable to concentrate or to think. They've . . . the docs there have been asking her to work on it." He frowned. "It worries me, Taji."

"I can understand why," he said, becoming concerned himself. He had thought that this would be a fairly direct phase of the investigation, but now he realized that it would not. He put his mind on his driving and let Dale Reed talk as they made their way to the private hospital where Irene Channing now lived.

There were three separate security stations to pass before they were admitted to her room.

Dr. Galen Simeon was already with Irene, his lugubrious face looking more like a basset hound's than usual. "It is distressing, Missus Channing," he was saying as Dale and Jeff came through the door.

"Irene," Dale said, going to her and kissing her, outwardly unconcerned about being observed.

She returned the kiss. "I'm so glad to see you, Dale," she said. "How's Steve? How's Brice? Are they doing all right?"

"I saw them yesterday. They're fine. I'm scheduling them for blood work and a full PAST scan next week. I'll let you know what the results are." He had her hands in his.

"No matter what?" she insisted.

"No matter what," he promised.

"And Edith? I need to speak with her. They're not going to allow her to visit, but I have to—"

Dale interrupted her. "I'll call her. And I'll explain to the staff here that Ms. Kentish is your attorney, so that you won't have to go through this anymore." He slipped his arm around her shoulder and drew her as close as he could, sitting on the edge of the bed. The draperies were drawn and so the room had a muted light in it, as if it were under water and these two were lost sculpture of another time lying on the floor of the sea.

"Doctor Reed." Simeon was short of patience, but his urgency stemmed from something more than that. "I haven't finished here. I have others to look after; Missus Channing is not my only responsibility."

Jeff stepped into the breach. "I'm Jeff Taji from the National Center for Dis—"

"Oh, yes," Simeon cut him short as he came forward, hand extended, a look in his eyes that probed Jeff even as he went through the proper form of good manners. "A pleasure. I'm curious to hear about your latest work on this difficult disease."

"Certainly. I'll be grateful to hear your views as well. I'll do what I can to fill you in on my own end of the work," said Jeff, drawing Galen Simeon to the farthest point in the room. "I want to have a look at the tape you have on Missus Channing. I realize you haven't yet determined what the cause of this is, but we have found a few more survivors of the disease and we're extremely curious about the aftereffects of TS." He hesitated. "We're trying to keep these developments as quiet as possible. It's bad enough to have so deadly a disease, but the possibility of becoming a freak if one survives it . . ."

"You're certain that happens in all cases?" Simeon asked.

"No. That's part of the trouble. We find survivors very slowly, and when we do, testing them is awkward, to say the least. We don't want to give rise to more ... problems than we've got."

"Not surprising," said Simeon. "I think it would be of great interest to more than you," he added pointedly. "How fast is TS spreading; do you know?"

"Faster than is being admitted publicly, though after John Post's regular reports, I doubt the public is fooled very much. They know about his son, and they trust him. Our figures indicate that we have over a hundred thousand cases in the U.S. with another fifteen thousand in Canada. By that, we mean cases that have been diagnosed. Who knows how many people out there could come down with it in the next year or so?"

"And the fatality curve remains about the same?" Simeon asked.

"About the same. We will need more time to find out how constant it is, of course." Jeff sighed. "So far, we haven't been able to isolate the trigger."

"That's not good," Simeon said, his haggard Russian features growing more careworn. "You have another problem, in case you were not aware of it."

"Which problem? I could name dozens." Jeff thought that he was referring to the emotional involvement of Dale and Irene, and was not alert to the warning, so that what Simeon said next was shocking.

"There are ESA men nosing around here. They're trying to get their hands on Irene Channing. Luckily she is a well-known and wealthy woman, and she can insist on privacy, and get some protection from us. At least she can so far. There may be other survivors who are not as fortunate."

"How do you mean?" Jeff demanded, keeping his voice low so that he would not disturb the two on the bed.

"I mean," he said with great precision, "that apparently the ESA has come to believe that the survivors are strategically important to the country. They are a tightlipped lot, but I gather that Missus Channing isn't the only one to have developed psychokinetic abilities, and they are determined to . . . to have control over their skills, and to direct their use." He waited, letting this sink in.

"No one in Atlanta has said . . ." Jeff's phrase trailed off. "But they wouldn't, would they? We might blow their cover, we might tell the world. Hell, we *would* tell the world."

"A consideration," said Simeon. "And they have also concealed the statistics of TS in the armed forces for similar reasons. They want to cull out the secret weapons, and those who do not survive—at least so far—are considered to be acceptable losses."

Jeff did not want to believe what he was hearing. He tried to muster arguments to deny it, but none of them were wholly convincing. He took a deep breath. "I'm going to have to find out more about this."

"You will in any case, I think." He rubbed at his long jaw as if he wore a goatee. "I don't want to be a harbinger of doom, but it strikes me, Doctor Taji, that every one of you working on this investigation had better be as careful as you possibly can, not only for your health, but your safety as well. The Executive Security Agency isn't going to be thwarted by a few determined doctors if they really want the TS survivors. I'm telling you this because I know what we've had going on here. I haven't said anything to Dale," he went on as he saw the skeptical look in Jeff's eyes. "Dale might do something foolish because of his involvement with Irene Channing, and that would not help anyone."

Jeff nodded slowly. "All right; what's happened?"

Simeon lowered his voice. "In the last two weeks there have been nine new lab techs here, all of them from outside of the Dallas–Fort Worth area. Everyone else in the lab defers to them and they are permitted to work with minimal supervision. Two days ago I caught one of them rifling the PAST scan files. When I reported it, I was told that I had made a mistake. Up until then I was afraid I was being paranoid; now I think I was being naive."

"It could have been something else," Jeff said without any conviction.

"Certainly. That's what I've been told. But those lab techs aren't here to find out what's new in geriatric medicine or new ways to dry out rich drunks, so I have to assume that Missus Channing is the reason for all this. The military wants to find out how to make psychokines. You ought to see the lab techs. You'd know what I mean." Simeon lowered his eyes. "I quit smoking eight years ago, but right now I would love a cigarette."

Jeff nodded sympathetically, though he had never smoked. "I know the feeling," he said, recognizing the anxiety the admission concealed.

"There's one who seems to be in charge of the others, a man in his mid-thirties named Kiley. You would have to see his eyes to understand, but he is a machine." Simeon looked toward Irene and Dale, giving Jeff a warning gesture with his hand. "I would like to borrow Missus Channing for a few minutes, Reed."

Dale had risen and was standing by the bed. "All right. I'll come with you."

"As you wish." Simeon took a terry cloth robe from the closet. "You can walk on your own, Missus Channing," he said as he gave the robe to Dale, who held it for her.

"You know, there's really no reason to keep me in jammies all the time," Irene said. "I'd feel a hell of a lot better in slacks and shirt. I don't like thinking of myself as sick anymore. I think it's slowing down my progress."

The three men walked with her down the hall. "I'll see what can be arranged," said Dale. "I should have thought of it before now."

She slipped her hand into his. "You're a love, do you know that?"

"We aim to please," Dale told her, ignoring the two other men.

They arrived at a small therapy room equipped with

whirlpool baths and a wall of double doors leading to small saunas. Beyond that stood four massage tables and some mild exercise machines.

"I would like it if you'd try the rowing machine. Nothing too strenuous, but enough to get your muscles into gear. If you start to feel dizzy or sore, stop at once," said Simeon, looking not at Irene but at Dale, daring him to object.

"I'll send for Naoko," said Dale, and started toward the door.

"Naoko has been replaced," Simeon said with no emotion at all.

"But—" Dale came back toward them. "She's the best masseuse we have. Why replace her?"

"It wasn't my decision," Simeon said coolly. "I wasn't consulted. There's a Francis Bethune in her place. If I were you, I'd ask for Narmada Parvi—she's very good." He did not add that she had been with the hospital for more than ten years and was therefore relatively safe.

"All right. Is she here?" Dale said, perplexed.

"What's going on?" Irene interrupted. "Why is Naoko gone and why don't you want me to have the new man? It has to do with that fellow Kiley, doesn't it? Ever since he came here, I feel like I'm being watched all the time. He gives me the creeps."

"Narmada's worked on you before," said Simeon evenly, his tone even faintly bored, but his eyes warned her to be cautious and not argue.

"She's fine," said Irene, picking up on Simeon's unspoken signals. "I'm not up to having more strangers around me. I've had nothing but strangers since I got this damned TS. Aside from Dale, I haven't seen a truly familiar face in months."

"Narmada it is," said Dale, who had watched the silent exchange with growing apprehension. "I'll be back in a couple of minutes."

"Now then, Missus Channing, the rowing machine. Use that one, please, and no more than a dozen repeats. We'll see how you're doing when you're through." As she pulled out of her robe and took her place on the machine, Simeon pulled Jeff aside and said very softly, "The room is bugged. Possibly photographed as well."

Jeff raised his voice enough to provide something for the listeners, "I can understand your concern. But if her temperature remains normal, I don't think you should hold her back. Lack of exercise might be more of a problem than you think."

"Her blood work isn't normal yet," Simeon said with a quick, relieved smile. "I don't want to take any chances."

From her place on the rowing machine, Irene hesitated in her workout to ask, "How is Doctor Picknor? When I heard he was in the hospital, I was . . . I felt so guilty."

Simeon strolled over to her. "He's holding his own. He's signed a Public Benefit contract and they're starting with some new therapy tomorrow. He's more useful than many of the others, since he's a physician."

"Being a physician didn't stop him from coming down with TS, and being one isn't going to cure him. The statistics on nurses are horrifying," Jeff said. "Twenty percent of the victims of TS have signed Public Benefit contracts and we still aren't getting anywhere. All we have is more sick people we can try things out on. It's all well and good to have the Public Benefit contract, but God! it would be better to have something to offer the people who sign them." He looked away, and when he gave his attention to Simeon again, he was less caustic. "I was out of line to talk like that."

"You're under the gun," said Simeon, slightly startled that he would receive an apology.

"Aren't we all. It's no excuse for . . ." He shrugged and dropped his voice. "About the PK?"

From the rowing machine, Irene groaned. As both men turned to her, startled, she said. "Sorry. Sore muscles."

Simeon took a moment to collect his thoughts again. "It exhausts her, but she is gaining more control all the time."

His eyes were apprehensive. "I don't know how long we can keep the ESA out of this."

"We'll find a way," said Jeff, not at all sure how. "I want daily reports on her progress, with blood work and test results as they're processed. I need to know what's going on here. I haven't enough data to begin to know where to start on the cases like hers."

"You're worried about her, aren't you?"

"I'm worried about all of them. The survivors . . . I don't know what to say about them. What's the old expression? out of the frying pan into the fire? Most of them are worn out from illness, and to have this . . . this ability turn up, well, the few we've identified are scared. Who can blame them?"

"Frying pan into the fire," confirmed Simeon. "I haven't seen much on the other survivors."

"There aren't very many of them," Jeff said reluctantly. "This disease has about an eighty-six percent fatality rate, at least that's the current figures. Survivors are only now showing up, and with TS spreading the way it is, we haven't the time or the staff to go looking for them. We hope that someone notices them and lets us know about them."

"Is that all you've been able to come up with? I know that the teenagers seem to come down with it faster than adults, but to have so high a fatality rate. . . . Hell, once you're thirteen, it sounds pretty hopeless."

"There are a few people who are apparently past puberty and still immune. We're trying to find out why. We can't work out a similarity, except that none of the survivors have O-type blood and all those who are apparently immune do." He shook his head slowly. "But find the sense in that, will you? If all it takes is O-type blood to be immune, most of the population would be safe."

"Rh factors?" Simeon suggested.

"Nothing so far. We're going for genotypes next. The genotypes may be a long shot, but—" He looked over at Irene. "Missus Channing, how do you feel?"

She stopped rowing. "Like I've dug up an entire back yard," she said, pressing her forearm against her face. "I can't believe how weak I am."

"You're doing very well," Simeon said as the door opened and Dale returned with a small Hindu woman. "We're almost ready for you, Narmada."

"Good," said Narmada with a smile. "It is wonderful to see Missus Channing so much improved."

Jeff heard the lilt in her speech and asked, "Where are you from, Narmada?"

She beamed at him. "We came from New Delhi, many, many years ago. I was only eight." She was too polite to ask where he came from, so he volunteered.

"My family left Iran when I was young, too. We aren't Moslems, let alone Shi'ites." He indicated Irene. "Have you worked with her before?"

"Oh, yes. Very fortunate lady is Missus Channing. She has lived." Narmada went and stood beside her. "Come. If you are ready."

Dale was helping Irene up from the rowing machine. "I have a feeling you'll be back at work full-time in another month, Irene." He wrapped his arms around her.

Irene returned his embrace, but when they broke apart, she said to Jeff, "What has always amazed me about Dale is that all through this, he has never once acted as if he was afraid of TS. He never behaved as if he could catch it from me, or as if there was any danger. When I think of the way everyone else behaved, it . . . humbles me."

"Irene, don't," Dale protested fondly.

"It *is* remarkable," said Simeon to them both.

"What's to fear from an environmental disease?" Dale asked a little too blithely. "The air will give it to me quicker than she will."

Narmada came and took Irene's arm. "Excuse me, but it is time for the massage. You should not stand idly after exercise; it will make your muscles stiff." So saying, she led Irene over to the massage tables.

"How has she been doing?" Dale asked, indicating the rowing machine.

"Fine," Simeon said.

"She looked good," Jeff agreed.

"And the other? What about that?" Dale looked scared for the first time. "Is she still . . . doing that?"

"I don't know about today," Simeon answered. "But we have the tapes from yesterday, and she certainly was doing it then." He tried to give Dale the same sort of unspoken warning he had given Jeff, but Dale was not paying enough attention.

"How could something like that happen? Can you tell me that? How could she get that kind of . . . talent from surviving TS?" He was becoming nervous and he would not meet Simeon's eyes.

"We don't know." Simeon folded his hands and looked toward the clerestory windows. "I think we ought to discuss this later, Dale. You don't want to upset Missus Channing, do you?"

"No," said Dale at once, looking quickly over his shoulder to where Narmada was draping Irene with light blankets while she prepared to begin her massage. "She's lost a lot of weight," he remarked inconsequently.

"That's to be expected." Jeff wondered if Dale knew there were listening devices in the room. He certainly did not act that way.

"I think she's gained a little of it back. She needs it." He folded his arms. "Doctor Taji"—the formality shocked both Jeff and Simeon—"I'd like to have access to all the TS records you have for this region. I might be able to spot something you've overlooked. I want to do something. You can understand that, can't you?"

This abrupt petition was so unexpected that it took Jeff a little while to frame his answer. "Let's discuss it later. I have to make a few phone calls to find out what we're permitted to release, and to whom." He was aware that he could shift the response from positive to negative, depending upon whom he called: Susannah Ling would certainly permit the information being released; Patrick Drucker would just as certainly refuse.

"Fine. That's fine." He looked from one man to the other. "I want her to be better. I want her to be well, to be over this."

"So do we," said Jeff. He took a step toward the door. "Where are the records? I want to go over her entries for the last two days."

"I'll show you," Simeon offered at once. "Dale?"

"I want to stay with Irene a little while. I'll catch up with you." He moved away from them, toward the massage table.

As soon as the door closed behind them, Simeon said, "I don't know what to make of Dale these days. He was staunch as a pioneer through the worst of it, and now he looks as if he's about to cave in."

"Maybe he's the sort who goes to pieces after an emergency. I'm a little like that myself." They went quickly down the hall, neither man paying much attention to others around them.

"It's more than that. He said something the other day that worried me then. He said he thought TS had changed Irene, had turned her into someone he didn't know any more. Mind you, that was after a third brass monkey, so who knows how much of that was booze and how much was his real thoughts." He indicated a door on the right. "That's medical records. There should be two techs and two transcriptionists on duty."

"Okay," Jeff said, recognizing the note of circumspection in the information.

There were three techs in the room, one of them wearing a badge that said Kiley.

"Doctor Simeon," said Kiley, coming to greet him with the kind of stiff-legged walk a guard dog might have.

"This is Doctor Taji from Atlanta. He's with me." Simeon could not quite sustain the faint air of superiority that he most often used to put staff members in their place.

"Doctor Taji," said Kiley in a way that made it obvious that he knew precisely who Jeff was.

"Which monitor may I use?" Jeff inquired in a manner that Susannah had once described as his preoccupied mode. "I need to review some material."

"I'll be happy to get it for you," said Kiley, his eyes, as Simeon had said, like stones.

"No, I won't trouble you. Since I don't know yet how much of her records I'll have to access, it's hardly fair for me to take up your time. Thanks, anyway." With that, he went and selected one of the monitor stations and sat down, seemingly oblivious to the anger he had inspired in Kiley.

By the time they left the records room, some forty minutes later, Jeff had discovered that almost a third of Irene Channing's test results had been put under seal. He told Dale about it as they drove back into Dallas.

"They're being cautious," said Dale.

"Come on," Jeff chided him gently. "You know better than that. They're trying to put a lid on her. And they're doing a pretty good job of it."

"Well, they don't know what's going on," Dale said weakly.

"Dale, what's wrong?" Jeff demanded. "What's bothering you?"

Dale stared out the window of the Comet; when he spoke, he said, "I think you ought to check her kids yourself. I think you could find out something that way."

"Her kids? Why?"

"Because she got it and survived it, and her teenaged son hasn't got it at all. Steven doesn't have a trace of it. Who knows about Brice—he's still too young, in any case." He checked the crease in his trousers. "She got through the disease and ended up with a power and her kids don't have it. It's not like any other case I've ever seen."

"TS hasn't been around long enough for that to be necessarily significant," Jeff reminded Dale as he honked at a speeding cyclist.

"Yeah."

Jeff thought for a couple of miles. "All right; I'll check the kids out myself."

For the first time since they left the hospital, Dale's expression lightened. "Thanks.

Weyman Muggridge and Edgar Haliburton

Propped up against the pillows in an isolation tent, Edgar Haliburton looked dreadfully thin and pale. He tried to raise his arm in greeting as Weyman came through the door of his room, but he was not able to. "Doctor Muggridge."

"Doctor Haliburton." Weyman came and stood beside the bed. "They tell me you've signed a Public Benefit contract."

"They're trying a new combination of antibiotics on me right now. I don't think it's doing much good, but it has reduced the secondary infection risks." He indicated the chair near his bed. "Sit down. I appreciate your coming."

"Well, your request came the same day the names of some of your patients cropped up. I thought it was worth seeing you." Weyman straddled the chair, his arms laid over the back and his chin resting on them.

"Patients?"

"The Grey family."

"Oh. Yes. Marilee and then Jared. A terrible thing. It was the first time I saw TS. I didn't know what to make of it." His old eyes, once flinty, were now distant and ill-focused. "I couldn't have anticipated the danger, the potential, could I?"

"None of the rest of us did," Weyman pointed out.

"Not that that's an excuse. There were plenty of warnings, but we weren't seeing them." He levered himself a little higher on the pillows.

"Twenty-twenty hindsight," Weyman agreed. "About the Greys?"

"A terrible thing for that family. There was trouble not long ago with her former husband, and they were starting to put their lives in order from that. When the daughter died, they were able to get through it, but then when the boy came down with TS as well, the strain was almost too much. For a while I wasn't sure they'd be able to stay together. I thought it would be too demanding, and have too many tragic memories." He stopped, breathing hard.

"Take your time, Doctor Haliburton." Weyman hoped that his tape recorder was picking up all of his remarks. He did not want to rush Haliburton, for he was sure that that way some minuscule but vital piece of information might be overlooked.

"I don't have a lot of that to spare," said Haliburton. "And I'd feel better if you'd call me Edgar."

"Anything you like," said Weyman, softening to the other man. "In your letter, you say that you think that there were not one but two separate outbreaks of TS in Southern California. You believe that the outbreak in the San Fernando Valley was not the same as the one in San Diego. Can you tell me why you think this?"

"Well, hell," said Haliburton. "Geography, for one thing. It's not like San Diego's Covina. Or even Ventura, for that matter. They are over a hundred miles apart. What confused everything was the outbreak in the Immigration Compound. It was assumed that there were Illegals carrying TS coming into Southern California and spreading the disease. And I think that's bullshit."

"For an environmental disease, I'd have to agree."

"I also think that the environmental disease notion is at least half bullshit." Haliburton folded his hands. "I want to go on record saying that I am convinced that the San Diego outbreak and the San Fernando Valley outbreak are two different sites with two different triggers." He stopped to cough. "I think you have to—" This time he could not make himself continue.

"Edgar?" Weyman ventured when Haliburton stopped coughing.

"Look," he said when he had adjusted himself on the pillow, "this Illegals notion is ridiculous. I've outlined this in my report. The assumption that Illegals were carrying some kind of triggering infection is absurd: if it was right, then half of Laurie Grey's Girl Scout troop ought to have come down with it before anyone."

"What do you mean?" Weyman demanded, suddenly tense.

"Last September, Laurie Grey's troop did volunteer work at the Immigration compound—you know the sort of thing, making sure the food boxes get distributed, holding children while parents are being examined by the docs, helping out with the ones who are upset—and they were okay. If the Illegals were carrying it, all the girls should have come down with it. As it was, Laurie's family had it, but not Laurie, and she was the one who was exposed. And for a while TS was confined to one neighborhood. That's why I say the San Fernando Valley site isn't related. If it really is toxins, that's another matter, but you'll pardon me if I say that it doesn't look that way." His voice had been growing fainter and fainter so that at the last it was barely more than a whisper.

"Doctor Haliburton?" Weyman said, starting to get up.

"Not yet; I'm still here," said Haliburton. "I've been thinking about this. I haven't had anything much else to do except the two-hour check. I can't reconcile what I've learned with what's been assumed." He stopped, closed his eyes and took a long, deep breath. "I go along with the environmental trigger. I read what your office released last week. That makes sense. But the rest of it doesn't jibe with what I've found out."

"Go on," said Weyman, now very much interested in what he had to say. "Tell me as much as you can."

This time Haliburton took a little while to prepare himself. "From what I've read, this stuff is starting to spread, and that certainly eliminates the contamination theory, unless you have something so powerful that it can be carried in some way, such as on clothes. But if that's the case, it doesn't make sense that no kids under twelve get it." He looked over at the clock on the wall. "They're going to be in shortly; can we wait until they finish with me?"

"If you like; sure." Weyman stood up. "I'm grateful, Edgar. I want you to know that."

"Kind of you," said Haliburton, shifting again, trying to make the pillows more comfortable. "I wish I could have one of those fancy water beds they have in the physical therapy department. My skin's becoming supersensitive and I can't find a position that's comfortable for very long."

"I'll be back in half an hour—is that—"

"Just about right," said Haliburton. "I'm looking forward to it, Doctor Muggridge."

As Weyman stepped out of the room, he saw three nurses coming toward the room. On impulse, he stopped them. "How's he doing? Not what it says on his chart; what you know as his nurse."

"I don't know," said the oldest nurse. "I only got his case yesterday. We've got nine nurses on this floor alone out with TS. You know what that means. We're trying to get help from areas where they don't have much TS, but not many nurses are willing to come." She made a point of looking at her watch. "We're on a tight schedule, Doctor Muggridge."

"I'll let you get on with it," he said, taking the unsubtle hint.

The nurses were almost through the door when the oldest turned back to Weyman. "I'll let you know what I think when we're through. Stop by the station before you go; I'll talk to you then. It might not be very reliable."

"Thank you," Weyman said sincerely, surprised at her change of heart. He went down the hall toward the floor monitor station, and on impulse, asked to borrow the phone.

On the third try, he found Sylvia at the hospital at the Naval Air Station. "What's wrong?" she asked when she heard Weyman's voice.

"Nothing as bad as you're thinking," Weyman answered. "But I've been talking to Edgar Haliburton, and he's got me to asking a few new questions. I think he's on to something. He thinks we've got TS back to front. I want to go over the records again, the way Jeff suggested we do, looking at the first cases. I might have a lead on this TS stuff and I want to check it out."

"What is it?" she asked, calmer and more curious.

"Damned if I know yet. There's something I'm not seeing, but it's there. It's as if I'm an out-of-focus lens." He slapped his thigh with aggravation. "I hate getting like this."

"But you're okay?" She made no attempt to hide her anxiety. "Weyman?"

"Sure. What about you?" He was gently teasing.

"It's this place, all the military. You know me and uniforms. Half the time I want to jump out of my skin. And Tolliver is being so damned polite and soft-spoken that I keep thinking he has thumbscrews in his pocket."

"He doesn't," said Weyman, wondering for the first time if Commander Maurice Tolliver might be concealing something worse.

"That's what you think. It's always a bad sign when they're nice to you," she countered. "Does this mean you want to cancel dinner tonight?"

"It means I think we better pick up something to eat and get back to the PHES complex. I want to get on the Atlanta records and that's the best place to do it. Probably the best time, as well." He could feel the frustration building in him and he began to hope that Edgar Haliburton would provide the key to this deadly puzzle.

"Weyman, I've got to get back. I don't like to—" She sounded embarrassed and he immediately felt sympathy for her.

"No problem. Do you mind keeping me company tonight?"

"Fine. I'd like that." She hesitated. "You sound a little tense."

"That's good—I'm a lot tense," he answered, going on quickly, "It hasn't anything to do with you. I'll see you later. Good luck with the brass."

"I'll need it," she said uncertainly.

"You'll do fine." He smiled at the receiver, hoping she could sense it.

"Thanks. See you later."

"Later," he agreed, and hung up.

It was forty-five minutes later when he was allowed back in Edgar Haliburton's room. There was some new equipment beside his bed and his isolation tent had been changed so that now he appeared to be wrapped in an enormous cocoon.

"How are you feeling?" Weyman asked. He could see that Haliburton's face was ashen and drawn, but he did not want to give any indication of alarm.

"Like the hind end of a bear," said Haliburton. "Don't worry about it; it'll change soon enough. They've given me something, one of those stabilizers they used to give AIDS patients. I'll cope."

"If you'd rather postpone this?" Weyman said, praying that Haliburton would not.

"Chances are I'll be worse tomorrow. Let's get on with it," he said testily. "Ask away."

"You were telling me about the Greys. That's the name, isn't it?" Weyman came back to the chair and sat down.

"Yeah. Jonathon and Catherine Grey, four kids, three

from his first marriage, and Laurie between them. She's a dancer." He stared at the ceiling. "You know, when the quake struck, I was in a clinic and the lighting fixture fell. It hit my shoulder. Hurt like hell. But if it had hit my head it probably would have killed me."

Weyman kept silent. He adjusted the volume on his tape recorder and watched Haliburton, part of his attention still wrestling with the questions that were half-formed in his mind.

"I think the hardest thing about dying is having to give up so much. Not life, not life. But things like my two cats and the neighbor's kids and Hunan food and my favorite loafers and letters from my cousins and walks on the beach and sleeping close together after sex. I'm not through with any of those things yet." He botched a chuckle. "So tell me. What can I do for you while I'm still here?"

"What you were saying about Laurie Grey and her Girl Scout troop. You said they did community service work with Immigration last September." He sensed that this was the right place to begin.

"They did. And TS started showing up a little later, mostly among those with other health problems, things like poor nutrition and intestinal parasites. You know the kind of things Immigration handles." He rubbed his chin. "They gave me a lousy shave this morning. They won't let me do it myself. Stupid precaution, if you ask me."

"Perhaps the Girl Scouts weren't exposed," Weyman suggested.

"Maybe, but I doubt it. That stuff seems to have a pretty long incubation period, and that means that it was probably present when the Girl Scouts were there, if it was there at all."

"What about the other way around? What if the Girl Scouts had the trigger and the people in the Immigration Compound got it from them?" said Weyman, expecting Haliburton to dismiss the idea as ridiculous.

"Could be," said Haliburton. "Look what happened with

the Greys. And more than half the girls in the troop have TS now. It's one possibility." He turned and looked directly at Weyman. "If I were you I'd run a full series of tests on every girl in that troop, and their families as well. I don't know what I'd expect to find, but I'm convinced I'd find something."

"Sounds promising," said Weyman sincerely. "I'll keep you posted."

"Thanks," said Haliburton with real gratitude.

"Any time." He knew he ought to leave but Haliburton was reluctant to let him go.

"That's one of the things I hate about being a patient—suddenly everyone treats you like a deaf six-year-old. They do things to you and won't say why, they won't tell you what they're finding out, and the nurses behave like nannies half the time and drill sergeants the other half. I know I was as bad as any of 'em. I used to tell myself I was more understanding and informative, but I was kidding myself."

"Are you sure? Could be you're being too hard on yourself." Weyman rose and came to the side of the bed.

"I'd like to believe you, but my memory's too good for that." He started to lift his hand again then let it drop back. "Let me know about the Girl Scouts."

"Yes. I will." He left the room and went to the nurses' station. He was somewhat surprised to find the nurse he had spoken with waiting for him.

"Doctor Haliburton's a spartan—he'd let that fox eat his guts out and not make a sound," she said. "But TS has its hooks in him all the way. His fever's been hitting one hundred four since Monday and there isn't anything we've found that can control it."

"What about blood chemistry?" Weyman asked.

"Same as all of them. It's coming apart. I'll be surprised and sad if he lasts another ten days." She read his face well. "Yeah, sad. He's miserable and it's going to get worse. I'm sad that he's suffering."

Weyman nodded. "I know what you mean."

"I'm glad he's doing Public Benefit because it makes it a little less futile. For him. And that's what counts." She looked up as a light came on the display panel. "Gotta run. I'll give you a call if there's any change. I can reach you at PHES, can't I?"

"Yes," Weyman said to her back.

PART VI

May–June, 1996

Jeff Taji and
Mason Ross

Harper Ross glared across the table at Jeff Taji, his hands clenched on top of a stack of printouts. "These figures have to be wrong. The readings aren't accurate. Have you checked the equipment?"

"Yes; so have you." Jeff felt bone-weary. "There isn't an error." He put his hand to his eyes. This interview was going more badly than he had feared; he had not found the proper things to say to Harper, to help him accept what the most recent tests had finally and incontrovertibly revealed.

"There's got to be. Mason a TS carrier! It's ludicrous." Harper hit the table twice. "If he's a carrier, how come no one noticed until now?"

"We weren't looking for carriers. That's our fault," said Jeff. "And the confirmation wasn't available until we started comparing his previous tests with the full PAST scan." He saw resistance in Harper's face but could not blame the man for his feelings. How would he feel if it were one of his kids in this predicament, he asked himself. How would he bear it?

"How many others do you think there are out there? What makes you choose him?" Harper choked out the question, unable to look away from the printouts.

"We don't know." Let it be few, he added to himself. "We've found Mason because of Kevin. We're tracing back to the first cases in all the areas where there have been outbreaks. We have thousands of cases to check yet. That we found Mason so soon was more luck than we deserve."

"I assume you're looking?" The question was far more painful than sarcastic. Harper slapped the papers down and got up from the chair. "There's a mistake."

"Not in the figures. Not in the case." Jeff shifted his position so that he could watch Harper.

"I'll find an answer to this. We've come a long way for a short time. There's more information now and we're learning more every day. It stands to reason that we'll make breakthroughs." He was speaking to the air, paying no attention to Jeff. "There's got to be an answer."

"Yes," Jeff agreed softly. "But in the meantime—I'm more sorry than I can say, Harper—Mason has to go into isolation. At once. It's the only thing we can do, at least for the time being." This was the part he had dreaded, and from the expression on Harper's face, he had been right to do so.

"Don't give me that crap!" Harper rounded on him, the full weight of his frustration and outrage falling on Jeff. "Don't take that superior attitude with me. I've been working on TS since Kevin died, and I'm sick and tired of your assumption that all you have to do is flash your Atlanta credentials and the whole world will do what you tell it to. Who are you to send my boy into isolation because of a few questions, a few unusual readings in his PAST scan? What makes you think you have any right to do this?"

"I wish it weren't your child. I wish it weren't anyone's child," Jeff said. "I wish TS had never happened."

"And that's supposed to make it okay?" Harper's voice had risen and his face was flushed. He moved awkwardly, as if his body was not entirely his own. "I won't let you get away with it."

"Harper, it's not a question of anyone getting away with anything." He stretched, trying unsuccessfully to ease the tension that was building in his neck and shoulders. "I don't know what to say to you." He heard his shoulder pop as he moved: was that stress or age?

"For starters, you can pull a few strings to keep my kid

out of isolation," Harper insisted. "Damn it, Jeff, you can't pack him off like some kind of criminal. There are laws; he has rights."

"I haven't the authority to keep him out of isolation, and you know it." Jeff put his hand to his head again. "Even if I could, I wouldn't, not with a disease like this one."

"How righteous." Harper swept the printouts off the table with one long arc of his arm. "You proper bastard."

Jeff watched the paper slither over the floor. "Harper," he said quietly, "consider this a moment: suppose Mason knew about his condition—do you think—"

"He's not going to know! I won't let you do that to him!" Harper was shouting, his face working with emotion.

"—do you think," Jeff persisted, "he would want to carry TS to one more person than he already has? Don't you think he's going to have trouble enough with his feelings now? Don't you think he would want to isolate himself if he understood what was at stake?"

"Oh, that's a very pious attitude," Harper scoffed. "Mason's thirteen. He's been in the top of his class for years. He's a popular kid. You're proposing to turn him into a laboratory animal. What's wrong with you? Don't you see what you'd do to him?"

"I'm thinking about your son. You might not believe that, but it's true." He held Harper's eyes with his own. "Your son is a carrier of TS. That is a fact. TS is a deadly disease. That is a fact. For his own protection, if not for public safety, Mason has to be placed in isolation, as do any and all carriers of TS."

"Why so institutional? Why does it have to be in Atlanta, on the other side of the country? Why not let him stay here, under an arrangement of some kind, maybe house arrest. Why do you have to take him away from us." Harper was not so angry now, but his desperation was plainer.

"For one thing, no one can guarantee you won't get TS.

You've been exposed to it, and there are signs that you could develop it. You can't screen everyone who has any contact with him or other family members all the time, not full blood work and PAST scans and the rest of it, to say nothing of the tests we're developing and trying. The hospitals are already having trouble, and adding another layer of regular tests would be more than they can handle. Think about what would have to be done, each day, every day. That simply isn't possible, is it?" Jeff hesitated, worried about how Harper would respond to his next argument. "And there is the question of his protection. There are people out there"—he gestured toward the windows and the city of Seattle beyond—"who might want to exact vengeance on your boy because someone they loved died of TS. Can you be certain you could deal with that?"

"That's being a little extreme," said Harper carefully.

"People under stress are extreme by nature. Most of them will want to have the chance to claim their pound of flesh." In a remote part of his thoughts, Jeff tried to decide if that was a mixed metaphor, and decided that it wasn't, it was merely bad use of language. "Your son would have more to deal with than his own doubts and guilt."

"Mason's not like that," Harper declared.

"If he's any kind of a human being, he is," Jeff said, deliberately harsh. "How did you feel when you were a kid and you hit a squirrel on your bike? How did you feel when a friend caught your summer cold? Well, that's just the tiniest part of what Mason is going to feel. You want to deny he's a carrier, but for him it's apt to be more of a crusade, an expiation. It's not an uncommon reaction, particularly in young people. He's going to need your help, not your denial."

"That's a well-rehearsed speech, Doctor Taji," said Harper, sneering. "Do you use it on all your difficult cases?"

"I don't like to make speeches at all," said Jeff, refusing to rise to the bait. "I know people you can talk to who can explain this better. There's a Doctor Loren Protheroe who specializes in cases like this. He's already been assigned to the TS carriers. He'll know more than I do. Let me give you his number." He moved forward in his chair, reaching for his pen.

"Wait just a minute," said Harper. "I want to get a few things straight with you." His manner was outwardly calmer, but it was clear he was smoldering. "You're prepared to take Mason no matter what, in part because you think he could be the target of something like a lynch mob. You're not confining him, you're sparing him hurt and dishonor."

"If that's the side effect, then fine: my purpose is to save lives, including your son's, if I can," said Jeff, making more of an effort to keep control of his temper. "Harper, I have to go see Mason. You can come with me or you can stay here, but if you do come with me, I hope you won't decide to fight with me. What Mason has to hear is going to be hard enough without you being distraught."

"*Stop it!* Just stop it," ordered Harper. "I can't handle this."

"Harper," Jeff went on, "we haven't time to smooth the way as much as I'd like. There is too much risk—can't you understand?—in leaving Mason out of isolation." He got up and reached for his attaché case. "Mason's a smart kid. You've said so yourself. He has so much going for him. If anyone can handle this, he can. I'm depending on you to give him a break, so that he'll have a chance to come to terms with his condition. Will you do that?"

Harper stood looking down at the printout he had shoved aside. "You really are convinced, aren't you?"

"If it were any kid but Mason, you'd be, too," Jeff said gently.

"No," Harper said. "No, I don't think I could ever see things in the cut-and-dried way you do, Jeff. Maybe that's the difference between a professor of criminology and an epidemiologist."

"Maybe," Jeff said. "You ready?"

"You go ahead. I have to . . . think this through. I'll be along in a while, and I'll spend a lot of time with him then." His face was sad and when he looked at Jeff, he could not speak at all.

"If that's what you want. I'll tell Mason you're on the way." The last was almost a question.

"Thanks." He looked away, toward the windows.

It took Jeff almost ten minutes to get to Mason's room, part of that time spent in putting on the quarantine gear that was still required for TS cases. As he checked the cuffs at wrist and trousers to make sure the elastic was sufficiently tight, he did his best to compose himself, to gather his thoughts before he had to face Harper's son.

He found Mason sitting up in bed, wearing pajamas and watching television. "Doctor Taji?" Mason asked as Jeff got nearer his bed. "Everyone looks like they're from Mars in those rigs."

"Worse than that," said Jeff, selecting one of two chairs in the room. "How are you feeling?"

"Not bad," Mason answered, doing his best to hide his own puzzlement. "No one has said anything about my tests."

"That's what I'm here for," said Jeff. "They leave those kinds of talks to me." He wanted to ask Mason to turn the TV down or off, but could not bring himself to deprive the youth of his entertainment. "What are you watching?"

"One of those real old PBS reruns. The one about that spy, Sidney Reilly. It's real good. They're doing a whole bunch of those old mini-series on PBS right now. Next week they're doing that *Wuthering Heights* they did five years ago." As he spoke, he watched Jeff in a guarded, secretive way. "I got a kick out of it back then, even though we had to watch it for English at school."

"I hope you'll enjoy it as much now," said Jeff. He tried to find a natural position to sit in and only succeeded in wadding up the quarantine garments more uncomfortably.

There was the sound of metal slamming against metal in

the hall; Jeff winced and Mason did his best not to react at all.

"Have I got TS?" Mason asked suddenly.

"Not exactly," said Jeff.

"How can I not exactly have TS?" Mason wanted to know. "You don't have to try to make it easy for me, Doctor Taji. I've come to terms about Kevin. A lot of my friends have got it now. You can tell me whatever I have to know."

"All right," said Jeff, gathering his thoughts. "You remember back when your brother died, we were all pretty sure it was the result of an environmental toxin. I found the abnormalities in the blood and the ACTH and—"

"Yeah, I know about that. Dad's told me about it, when he comes home from work. It's almost all he talks about these days."

Jeff held up a hand, silently recommending patience. "Identifying the nature of the symptoms was how the disease ended up with my name. We then thought that we had a cumulative or synergetic toxin—that is, a two-stage contamination—and then we changed our minds again and tried to find out if there was a genetic or a biological trigger. The trouble is, the Standard Public School Blood Screen hadn't provided any warning or early information, and that's what caused so much confusion." He was finding it increasingly difficult to go on. "And now we have to admit that what we have is a mutant disease, highly communicable, that at least began with carriers."

"Carriers? You mean like that lady who had typhoid and worked in kitchens? That kind of carriers?" Mason clearly did not accept this notion. "How can something that spread the way TS has spread be because of a carrier?"

"Because once you reach the second stage of the disease, you become a carrier as well, until the fever starts." Jeff leaned forward and braced his elbows on his knees. On the TV screen, an actor who looked uncannily like Josef Stalin was writing out a document.

"You think someone in the family might be a carrier?" Mason asked, for the first time looking frightened.

"We know someone in your family is a carrier," Jeff corrected as gently as he could.

"Dad?" Mason said, his voice rising an octave. "Is that why he's not here?"

"No," said Jeff. "No, it's not your father. I've been trying to find the right way to say this to you, Mason, but there isn't any right way. You're the carrier, I'm afraid, and there are some measures we must take at once for everyone's safety."

Mason was stunned. He was shaking his head, hardly moving, but still shaking his head, his eyes taking on the odd shine of inner terror. "I can't. I wouldn't."

"It isn't you, Mason," Jeff said, getting up and approaching the boy. "It's a peculiarity in your genetic structure. We need to know more about that, if we're going to make progress toward controlling and curing TS."

"Un-huh," said Mason, now becoming more remote. "I can't do . . . I wouldn't."

"That's why we're counting on you to help us." Jeff said, his persuasiveness growing stronger. "And we're going to need all the help we can get. The risks are so enormous, and so far we haven't found other carriers, though there must be others."

"Sure," said Mason with the heavy cynicism of the young.

"Really. You haven't been to San Diego and Los Angeles and Idaho and Dallas recently, have you? What about Portland?"

"Dad went to Portland last week." He said it with the kind of determination kids usually reserve for claiming important prizes.

"And he'll have to go again soon, I'm afraid," said Jeff, thinking of Max Klausen, who had been transferred to Intensive Care the day before.

"But Doctor Taji, I haven't done anything. I never got sick. It's a mix-up. *It's a mix-up.* It has to be a mix-up."

There was a tightness in Jeff's chest, as if something hot was gathering under his sternum. He wanted to comfort Mason, to promise him that it would all be fine soon, but he could not do that in honesty. "Yes, there's been a mix-up, but it happened before you were born. Somehow, in some way, a kind of trigger got built into your genes, and now it's been . . . activated. As it has been for others, or so we suspect. We have to find the carriers and then try to find out what happened to make them carriers."

"Do you really think there's other carriers?" He asked it with a mixture of anticipation and contempt, not knowing what answer he wanted.

"Yes, I do," Jeff said candidly. "I think there may be a couple hundred carriers out there."

"But what caused it?" Mason asked, very tense.

"I wish I knew. We're going to have to do a lot of checking. It could be that the toxin we've been looking for all along was something that affected one or the other or both of your parents. It might be that you were in the wrong place at the wrong time while your mother was pregnant, or that your father worked on the wrong site at one time. We won't be able to do much until we identify most or all of the carriers."

"Don't call me that," Mason objected.

"What?" Jeff asked.

"A carrier. I'm not a carrier. I'm someone with a communicable disease. That's what you call it, isn't it? I've been reading up, since Kevin got sick. For all you know, I've got TS but it's taking longer to develop." He was not speaking very loudly but there was such defiance in his behavior that Jeff was startled by the boy's intensity. "It could be that, Doctor Taji. Why should it be different for me than it is for all those other kids out there?"

"I don't know, Mason," Jeff said quietly. "But it is. If you'll help us, there's a chance we can find out why." He leaned forward. "You're not the kind who needs easy answers; you know enough about TS to be certain that if there were an easy answer, we would have found it by now."

Mason looked away from Jeff, his eyes directed, unseeing, at the television screen. "I don't want . . ." The words drifted off.

"You don't want to have TS?" Jeff guessed. "You don't want to have given it to someone—anyone?"

"I guess." He dragged his sleeve cuff over his eyes. "I don't have to . . . it's so hard and . . . I don't have . . ."

"Mason," Jeff said with stern affection, "understand me: you did not knowingly harm anyone. You are innocent of any wrongdoing. It is not a crime to have a disease. You did not plan any of this. You are not responsible for what happened."

"Aren't I?" he asked miserably.

"No. Whoever caused the mutation is to blame, not you. And if it is a natural mutation, then no one at all is to blame." He said this with conviction, as if his tone of voice could instill a similar sureness in Mason.

"Does a natural mutation show up like this, in lots of places at once?" Mason inquired. He was doing his best to sound mature and in control of himself, responding to Jeff's certainty, but there was a breathiness that gave away the depth of his emotions.

"No," Jeff admitted. "Not that I know of."

"Then somebody did it," Mason said, sitting straighter once more. "I've been reading, and it says that natural mutations rarely occur in more than one place at the same time."

"Very likely. But we may never find out who or how." It was not easy to say this, to voice a profound concern which had taken hold of him in the last week. "There's been too much time."

"But you'll try," Mason said urgently.

"Oh, yes. I give you my promise that I will try. I'm as

worried as you are—though you might not believe it." He got up and came to stand beside the bed. "I'm not going to give you a lot of useless talk on how important it is to be brave, or that you have to be grown-up about this. I hope you can find a way to deal with this because . . . because you have to. If you let yourself give way to anger or despair, then there's nothing we can do. If you can keep charge of yourself, we have a chance, all of us, to end this sooner." He paused. "I know I'm asking a lot of you, and I have no right to assume you'll be willing to help us. If you can't, that's the way it is. I know we're asking a lot of you—more than we have any right to ask. No one knows how to respond in situations like this, no matter how old they are or how much experience they might have had."

"Oh?" The expression in Mason's eyes made Jeff shudder inwardly. "But you want me to say I'll help you, don't you?"

"Yes," Jeff admitted. "You'd have to do the same thing, if you were in my position."

"What if I say I won't? What if I decide that I don't want to work on your project?"

"I don't have any recommendations on how to come to terms with being a TS carrier. I don't know what to tell you that might help." He put his hand on Mason's shoulder. "I am very, very sorry, Mason."

The boy did not react at once, and when he did, he would not look at Jeff. "Does that mean I'll get TS? After a long time, I'll get it?"

"We don't know," said Jeff with terrible honesty. "But at present, I doubt it. Whatever effect the mutation has had, it seems to have stopped the disease from spreading in you. That was one of the anomalies that made your case unusual."

"How, unusual?" Mason demanded. "Isn't it unusual enough that I'm carrying TS?"

Jeff studied Mason, and decided that Harper's son had more to bear than he could carry already. To be told now that Harper had shown signs of early-stage TS would be intolerable. "It's not just unusual: it's tragic. It's part of epidemiology that I wish I never had to deal with, and that I would give anything not to have to tell you."

"Sure." The boy was retreating, looking for solace within himself.

There were a few more matters to be addressed, and Jeff determined to finish them as quickly as possible. "I'm arranging to transfer you to Atlanta, not only for more detailed research, but to minimize the chances of spreading the disease any more than it already has been spread."

"Great," Mason said between his teeth, wrath in his eyes. "Atlanta in the springtime. Great."

"I wish I didn't have to, Mason. If I thought it would be safe, I wouldn't do this. I wish you'd believe me." His whole body felt heavy and he was not able to keep his grief out of his voice, or his demeanour.

"I want to talk to my father." It was a flat demand, closing their conversation with the finality of a slammed door.

"He wants to talk to you," said Jeff, the clammy chill of defeat seeping through him.

"Good." He reached for the TV remote control and turned the volume up so that conversation was difficult.

Jeff waited beside Mason's bed, hoping that the boy would give him another opening. He was so young, thought Jeff. There were a few tokens of puberty on him—a brown fuzz on his upper lip and the edge of his jaw, an occasional shift of register in his voice as new depth and power emerged—that marked his emergence from childhood so that Jeff had a brief notion that perhaps growth-retardant hormones might help him. Sternly he reminded himself that was impossible. "I'll see you later," he said when Mason remained stubbornly silent.

Mason nodded once and did not pay any attention as Jeff went out of his quarantine room.

Dale Reed and
──── Steven Poulakis Channing ────

Coming into Atlanta their Lockheed Execu-jet was given priority landing clearance, so they arrived fifteen minutes before the car from the National Center for Disease Control Environmental Division came to pick them up.

Dale did his best to keep both of them from becoming anxious. "They've arranged special quarters for you and the other kids who'll be here," he said, keeping with a theme that had formed the bulk of his conversation since Tuesday.

"You said, Doctor Reed," Steven reminded him quietly. He looked around the enormous runways, his eyes narrowing in the brilliant sunshine. "It's a big place."

"The main terminal," Dale said, pointing out the sprawling building two miles away, "is the fourth busiest airport in this country. It's the major American departure point for Africa and the east coast of South America." He was glad to have something to talk about that did not concern the isolation quarters Steven would be entering.

"Is TS there yet? In South America or Africa?"

The question stunned Dale and he did not answer it at first. He put his hand out on the metal flank of the six-seater jet which had brought them to Atlanta and tried to think of a way to answer the question. "I really don't know," he said. "We have been told that there are cases in Europe now—not very many."

"And how many of us kids have they found?" He no longer sounded nervous.

"You and five others. There may be more, but so far it's you and five more."

"Six kids. And how many people are sick? John Post said that it was over one hundred thousand." He paced a few steps away and then looked back at Dale. "Will they let Mom come to visit me, since she's getting over TS now?"

"I hope so," said Dale, more worried about Douglas Kiley and the ESA men who were so diligent in their guarding of Irene Channing than the isolation quarters her son would occupy.

"They better," Steven said darkly. He was taller than he had been six months ago; his gangly frame had stretched up four inches in the previous year and showed no sign of slowing down. He had started shaving and had developed the first sprinkling of acne.

"I'll do everything I can to arrange it. I promise you." He had made a similar promise to Irene before he left her for the three days he would be gone.

"Besides Mom, how many others have survived TS, do you know?"

"No. According to what Doctor Taji told me, they think that there may be over fifteen hundred now." It was not easy to make that very low figure sound encouraging, but Dale did his best.

"Un-huh," Steven said, pacing again.

A black Honda Sturgeon approached, the horn announcing its arrival. Its personalized plate said CAVIAR. It drew up near the jet and came to an idling stop; Jeff Taji got out. "Sorry I'm late," he began.

"We're early," Dale countered. "They let us land as soon as we used the magic initials NCDC." He put his hand on Steven's shoulder. "Steve, you remember Doctor Taji, don't you?"

"Hi," Steven said diffidently, taking Jeff's proffered hand after a moment's hesitation.

"Hello," said Jeff. "Did you have a good flight?"

"I suppose so," Steven said, trying to be as adult as possible.

"I've been in planes so much in the past two months that I'll probably try to lower the landing gear when we park." Jeff's smile—its apparent ease belied the tremendous effort it cost—was warm and encouraging. "Where are your things?"

"In the plane," said Dale for both of them.

Jeff nodded. "Unless you need to have them with you for some reason, I'll arrange for them to be brought to ... your quarters." He indicated his car. "Is that okay?"

"Fine," Dale said, his hand squeezing Steven's shoulder to prompt him to agree.

"Yeah; fine," he echoed dutifully.

"There are a few things that have to be checked. You understand," said Jeff, who did not want to discuss the analysis that their luggage would undergo. "Three of the others are here already," he went on as he strode toward his car. "There's a girl from San Diego who's a dancer, and twins from a small town in Oregon." Privately he wondered how the Fundamentalist Barenssens would get along with their less rigid companions, but he would not let himself dwell on that problem. He opened the back door for Dale. "You see, we have company."

Loren Protheroe smiled from his seat in the back. His face was as comfortable as a good pair of hiking boots. "Hello, Doctor Reed," he said, his eyes shifting at once to Steven. "And Steve."

"Hi," said Steven as he got into the front seat.

"It's going to take about half an hour to reach the facility. The traffic isn't bad this time of day, but it's about twenty miles from here." He fell silent as a huge Egyptian Air 767 lumbered down the runway, air and engines screaming as it braked.

By the time the noise abated, Jeff was driving toward the side gate that serviced the private planes of the NCDC. He had put on dark glasses and looked more like a diplomat or high-class crime lord than a doctor. As he turned toward the freeway, he said, "There are two other kids coming in tomorrow; one from Los Angeles and one from Seattle."

"Oh," Steven replied.

"You're all about the same age," Jeff went on, determined to keep even a semblance of conversation going.

"I was born on October twenty-fourth in nineteen eighty-two," said Steven as if reciting in class.

"You're the youngest. The twins are the oldest: they were born on the twelfth of October." He did his best to be cheerful. "In a way your birthdays have been a big help. Once we knew what to look for, we could eliminate a lot of people from our search."

"Un-huh," Steven muttered.

"Steven," Loren Protheroe said from the backseat, "I'm going to be working with you kids while you're here."

"You're a shrink, right?" Steven said, turning as much as his seatbelt would permit.

"Right." Loren smiled.

"Why do I need a shrink? Isn't it enough that I'm a TS carrier? Or does it make you crazy, too?"

"Steve!" Dale admonished him.

"It's okay," Loren said, addressing both Dale and Steven. "And, no, Steve, you're not crazy. But you're going to have to live a very strange life for a while, and sometimes it helps to have someone to talk to."

"A shrink," Steven jeered.

Loren refused to be goaded. "It beats talking to the walls."

"Shit." Steven folded his arms and glowered out the window.

For the next few minutes they rode in silence, then Dale took up the gauntlet. "About these other kids; what are they like?"

"Pretty much what you'd expect, a mixed bag," said Loren, not quite sighing. "In circumstances like this, it's a little difficult to assess them."

"I'll bet," Steven said quietly, but loudly enough to be heard.

Dale resisted the urge to repeat Irene's instructions to her son. "Have you worked out a routine yet?"

"To a degree," Loren said. "We're not quite prepared for everything, but I think we've made a good start. The facility is far enough away from the city that we can guarantee security, and there's enough recreation that I don't think the kids will be at too much of a disadvantage. We have two swimming pools for them, and an athletic court; even horses, if they want to ride." He said nothing about the problem of companionship and the difficulties of such limited social contact.

"What about classes?" It was something Irene had wanted to know, and Dale saw Steven flinch. He told himself to be patient, to keep calm. "Will it be school as usual?"

"Not quite as usual, but close enough. We'll do standard eighth- and ninth-grade studies plus whatever additional study the kids might want. We're trying to find a dance teacher for Laurie Grey, and a swimming coach for Gail Harmmon."

Steven slid further down in his seat, sulking.

"We've got a small woodshop and a potter's wheel for crafts, and over two thousand videotapes. Each room has a three-foot TV and a CD player." Loren saw that he was not getting far with Steven. "And every kid has a telephone, so he can keep in touch with his family."

"My Mom's in a hospital," Steven announced loudly. "She isn't allowed to have many calls."

"I've already arranged things for you," said Dale. "I told you that on the plane."

"It doesn't mean it'll work," Steven said, his chin lowering onto his chest. "They'll tell me she's in physical therapy, the way they've always done. And Brice is at boarding school. I won't get to talk to him very much."

"What about your friends?" Dale said, and in the next instant wished he had bitten off his tongue.

"My friends are dead," Steven said. "They got TS from me and they're dead."

There was nothing that anyone could say that would soften what Steven had said; Loren did not make the attempt.

"In time you might want to talk about your friends," he said. "Not right now, but later, when some time has gone by."

"Talking won't make them not dead, will it?" Steven demanded.

"No. But it might make your grief a little less painful," Loren said. "We're about halfway there."

"Rooty," Steven said.

By the time they turned in through the tall, guarded gate, Steven was looking more frightened than irate. Jeff parked in front of the medical building and indicated the two long buildings that flanked it. "Those are your quarters. The staff has quarters on the third floor of the medical building. Each of you has your own . . . apartment. You have a main room, a bedroom, a workroom, a bathroom, a lanai facing the pool, and a small kitchen. Food service will be available around the clock in the central kitchen and you will have twenty-four-hour access to the medical staff."

"Sounds like I'm sick, after all." Steven stood beside the car, shading his eyes as he looked at the place. "Where are the athletic courts?"

"The far side of the swimming pool," said Jeff. "They can be used for tennis, badminton, basketball and croquet. The stable's beyond that. We have eight horses for you and the staff." Not very long ago this facility had been used by a group of AIDS victims who were testing the various treatments available. Now, with AIDS all but extinct, the facility was being turned over to these continuing victims of TS.

"It's not bad," was all Steven would say for it.

"I'll get you started," offered Loren.

"I will," Dale corrected. "I told Irene Channing I'd make sure he was off to a good start here."

Loren shrugged. "Whatever you like. First stop is the lab."

"Oh *no*!" Steven wailed. "Not again!"

"It won't be as long as the other times. We just need a few things from you to compare with the records we already have," said Jeff as he started up the three shallow steps to the door of the medical building. "The sooner you start, the sooner it's over with."

"Come on, Steve," said Dale, not quite dragging the boy into the building.

The four staff nurses were quick and polite without being falsely cheerful and in less than forty minutes, an orderly was escorting Steven—with Dale in tow—through his quarters.

"There's an intercom and a buzzer. You can use either of them to call the main building, or to reach any of the other facilities. To call other rooms, use the phone." The orderly was not dressed in lab whites but in khaki chinos and a Hawaiian shirt, and his nametag was embellished with a drawing of a unicorn. "I'm Ted Brazios; Ted for Edward and Theodore—that's my first and middle name. I answer to Ted and Hey You."

Steven would not smile. "Thanks," he muttered, taking the key that Ted held out to him.

"Dinner's in three hours in the main dining room, on the other side of the pool, the second door from the left end. If you want to have Doctor Reed come with you, that's fine." He gave Steven a thumbs-up sign and left.

"How long am I going to have to stay here, Dale?" Steven asked, taking strange consolation in being able to call Reed by his first name.

"I don't know, Steve; I wish I did. Not long, I hope." His sympathy was so strong that he felt tears well in his eyes; he blinked rapidly to control them.

"Yeah." He looked around the room, noting its pleasant furnishing. "He said there were fifteen apartments like this in this wing. I'm in junior high and I have my own apartment. I wonder who else they're expecting." He dropped onto the copper-colored sofa.

"I don't think they know, Steve," Dale said, uncertain if he should remain standing.

"They're playing it by ear, huh?" His voice broke, going from alto to baritone and back again.

"Wouldn't you?" Dale decided to sit down and selected a low-slung Italian chair; he got into it awkwardly and found it very comfortable. "They've made mistakes with TS. We always make mistakes with new diseases. They don't want to do it again if they can help it."

"So why fifteen rooms if there are only six of us, and two are twins?" He was nervous; his right foot, propped at the ankle on his left knee, was jiggling.

"They may be more than six."

"And maybe they're up to something." He stared morosely at the TV and snapped his fingers a few times. "Well, at least there's some girls coming. That's something." He was not as eager as he sounded, but he had just reached the age when girls were supposed to be less of a pest than they had been.

"A dancer and a swimmer," said Dale.

"What if they like the other guys better? What am I going to do?" He got up abruptly and went to the sliding glass doors that led out to a tiny patio. "It isn't like I can ask one of the nurses on a date."

"Worry about that when it happens," Dale advised, then went on in another voice, "I know you're worried about what's going to happen to your family. Well, remember that for the time being, they're safe. Your mother's gotten over TS, and your brother isn't old enough to catch it. I'll keep my eye on both of them. If you want to talk to me about them, you can call me at any time. You have my private number and you can use it whenever you want to."

"Okay; yeah." He stared down at his shoes. "You're right, I am worried. I don't like Brice being sent away like that, and I don't like Mom being kept in a hospital like some kind of . . . of invalid."

"She won't be. I'll make sure that as soon as she's ready, she gets out of there. I'll look after her, Steve." He had to work on sounding confident and undisturbed.

Steven continued to look down, and then, quite suddenly, he asked, "Are you going to marry my Mom?"

"If she'll have me," said Dale, taken off-guard by the unexpected question.

"Okay." Steven turned and gave Dale a hard look. "But while I'm in here, you've got to keep those shit-faced ESA guys away from her."

Dale nodded once. "You've got my word on it."

Gail Harmmon and Loren Protheroe

Still dripping from her morning laps, Gail stood in the patio door of Loren's office. "Why do you want to see me?" she asked when he did not respond to her presence.

"It's your second week here and you haven't talked with me," said Loren in his easiest conversational style.

"So what?" She did not come one step farther into the room.

"I thought you might like to talk, that's all." He looked toward the Sixties-fashion beanbag chairs scattered about the room like so many oversized soufflés.

"I don't need a shrink," she said. "I just want them to do whatever they're going to do and let us out of here."

"That's what they're trying to do," Loren said in the same steady way.

"Are they making any progress?" Her head angled up more sharply.

"They think so," he answered, telling the truth but withholding the doubts that plagued all the staff at the quarantine facility.

"So how long will it take?" she asked.

"There's no way to tell—a few months if we're very lucky." He cleared his throat. "I won't kid you: it could be a lot longer."

"A year? Two years?" For the first time she sounded distressed. "I can't stay here for two years. That's grotty."

"You and the others have to stay for as long as it takes." He was still affable but there was a stern undertone that had not been present earlier.

"And you guys? Does the staff have to stay here a long time, too?"

"We all volunteered to be here," he said. "We can ask to be transferred, or we can be ordered out."

"Because you get sick?" she guessed.

"That's one reason." He let her consider that before he went on. "Some of us do get sick. It's a risk we take. But if we didn't think it was worth it—if we didn't think *you* were worth it, we wouldn't have volunteered. How's the swimming?" he changed the subject without missing a beat.

"Okay, mostly. It isn't much fun without someone to swim against, and the other kids aren't all that good." She slouched forward. "That guy Mason is about the best, but I can beat him easy."

"Well, you were in pretty classy competition last fall," Loren said, indicating the seat nearest his desk.

"That was last fall." She folded into the shapeless chair and leaned back enough so she could look at the ceiling instead of him. "Hey, you've got posters on the ceiling. That's neat."

"For people like you, who'd rather look up."

"Yeah," she said, glaring at him.

Loren fiddled with a stack of papers—he did not mention they were the latest test results of the six kids in his care—and changed the subject again. "You been out to the barn? There's a couple pretty good horses out there."

"I don't know how to ride," said Gail resentfully.

"You can learn. Laurie is pretty good; she could teach you." He began deliberately to doodle on his desk blotter.

"You're funny for a shrink." She stared at him a while. "They said at dinner last night that there's TS all over the country now. It was on the news."

"Not surprising," Loren told her as he continued to let his pen travel over the blotter. "A disease like this makes news, unfortunately."

"It's not right," she stated.

"You mean because of you? So far we've been able to keep you kids out of the news, and that hasn't been easy. Your families' names haven't been mentioned and the information about initial carriers hasn't come up. Think about that for a bit, will you?" He waited, knowing that she would eventually have questions for him.

"Why'd you volunteer?" she asked him after a little time had gone by.

"Oh, a number of reasons. My dad has TS. Two of my cousins have died from it—they got it early, last December. I want to do what I can to stop it." He set his pen aside.

"Like keeping us locked up?" she challenged.

"More like keeping you in isolation so that the disease doesn't spread and so you don't become targets for a lot of very unpleasant attention." He pushed his chair back and came around his desk; as he dragged one of the beanbag chairs close to hers, he continued, "I don't like to think that there are people dying who don't have to. And I don't think any of you kids wants to have to—"

"Dad said that I couldn't have known about it. I couldn't have known. It . . . I didn't." The last was pleading.

"No, you couldn't. But it's natural for you to have trouble accepting that. You said when you arrived that you would rather TS had killed you than your brother. I want you to know that I understand how you feel that, and why you feel it." He pulled his legs up tailor fashion and watched her. "Are there times you blame yourself even when you know it isn't necessary?"

"God, you sound just like a shrink now," she complained.

"That's what I am." He was content to wait for her to talk some more.

Finally she gave in. "What am I supposed to say? That I feel guilty? That I hate myself?"

"Do you?" he asked.

"You're corny. You're like something out of a bad movie." She folded her arms. "Do they teach you how to ask those questions in shrink school?"

"Yes, among other things," he said, and smiled impishly. Since he had a pixie face, this did not seem wrong, and in spite of herself, Gail smiled.

"You look funny," she said.

"So they tell me," he agreed, leaning back and staring at the ceiling as she had done. "I like the one of Alain Wilding," he said, indicating the provocative young Canadian actor who had risen to astronomical heights in the last two years.

"I like John Castle," she said, choosing the middle-aged British actor rigged out in eighteenth-century laces and velvet. "I like it when he smiles."

"Why him?" Loren asked.

"I told you: I like his smile. He doesn't do it very much and when he does it's special. Most of the time, he does a sly grin. His smile isn't sly at all." She cocked her head as she studied the poster, her face thoughtful. "I saw the movie that's from. He was sneaky. I liked it."

"We can get it for the video equipment, if you like," offered Loren.

"I don't know," she said dreamily. "Sometimes remembering is better." For a few seconds her eyes were far away, on scenes only she knew.

Loren nodded. "Yes, sometimes it is."

Gail was quiet again for a short while; then, while she continued to stare absently at John Castle's picture, she said distantly, "My mother's best friend—Erin Donnell?— two of her kids died of TS, and now she's got it. She told my mother that I'm worse than a murderer."

"When did this happen?" Loren asked, keeping his voice level. He had been prepared from the beginning to hear this and worse; though it distressed him, there was no reflection of that in his manner.

"The day before I left to come here. Mom was upset and she yelled at me and at Erin and then she called Dad and yelled at him, too. She's been yelling a lot since he moved out." It was as if she were talking about something slightly boring that had happened long ago, not the disintegration of her family. "Mom's tested positive for TS, too, hasn't she?"

"Yes," said Loren softly. He sensed rather than saw the powerful emotions behind Gail's apparent lack of interest. Steven Channing behaved much the same way.

"Does that mean she's going to die?" Gail's voice had shrunk to a whisper.

"We're all going to die. It's merely a question of how and when." He hesitated, uncertain of how best to proceed. Then he took a chance. "You know, for about fifty years, we forgot how vulnerable we are. We had vaccines and antibiotics and all the rest of the pharmacological weapons to stop things that used to kill regularly. We were getting somewhere with cancer and had a handle on heart disease. And then along came AIDS and reminded us that we can't hold off dying forever. As soon as we got that under control, TS shows up, and the increase in such puzzling diseases as polyarteritis. The Tunis Flu Two and Three wasn't in quite the same league, but it left its mark." He waited to see what she would do. "Illness happens to people. No matter what we do, we can't get rid of it."

Gail huddled more deeply in her beanbag chair. "So we're part of a long string of disasters?" She flung the question at him like a gauntlet.

"No," he countered. "No. That's not it at all. I was hoping to show that you aren't responsible for the disease you carry, that disease is a fact of life." He shrugged.

She started to tremble as if she were suddenly very cold. "I don't want to think about that. It makes me mad and sorry. I don't like anything like that. I just want to get better and go home, and not have anyone else die from TS."

"That's what we'd all like, Gail," Loren said. "That's what we're trying for, all of us."

"But how can I go home if my Dad's gone and my Mom's dead?" she wailed. "What's the use."

"Your Mom isn't dead yet and your Dad hasn't vanished." He trusted that Brandon Harmmon would relent and call his daughter in the next few days. "When you talk to him, you can ask him how he's doing. He cares about you, Gail, and he cares about your sister. You know how important he is to you—you're important to him, too." He devoutly hoped this was so.

"He won't call," she said miserably. "He told Mom he didn't want to have any contact with me. He said it's my fault that Eric's dead, and it is, *it is*. Eric had TS, and he had to get it from me. Maybe Adam and Axel are right, and this is God's punishment on us."

"Why would God be punishing you?" Loren said, going warily now, for he was not having much success with the religiously rigid Barenssen twins.

"Because of the wickedness of the world. That's what they say. If the world wasn't sinful and wicked, there wouldn't be any TS or anything else bad. They said that the only way to get rid of TS is to repent and pray for all the sinners who have visited this on the world. They said praying is the only thing that can help. They prayed until ten o'clock last night. Four hours they prayed, and they said it isn't enough." She scrunched into a fetal ball, letting the chair surround her.

"Do you think that having TS will cure wickedness?" Loren asked.

She hitched up her shoulder, and did not answer directly. "Mason got mad at them. He said that it was bad enough that we carry a disease, but it doesn't make any sense to confuse a disease with moral judgments." She wiped her nose. "Sometimes Mason's as strange as Adam and Axel are."

"And how does that make you feel?" he asked.

"Will you stop those dumb shrink questions?" Her face turned more sullen. "What if they *are* right, and God *is* doing this to us? What if we can't ever cure it, and almost everyone will die because of us?"

"That's not going to happen," said Loren, wanting it to be so. "We're finding out more about TS every day, and we think we can slow it down, if not cure it completely. We developed the AIDS vaccine, didn't we? Then we can develop a TS vaccine, too."

"Are you really sure?" Gail moved so that she no longer looked in Loren's direction.

"Yes. If I weren't sure, I wouldn't have volunteered to work with you." He spoke calmly, but it was an effort. It had been agreed at the start that only those who tested positive for TS would be accepted to work with the carriers, and that they would have to sign a Public Benefit contract. Loren had wanted the carriers to know that, but a decision made higher up in the NCDC had vetoed his idea. He was more convinced than ever that the kids had the right to know.

"What if you get it? What if you die?" She directed her question to the opposite wall. "I heard that Alain Wilding has TS. That's why they're doing reruns of his old shows all the time."

"Yes, he does," said Loren after a slight hesitation. "He's doing Public Benefit."

"That started during AIDS, didn't it?" she asked, still facing away from him. "There was that big suit, wasn't there? My Dad said that it was pressure politics and that . . . that no responsible adult . . ." She frowned, trying to recall her lawyer father's explanation of something she had not understood at the time and only partially grasped now. "He said it was about individual rights and civic responsibility. That someone would have a civic duty to report contaminated water and if they didn't, it would be their fault if people got sick and died. He said that people sick with AIDS had a responsibility to help in getting rid of it. He said the Supreme Court had done the right thing."

"Yes. It probably would have taken longer to get the vaccine if the Public Benefit contract hadn't been okayed by the Supreme Court." He paused. "Your parents all signed Public Benefit contracts for you and for themselves."

"That's what Mom said. Dad got mad at her for doing it." Abruptly she turned and looked at him. "Sometimes I want to scream."

"Go ahead, if you like," he said.

"No," she decided after considering it. "That's dumb."

"You might feel better if you did," he suggested.

"It wouldn't do anything." She struggled out of the chair. "I want to get some lunch."

He had the good sense not to push his luck with her; he patted the beanbag chair he was in and asked, "Mind if I tag along?"

"If you want. It's probably going to be spinach and eggs again." She made a face.

"And cornbread muffins," he told her.

"Oh." She considered that information. "That's not too bad, then." Without waiting for him, she went to the door.

After a moment, Loren heaved himself out of the beanbag chair and followed after her.

Weyman Muggridge and
———— Jeff Taji ————

"Well," Weyman sighed as he looked at the printouts. "I guess the other shoe's dropped."

Jeff could think of nothing to say. He shook his head at the figures and caught his lower lip between his teeth. Finally he spoke. "It's very early. It might take a long time to develop. Portland's coming up with things that seem to slow it down."

"Tell that to Max Klausen," Weyman snapped, then stopped. "Sorry. Cheap shot. Max was a real hero."

"Yes, he was. And his research has been paying off. You've seen the projected curves. They've doubled the time for second stage development, and that's real progress. You'll qualify for the program." He wished he had more encouragement to offer. "We caught this early enough that we can probably slow it down some more. The developmental time can be——"

"It fucking well better take a long time to develop." He slapped the printouts down on his desk. "I've got plans that do not—emphatically do not—include TS."

"There's always a risk," said Jeff for want of anything better.

"That's comforting," said Weyman sarcastically. "Look, I just promised a very wonderful lady that I would not leave her. I'm going to keep that promise; don't ask me how."

"I hope you can keep it," Jeff said with great sincerity.

"No hope about it, Jamshid." Weyman rarely used

327

Jeff's Persian name, and only when he was making the strongest possible point. "I am going to keep my word."

"What about a Public Benefit contract?" Jeff suggested.

"I don't think so. It takes too bloody long, and I don't want to lose a minute. I think I'm going directly to the lab and start kicking some ass." He touched the printouts with the tips of his fingers, as if the information on the pages was as dangerous as TS itself.

"The lab here?" Jeff asked, thinking of the pressure that had been put on them in recent months.

"Hell, no. I'm going back to San Diego. It's a major outbreak site, and there are all those military labs there. I want a general access order for all the military installations; that way I can get three or four separate experiments going at once without any risk of crossbreeding. I can even set up adversary experiments and save us all some more time." He tossed his head. "What about transfusions? How's that going?"

"It seems to help with those who don't have type-O blood. With type O, most of the time, it doesn't do much good." Jeff felt renewed puzzlement as he reported this. What was it about TS that was so mysteriously linked to blood type? None of the experiments so far had provided any clue. He thought of those survivors they had located and recalled that none of them had type-O blood. It was one of the oddest parts of this perplexing disease.

"What's on your mind?" Weyman asked, cutting into Jeff's thoughts.

He sighed deeply before answering. "I keep thinking that we'll find something so obvious that we'll all be outraged that we didn't see it before. But that's wishful thinking, isn't it? A disease like this one never gives you dramatic solutions. You assemble minutiae and sift through it, and you're left with little bits of this and that which might or might not fit together."

"Welcome to medical research. And at least you've got a good track record for minutiae-sifting. You found the culprit behind Silicon Measles." He clapped Jeff on the shoulder. "You defined the nature and parameters of TS. I'm depending on you to come up with the solution." It was apparent that Weyman was only half-joking.

"Thanks," Jeff said heavily.

"By the way, I hear you're going to do an interview with John Post next week, national coverage." His smile was not a happy one, all teeth and no eyes.

"Yeah. Lucky me," said Jeff. "For once Patrick Drucker turned down a TV appearance. That's not real promising."

"It's rare," Weyman said with a sardonic quirk to his brow. "Have you got advance information on the show?"

"Enough," said Jeff. "I'm trying to think of how to explain TS without making it sound worse than it is."

"What would make it worse?" Before Jeff could speak, Weyman went on, "You mean, it could be caught by kids under puberty? It could have no recovery at all instead of about twelve percent, so far? You mean that maybe the government wouldn't be up to something with the few survivors we know about? By the way, are you going to get into the question of the disappearing survivors, or are you going to save that for later?"

"John Post tried to get an interview with a survivor, and the only one he's been able to reach is Irene Channing; she's not being permitted to speak because one of her kids is a carrier, and there's already been a provisional ruling that the names of the carriers will not be released to the public." He held up his hands to show he was helpless.

"They'll find out. You wait. One of those supermarket tabloids will have a cover story, and then a month later, *Time* or one of the other super-legits will report on it, with all kinds of legally hedged language, but everyone will know about the carriers. Period." He looked at the printout. "Right now, I'd be on the reporters' side, but that's right now. In a week or so, I'll be on the kids' side again."

"They're going to need it," Jeff said gloomily. "By the way, Theresa Ann wants to get a few more samples from—"

"Oh, no!" Weyman moaned dramatically.

"Oh, yes," Jeff said firmly. "You've been following her work: she's demonstrating how TS works on the blood, and that is very likely going to be the key to controlling this stuff."

Weyman took a deep breath and let it out slowly. "Theresa Ann is about the best we've got on the DNA squad," he allowed, "but that woman makes my skin crawl. I don't think she knows there are human beings attached to the tissues samples she's so enamored of."

"Probably not," Jeff allowed. "But those tissues samples are holy relics to her, and she's worked a few miracles before."

"You mean Aames Catalepsy?" Weyman asked. "Yeah, she called that one. And got it named for her. I give her credit: finding a food-stabilizing additive that brought about catalepsy in persons with a certain allergic history was drawing to an inside straight and winning. It doesn't change the fact that she gives me the creeps." He frowned at his hands. "Besides, I want to get a hold of this for myself. I have a vested interest. You found and described the shit, but I've *got* it and I want to blow it out of the water."

"I hope you do," Jeff said with feeling. "Come on: I'll go with you. It won't to do keep Theresa Ann waiting." They went toward the door together, Weyman holding the printouts in his hands.

"I don't want you to say anything to Sylvia just yet. Let me handle it, okay?"

"I wasn't planning to say anything," Jeff told him. "What would be the point? It's up to you. I've only met the woman once."

Their elevator was mercifully empty and they continued to talk as they rode to the isolation labs in the basement.

"How're your kids taking the move?" Weyman asked.

"They're philosophical. They're both grown up enough that going to Europe is thrilling. As soon as they tested free of TS, I made sure they got away. I have pressure enough without having to worry about them as well." He slipped his hands into his pockets. "I know that some of the department thinks I'm not playing fair, sending my kids away during this epidemic. They think I'm using my position unfairly."

Weyman nodded. "Claire Lui sent her kids to relatives in New Zealand and no one minds."

"She's an executive secretary, not a doc, and for some reason that's supposed to make my family fair game. Well, they've already got my wife. The terrorists who killed her haven't been caught yet. I don't intend to make another sacrifice to the general good, especially since I can't see that it would be worthwhile. All we'd gain from it is another set of figures to add to the statistics." He had started to jingle the keys in his pocket, but he noticed how loud they were and stopped.

"It bothers you, doesn't it?" Weyman asked.

"All right; yes, it bothers me," Jeff said with asperity. "But that doesn't mean that—"

Weyman would not let him finish. "Why does it bother you? What makes you feel guilty? Do you think you're doing something wrong in doing your best to keep your kids alive? You haven't said that you think everyone ought to wait around to catch TS." He patted Jeff on the shoulder. "Come on. It's okay."

"Drucker wouldn't agree with you," Jeff said bitterly. "He was one of those who were . . . unpleasant about it." As the doors opened, he stopped talking.

"Drucker's an ass. Everyone knows that." Weyman did not lower his voice or make apology for his bald-faced statement.

"It's hard enough working with him as things are," Jeff objected as he gestured to Weyman to lower his voice.

"Well they aren't going to get any easier, so you might as well have your cards on the table." He hesitated at the door to Theresa Ann Aames' laboratory door. "That woman reminds me of a lizard."

"Go in and get it over with," Jeff recommended. "I'll bring you a cup of coffee. Black okay?"

"You're chicken," Weyman announced. "You don't want to have anything to do with her, either." He opened the door and called out, "Yoo-hoo, Doctor Aames!"

"You're clowning again," Jeff said.

"It's that or shit in my pants," Weyman made a show of explaining. "If you come back and I've dropped dead, you can blame it on Induced Aames Catalepsy. It's a rare form of the disease brought about by spending time in her presence."

"I'll keep that in mind," Jeff said.

Weyman made a face before he closed the door and Jeff went on to the lounge at the end of the hall where he took the time to brew fresh coffee for himself and Weyman. He appreciated the bravado Weyman was displaying but was glad of a respite from it. As he poured out coffee into styrofoam cups, he tried to imagine how he would feel in Weyman's position and decided that his colleague was handling his predicament more successfully than he would if he had TS.

"About time," said Weyman when Jeff came around the corner of the lab partition. "In another ten minutes I would have been comatose." He reached out for the coffee cup and had to steady himself.

"Doctor Muggridge," admonished Theresa Ann Aames, sounding like an ancient school librarian instead of the attractive woman of thirty-four she actually was.

"Sorry. I'm not supposed to move quickly, am I?" He sounded too bitter to be funny, but Jeff knew he was expected to smile.

"Pay attention to her," he warned Weyman.

"And Doctor Taji," said Theresa Ann as if neither man had spoken, "I must take another blood sample while you're here. I have not been permitted to use your samples for the last ten days and this will not do." Her immaculate lab coat made her look more like an advertising executive's notion of a physician instead of actually being one. "It will only take a moment or two. I will have Albert tend to it at once. Albert!"

"I'll come back later," Jeff said.

"That's useless bother," commented Theresa Ann brusquely. "You are here now and it will take less than five minutes. Albert!"

Her senior lab assistant, a second-generation Cuban, came around the partition. "Doctor Aames?"

"Take a standard blood sample and a second comparative sample from Doctor Taji." She pointed to her intended victim.

"You don't have—" Jeff began, doing his best to ignore Weyman's laughter.

"It will be over before you can think of it," said Theresa Ann. "Albert is very efficient." She indicated a padded chair, not unlike those used by dentists. "Sit down, please."

Weyman was finally on his feet. "I'll get you some coffee, Jeff. I'll be back in a couple minutes." His good-natured malice did more to goad Jeff on than the blithe certainty of Theresa Ann.

"I'd like some cream in mine this time," Jeff made himself quip. "Thanks."

"No problem," said Weyman, going toward the door and leaving Jeff to the ministrations of Albert and Theresa Ann.

Sam Jarvis and
Dien Paniagua

Dien stood in the door of the hospital room and fiddled with her quarantine mask, using this simple task to postpone entering the room. Little as she wanted to admit it, she was afraid of what she would see, for now that Sam had TS, she felt that her bastions had crumbled beyond repair. When she could delay no longer, she stepped inside and called out, "Sam? It's Dien."

He turned to stare at her. "Hi, Dien," he said after a moment. "It's good of you to come."

"I'm sorry I had to," she admitted, taking much of the blame for his disease onto herself, though she knew it was folly.

Sam looked up at the ceiling through his isolation tent. "My kids were here yesterday, but I've told them I don't want them taking any chances. We're still not sure we know how this stuff spreads and I don't want to increase their risks. Do I?" He winked at her. "Harper Ross is coming by this evening. So far he hasn't got sick; that's something."

Dien pulled up a chair and sat down, her face set into a smile that was as fixed and rigid as concrete. "I've asked for your lab records."

"Good; good." He coughed once. "I signed a Public Benefit contract yesterday. A little late, but better than not doing it at all. I guess after Max died, I couldn't accept that it could happen to me. I decided that I simply wouldn't get it." He tried to laugh and ended up coughing. "They tell me my blood's breaking down faster than in most cases. I've been running on empty for the last week, it seems." He waved his hand, brushing his fingers against the plastic hood that enclosed his upper body. "I should have been in one of these days ago."

"You'll do fine," Dien said automatically, without thought.

He caught her at it. "You really think so?" As he saw the stricken look in her face, he relented and changed the subject. "What about that coach? Have you had any luck finding him?"

"No," she admitted. "Atlanta has put in a form request to the VA to get a fix on him. I was told that this was not met with any serious cooperation." Her body felt cold in the warm room. "A goose just walked over my grave," she said, repeating what her paternal grandmother had said so many times.

"I know the feeling," said Sam. "Have you even located Jackson?"

"No, nor any of the other survivors except that Channing woman in Dallas, and she's being watched day and night in a private hospital." Dien finally made herself speak. "Do you think they're trying to keep the survivors in isolation? What's the reason for it?"

Sam took two deep breaths as he prepared to answer. "The thing is, they probably have the same ability that Missus Channing does, or something like it. Harper has some test results that his grad students are analyzing right now, and they suggest that all the survivors we know of have some psychokinetic abilities. That's very, very disquieting," he said, drawing out the last words.

"Because of danger to others?" Dien asked hopefully.

"No, and you know it. Someone wants them for what they can do. Which might explain the problems we've had in getting emergency funds for finding a vaccine. We've got megabucks coming out of our ears for cure, but not a vaccine. We're being blackmailed, manipulated. We're being set up. Someone, somewhere in government wants this stuff stopped, but not eliminated. Someone wants the psychokinetic effect retained and to have more people with that ability." He slapped his arm weakly against the sheets. "Fuck them all! They're using people like robots. I *hate* that."

"Is there anything I can do to help?" Dien asked, meaning it sincerely.

"You might try to talk to Jeff Taji; find out everything he knows and use his contacts with the media. Someone in the press or TV news must want to do an exposé." He folded his arms over his chest, as if to conceal his pain. "We need to wake the public up to the risk. We need to let them know that this isn't being treated like AIDS or Tunis Flu. This is somebody's gold mine, and that makes it more dangerous than Bubonic Plague and smallpox and cholera all lumped together, because there are people in the government, somewhere, who want TS to continue. And I have to tell you, Dien, it scares the crap out of me every time I think about it." He leaned back, deliberately calming himself. "Those ACTH irregularities—they're the key to all this. We ignore it because we don't know what to do with it, but the fact of the matter is, that's the secret, at least to the survivors. TS changes the chemistry of the blood—we all know about that and accept it—but it changes the chemistry of the brain as well, and we stay away from that because it's so baffling." He stopped, breathing quickly.

"You're certain about that?" Dien asked, because it confirmed her own assumptions. "What if it has to do with the sexual hormones instead of the brain?"

"They're interrelated," said Sam when he had air enough to speak. "But if it were just sex hormones, then the balance of estrogen and testosterone would be in some way indicative and that doesn't appear to be the case." He paused to take a deep breath. "I've had Harper and his grad students working on it, and so far, they can't find any specific correlation between the balance of sexual hormones and the onset of TS. All you have to do is enter puberty to be a target."

She closed her eyes, willing herself to be sensible and steadfast. When she opened them again, she said, "Is there anything I can get for you? Anything I can do for you?"

"You can make sure they get all the information they can out of my body before they bury it. Harper knows where my will is and my kids have copies of it, in any case. Not that it matters all that much anymore." As he said that last, his gaze drifted toward the window. "You know, I'd appreciate it if you'd set some time aside to help out with the orphaned kids who are left. They're so young, aren't they?"

"Yes," said Dien, thinking of her own child. "And there are a lot of them."

"And there'll be more before we're through. I hear that KDAL ran a week-long report on kids there in Texas, looking for foster homes for them. Trouble is, most people are too scared of them to take them in, and most of the facilities for kids are awful and overcrowded already." It was an effort to continue speaking, but he forced himself to go on. "Listen to me, Dien. We're going to have a whole generation in this country who will have no older family whatsoever. That's going to make a mark on the country in ways none of us can anticipate now. And we're not facing that. We're more worried about those six kids in Atlanta than those hundreds of thousands who have lost their families. I got to tell you, that frightens me." This time he needed almost a full minute to recover. "It's what comes of having all this time on my hands."

Dien listened to what he told her and wished that she had the courage and strength of character to take in two or three of the TS orphans. It wasn't just the question of money, she told herself, offering acceptable excuses: she was a single parent who had little enough time to spend with her child as it was; to add more children would only serve to increase the neglect. She decided that her argument sounded like the rationalization it was. "Sam?" she asked.

"What?" He sounded faint and far off.

"If you had the chance, would you take in any of the orphans?" She dreaded his answer.

"Me? You mean, problematically?" He gave a nasty, sardonic wag of his hand. "If I had the chance, I don't know what I'd do. I'd like to think that I'd have the guts to take a few of the kids, but that's easy for me to say, here, now. Fact is, I don't know." When he had stifled his cough, he said, "I think I'd try. Because I felt guilty for being alive, I suspect. And that's a crappy reason to help anyone."

"But those kids do need help," Dien said more urgently.

"Sure. Sure they do. And I don't want to leave them to the tender mercies of the state. Trouble is, who's to say that being a . . . a compensation would be any good for the kids? In another fifteen years, we'll have an answer to that, but by then, the stain'll be set." There was a buzz on the intercom by his bed and both of them jumped at the sound.

"Doctor Ross is here, Doctor Jarvis," said the crackly voice of the head nurse on the intercom.

"Send him in." Sam gave the order automatically, doing his best to ignore the interruption.

"You already have one visitor," admonished the head nurse's voice.

"So I'll have two. Send him in."

"Maybe I'd better leave," Dien offered.

"Why?" Sam asked. "You're going to need to talk with Harper sooner or later, so you might as well do it now. This is as neutral ground as you'll find." When he did his best to chuckle, the sound he made was horrible.

"You need your rest," Dien said, starting to rise.

"Sit!" Sam commanded. "I don't think I'll have a chance like this again, and I want to make the most of it before they turn the sod over me."

"Jesus," she muttered, unable to deny his condition, but annoyed at how blatantly he traded on it.

"Maybe him, too," said Sam, and locked his fingers behind his head. "You two should have been comparing notes weeks ago. I'm not going to let you get out of it now."

"But Sam—" Dien protested just as the door opened and Harper Ross stepped through.

He had lost more than twenty pounds in the last three months; his clothes made him look like a scarecrow. His face was pasty in the first visible touch of TS. He halted as he saw Dien sitting by the bed. "Sam?"

"Sam, meet Doctor Paniagua. I think that means bread-and-water, doesn't it?"

"Yes," said Dien, her defensive attitude shaken by this unexpected and mundane question.

"This is Harper Ross. He's Mason's father," Sam added, to remind Dien that she would have to use some diplomacy when dealing with the professor.

"Hello," said Dien, holding out her hand.

Harper held his printouts more tightly. "Hello."

"If you're going to act like that, I'll have you both thrown out," said Sam in his most conversational manner.

"Doctor Paniagua," Harper capitulated, holding one hand out to her.

She took it. "Professor Ross." They shook hands in some embarrassment. "I've almost finished my business with Doctor Jarvis. I'll leave you alone shortly."

"No, you won't," Sam informed her. "We've got a lot of work to do and I haven't much time to do it in. We have some survivors we need to find ways to locate and there are a lot of kids out there who need our help, right now." From the ragged sound of his voice it was clear he was exhausted, but neither Harper nor Dien was willing to state the obvious. "Sit down, Harper."

There was a very uncomfortable straight-backed plastic chair by the bathroom door; Harper retrieved it and placed it next to Sam's bed, opposite Dien. "I've got as much information as I can find, but it doesn't tell us very much," he began carefully.

"That's important—that they're concealing information." Sam looked briefly at Dien with a faltering I-told-you-so grin.

"It looks as if they're concealing information," Harper said, refusing to be forced into an opinion he did not share.

"For the time being, we'll go along with looks," said Sam, nodding once to punctuate his determination. "You'd better find out from Atlanta who's putting pressure on whom about the survivors. Until we have the answer to that, we'll be in no position to change anything."

"The money's on the ESA," said Harper, reluctant to admit that much. "They're making surveys of all hospitals with TS patients in them, or so the reports say."

"Maybe they're trying to protect themselves," said Dien softly, to stop Harper from taking over completely.

"Protect themselves how?" Sam demanded, his eyes alert as he struggled to get his body to respond.

"Well, suppose this is the side effect of . . . oh, some

kind of testing done years ago. Done before Steve Channing was born—"

"October twenty-fourth, nineteen eighty-two," Harper supplied.

"Yes, before then," said Dien, flustered by the interruption. "Suppose they know that the government or military was doing experiments that might—I said *might*—bring about these symptoms? Suppose they're doing their best to stop anyone finding out. If they only *suspect* that this might be the case, they can't afford to take chances, can they?" She addressed all her questions to Sam, knowing that if she had to face Harper, it would be more than she was prepared to deal with.

"Suspect?" Harper echoed derisively. "Might?"

"We haven't any proof," Dien reminded him stubbornly. "You think it's easy to ask these questions?"

"Isn't it?" Harper asked.

"No," Dien said. "I don't like to think that the government is so . . . so isolated that there are people in it who cannot recognize statistics as human beings, and cannot see that what they are damaging is lives." She put her fingers to her mouth, as if to block any more words from escaping.

"You're making a number of assumptions that could bring about a lot of trouble," said Sam, motioning Harper to be silent. "Once we ask them, there will be no way to retract. And if you're right, then we may have to confront issues far beyond the medical ones that are already more than we're ready to deal with." He waited for Dien to continue.

She began hesitantly. "But . . . if there are governmental considerations . . . if they've had a hand in TS, any hand at all, then . . . they share responsibility for what's happened. They can't be excused. If they're trying to throw us off the track, it could mean that they're afraid of what we could find out about them. And if they are involved, then we must find out. Otherwise TS will continue to wipe out thousands of Americans every week."

"And Canadians, and Europeans, and Orientals," Harper

added gloomily. "We got the most recent World Health Organization figures yesterday. They're pretty discouraging."

"It's spreading," said Sam bluntly.

"At an increasing rate," Harper confirmed. "Nine thousand cases in Europe, over seven thousand in Africa, over thirty thousand in Canada, and probably another twenty thousand in Asia." The printouts were offered as if into evidence.

"That's the first upswing on the curve," said Sam. "Give it a month or two and the increase will be staggering."

"I don't want to give it that long," Dien objected. "I want to stop it now. Today. This minute."

"Yes," said Sam. "And we'll work on it." He motioned to Harper. "You're the criminologist. What do you think about the chance of governmental interference?"

"Not much," Harper said without apology. "And I'll tell you why. They were taken by surprise as much as we were. This tends to make it look like they had not planned on TS, or anything like it. I'm willing to admit that they might have done some experiments in the past that might be responsible in some way for the outbreak. They certainly have been monkeying around with the genetic components of ESP and the like. So it's not impossible that one of their older experiments went awry and we ended up with TS. But I'll bet my last drop of blood that TS was a side effect, not a primary development of whatever they were doing with the genetic material." He had risen as he spoke and now he paced restlessly around the room. "That could account for the unpredictable behavior, and it would explain why President Hunter had trouble getting an investigatory commission together—none of the security guys want to get caught in the crunch."

"And why is that?" Sam asked with a decidedly rhetorical air.

"They weren't expecting TS," said Harper. "They were on the lookout for something, but not TS." He came to a halt near the foot of Sam's bed. "It makes sense," he insisted.

"Of a sort," Sam agreed. "All right. Talk to Jeff and see what he can turn up about experiments in the early 80s with DNA or basic physical chemistry. They probably took that approach, because that's one that was more academically acceptable back then."

"Sam," said Dien, her concern showing in the softening of her voice. "You're worn out."

"True enough," Sam admitted. "All right, tell you what: you two compare notes and report back here after dinner. I want the strongest possible case made for governmental cover-up, or security division interference. Anything that will help us gain access to the information we have to have." As he paused to catch his breath, he could feel his pulse flutter in his neck. "Not now," he whispered.

"Sam, if we do what you want, we'll be on such thin ice that paper'll be more attractive," Harper said. "If we're wrong, then we'll destroy our credibility. You know how merciless the security agencies are."

"It doesn't matter," said Sam.

"They could block what research is already going on," Harper went on. "You know that they can influence how much gets spent on what."

"I also know that Palmer Fields did a lot to change that," Sam reminded them. "Things have been different since ninety-three, thanks to Fields. A phone call or two and Fields would be on their case again, especially for something like this. You know as well as I do that the Pentagon can't take another Pentagate scandal. And stopping or influencing research on TS would make Pentagate look like nothing."

Dien stared at Sam. "Palmer Fields doesn't talk to people like us. Even if we had something to offer him, he wouldn't take it on."

"If he didn't, John Post would, you can be damned sure," said Harper, his eyes narrowing as he considered what Sam was telling him. "All right, so we look for the good guys and we tell them that there might be bad guys.

They find out one of the carriers is my kid and they ignore me."

"No, they won't. Not if you tell them where you're working and what you're working on. Since the names of the carriers haven't been made public, you have a good chance to be heard without the association getting made." Sam had to stop. He panted and slowly a little of the color came back into his face.

"We'd better let you get some rest," said Harper. "We'll come back later, after we've cobbled some kind of plan together." He looked at Dien and saw her nod of assent. "Don't worry, we'll find a way."

"I'm counting on it," said Sam, his voice so soft that the air conditioning was louder.

When they had got out of their quarantine suits, Dien and Harper met again near the elevators, both taking a little time to size the other up. Harper tried to think of something to say. "Sam tells me you have a kid."

"Yes," she said. "He's . . . he's with one of my cousins in St. Louis. I sent him there last week." Her eyes revealed her sadness far more than her words. "It's safer."

"How old is he?" Harper asked, thinking of his own surviving sons.

"Three years, two months." She looked suddenly defensive. "He's not old enough to get TS. I know that. But I want him to have as little exposure as possible. No one knows how long the incubation period on TS is, and I don't want to take chances."

"A good point," said Harper as they stepped into the elevator. "What are we going to do about Sam?"

"You mean in regard to a possible military side to this?" Her eyes hardened and the line of her jaw became firmer. "If there's any association, any association whatever, then I want to have them answer for it. And I'll use Palmer Fields or President Hunter or anyone else to do it."

"Sounds like a tall order for someone," said Harper, his brows lifting at the determination Dien showed.

"What's the alternative?" she challenged. "Wait until TS

has wiped out half the people in the country? Why are we all working ourselves into exhaustion if that's the only thing we can do. I can't believe that there's no hope, no solution, and I *won't* believe it."

Harper accepted this. "All right, but fighting TS alone is more than a full-time job. If you want to take on the Pentagon as well, you're not going to have energy enough to tie your shoes." He stood aside as the door opened and followed her toward the cafeteria.

The room was messy and the serving line was staffed by two cooks' assistants instead of the usual four. The cashier said, in response to a mild criticism Harper made, "We've got more than half the staff out, either sick, or with sick family, or so scared that they can't be here. So take care of your trays and if you want more coffee, you get it yourselves."

"Thanks," said Harper, chagrined.

"You see what we're up against?" Dien asked, nodding once in the direction of the harried cashier.

"I see the figures every day," Harper said.

"Not the figures, the reality. This is the reality. Sam is the reality. And Coach Jackson missing is the reality. That's what we've taken on." She sat down abruptly, as if this admission might overwhelm her.

Harper sat opposite her. "There has been progress made," he reminded her.

"Maybe, but we're losing ground. We need to buy some time. If we knew what this was all about, where the DNA modification came from, and when, we could buy a little time, and that might be enough." She made herself stop. "Read any good books lately?"

Harper stared at her as if she had suddenly grown an extra limb or turned bright blue. "What? Books?"

"We've got to talk about something else for a little while," she said reasonably. "High stress and food don't mix. And it won't take much to bring on a bad case of job burn-out if all we talk about is how many people are dying from this disease." As Dien said this, her face began to relax, her features to regain some of the softness they usually held.

"You might be right," said Harper.

"Damn right," Dien said at her most angelic. "So? What about good books?"

Laurie Grey, Mason Ross and Jeff Taji

By ten at night the laboratory at the Control Facility—as it was vaguely and euphemistically known—was as close to deserted as it ever was; a skeleton staff of nine worked through the night, comparing data on the six teenagers living in their care. The head technician for the night was a massive black man called Ace by everyone except his records card, which had his full name: Horace Percival Hardy. The card also listed his academic credentials, which included two M.S. degrees and a Ph.D.

"Hi, Doc," he called out as Jeff Taji was buzzed through the security door. "Where you been the last week?"

"Don't ask," said Jeff. "Utah. Texas. California twice. Wyoming. Ohio. South Carolina." He ran his fingers through his thick hair; it was noticeably greyer than it had been a month ago.

"What fun," Ace said untruthfully. "Rather you than me. What's up?"

"I'm just checking in. And it's time for another full set of blood work for me." He looked around at the apparatus. "How's it going?"

"We're trying some new blood studies. Quiggly came up with a new way to track TS in the blood. So you're going to be one of the first other than the staff and the kids." He indicated a covered table where a large number of labeled glass containers were lined up. "Care to have a look?"

"Why not?" Jeff asked. He took off his jacket and hung it in the small closet at the front of the room. "It's got warm."

"It's June; what did you expect?" He grinned. "I love it when it gets hot. I love the way it feels. The air is so soft and . . . cuddly."

"Cuddly?" Jeff repeated, not certain he had heard correctly.

"Yeah. You know what I mean. Jessie and I, we make a picnic and go out into the country and let the heat soak into our bones." His smile faded. "Not this summer, though."

"I'm sorry." Jeff hesitated before he asked the next question. "How . . . how is Jessie?"

"Holding her own," said Ace slowly. "I keep hoping we're going to find something that will help while there's time." He drew up one of the tall drafting stools that clustered around the tables. "I never thought it would be faster with her than me, and that's God's own truth."

Jeff could think of nothing to say. "I've run out of ways to tell everyone how sorry I am. I say the words and they don't seem to mean anything. But I *am* sorry. I really am."

"I know that, Jeff. If you weren't sorry, you wouldn't be here." He turned and busied himself collecting his equipment. "You want to roll up your sleeve for me?"

"Not really, but I'll do it anyway," said Jeff, trying to lighten the tone of their conversation.

"But you'll do it anyway, right?" Ace said, speaking with Jeff, readying his equipment. "It won't take more than a minute."

"Fine," said Jeff. He did as requested and rolled up his sleeve, staring at the ceiling while Ace drew blood quickly and efficiently. "How're things doing around here?"

"Mezza-mezza," said Ace as he prepared slides and test tubes. "It's those twins. They're so damned religious. They show up everywhere and pray. Trouble is, I think they're bright. That makes it hard to get through to them, because of the way they're trained. They've been given answers and they know how to argue. They'd be a credit to the Jesuits." He put labels on everything he had prepared. "They depress the other kids—let's face it, learning that you are the cause of people having TS would be hard to take if you were the best-adjusted adult on the planet. To be a teenager and have to come to terms with carrying TS, well, fuck it all to hell, Doc, they're having trouble with it."

"And the Barenssens make it worse?" Jeff asked while he rolled down his sleeve.

"Sure. All that guilt, guilt, guilt, and begging God to forgive them and show them how to be free of their guilt, guilt, guilt." He struck his chest lightly with his fist. "Funny thing is, in some ways they're doing better than the other kids. They've been through the hellfire-and-brimstone Fundamentalism that set them up for catastrophe. Strange boys, both of them. Axel and Adam. They say that they're responsible for their mother's death, and that had nothing to do with TS. They say they're the reason for their aunt's death. She died of TS, and they show that as proof positive." He set his specimens in their proper places. "This new test will show results in an hour or so, if we're on to anything."

"What are you looking for?"

Occasionally Ace took on the manner of a first-class lecturer, speaking as if to a large class of intelligent students instead of to a single colleague. "We're trying to identify the specific rate of breakdown, the course of non-absorption that would account—"

"I get the picture," said Jeff.

"Assuming we can isolate that factor, then we might be able to find a way to slow it down or stop it. That's not a cure, exactly, but it is an effective treatment." Ace indicated the covered specimens. "You'd be amazed how fast we can duplicate the TS damage here. We can duplicate complete blood chemistries and isolate all factors. We can do in a couple of hours what takes months to do in the body."

"It's that new equipment from Lucas Medical, is it?" Jeff asked.

"They're the most innovative people in the field," said Ace with genuine admiration. "When we find a cure for this, they should have at least half the credit, because of what their equipment has allowed us to do."

"Write them a letter," said Jeff. "I mean it. We need to give full credit where we can. There's enough of a morale problem without getting—"

"Tight-assed?" suggested Ace.

"Something like that," Jeff agreed. He was looking down at the blood samples. "Will you look at that." The specimen he indicated was showing visible signs of alteration. "How long ago did you draw blood on . . . whoever that is?"

"It's Loren Protheroe," said Ace softly. "I didn't draw it, but it was taken about five hours ago. We're going to have to transfer him to a hospital before long. He won't like it, and he'll probably fight it, but I don't think he's got more than two weeks before he'll need constant care."

"That's going to be hard on the kids," Jeff said. "Protheroe's been very important to them."

"Yeah, like their families," said Ace. "Don't tell me I'm out of line—I know that." He was about to go on, but looking up, he fell silent and motioned to Jeff to do the same. "Mason and Laurie. They're outside."

"Are they coming in?" Jeff asked.

"There's no reason to keep them out. Mason's been pretty helpful around here. Laurie hasn't been much interested until now. I think she's getting interested in Mason." The admit buzzer sounded and Ace looked around deliberately and waved.

"How long do they usually stay?" Jeff wanted to know.

"It varies. But this late at night, not much more than an hour or so. Mason's been coming in twice a day for the

entire week, following the testing. He's a bright kid, Jeff."
Ace buzzed the two teenagers through.

"Hi," Mason said to Ace, then held out his hand to Jeff.
"How are you, Doctor Taji?"

"Tired," Jeff said honestly.

Laurie Grey hung back; her years of dance made even
her uncertainty graceful. "Is it okay to be here?" she asked
Ace.

"Sure; it's fine," said Ace. "We were talking about these
new tests, and we were going over the blood samples. You
kids' specimens are here, at the left side of the rack. You
can see that the responses of your samples are different
than the others." He had lapsed into his lecturing mode
again; Jeff wondered if at the end of it, Ace would give a
quiz.

"Are you using anything to act against the TS?" Mason
asked, looking at the specimen racks through the clear
cover.

"No, we're using techniques to speed up the TS. We're
trying to establish the breakdown pattern in the blood. If
we can find a consistent pattern, then we can—"

"—think of something that will stop the breakdown,"
Mason finished for him, nodding his enthusiasm. "One of
us should have thought of that before." It was apparent
from the tone of his voice that the one he thought should
have done it was Mason himself.

Ace was not willing to let Mason indulge in self-recrimination. "It's just one of a series of tests, Mason. We can't
look for solutions in one place only. We haven't the time
for that. You remember last week we did those sedimenta-
tion tests, to analyze changes in blood and urine? That
might show us the way as much as this test."

"But this test is so *obvious*," Mason insisted.

"It's also very new equipment that did not exist until
four months ago. We couldn't have made the test even if
we'd thought of it. If hundreds of skilled technicians and
engineers as well as thousands of doctors didn't think of it

until now, why should you have?" Ace gestured to Laurie. "Do you want to see this?"

"I guess," she said, staring. It was apparent that the lab exercised a dreadful fascination over her. "It's so spooky, looking at blood like this. It's like it's alien, from outer space."

"That might make our problem easier," said Jeff. "Then we wouldn't have to treat people, just blood." He turned to Mason. "How's it going?"

"It's okay. I talked to Dad yesterday. He's going to the hospital in a couple of days." His face paled but he remained resolutely calm.

"That's too bad," said Jeff sincerely, thinking he ought to call Harper Ross before that happened.

"I wrote to Mom, but I haven't had an answer from her. I tried to talk to Grant, but he hung up on me." Mason turned away from Jeff, his eyes hurt and distant.

"Mason?" Laurie asked.

"I'm okay," he insisted, choking the words out. "I'm okay."

She moved a few steps closer to him. "Your Mom'll come around, you'll see."

"Un-huh," he said vaguely.

"You kids want to stick around, or do you need some time alone?" Ace was able to make this sound like an unimportant question, no more significant than whether they would have honey or marmalade on their toast.

"I want to stay here," Mason said quickly and firmly. "If I sit by myself doing nothing, I'll . . ."

Jeff patted him on the shoulder, realizing that Mason had got taller in the last two months. "I know how you feel," he said. "Every time I think I'm too worn out to go on, I think of how I'd feel if I *didn't* go on."

Ace shook his head. "That's not always smart. You work too hard, you get too close to the problem, you lose perspective." He got back on his drafting stool. "You need a balance, Mason. You too, Jeff."

"It's not easy," said Mason. He gave his attention to the

blood samples. "Have you found out what makes ours different yet?"

"You mean beyond the DNA modification?" Ace began. "We're reasonably sure that the mutation was triggered externally, which is why your case is still part of the Environmental Division and not with the big boys at the main Disease Control Center. We've also determined that the exposure happened *in utero*, as we first suspected. That in part accounts for the closeness of your ages. Whatever carried the modifier was available only for a limited time." Ace did his best to include Laurie in his impromptu lecture, though he found most of his response was coming from Mason.

"Do you think you'll find out what caused it?" Laurie asked, her mesmerized gaze on the specimen racks.

"If we knew what to look for, perhaps," said Jeff. "That's part of what we're working on, but realistically, unless we're incredibly lucky, we may never know. We have established that your parents were not in the same place at any time during your mothers' pregnancies. As far as we have been able to determine, your parents did not have any common links at that time, aside from the fact that they were all west of the Rockies. That isn't enough." He indicated the machines around them. "We're hoping all these guys will give us a clue."

"And if they don't?" Mason challenged.

"Then we'll do our best to find a cure without knowing the cause. The cure is what matters in any case; it would be helpful to know the cause in terms of prevention of similar outbreaks." As soon as he said it, he could see that the two kids were upset at the idea.

"There could be another outbreak of TS?" Laurie demanded, her voice suddenly so high it was almost a squeak.

"Yes. We have to be prepared to deal with that. Or there might be something else."

"Who'd want to give a disease like this?" Laurie persisted.

"People who don't care," said Mason, his young face harsh now, his eyes filled with anger and betrayal.

All four of them were silent; the hiss and hum of equipment, the soft clicks from monitors and clocks were suddenly very loud in the laboratory. In the adjoining room, someone started to whistle.

"Doesn't it make you frustrated?" Laurie asked Ace.

"Sure as hell does," said Ace amiably. "But I can't let a little thing like frustration stop me. We'd all be hanging around caves and eating grubs if we let frustration stop us."

"And the people who did this? What about them?" Mason accused them all with his question. "Are you going to let them get away with it?"

"First things first," said Jeff, hearing a second whistler in the next room. "We have a disease to stop, and then we can go looking for the people who might be behind it."

"Might be?" Mason said, clearly not convinced.

"Yes, might be," said Jeff. "We can't rule out accident, or a freak combination of . . . oh, toxins or contaminants, that resulted in the change in your DNA." He looked toward Ace. "Or have you been able to rule that out?"

"Not yet," Ace admitted. "It's a long shot, but not impossible."

"But how come us? Why did it happen to us?" Laurie wailed.

"We don't know," said Ace. "It was an accident. Your parents didn't set out to change your DNA and you didn't select the DNA that brought this about. It was an accident."

"I want it over with," said Mason. "Before everyone I ever knew is dead." These last few words were desolate.

Ace put his hand on the cover that protected the table where the specimen racks stood. "We're doing our best."

The wiles inthe other room had attempted a duet which had failed and now they were laughing together. One of them was doing his best to find a new melody, but the tune was interrupted by chuckles.

"What do you think you'll get out of this?" Laurie

asked, clearly trying to move their conversation onto safer ground.

"Another piece of the puzzle," said Ace. "Most scientific breakthroughs aren't sudden dramatic changes, but the result of hours and hours and hours of painstaking analysis of detail. The first part of that analysis is trying to determine the parameters of the problem, because until you do that, you can't tell what is and isn't part of the puzzle."

"My dad had one of those puzzles," Mason said, making an effort to contain his anger. "You know the kind? It was round and all red and it took forever to put it together. You're talking about something like that, aren't you?"

"Yes," said Ace. "But in this case, you can't be sure that if something is red it's part of the puzzle, or that all the pieces of the puzzle are in the box. It's a good analogy, Mason."

"Thanks," he muttered.

Laurie had been staring at the blood specimens. "What does it mean when it changes color like that?"

"It means that TS is present," said Ace, deliberately emotionless.

"Look how many," she said softly.

"Too many," said Mason, his eyes accusing both Ace and Jeff of terrible acts.

"And these?" Laurie pointed to those belonging to the carriers. "They're ours?"

"Yes," said Ace.

"What about this one?" she asked, indicating Jeff's blood specimen.

"That's mine," said Jeff. "Just taken."

"But it doesn't look like the others," said Laurie. "It looks like . . . just blood."

"That's because it hasn't had time to change yet," said Jeff, wondering how great his risk was. He had been expecting to find TS in his blood for the last two months.

"Give it time," said Ace. "It'll take a while before you can see what's going on."

"If all these other specimens have changed this way,"

said Laurie, puzzled and distant, "does that mean that they all have TS?"

Ace sneaked a look at Jeff before he answered, "It means that TS is present, yes. The disease might not be active, but it is present."

In a very small voice she said, "Oh."

"If it doesn't change, what would that mean?" Mason asked, some of his outrage lessened by curiosity.

"I don't really know," said Jeff. "Resistance, probably."

"What about immunity?" asked Mason. "Aren't there some people who're supposed to be immune to TS?"

"There are a few," said Jeff cautiously. "We don't know why they're immune, or if the immunity will last, but they do exist. Now that we have the equipment we can study blood factor by factor, until we find the answer." He could hear the sound of conversation in the next room but was unable to make out the words or the sense.

"What if the immunity lasts? What about that?" Mason pursued, his attention more fully engaged.

"Then we'll do our best to find out everything we can about the immunity and see if there's a way to duplicate the conditions or the factors present in the blood that results in the immunity." Jeff glanced at Ace. "Immunity might give us a clue to a cure. It would also give us . . . hope."

"Then why aren't you studying more immune people?" Laurie demanded.

"Because we have only four people who tested immune to TS who've signed Public Benefit contracts. It's a lot trickier to get the court to approve those contracts when the person isn't in immediate physical peril. Some judges won't permit altruistic Public Benefit contracts, because they believe it isn't within the purview of the courts to do so. There are families who have sued for wrongful death and won settlements because Public Benefit contracts were signed by men and women who were not at physical risk until they undertook the terms of the contracts."

"That doesn't make a lot of sense," said Laurie. "If they

want to help out and they can help out, why aren't they allowed to?"

Jeff pulled up a standard office chair—unlike Ace he was not comfortable on the tall drafting stools—and sat down, looking squarely at the two kids. "Ten years ago, there was no Public Benefit contract at all. There were plenty of people out there, physically ill and willing to do anything that might advance the understanding of their disease and give them a chance, no matter how slim, at recovery. The courts then would not permit it because it was seen as part of the 'cruel and inhuman punishment' prohibitions, and as worse than laboratory use of animals for experimentation. That prevailed until the AIDS crisis, because AIDS was so very deadly, and there were so few ways to slow it down. If the courts had not approved the Public Benefit contract—and the Standard Public School Blood Screen—AIDS might still be killing people everywhere."

"Why would anybody object to those things?" Laurie asked, more baffled than ever.

"For many reasons, but I've told you what the usual legal reasons were." He looked over at Ace. "And without the Public Benefit contract, most of the staff would not be allowed to work here."

"Yeah," said Ace. "To work here you have to test positive for TS. The only exceptions are people like Jeff Taji there, who had to sign an exemption agreement with the Disease Control Center when he went to work, holding them blameless if anything happened to him because of his occupation. Right?" This last was directed to Jeff with a large smile.

"Right," said Jeff wearily.

Ace got off his stool. "I need a cup of coffee. Any of you like one? Or an orange juice?"

Both Jeff and Mason opted for coffee; Laurie wanted the orange juice.

"I'll come with you," Mason volunteered. "I'll help carry things."

"Good idea," said Ace, patting Mason's shoulder with a dinner plate-sized hand as they went into the long hall that ran the length of the floor.

"I heard my Dad's in the hospital," said Laurie after more than three minutes of silence.

"That's too bad." Jeff did not know how to draw her out and knew better than to force her to speak.

"I guess it would have happened anyway, but I feel like I did it to him. I mean, the way TS is all over the place, it doesn't matter that I carry it, does it? It would be in San Diego whether I had it or not, wouldn't it?" She was pleading with him, though she sounded as if she were giving a report in class. "I didn't make him sick, did I?"

"No," said Jeff; his uncertainty must have shown more than he thought, for she started to cry.

"It *is* my fault." She continued weeping, though with hardly any sobs.

"It's the fault of TS, certainly, but it is not your fault that you are a carrier." Jeff thought of his own children in their European haven with their aunt. "It's hard to accept that these things can happen, especially if they happen to you."

"Adam Barenssen said we're the instruments of God's vengeance against the sins of the world." She wiped her face. "I told him he's wrong, but sometimes . . ."

"Sometimes it gets to you, and you're afraid that he could be right?" Jeff guessed, recalling the reports he had read on the Barenssen twins and their relentless insistence on the religious purpose of TS.

She nodded. "I hate it."

"Small wonder," said Jeff, not caring what *it* she reerre toI told Adam not to talk to me any more, but he still does, and so does Axel." She folded her arms, looking very young. "They said it wasn't safe to be around the horses because we'd make them sick, too."

Jeff shook his head. "It doesn't work that way. So far as we know no animal except laboratory mice and hamsters has got TS, and they were made to get it. You can spend all the time you like with the horses and they'll be fine." Privately, he hoped this turned out to be true. Blood tests on the horses, dogs and cats at the Control Facility had yet to reveal any trace of the disease, but the tests continued, and would continue for some time to come.

"I couldn't stand it if dogs and horses got sick, too."

"I know, Laurie; I know," said Jeff, miserably aware of how little consolation he could offer her.

Ace and Mason came back with large containers of coffee—one orange juice—and Mason announced, "Ace said I can stay here as long as I want tonight and help him. He'll show me how they get all the specimens ready and what they look for. Maybe I can help you guys find a cure, after all."

"That sounds very interesting," said Jeff, giving Laurie an encouraging half-smile.

"Yeah," said Mason with determination. "We're starting with the covered racks—including *your* specimen, Doctor Taji."

"You let me know what you find out," Jeff said as he took the styrofoam cup the boy held out.

"I'm going to learn how to write up the reports, too. If I can do that I'll be—" He stopped himself and would not go on.

"Tell you what, Mason," said Jeff as if he had not noticed the way he had broken off his words, "you do the paperwork on my specimen and show it to me at breakfast, okay? We can talk about it then." He got up. "In the meantime, I have some paperwork of my own to do, and I'm tired. You night owls can keep going until four in the morning, if you want. I'm going to bed." Taking his coffee with him, he left Ace and the two kids in the lab, and in an hour he drifted into sleep with papers spread around him.

He was awakened at ten minutes to seven.

"Doctor Taji, this is Mason Ross. I think you better get up to the lab right away." The boy's voice was husky with fatigue, but his excitement and concern overrode his exhaustion.

"Mason?" Jeff said, shaking his head and rubbing his eyes. "What's the matter?"

"Your blood specimen? The one Ace took last night?" His voice cracked with excitement.

"I remember," Jeff said with cold dread in his chest.

"It didn't change. All night long it didn't change."

Dale Reed and Irene Channing

Her first impression was of the musty smell of the room. Irene looked around the cabin and turned to Dale. "When were you up here last?"

"Four weeks ago, but only for the night." He dropped the suitcases by the worn and stained leather couch. "I told you it wasn't fancy."

"And you sure didn't exaggerate," she said, trying to make a joke of it. "Mice in the kitchen, too, no doubt."

"Probably. And 'possums in the woodshed." He suddenly doubted his decision to bring her here. "If you'd rather go back to the hospitl, Il al Galen Simeon and make arrangements."

"Hell, no," said Irene in rallying tones. "You should have seen the place I had in Winnemucca, right around the time Steven was born. That was after Tim moved out and went to Arizona. I had this three-room shack and . . ." Her eyes grew distant and she made an effort to put those memories behind her. "Thank goodness that's over."

Dale accepted this with reservations. "How long did you live there? Isn't it—"

"—out in the middle of nowhere? Pretty much. I lived there until I came to my senses and realized that no matter how good my work was, no one was going to give a damn in that part of Nevada; or no one who could help me. No one was going to truck out to Winnemucca and search for a painter. And no one in Winnemucca had the contacts that might find an outlet for my work. I don't mean that quite the way it sounds. Nevada can be beautiful in a stark way, and for a time it was exactly what I wanted to paint, that clean, honed landscape with its shadows and rocks equally hard-edged. There were actually a couple of Indians there who liked everything I did. They had very keen eyes, though not educated." She stopped. "I'm sorry, Dale, I'm rattling along like . . . like nothing sensible."

"You're nervous," he said, reaching to close the door.

"Yes," she admitted. "It's silly. I can't understand why I should be so nervous. I'm not a convent-raised virgin. I'm not naive. But I don't know what's happening. You'd think I reverted to age sixteen." Deliberately she took the time to study the main room of the cabin. "Does the fireplace work?"

"The chimney was cleaned in February," said Dale. "I haven't had it checked since. If there aren't critters living in there, I suppose it's fine."

Her skin paled. "If there's a chance that you've got something living in it, then let's not use it. I don't want to hurt anything."

"I'll have a look later. But do you want a fire? It's summer, for God's sake. You said you were roasting in the car." He was as keyed-up as she was, though he did his best to conceal this.

"Later, it might be nice. If it's not too hot at night." She had brushed off the seat of the leather couch and now she sank onto it. "If you've got some Murphy's I'll clean this up for you," she offered.

"It could use a good cleaning. I think there's an old tub of Murphy's in the kitchen somewhere. You don't have to do it if you don't want to."

"I *do* want to, that's why I brought it up," she said with a touch of irritation. "This couch might be old, but it's very well made and it needs care. A couple hours of washing and buffing would be . . . fun."

"If you're sure you're up to it, we can think about it. And I'll see if we've still got some Murphy's."

"We can get some in town," she said without thinking, then looked over at him. "I'm sorry, Dale. I didn't mean that. If we have to get something, I'll let you arrange it."

"Thanks," he said, a trifle stiffly. "I don't want you being hounded any more. That's why we're here, remember? I want you to be able to work and get . . . control of this thing you do." By the time he finished talking, he was on the couch beside her. "I've arranged to have messages left at a general store at the lake. They do message holdings and act a little like a private post office."

She let her head drop onto his shoulder. "Do you think it's safe? Really? Do you think they won't find us?"

"Oh, they might," said Dale, his lips brushing her forehead. "But we're a low priority for a while. They have their hands full with TS."

"What about you?" she asked gently. "You have patients and they need you. You can't walk away from them. TS is all over now, and you're still healthy. Aren't you?"

"Healthy?" He looked over her head, his eyes fixed on some point beyond the shuttered window. "So far."

For a little while she said nothing. "How have your tests been?"

"We can talk about that later, when I've had the most recent results." He took her hand and kissed it. "We'll worry about this when and if we have to. Okay?"

"Okay," she said.

He moved his hand through her hair, loving the texture of it, the way it slid through his fingers. "I've got to unpack the car."

"I'll help," she said, not moving.

Reluctantly he moved away from her. "No, you stay here. I'll take care of it."

"Dale, don't wrap me up in cotton batting. I was going nuts in that hospital because everyone tried to keep me from doing things other than the prescribed exercises and the reflex tests. They wanted to get more on the PK, not on me or my work." She rose from the sofa. "I don't know what to say. I don't know how to describe to you the way this made me feel. I can't think about the life I've had to lead. If I do, I'll throw myself in front of a train, I swear I will." Her hands were up at her face and she moved away from him. "If you turn me into a freak, I won't have anything left."

"You have your kids," he reminded her desperately.

"One of them is off outside of Atlanta somewhere, and I won't get to see him again for a long time. The other is with relatives and . . . poor Brice." She closed her eyes and struggled to bring her turbulent emotions under control.

An old glass ashtray in the shape of a cuspidor rattled to the edge of the endtable and smashed, shattering, onto the floor.

Dale stared at the wreckage. "Irene, calm down, will you?" The words were low and steady, though the muscles of his face were tight.

"I didn't mean . . ." she faltered. "I truly didn't, Dale." When she looked at him, there was shock and supplication in her eyes.

"I know, love." He moved slowly toward her and put his arm around her shoulder. "It's been a long, tough haul and you're entitled to a few rough times. Don't worry about it. I'll clean it up."

"Let me," she said quietly. "I broke it."

He looked at the shards of glass. "Maybe we'd better do it together. It could be quite a job."

"Let me sweep it up, first," she pleaded. "Then we can damp-mop or whatever needs to be done."

"Fine," he said woodenly. "I'll get you the broom."

While she swept, her expression a fixed one of single-minded determination, he brought in the rest of their baggage and supplies from the car. He took time to put the perishable groceries in the little refrigerator, silently praying that the ancient machine would continue to work for a

little while longer. When he had done that chore, he prepared the mop and carried it and the bucket into the front
room where he found Irene sitting on the couch again,
staring at the floor.

"I think I got as much as . . ." She let her words fade.
"Dale, I'm so sorry I did that. I tried not to, please believe
me."

"I believe you," he said, putting his hand on her
shoulder. "You watch while I take care of this." He was not
deft with household equipment, but for the next quarter
hour he did his best with the damp mop. For the most part
he managed well, though he did succeed in cutting his
thumb while being careless in wringing out the mop: he
found a prescription bottle for the latest analgesic in her
purse and took two.

"You did a great job," said Irene as she helped to ban-
dage the cut.

"Thanks," Dale said as he watched her, flattered and
exasperated by what had happened. He let his gaze drift
around the kitchen, noticing for the first time how small it
was, and how there was a persistent odor of slightly sour
milk in the room. It shamed him to think that he had
brought Irene here with so little preparation for what the
place was like, but he had been desperate to get her out of
the hospital and away from Douglas Kiley. Now that he
had the leisure to examine their predicament he was not at
all convinced that this cabin was the safest place he might
have chosen.

"What's the matter?" She was still holding his hand, but
now her eyes were focused on his face, caught by the remote intensity there.

"I'm worried." He knew that it was useless to fib about
it. "I can't help thinking that one of those ESA agents will
knock at the back door and oh-so-politely inform me that
they need your skills to study as part of their job, and that
once you're gone, I'll never be able to find you again."

Her smile trembled. "You're so dear. Don't fret about
me, Dale. If they caught me, I wouldn't let them keep me.

I'm getting good enough that I could probably get out of any place they tried to hold me. Besides, now that the news media are investigating TS, it's only a matter of time before they find the other survivors. It'll all be out in the open soon, no matter what anybody does. There've been too many victims of TS for the media to ignore it any more." She reached out for one of the old-fashioned straight-backed chairs and sat him down in it. "In a couple of weeks, we can go back to Dallas if we want. No one will touch us then."

"Okay," he said doubtfully. "In the meantime, what about dinner?"

"You mean you dragged me all the way out into this wilderness just to find out if I could *cook*?" Her mock indignation coaxed a smile from him.

"It's as good a time as any." The pain of the cut had subsided so that it no longer lanced up to his elbow every time he moved his hand. "I'm out of service for tonight."

"Convenient," she said with a shake of her head.

"Actually," he said, "I had planned to do the cooking, at least for a while. So that you could start painting again. I've missed seeing your work."

"I've missed workin,"h countered. "Where do you keep the pots and pans, and what are we going to have to eat?" With her hands on her hips and her hair tied back with a scarf, she looked like an advertiser's idea of a woman roughing it; Dale could not help grinning at her. "And what's that all about?"

"Nothing. The pots are in that bin beside the sink. You pull out the top so it can tip open. The pans are in the deep drawer at the end of the counter. There's also a teakettle and a coffeepot, if you're interested." He could feel the painkiller she had given him take effect, making him feel muzzy, so that it seemed he was watching the room from the wrong end of a telescope, turning everything distant and small.

"Are you doing all right?" she asked as she opened the bin.

"Yeah," he said abstractedly. "I was thinking of something, that's all."

"Thinking of what?" she asked.

"That it's good to have you here." It was not the truth but it was far from a lie. "I think I'm going to need a nap."

"Let's wait dinner, then," she said at once, glad to have the opportunity to abandon her attempts in this unfamiliar kitchen. "How about three hours? You brought an alarm clock, didn't you? We can set it for seven and be having dinner by eight. Very fashionable hour, once upon a time."

His thoughts were jumbled; he felt disoriented as he got to his feet. "You're probably right," he said as he strove to keep his balance. "Jeez, what's in those pills?"

"They're the ones Simeon gave me, for after my physical therapy, so that I could sleep without having trouble with muscle aches." She tugged at his good arm. "Come on, tell me where the stairs are."

"Over in the corner of the main room, that door beside the chimney." He permitted himself to be led, all the while thinking that he ought to do a better job of taking charge.

As she opened the door, Irene made a face and waved a hand at the dust that billowed out. "What a place this is."

"I probably should have had someone in to clean it, but I didn't want anyone to know I'd be here." He could hear the way he sounded—sleepy, half-drunk. As he walked, his steps were uncertain. "How much of this stuff . . . did they give you . . . in the . . ."

She had managed to get him up the first four steps. "In the hospital?" she guessed when he trailed off.

"Yep," he said with a silly smile. "What is it?"

"I forget the name. Simeon prescribed it." She watched him in growing alarm, her curiosity fading into apprehension. "Dale, are you okay?"

"Yep," he said, refusing to climb any further. "Lemme siddown."

"No, you're going to bed," she said with determination, trying to raise him.

"Y'r not so hot. Wi' wha' I seen . . ." He waggled a

finger at her, his silly smile beaming at her from where he had slumped on the stairs.

"Dale, Dale, *please*," she insisted, pulling on his arm again. Then, knowing the difference it had made with her, she reached out and deliberately pressed his bandaged thumb.

"*Fuckaduck*!" he roared, bolting upright. "You *bitch*! You sadistic—" He lurched several steps after her, his eyes no longer in focus, and the swipes he made to catch her went wild as he strove to keep his balance.

She was trying to choose which room to put him in when he caught up with her, pinning her to the wall, her face pressed to the wood, his weight all but collapsing on her shoulders. "Dale, don't," she protested.

"You c'n move me," he taunted. "You c'n move me if y'want." He shoved his weight against her back, chuckling at the idea. "Go 'head. Move me."

"Dale, get back. You're hurting me." Little as she wanted to admit it, she was starting to be frightened.

"Y'hurt me." He gave a strange sound and dropped abruptly to his knees. "Shit, it hurts."

She turned, frightened but determined not to let it show. "What? your hand?"

"No." He panted for several seconds. "My head. Christ!"

"Dale!" She knelt beside him, her fright now far more for him than for herself. "Dale, what is it?"

He held his head between his hands, pressing at the temples. "God. God. God. Oh, shit." The words came out in gasps, all but senseless.

She took hold of his wrists. "Dale, what is it? Dale!"

He turned his blurred, bloodshot eyes on her, and there was a hint of lucidity in them. "Honest-to-God, I love you, Irene. And you scare bejesus out of me." With that, he fell on his side, already in deep, troubled sleep.

Irene sat watching him, undecided about what to do. She knew it was probably safe enough to leave him where he was. Out of habit and the need to do something, she got up and went into the nearest bedroom. Here there were three pillows in plastic bags and a stack of blankets, also in bags to protect them from mice and moths. She chose the top one arbitrarily and took it to Dale to cover him. Her hands shook as she saw him writhe and mumble fragments of words, clearly in the grip of a nightmare. What kind of drug had she been given? It killed pain, but what else did it do?

When Dale woke up the next morning, he was silent, depressed and chagrined. "Whatever I told you," he said when he was able to broach the subject, "pay no attention. I didn't . . . I didn't know what I was saying."

"Then you remember what you said?" Irene asked, doing her best to keep the question curious and light.

"No," he admitted. "Not really. I can remember speaking—shouting—but I can't recall what I said."

"Don't worry." She handed him a cup of coffee and sat down opposite him at the kitchen table.

"Did I sleep on the floor all night?" he asked a little later.

"I couldn't get you into bed," she said, which was the truth as far as it went. She did not mention the nightmares that had plagued him until the early hours of the morning, nor did she tell him what he had cried out during the worst of them.

"I'm . . . I apologize, Irene. I . . . I never thought that it would turn out this way." He had drunk half the coffee but could not yet force any more down.

"Dale," she ventured when she finally got up to fry eggs for them, "what's in those pills? They're supposed to be painkillers with a muscle relaxant, at least that was what I was told."

"Galen Simeon said that was what he had been prescribing. According to the records, you were getting a standard drug. I've taken it myself and never had anything like this happen before." He stared up at the ceiling. "When we left, they didn't . . . Where did you get your supply? Did you go down to the dispensary?"

"Didn't you?" she asked, mildly shocked.

He shook his head. "Tell me."

"One of the nurses brought my things to me, and said that there was a supply of my prescriptions, with dosages and uses on the labels. I . . . I thought that you had arranged for it." She did not like the suspicions that were growing in her mind.

"No," he said, his eyes on his coffee cup while she worked on breakfast. "Did you have any nightmares while you were there? That you can remember?"

"Not that I can remember. Doctor Simeon said that all things considered, I was doing pretty well that way. He told me that there were some odd brain-wave patterns during sleep, but no serious disruption." She was putting a doublept ofbuter into the warm skillet. "Up or over?"

"Huh?" He glanced her way. "Oh. Up and basted, please."

"You got it." As she cracked eggs, she said, "Is there any way we can find out what that stuff is?"

"Sure," he said dubiously.

She heard the uncertainty in his voice. "What's the matter?"

"Nothing," he said without conviction, and relented almost at once. "If I take them to be analyzed, we might be traced. How much of that stuff can be floating around out there?"

"Not much, I hope," she said. "And so where does that leave us?"

He shook his head and fell silent, remaining that way until he had mopped up the last of his egg yolks with a sliver of toast. "It's risky," he said in the quiet.

"What's risky?" She was startled to hear him speak.

"I'm going to the general store and make a couple of calls, one to Simeon." He was feeling more himself now that he had been able to eat.

"Are you sure that's wise?" she asked, very cautious now.

"I've got to know what did this. It was bad enough for

me, but what might have happened to you if you'd taken one? Have you thought about that at all?" He banged on the table with his fist out of the urgency consuming him.

"Yes," she said in an undervoice. "I thought about it a lot last night."

"So have I, this morning." He finished his second cup of coffee. "There are questions I have to have answered before we get in any deeper. Which is why I am also going to call Jeff Taji in Atlanta, or wherever-the-hell he is, and see if he can find out what's going on."

Irene looked up at him, some of the color fading from her face. "No, Dale, please don't."

"We can trust him. Christ, we have to trust someone. We can't take on Douglas Kiley and all the ESA by ourselves. We have to get some help."

"How do you know Taji will help you?" She made the question hard and accusing.

"I don't. But if we don't get help, we might as well go back to Dallas right now and wait for the Feds to show up and take over. Do you want to do that?" The tenderness had come back into his eyes; he reached out and ran his fingers along her jaw to her chin. "Irene?"

"No," she sighed.

"What else can we do?" He asked it openly, without guile.

She shrugged, then got up and began to stack the dishes.

PART VII

June–August, 1996

Commander Maurice Tolliver _____ *and Patrick Drucker* _____

In the sultry afternoon the clouds hung, waiting, growling from time to time with impatience and menace. All of the South was in the grip of this oncoming storm, and Atlanta had taken on a wan greenish tinge as the weather clotted in.

"I hope I'm not an inconvenience," Commander Tolliver said as he and Patrick Drucker entered the conference room adjoining Drucker's office.

"Of course not," Drucker said, taking great satisfaction in having an officer defer to him. "We're all up against the same problem, aren't we, Commander?"

Tolliver gave a single slow nod. "In some ways I must agree."

Drucker was adept at nuances and sensed that Commander Tolliver had a criticism to offer. "Take a seat, Commander, and tell me what my Division can do for you." He thought that the proprietary *my* was a nice touch, one that reinforced his authority without being too obvious about it.

Tolliver gave Drucker his smoothest slight smile. "Oh, I think we can put this in the realm of joint projects, Doctor." He sat so that nothing disturbed the perfect, sharp creases in his uniform trousers. Everything about him was impeccable, which roused both envy and admiration in Drucker, who often suffered in humid weather.

"What's the nature of the project?" Drucker inquired as he sat at the head of the table.

"It's related to the TS carriers you have and some of the

patients we've been seeing," said Tolliver, letting the words roll out of him easily, as if this were polite after-dinner conversation.

"And what about these patients?" Drucker asked, trying to achieve the same ease, but botching it so that he sounded as if he were trying to sell questionable stocks.

"You're interested in them; we're interested in your project here." He did his smooth smile again. "It could well be a matter of national security."

"You mean that some of your research might be involved," Drucker corrected the Commander.

"We haven't acknowledged that, and we are not convinced that it is an applicable consideration."

"Meaning?" said Drucker, growing restive.

"It is possible, of course, that whatever triggered the outbreaks of TS could be remotely associated with some research that was carried on about ten to fifteen years ago, having to do with . . . well, with extrasensory perception. There was reason to think it might have a genetic component and there were efforts made in various places to determine if this was the case." He put his hands, palms down, on the table. "I'm sure that our interests are sufficiently in accord that we can work out agreeable terms that . . . shall we say, prove satisfactory to all parties?"

"What sort of terms are you suggesting?" asked Drucker with suspicion.

"There are variables which enter into it, of course," Tolliver went on as if he was not aware of the interruption. "You have your obligations as we have ours."

"What are you proposing?" Drucker asked forcefully.

"I am proposing that we exchange information, some of it crucial, some of it pro forma. And that we establish certain areas that could be described as isolated, as those six children are isolated. I can supply the address of the facility where they live, if you like." This last offer was said nonchalantly; it was the wrong tack to take with Drucker.

"You're trying to blackmail this Division," he said

bluntly. "You want us to do your dirty work for you, and you're selling your own brand of snake oil."

"I'm proposing a joint exploration," Tolliver said with a little more force than before.

"You're trying to take over our work on TS, aren't you?" Drucker resented Tolliver's polish as much as he resented the intrusion on what he saw as his territory. "It's not going to work, Commander. Not you or any other branch of the military is going to get their smarmy hands on TS."

"You're misinterpreting my remarks," said Tolliver with the same delivery he used for testifying before Congressional committees. "We have no intention of—"

"Bullshit," Drucker shot back. "You're trying to cover up something. It's like that nerve gas and the sheep, twenty years ago. It's like that radioactive site you kept claiming didn't exist in Ohio. It's the same damned thing, only now you're trying to get out of TS."

"We want to keep the public informed and to offer treatment, of course, but this disease has certain characteristics that make it . . . different than others that have developed in the last century." Tolliver concealed his aggravation with skill. "You are determined to find a cure for it as soon as possible, as was done with AIDS. That is correct, isn't it?" He deliberately controlled the length of the silence.

"Naturally," Drucker said, worried that the admission might strengthen Tolliver's position in some way Drucker did not yet understand.

"Our goals are not so different as yours. We want to see the disease cured." He paused again. "Cured, but not wiped out."

Drucker's face suffused with color. "What!" he demanded, coming half out of his chair.

"We want to lend you all our assistance in finding a cure, a treatment, but . . . there are a number of reasons we would encourage you to look for a treatment and turn your efforts to a vaccine later." He cleared his throat delicately. "Doctor Drucker, you don't appreciate the particular side effects of this disease."

"And I'm not likely to as long as you and your lackeys in uniform keep making off with the survivors. We have a motion in to the White House. President Hunter has already said that he plans to enforce our request that you release all the survivors you have in your keeping. We need to examine them and—"

"Ah, yes," Tolliver said, meeting Drucker's eyes squarely. "That famous motion of yours. We have reviewed it and we have made a counterproposal. You might say that's the reason I'm here, Doctor Drucker."

Patrick Drucker was by nature a guarded man. He often looked for the barb in the compliment or the challenge in the question, leading to his reputation for being abrasive and something of a martinet. Now he gave free rein to his suspicions with a single contemptuous word: "Crap."

"You haven't heard me out, Doctor Drucker," Tolliver said at his most unruffled.

"I don't need to hear you out, buster. You're like all those other buzzards in uniform who think the population of this country is there for testing your kill theories, and that the NCDC is a branch of your 'nonexistent' biological warfare department. Well, this time you're going to have to go find someone else to roll over for you. The Environmental Division isn't going to play your game, Commander." He had kept himself from shouting, but his voice was loud enough to bring his secretary to the door.

"Is anything wrong, Doctor Drucker?"

"No, Claire. Thanks. Leave us alone and be sure we're not disturbed." He waved her away and turned on Commander Tolliver once again. "You came to the wrong place, Commander, and I am going to see that you bear the full responsibility for what you have suggested we do for you."

Tolliver drew a long breath. "As I recall, I didn't have the opportunity to suggest much of anything; certainly not anything that would have weight with those . . . outside of this room."

The confidence of his opponent unnerved Drucker, and

he tried to cover this with anger. "You suggested that we treat TS rather than develop a vaccine."

"So would most advisors in a situation like this one. TS has too high a fatality to provide enough time to do vaccine studies. From what I've heard, the most promising work is in synthesizing a blood factor that will function like the genosubtype-h in those with type O."

"How the fuck did you learn about that?" This time Drucker got to his feet; he leaned forward, his hands splayed on the table, taking the weight of his upper body. "Who told you?"

Tolliver countered with an expression of wounded honor. "It wasn't supposed to be a secret, was it, Doctor Drucker?"

"It wasn't supposed to be general knowledge, either," he declared. "How did you find out about it?"

"We requested information at the active level," Tolliver said. "Both those of us in the military and the Executive Security Agency have made such requests."

"You mean you've been bribing nurses and lab assistants," Drucker said heavily. "We developed the information less than a week ago. If we weren't so short-handed, I'd fire every single person in this Division who spoke to anyone in the military or security services." He sat down once more, still breathing a little heavily. "You've abused your authority, Commander Tolliver. I'm going to inform President Hunter of it. And the leaders of the Republican Party, as well. This *is* an election year."

Tolliver made himself laugh though he would much rather have struck Drucker across the face. "It cuts both ways, Doctor. If you want to play political hardball, you'd best remember that once you're in there's no way to get out." He pressed his hands together. "If you come to your senses, you can reach me at the number on my card at any time of the day or night. We can still work out a program that will be mutually beneficial to you and to us, and will also afford a high level of public safety."

"So long as all the survivors are put into your tender care," Drucker finished for Tolliver.

"Those who survive develop certain valuable talents," said Tolliver. "You're aware of the skills they've shown. What they can do is of enormous benefit to the security of this country, and for most of those survivors, a protected life is welcomed."

"You mean," said Drucker, using his phrases to batter at the imperturbable Tolliver, "that you want to isolate them so that you can control how they develop and use their psychokinesis. You want to be in charge of that. When you hide behind the smokescreen of national security, what you are doing is turning these people into weapons."

"Doctor Drucker, in their position, what would you do?" He had not lost his gloss; if anything, it was brighter now, like the shine on a razor's edge.

"I'd want to make up my own mind, not have you ghouls do it for me." He pushed the intercom button. "Claire. Have Ms. Ling join us here." It was his habit to speak of Susannah Ling as if she was his inferior and not his boss.

"Right, Doctor Drucker," said Claire Lui.

"It won't change anything, having Ms. Ling present," said Tolliver, his manner now faintly condescending.

"Then you won't mind if she listens in," Drucker said. "I think it's time that we had this out in the open."

Tolliver was about to speak when a flash of lightning caused the lights in the room to dim for an instant; less than two seconds later thunder drummed.

"Your plane might be delayed," Drucker pointed out to Tolliver, taking petty pleasure in seeing Tolliver thrown off his stride.

"A storm like this won't last long," Tolliver stated. "What I had intended to say was that you haven't had much time to give my proposal any serious thought. You're being impetuous"—inwardly he decided that few words could apply less to Patrick Drucker—"in your decisions, Doctor Drucker. I would be very disappointed if you had to change your mind after the machinery had been set in motion. Why don't you take a day or two to review what I've said before you—"

"Why don't you jump off the roof?" Drucker suggested. "I won't have you manipulating this Division. That's all there is to it." For the last five years he had regarded the Environmental Division as his personal fiefdom and he resented any attempt to alter that. "You will not be allowed to abuse our work in any way. Is that clear?"

"You're overreacting, Doctor Drucker," said Tolliver.

"Is that clear?" Drucker demanded so loudly that the discreet knock on the door went unnoticed.

"What's the trouble here?" Susannah Ling asked as she entered the room. "Who is the . . . Commander, Patrick?"

Commander Tolliver had stood out of habit when Susannah came in. He watched her narrowly, for he had read enough about her to know that her attractive facade and soft Southern accent were deceptive. "Ms. Ling," he said as he extended his hand. "I'm Commander Maurice Tolliver."

She shook hands with him and sat down, then regarded Drucker with veiled impatience. "Well, Patrick? What was so urgent?"

"He knows about the O-subtype-h experiments," Drucker blurted.

Susannah remained unflustered, but privately she was shocked. "How did you manage that, Commander?"

"We conduct our investigations, too, Ms. Ling." Tolliver said, dealing with her more carefully than he had with Drucker.

"I'll just bet you do. What's the rest of it?" She leaned back in her chair and listened for the next half hour as Drucker and Tolliver took turns explaining their positions while the thunder punctuated their dispute.

"Did you seriously expect the National Center for Disease Control to go along with your scheme, Commander?" Susannah asked when all the arguments had been presented.

"Hardly a scheme, Ms. Ling."

"Would conspiracy suit you better?" she countered. "For the record, Commander, I am going to lodge a formal complaint with the President and with Congress on the conduct of the military during this health emergency. Not only did you knowingly conceal information that might have bearing on the outbreak of this disease, you have systematically kidnapped the survivors for your own purposes. That is going to stop, Commander Tolliver. You will be forthcoming with any and all information requests we make of you and if there is the least suggestion that you are not cooperating to the fullest extent, or that you are interfering with any TS patient, I will personally see to it that you are brought up on formal charges." She rose and smiled as Tolliver did likewise.

"You can't hope to accomplish any of that," Tolliver said with false gallantry.

"On the contrary, I will do all of it," said Susannah. "I have already been assured of the fullest support from President Hunter as part of his Public Benefit contract." She saw disbelief and shock in the two men's faces. "That's right, gentlemen. President Hunter has TS."

Susan Ross and
Elizabeth Harkness

Lights had been set up in the living room and the furniture rearranged to show the view out the tall windows. Six men in jeans and sweatshirts fiddled with the television equipment while a thin, fussy woman put the finishing make-up touches on Elizabeth Harkness and her subject, Susan Ross.

"Are you nervous?" Elizabeth asked as the last of her powder was brushed off her face.

"Yes," said Susan as she stared at her hands; she had bitten her nails off to the quick or she would probably be chewing them now. "How do you do it?"

"It's like anything else in this world; you do it long enough and you get used to it." She stood up and straightened her navy-blue suit, one of those Italian creations that managed to be both tailored and ineffably feminine at the same time. "Are we ready, everyone?"

"Give us two minutes," the head technician called back. "We need voice levels on you two. If you'll sit down the way you're going to for the interview?"

As Susan stumbled toward the couch, Elizabeth said, "Do you have any pictures of your family? A photo album or a portrait in a frame? Anything like that?"

"There are a few pictures in the bedroom, I think," Susan said uncertainly. She had returned to Seattle only a week ago and still felt like a stranger in her own house. "Should I go get them?"

"Yes, please," said Elizabeth, and sat down in the armchair next to the flagstone fireplace. As her button mike was secured, she touched her hair, trusting that it looked shiny enough under the lights.

Susan was back carrying two framed pictures, one a candid shot taken at a picnic several years ago, the other a formal portrait that was not quite two years old. She offered these to Elizabeth. "Will either of these do? They're the only ones I could find."

"They're fine," said Elizabeth. "Betsy, can we set these on the coffee table? Somewhere the glass doesn't catch the light so we can see them." She indicated the end of the sofa. "Sit down and try to relax, Susan. I know it's hard, but it'll all be over in about fifteen minutes. Then we'll have your house cleaned up for you and you can get on with your life."

"Can I?" Susan asked of no one in particular as she sat down and tried to find a position that was comfortable.

The preparation continued, and just as the chaos stopped, Elizabeth leaned over and patted Susan's arm. "Don't worry. You are doing the right thing. You're being very brave."

Susan tried to smile. "Thanks."

"Thirty seconds," the head technician said. "Elizabeth, move a skosh to the left."

"Okay, Freddie," she said as she complied.

"Tape is rolling," he announced.

Elizabeth directed her smile to one of the two cameras set up in the living room. "Good evening; this is Elizabeth Harkness in Bellevue, Washington. Tonight I'm in the home of Susan Ross, whose son Kevin was one of the first victims of Taji's Syndrome." She turned toward Susan. "Missus Ross, thank you for letting me intrude at this time."

"It's good you're here," said Susan in a low voice.

"Missus Ross," Elizabeth went on for the benefit of the audience, "has lost two sons and a husband to TS, but her loss is greater than that. Will you tell something about it, Missus Ross?"

Susan stared at the wall on the other side of the room, trying not to be mesmerized by the lights and the cameras. "Kevin was the first, back when no one knew what Taji's Syndrome was, when it didn't even have a name. Kevin got sick. We thought it was mono."

"You took him for treatment?" Elizabeth prompted.

"Yes. To Sam Jarvis. He's dead now, too." She saw that she had been twisting her skirt between her hands and made herself stop. "It was puzzling, the way Kevin died. Sam wanted to check it out, you know how doctors can be. He and Harper decided—"

"Harper Ross was Missus Ross' husband, a professor of criminology at the University of Washington," Elizabeth explained for the benefit of the audience.

"Yes. He thought Kevin's dying was a crime and wanted to treat it like one, so he and Sam started doing research together. Sam did the medical part and Harper worked on compiling information about Kevin's case, and the new cases that started to appear." She stopped and blinked. "I . . . I went with our second son Grant to California. He was . . . he was in a drug rehab center there and he needed to have someone with him." She squirmed as she admitted this, her guilt showing in the way she shifted against the cushions.

"It must have been very difficult to leave your husband and son at a time like that," Elizabeth commiserated.

"It was awful," said Susan, tears welling in her eyes. "It was the worst thing in the world."

Elizabeth handed a small linen handkerchief to Susan. "If this is too hard, Missus Ross—" she began, though without the least intention of discontinuing the interview.

"No, no. I need a second or two, that's all." She wiped her eyes and gave herself a little shake. "This matters too much to let anything stop it."

"What happened while you were gone?" Elizabeth asked, getting the interview back on track again.

"First we were told that what had killed Kevin was an environmental toxin of some sort, and then they said it was two toxins." She shook her head.

"That was the first assumption about TS, wasn't it? That it was environmental in origin?" Elizabeth asked for the benefit of the audience.

"Yes. I suppose it made sense." She made a visible effort to collect herself. "Anyway, while I was with Grant, I had a conversation with Doctor Taji of the National Center for Disease Control in Atlanta."

"This is the same Taji as in Taji's Syndrome?" asked Elizabeth, wanting to be sure the viewers understood.

"Yes, the same one. He came to visit me while I was with my son Grant in California." She stared, unblinking, at the far wall.

"Wasn't that a bit unusual?" Elizabeth asked with a quick, inviting glance at the camera.

"I suppose so. From what Harper told me—Harper had been dealing with Doctor Taji and a number of researchers

while he and Sam Jarvis worked on their investigation—
Doctor Taji was spending time going around the country
getting more information on TS. Harper was convinced
that Doctor Taji was doing the right thing, asking all these
questions and taking all that time to travel. I don't understand why it had to be done face to face when there are
telephones and computers and all the rest of it. Harper said
that being there made a difference, and I suppose it does if
you're a doctor."

"What did Doctor Taji have to say to you?" Elizabeth
put the question to Susan in a deliberately unweighted way,
so that Susan's revelation would not be expected by the
viewers.

"He said that the National Center for Disease Control
was planning to run a full series of tests on those families
where the first TS deaths had occurred. He already had my
husband's permission for a full series of tests on our son
Grant."

"And Grant died . . . ?" Elizabeth pursued.

"Three weeks ago. Of TS. He and about nine of the
other kids in the rehab center died around the same time.
Once TS started in the center, it just kept spreading and
spreading. They closed the place about a month ago, but
by then it was really too late for most of them." She wiped
her eyes, folding the handkerchief with meticulous care.
"Grant lasted longer than they thought he would."

"So your husband and two of your sons have died from
TS," said Elizabeth, recapping.

"Yes," Susan answered on a single breath.

"Your other son? What about him?" This was what Elizabeth had been leading up to and she hoped that Susan had
good sense in how she broke the news.

"Mason. My other son is Mason Ross. He's thirteen,
he'll be fourteen on October twenty-second. He's . . . in
Atlanta now, or somewhere near there." Her voice had
grown soft again. "He went there before I could see him
again."

"Is this part of a Public Benefit contract, Missus Ross?" Elizabeth asked, still shaping their conversation.

"Harper signed a Public Benefit contract for him, but . . . but that's not why he's there. He's there because he's a carrier. Harper told me before he died that the investigation had found six and possibly seven children, all about Mason's age, who apparently were the first exposed to TS. All of them are carriers. Six teenagers." She started to cry, making a muffled apology to the sodden handkerchief.

"Hold the tape a bit," Elizabeth said before she gave her attention to Susan. "Come on, now. You're doing fine. We're almost through the worst of it and you're holding up real well. I want you to think about the good you're doing. I know it's hard, but keep your mind on what you're trying to do. Okay? Susan?" She put her hand on Susan's shoulder.

Susan nodded several times. "I just need a couple seconds," she mumbled.

"Take all the time you need," Elizabeth comforted as she looked at her watch and tried to figure out how much time they had to edit the interview before the first news telecast that evening. "Betsy, while we're waiting, get me some shots of the family photos, okay? I want to have them for emphasis."

"Coming right up," said Betsy.

Elizabeth did her best to sit still and wait though she itched to order Susan to get a grip on herself. While she sat, she sharpened up a few alternate questions in her mind. "Do you think you can go on, Missus Ross?" she asked when she thought enough time had gone by.

"I'll try," Susan promised. She wadded the handkerchief and raised her head. "I didn't mean to do that."

"It's perfectly understandable." Elizabeth gave a covert signal to Betsy. "You'll do fine."

"It's just that these last few weeks have been so awful." She sighed. "If Mason had been okay, I think I could have handled everything, but with him in that place, and a carrier, I don't know what to do. He's my son. He's the reason that thousands of people have caught TS. I know it wasn't deliberate or anything like that, but . . . it's horrible knowing that he had this TS in him all the time, and that once it began, it couldn't be stopped."

Elizabeth had hoped for something stronger, and so she prodded. "So in a way, you've lost all your family to TS, and you have to face the fact that your one surviving son is dangerous to everyone."

"What the hell happened?" Susan burst out, filled with rage and grief. "It wasn't supposed to be like this. We were doing fine. We were all doing fine. No one wanted to hurt anybody. It was . . ."—she fumbled for words to express the betrayal she felt—"so right. And then it all went wrong."

"Have you talked to your son Mason since he was taken to Atlanta?" Elizabeth said, pleased at the intensity of the outburst.

"A few times. It's hard to know what to say to him. There's so much I don't dare talk about. Sometimes he tells me about the other kids, and how they're managing. They were hoping to get away from TS there, at least for a while, but Mason tells me that the staff is all volunteers and that they all have tested positive for TS. So eventually they die." She looked away from the camera. "I used to pray that it would go back to the way it was, but now I only hope that it might be possible for some of us to escape this terrible disease."

"These other kids—what do you know about them?" This would be the capper, and it took all of Elizabeth's discipline for her not to smile in anticipation.

"There are two boys, twins, from Oregon, named Barenssen. There are two girls from Southern California, one from San Diego and one from the L.A. area. The girl from San Diego is Laurie Grey and the girl from Van Nuys is Gail Harmmon. There's a boy from Dallas: his name is Steven Channing and from what Mason said, his mother has actually survived TS."

"One of the lucky few," Elizabeth said dryly.

"But apparently he hasn't been able to reach her for a while. Mason told me that it was very upsetting for the boy. He's been staying in his room, at least that's what Mason said." She looked at Elizabeth directly, her face showing more puzzlement than any other emotion. "How did this happen? How *could* it happen?"

"We're working on finding out, Missus Ross," said Elizabeth, already doing the editing of their interview in her mind. "We have a crew working in Atlanta, trying to learn more about what's going on with your boy Mason and the others." She turned and addressed the cameras directly. "Those are the names: Adam and Axel Barenssen, Gail Harmmon, Steven Channing, Laurie Grey—and Mason Ross. These are the first, and in many ways, the ultimate victims of TS, for as long as they are alive, they will carry destruction within them. They will have to live in isolation, tended by those who will die from the disease they carry. What a terrible burden for these unsuspecting children." She turned back to Susan. "Missus Ross, we're very grateful to you for your courage in speaking out. We cannot thank you enough for the service you've performed."

"I just want to know what happened," Susan murmured, exhausted now that she had spoken.

"So do we all," Elizabeth said with admirable determination. "And we are determined to find out."

"Great," said Betsy as the blinding lights went out. "We can make the first news in the East if we hurry."

Elizabeth stood up. "Thank you again, Susan. You've got real guts."

"Umm." Susan sat staring at the pictures, her eyes distant and her manner gently remote. She only spoke again once as Elizabeth was getting ready to leave. "Did I do the right thing?"

But Elizabeth was already on her way and gave her no answer.

Jeff Taji and
Susannah Ling

After the TV screen changed from a close-up on the formal portrait of the Ross family, Susannah angrily pressed the remote control, turning it off. "If I ever get the chance to flay Commander Maurice Tolliver..."

"I'll help you," said Jeff from the other side of her office. "You're certain he's behind it?"

"He or part of his military club," she sighed. "They're putting pressure on us. And they're using every trick at their disposal." She leaned back. "Are you through here?"

He gave a wistful smile. "No. Not by half. There's another batch of tests to be run and some comparison screens to process."

"But you think this O-subtype-h technique will work?" She could not keep the anxiety out of her question.

"So far it's the only game in town," he said. "And for those with O-type blood, it seems to be working so far. The artificial subtype-h works in the blood without an adverse reaction. It might only mean that the TS is slowed down, but even if that's all it does, it buys us some time." He dropped his hand on the largest stack of printouts in front of him. "Do you ever think that last year at this time, we didn't know about any of this? TS hadn't happened yet? And now it's all any of us ever talk about."

"That's because it's communicable and deadly," said Susannah in her most professional manner.

"Yes," Jeff agreed. "But I used to talk about gardens and art and music and food and the newspaper. I haven't done that in weeks. Everyone I know is measuring their lives in

386

terms of TS. Sometimes I think that's the saddest thing about the disease."

"You can't let it get you down, Jeff," Susannah said.

"And it doesn't get you down?" he asked.

"I'm coordinator for this Division. It's supposed to get me down. That's what they pay me for." She had wanted this to be droll and amusing, but instead she heard how tired she sounded.

"Strikes me that we're both in need of a respite," said Jeff.

"But not yet?" She winked at him.

"Not until the chores are done," he said. "But if you're going to be up later, I'll give you a call before I leave if it isn't too late."

"Call me whenever it is," she said.

"Great." He got up and slung three of the stacks of printouts in the bend of his arm. "I've got to get back to it. I have a hunch we're going to have a lot of newsflack coming our way in the next couple of days."

"It's going to be longer than that, I'm afraid," she said.

"You can handle it," he said, and came near enough to bend down and kiss her forehead.

"Thanks for the vote of confidence, Doctor." She got up, smoothing her skirt as she did. "Off you go. I know you'll do the best you can."

"Thanks for the vote of confidence," he said as he let himself out the door.

Ordinarily by six-thirty the halls would be deserted and the half-staff that ran the facility at night would be working in offices and labs. In the last two months, this had changed. There was less staff as people continued to fall ill, but they worked constantly; six in the morning, eleven in the night, the halls were never empty and the sound of work echoed from office to lab to computer stations.

Jeff took the elevator to his lab floor, and almost walked into a large specimen cart being wheeled from the receiving area into the first of three testing labs. He muttered a word of apology as he continued on his way.

"I'm Rita, Doctor Taji," said a lab assistant Jeff had never seen before.

"Hello, Rita," he said, shaking hands briefly. "What became of Stan? Or don't I need to ask?"

"He's in the hospital," said Rita. "I've been reading the records for the last series of tests. They look pretty good, don't they?"

"If we weren't desperate, I'd say they look worth exploring, but right now, I'd say they're the best bet we have." He put down the printouts. "Do you want to go over these with me, or would you rather keep on with what you were doing?"

"I'm running the comparison samples. I'll look over the printouts later, if that's okay." She was bright and willing, and Jeff felt a brief pang that she should be subjected to something as pernicious as Taji's Syndrome. Then he reminded himself that they needed all the help they could get, and sat down to run through the figures he had been given.

It was almost three hours later that Rita came back from her work. "Doctor Taji?" she said as she approached the lab table where he was reading comparisons of ACTH readings in advanced cases of TS.

"What is it?" he asked brusquely, irritated at the break in his concentration.

"I think you'd better have a look at this," she said uneasily.

"What's wrong?" He was on his feet at once, his printouts forgotten.

"The control specimens . . . they're following the curve, but that new compound, the one that you and Doctor Hardy developed . . ." She was having trouble finding the proper description.

"What's wrong with it?" Jeff demanded as they went into the other part of the lab.

"Nothing. It's not like the other group, that's using the previous compound. Those specimens change very slowly, but the new ones don't appear to be changing at all." Her face lit up. "It could do it, couldn't it? It can work in all blood, doesn't it? I mean, it could be a cure?"

Jeff felt his heart go like a triphammer in his chest, but he reminded himself sternly that he could not jump to assumptions simply because he wanted to believe them. "We'll see. And there are some questions of side effects, even if it seems it could work."

"But the Public Benefit contracts will take care of that, won't they?" Her eyes sparkled. "God, if it turns out I was the first one to see the cure. That would be . . . be—"

"We don't know anything about cures yet, Rita," he said with the intention of dampening her enthusiasm. "We'll find out later if that's what's going on."

"But it could be a cure, couldn't it?" She would not abandon her hope that it was.

"Maybe, and that's all I can tell you. I don't know enough about it to have another opinion yet." He came up to the three large specimen racks and looked over the vast array of test tubes. "Now, show me what you want me to see." This was only a formality; he could see that one rack was virtually unchanged while the others showed the telltale alterations in color that revealed the presence of Taji's Syndrome.

"What do you think?" Rita asked, all but holding her breath for his answer.

"I think this is worth looking into." He went over to the closet and pulled out his lab coat. "Get Doctor Hardy on the line and tell him to get his ass over here right now."

"In those words?" Rita wondered aloud.

"If it doesn't bother you, it won't bother him," said Jeff with a trace of amusement. "Tell him that means right now."

"He's at—"

"The Control Facility. His extension is seventy-one and if he doesn't answer the phone, one of his assistants will. Let it keep ringing and they'll pick it up eventually." He was already starting to prepare a more complete assessment of the three groups of specimens.

"Right away. I'll do it right now," said Rita rather breathlessly.

"Good," said Jeff, and set to work.

It was not quite an hour later when Ace strode into the lab, his short-sleeved shirt sweat-stained and his face shiny. "What's this I hear about a cure? And who is that kid working your phones?"

"Rita, this is Ace Hardy," Jeff said for an introduction. "Come here. Well, do something about that shirt, get into a lab coat and then come here."

"That good, huh?" Ace asked sardonically. "This better be worth all the trouble," he threatened.

"I wouldn't get your hopes up unless I thought we had a chance," Jeff said seriously. "Go on; shower and get in here. How is it out there, anyway?"

"It's fucking hot is how it is. Those old brick buildings, the ones the tourists like so much? You can't get near them without feeling like you're in an oven." He stepped into the men's room, slamming the door emphatically.

"Is he mad at you?" Rita asked in bewilderment.

"Not that I know of," said Jeff, going back to his work.

Ten minutes later Ace was back, listening as Jeff outlined what they needed to do. "Let me give Jessie a call, so she'll know why I won't be able to visit her tonight," he said, and went to the telephone.

Shortly after eleven that night, Rita apologized profusely and went home to be replaced by a second-generation Cuban called Charlie.

"I'll take care of coffee, washing slides and sterilizing anything that needs it, so long as you don't call me Carlos. That's for the old folks, the ones who talk about Havana as if it was heaven." He then set to work in steady determination, all the while singing South American pop songs to himself under his breath.

By four in the morning, Jeff had a thundering headache and the muscles of his neck and back seemed set into a Gordian knot. In spite of it all, he felt jubilant. "What do you think?" he asked Ace as they checked the computer scan against their own notes.

"I think some Public Benefit contracts are going to get put to use. Starting with Jessie's. She's type O and if this stuff can help anyone, I want it to be her."

"What about you?" asked Jeff, trying without success to stifle a yawn.

"Don't I wish. I'm type A." He shrugged. "Some of us have to be."

"Yeah," Jeff said heavily, much of his elation evaporating in the realization that the discovery would not be able to help Ace, who had spent so much time on this work.

"First we see about potential long-term damage, and if it exists, how severe it is." Ace ticked off their projects on his spatulate fingers. "If there are no apparent side effects, or if the side effects are minor, then the next step is to prepare a warning and make the material available to everyone with the disease who can benefit from the material."

"Those with type-O blood," said Jeff, wishing he could reconcile his relief at the chance of a limited solution with his dejection for those who could not yet be helped.

"You know, President Hunter has type-O blood and this is an election year," Ace said with a sly smile. "Could be worth a shot, no pun intended."

Jeff tried to straighten up, groaning as he heard his neck pop. "I've got to call Susannah."

"At four twenty-seven in the morning?" Ace asked, pretending to be shocked. "The sun isn't up yet."

"Don't remind me," said Jeff, making his way to the phone and pressing Susannah's number from memory.

She answered after eight rings and her tone was curt. "This had better be important, whoever you are," she warned as she lifted the receiver.

"I wouldn't call at this ungodly hour if it weren't. I wouldn't be up if it weren't important," said Jeff.

"Are you still at the lab?" she asked, sounding concerned and contrite. "Jeff?"

"Still here," he confirmed. "I'm beginning to think I've taken root here."

"Very funny; now why are you calling?" Though her question was all business, her tone of voice was not.

"Ace and I have been working on these latest tests and we might—I said might, Susannah—have come up with something that will be . . . useful."

"You mean you've got a workable subtype-h over there?" She almost shrieked the question. "Is that it?"

"I hope so," said Jeff with more emotion than he knew. "It looks more promising than anything we've developed so far. I want to run more tests, but at first go, it's doing well."

"Oh, Jeff, that's . . . wonderful. That's great. Hell, it's better than any of that." She sounded as excited as a high school senior being invited to the prom.

"It hasn't proved out yet," Jeff cautioned her, though he was having trouble keeping satisfaction out of his voice.

"How soon can we make an announcement?" She was not quite so giddy now.

"Not quite yet, I don't think. You don't want to make promises you can't keep." Jeff rubbed his forehead and longed for three aspirin.

"But what if someone ferrets this out and breaks it ahead of us?" The apprehension was back in her voice now.

"You mean John Post? No worry there? If you mean Maurice Tolliver, I don't think he wants us to look good. He'd break it only if he thought he could discredit it later." Jeff looked up as Charlie sashayed by, dancing to his own whispered song.

"You could be right. I hope, I hope, I hope," she said. "Look, are you going to be there much longer?"

"Probably another hour or so. I want to put more data into the computer before I leave so that I have something to come back to this afternoon." Slowly he arched his back, feeling his muscles protest.

"Make it an hour and a half and I'll take you to breakfast. Be out in front." Then the breath caught in her throat. "Do we really have a chance, Jeff?"

"A chance," he said. "It's a chance."

"I wish I were still religious. I think I'd want to say thank you." She gave an unsuccessful chuckle. "Can I thank *you*?"

"Not yet. Maybe later," said Jeff, surprised at the intensity of his reaction to her words. "I've told Ace that Jessie can have some of the first batch if this passes all the control tests."

"Sure, fine." said Susannah. "I'll see you later. I've got to shower and get dressed. Wait for me."

"I'll be there," said Jeff, and hung up.

"She excited?" Ace asked as he regarded Jeff over the rim of his coffee cup.

"Thrilled. But we've still got a long way to go. The last eight attempts made it this far and didn't pass the follow-up tests." He was just starting to realize how tired he was; he was not at all sure he could stay awake through breakfast.

"Think of it like symphonies: the ninth is always the best." Ace waited for a response, and when he got none, he said, "Remember the warning you've given me, the one about not asking for trouble? For all you know this stuff will work just fine."

"And everyone with type-O blood will have a chance," said Jeff wearily. "And the rest will continue to die."

"At least it's type-O and not type-AB," said Ace. "It gives the chance to the greatest number of people." He narrowed his eyes. "What's bothering you, Taji?"

"I was just thinking about Max Klausen and Wil Landholm and Sam Jarvis and all the rest of them. It doesn't matter what blood type they had. They're dead. They didn't have a chance." He lowered his head.

"Yeah, and two hundred years ago you didn't have a chance with cholera or smallpox or rabies, and ten years ago you didn't have a chance with AIDS. Maybe this is only a limited chance for a limited number of people—so be it. You can't let that get in the way or you'll never get out from under." He got up and came over. "The trouble with you is you're worn out, Doctor, and you need to give yourself twenty-four hours off."

"I can't take twenty-four hours off," Jeff protested even as the prospect tantalized him.

"Sure you can. Take a sleeping pill and come up for air this time tomorrow." He regarded Jeff seriously. "Hey, we need our wits working around here, Taji. You got to take care of yourself. The tests on this stuff of ours are still ahead, and I can't handle them on my own."

Jeff nodded three times very slowly. "To hear is to obey."

"I'll believe that when I see it," Ace said. "Go in and shave if you're going to have breakfast with our boss. She may like you, but don't push your luck."

"Good idea," said Jeff as he got to his feet. He shuffled into the men's room and stood staring into the mirror for more than two minutes as if he did not recognize himself; his eyes were reddened, the stubble on his face revealed two wide stripes of grey below the corners of his mouth, there were hollows under his cheeks and the skin under his eyes was purple-blue. He reached down and turned on the cold water, splashing it on his face until he began to feel restored. Eventually he went to his locker and got out his shaving kit and a change of shirt, then went and put himself in order.

Sylvia Kostermeyer and Weyman Muggridge

At the far end of the room, Guy Derelli was talking to the press, extolling the hard work done by the staff of the California State Department of Public Health and Environmental Services, and indirectly taking credit for their diligence.

"Does that bother you?" Weyman asked Sylvia as they ate the broiled prawns that were being passed by red-jacketed waiters.

"Does what bother me?" Sylvia asked; she had been watching the television screen where the latest proceedings of the Republican Convention were going on. "That Cornice is making foolish promises?"

"No, that Derelli is hogging the limelight." Weyman put his arm around her.

"Oh, he deserves credit. He made unpopular moves in an election year and that takes guts. He might even have integrity for all I know." She nibbled thoughtfully at another prawn. "I hope that the Standard Public School Blood Screen has enough information to let us reach most of the population with type-O blood. I'd hate to see anyone die now who doesn't have to."

"Meaning everyone who doesn't have type-O blood?" Weyman asked, the question a trifle brittle.

"For the time being, yes," said Sylvia. "What's the matter? Are you feeling guilty because you have type-O blood and your Public Benefit contract entitled you to some of the first of the artificial genosubtype-h?" She read the answer in his eyes. "You'd better feel guilty about not telling me you were pre-TS. How could you do that to me?"

"I didn't want to upset you," he said, repeating what he had been telling her since she learned he had been given the gst-h. "You were afraid I'd leave you, and I didn't want you to think that would happen. I told you before I won't leave you."

She sighed and finished the prawn. "I never asked that of you."

"I'm volunteering. Actually, I'm proposing," he amended.

"What?" She stared at him.

"I'm proposing," he repeated.

"We're in the middle of a political cocktail party," she objected.

"I know. I'm still proposing." He gave her a swift, wide grin. "Well?"

"Proposing what?" she asked, her cheeks coloring.

"I like it when you blush," he told her softly.

"Proposing what?" she repeated.

"Marriage. What else would I propose?" He snagged two prawns from a passing waiter. "Here."

She took the prawn. "Thanks."

A flurry of applause caused them both to glance in the governor's direction and to see him give a genial wave to the assembled press.

"It's a pretty disappointing crowd," Weyman said as if agreeing with something Sylvia had said. "But look at the poor show for the Republican Convention. Everyone's scared of TS, and you can't blame them."

"I guess not," she said, sounding distracted. Her eyes were fixed on Governor Guy Derelli, but her thoughts were clearly elsewhere.

"I'm not going to be sidetracked," Weyman said with a little mischief in his eyes. "One way or another, I'll get an answer out of you."

"I don't know what to say," she said, still refusing to look at him.

A TV news crew with lights and cameras shoved by them; Weyman stepped between Sylvia and them so that she would not be jostled. "You could ruin the suspense and say yes."

She gestured with her free hand. "Weyman, that's what troubles me about you."

"That I propose here? I'll propose almost anywhere you like. Name the place." He nodded toward the door. "Want to go have overdone chicken and dessicated vegetables?"

"We have to. We're supposed to be here. Azada told me to attend." She finished the prawn. "You're confusing me."

"How so?" He slipped his hand through her arm and started toward the banquet room doors.

"By . . . by the things you do; by not letting those TV people near me, by opening my car door, by doing the laundry when I'm too busy, by making dinner or taking me out when we go late at night." The banquet room was set for two hundred, fifteen of those places at a long table at the front of the room in the full glare of the lights, the rest at round tables that seated ten.

"We're at table number eight," said Weyman, looking for the numbers. "It's on the other side of the room. Come on." He released her arm and took her hand, leading the way through the crush.

"See?" she accused him as they reached table number eight.

"What?" He was holding her chair out for her. "What's wrong, Sylvia?"

"*Nothing.*" She sat down and glared at the arrangement of plastic flowers in the center of the table.

"Pretty strange reaction to nothing. Or don't you like banquets?" Weyman asked, still unperturbed, as he took his seat. "If it's the TS, we can wait to see what the blood work tells us. I won't expect you to marry me if it turns out that you'll be a widow before you've got all your table silver."

She slapped her hands down on the table. "That's what I mean. That's it?"

This time he was truly puzzled. "What is it?"

"Your damned, infernal, automatic, addictive *considera-tion.* You act like the things you do for me are . . . are fun." She hurled the words at him.

"I like the addictive part," he said, and before she could say more, he added, "They are fun, Sylvia. Being able to do things for you is a privilege."

On the dais someone was testing the microphone; there were the traditional explosive taps and electronic squeals. The toastmaster, a local television anchorman, counted to five, blinked as a third bank of lights came on, and sat down.

Four more people came to table eight and sat down.

"I'm Jim Swayles; Immigration."

"I'm Jim's wife, Nina."

"I'm Sylvia Kostermeyer—"

"Doctor Kostermeyer—"

"—with PHES and he's—"

"Weyman Muggridge—"

"Doctor Muggridge—"

"—NCDC-ED."

"I'm Sherry Wood, County Health Department."

"I'm Jesus Dominguez, Immigration."

Weyman gave the kind of smile he usually reserved for especially boring staff meetings. "You'll have to pardon us. We were in the middle of a discussion and there's a couple points we need to clear up."

"Weyman, for God's sake," Sylvia said in a lower voice.

"If not here, tell me where?" He was all innocence.

Double doors to the left of the dais opened and the first squad of waiters rushed into the room, starting to distribute what had been called Frutti del Mare salad.

"Later; we can discuss things later. No one here wants to listen to this." Sylvia looked guiltily at the others. "I'm sorry. When he gets his mind on something, there's no getting him off it."

Nina Swayles smiled indulgently. "Jim's just like that, too."

"When, Sylvia?" Something in his tone revealed his determination.

"Tonight. We'll settle it tonight, okay? But not right now. Look. Mayor Talley is going to say something." Sylvia, who usually abhorred these dinners, found herself hoping this one would never end. She could feel Weyman beside her, and hated herself for relying on him to make polite conversation.

During his address after the puddle of whipped chocolate goo that was billed as mousse, Governor Derelli introduced several of those he labeled "medical crusaders," including Sylvia.

"Well, stand up for the Governor," Weyman prompted her when she faltered, blushing.

"You mean, you were one of those working on TS all along?" Dominguez asked with increased respect.

"Right from the beginning," Weyman confirmed. "She was one of the docs who insisted that the NCDC get involved." He clapped enthusiastically. "A lot of people owe her their lives."

"Weyman, stop it," she whispered as she stood, flattered and miserable at the same time.

"Not a chance. You deserve a lot more credit than you're ever going to get, lady, and I'm not going to let you throw away what comes to you, because it's yours by rights." He held her chair for her as she sat down.

The speeches dragged on until after eleven. By then the room was stuffy and the TV crews were openly restive since they had missed everything but the late-night news. Finally Mayor Talley thanked everyone for coming and expressed her gratitude for all that had been done to help the victims of TS. She gave special thanks to the gentleman at her right, Captain Jacob Lorrimer of the United States Marine Corps, for his work in opening military medical facilities to civilians during the emergency, and Captain Lorrimer nodded acknowledgement.

"What's the most beautiful stretch of coast along here?" Weyman asked as he held Sylvia's spangled sweater for her.

"La Jolla, probably," she said without thinking.

"Okay. We'll drive up there—you can guide me or you can drive, whichever you prefer—and we'll finish our 'discussion'."

She turned to him in dismay. "But—"

"You said later. This is later. Let's clear the air so we can both get back to work." He held her arm and guided them both through the crowd. "You can say yes right now, but you might as well get your questions answered, so you can say it in comfort."

"What makes you so sure I'm going to say yes?" She stopped walking, and he stood beside her.

"Because you're a very smart lady, and no matter how much I scare you, losing me scares you more," he told her very gently. "Which is good, because losing you scares me more than all the disease in the world, or all the disasters we face."

"Weyman—"

"God's own truth," he said, holding up his right hand to swear.

"All right," she capitulated with a sigh. "Let's go to La Jolla and thrash this out."

They drove in silence, the radio picking up Broadway tunes from a station in L.A. There was moderate traffic, most of it moving fairly fast, but Sylvia refused to be rushed. She turned off I-5 at Van Nuys and drove out to the coast road, heading north around the point.

"You can park any time," Weyman suggested.

"Can't we keep driving?" she pleaded.

"All the way to San Francisco, if it'll make you feel better," he said.

"All right," she said, taking up the challenge and heading up the coast. "Talk."

"First, I want you to know that if it turns out that my TS hasn't responded to the artificial sub-h, then I won't hold you to anything. I don't want you chained to me while I die. That's not part of the bargain."

"None of that 'in sickness and health' nonsense for you?" she asked, her eyes glittering dangerously.

"I didn't say that. I said that if I still have TS, the deal's off. Something, sometime, will kill me. Something, sometime, will kill you. If we're lucky, it'll be years down the line, and we'll go quickly, in our sleeps, from old age. It would tear me apart to see you suffer." He leaned back, hands laced behind his head.

"Lovely things you think about." She kept her attention on the road and paid little attention to the shine of the Pacific Ocean on her left, or Weyman on her right.

"You're a doctor; you think about those things, too." He

took a deep breath. "So. If I have TS, that's that. Anything else is a crap shoot and we'll take our chances, how does that sound?"

"Too noble for words," she answered.

He chuckled once. "I been called lots of things in my time but noble is a first. Tell me what's troubling you about this? Can you honestly say you don't want to marry me?"

She swallowed hard. "I had an aunt. She's twelve years older than I am. And she grew up with the old myths—you know, you go to school, you get a good job and you find a good husband and you have a good life and a good family. Only it didn't happen that way. She had a three-year relationship with a married man when she was in her late twenties, and then...there were no more relationships. She went as far as she could with the job, and then she was stuck, and there was nowhere to go. It eroded her. Every day she lost a little of her self-esteem because none of the payoffs ever happened, no matter how right she did things."

"Are you sure that's how she felt?" Weyman asked softly.

"Yeah. I'm sure. I read the letter she left. Because I found her after she killed herself." She took a deep breath. "I was sharing her apartment with her while I went to college."

"Oh, Sylvia." He reached over and touched the back of her neck. "God, the things we go through."

"Anyway," she said, while a part of her mind railed at her for revealing so much, "I realized then that the myths were dangerous and they could destroy you."

"And you decided that you'd never let them destroy Sylvia Kostermeyer."

"Something like that," she allowed.

"Even if you had to deny yourself what you longed for." He leaned back again. "We all lose things we love. That's the way it works. But to turn away from it because eventually we'll lose it means you never have it at all. For a very intelligent lady, that's rotten logic."

"How kind of you to point that out." Her hands tightened on the steering wheel.

"You don't believe it yet, but it is." He was silent for a time. "We're not through this TS crisis yet. We're only delaying the worst of it. And frankly, there's no way I can make it through all by myself."

"In fact, proposing to me is selfish of you," she expanded on his words.

"Damn right."

"And you want to marry me because then you can handle working on this epidemic." She shook her head.

"And the other epidemics we don't know anything about," he appended. "And all the rest of it. If I have to go through the rest of my life knowing that I botched it with you . . . Sylvia, I didn't propose out of convenience. It isn't convenient being in love with a woman who lives across the country from where I work. I didn't propose out of lust. If that were all I felt, or you felt, we'd both know it. I didn't propose out of pity. I don't pity you at all, though I am deeply saddened to know how difficult your life has been at times. I didn't even propose out of loneliness. That's the worst possible reason to propose, though because I love you I'd be very lonely without you; the thing is, Sylvia, the love comes first, not the loneliness; that's the difference." He put his left hand over her right one for a moment. "I've said my peace. If you can't say yes, even though you want to—"

"How can you be sure of that?" This time she did not sound as angry or as confident as before.

"Because I'm not deaf, dumb and blind; and I'm not stupid." He laughed. "If you're so worried, we'll take a year to live together, to work it out. Hell, we'll take two years or five or however many you want."

"Are you patronizing me?" she asked uncertainly.

He laughed out loud. "God *damn*, you are the most suspicious woman!"

She tried to find an indignant accusation, but started giggling instead. "You bastard," she laughed.

"Does that mean you will?"

"It means I'll think about it," she said, smiling and beginning to lose the tension that had gripped her all evening.

"While we live together," he added.

"All right, all right, all right, while we live together." Although she could not bring herself to say it, she suddenly felt idiotically happy.

Alexandra Porter

One of the older geldings was down with pidgeon fever, and Alexa was with the vet when the phone rang.

"Do you mind if I get that?" she asked as the ringing continued. "Elvira usually refuses to answer it."

"Sure," said the vet as she examined the swelling that stretched from the base of his neck to between his front legs. "This poor fella isn't going anywhere."

"I appreciate it," said Alexa, and hurried out of the stable toward the house at a fast jog.

"Porter Ranch," she answered, a little out of breath.

"Collect call from Harold," announced the synthesized voice. "Will you accept charges."

Alexa swallowed hard. "Yes. Yes, operator. I'll accept the—"

"Thank you; go ahead please," said the voice.

"Mom?" he said tentatively.

"Harold? Honey? God, it's good to hear your voice." She could feel tears on her face. "Where are you, Harold?"

"Near Penticton. That's in Canada." His voice was lower than she remembered it from six months ago and he spoke hesitantly.

"I know where Penticton is," she said. "How are you, Harold?"

"I'm okay. I guess. Yeah."

"Harold, what is it?" She tried to remain calm, but dread was poking its hot fingers on her spine. "Harold?"

"It's Dad." His voice broke and he started to sob. "He just collapsed. Just like that."

"Harold," she said, trying to calm him. "Harold, tell me where he is now."

"They took him to the hospital, about an hour ago."

"Which hospital?" Alexa asked, trying to keep her wits about her.

"I don't know. The big one near the old Peach Festival grounds. I didn't get the name. Mom, I'm sorry."

"It's okay, Harold. I'll tend to that later." She wanted to reassure him. "I'll call Penticton later and take care of everything."

The boy was sobbing and he could not put words together. "Oh, Mom . . . he's . . . he's . . ."

"I know what he is," said Alexa with feeling. "I'll make sure he's taken care of. Don't you worry about that. What about you? Where are you staying right now?"

"Dad's got a job here, with a man who runs an auction house." He said it in a rush. "Livestock auctions."

"And where are you staying?" Alexa persisted, not wanting to upset her son any more than he already was.

He was not able to answer for a few seconds. "We were staying at a motel until two nights ago." His breathing grew less rapid. "Dad got into a fight and the manager wanted us to leave."

It took all her self-discipline for Alexa not to come back with a sharp summary of her opinion of Frank Porter. That would accomplish nothing; Harold was upset as it was. To have his mother attacking his father in the hospital, no matter what their past relationship had been, would serve no purpose. "Harold, listen to me. I have to know where you are, where to find you." She was already thinking about the telephone calls she had had from Jeff Taji, offering his assistance with Harold if she should ever need it.

"We were . . . there's a kind of apartment in back of Dad's boss' garage. We went there last night. I guess he'll let me stay there a couple of days, until I know how things are with Dad. If not . . ."

"I'm going to catch a plane to Penticton"—or wherever the nearest airport was, she added to herself—"as soon as I can drive into Denver. I'll be there before tomorrow afternoon. You tell Frank's boss that your mother is coming, that I live in Colorado and that I'll take full responsibility for you. I don't want to have to work things out with a juvenile court, especially not in Canada."

"Dad's awful sick, Mom. The nurse told me that they think it might be that TS." He faltered. "Mom, is it TS?"

"There's a lot of it around," she answered evasively.

"I heard that there was a thing on the news about kids who carry TS." This time he paused nervously. "Dad got it into his head that I gave it to him, because I've been around kids who had it and I'm okay." Once again he was silent. "Mom, he's wrong, isn't he? It's because he's feeling sick that he says that, right?"

"We'll find out as soon as I get you home," she said. "I haven't any idea why some people get TS and some don't, and neither does anyone else," she added belligerently, though she knew it was not so.

"There's a treatment for it now, anyway." Harold was begging for reassurance, wanting his mother to exonerate him of his father's illness.

"Now you listen to me, Harold. Your father could pick up TS or any number of diseases, the way he lives. Why, it's amazing he hasn't come down with something long before now. He's been a lot luckier than he deserves. And if he tries to make you take the blame for what's wrong with him, you just ignore him, you got that? Frank is a jealous, spiteful man who'd do almost anything to get his way." All her resolutions about what she said about her former husband were forgotten. "I won't let him do anything more to you, Harold, that's a promise. He took you from me, but I'm taking you back. You hold on, son. I'll be there just as soon as I can arrange for a plane. You tell me where I'll find you and I'll be there."

Harold caught his breath. "Probably the hospital. You can find out its name."

"If it's on the old Peach Festival site, it shouldn't be too hard to find." She wanted to find the words to reassure Harold. "I love you, honey. I've missed you so much, and I can't wait to see you again. I . . . I bet you've changed."

He cracked a single laugh. "I'm a little taller—"

"A little?"

"Well, I'm about five-ten now. I got a bit of a beard, too. You probably won't like the clothes I wear or my haircut." He was doing what he could to apologize for what his father had done.

"It won't matter diddly to me, Harold. Getting to see you again is what matters." She was finding it hard to keep her voice even. "Now, I got two other calls to make, to arrange for things from this end, and then I'll be on my way to Denver. I'll be there tomorrow afternoon at the latest. I'll see you then."

"Okay, Mom. Thanks." That hint of embarrassment again colored his speech. "Thanks a lot."

"Any time," she said, and hung up while she could control her voice. She stood in the kitchen wiping her face, then she yelled for Elvira. "I want coffee, I want a suitcase packed for a couple days in Canada. I want a strong brandy right now."

Elvira appeared in the kitchen door.

"El hijo?"

"Si. Now get on it. Pronto, todo pronto."

"Coffee, brandy, packing," she said in very good English.

"Por gran favor," said Alexa, and picked up the phone

to dial a familiar number in Golden. She waited with impatience while she explained her business to a receptionist and a secretary, and then she reached Fenton Weeks, who had been her attorney since the whole miserable business with Frank began.

"Alexa, this is an unexpected pleasure," said Fenton Weeks when he came on the line at last.

"You, too," said Alexa, minimizing the formalities. "I just had a call from Harold—"

"Not again," said Fenton softly.

"He's in Penticton—"

"Where's that?" Fenton asked.

"Canada, either Alberta or British Columbia. He told me that Frank's in the hospital, pretty sick. I'm going to fly out as soon as I can get a plane, and I want to be sure there's no red tape waiting for me. You got that?" She had been speaking so quickly that she was suddenly out of breath. "Tony? You got that?"

"I don't know if I can do it . . ." he attempted to qualify his position.

"You do it, Tony Weeks, or you'll regret it, I promise you that. I want full court records sent up to Penticton so there's no question of who has the right to the boy. If I know Frank, he'll spin a story that'll tie things up for days if we don't nip it in the bud." She looked up; Elvira was handing her a cup of coffee. She mouthed "thanks" and listened to Fenton sputter.

"I'll do what I can, Alexa, but I can't make any promises. We have several questions of legal jurisdictions here and the law of the United States is not the law of Canada. It's a tall order and—"

"Then you'll want to get on it right away."

"I have other cases," he protested.

"When I first came to you, you didn't. You hadn't had a client in a month and you were willing to do almost anything. I took half my savings to give you a decent retainer and I've paid you that much every year since, plus your billings. Or had that slipped your mind?" She drank some of the strong, hot coffee, letting the roof of her mouth scald from it.

"I'll get on it in an hour. An hour, Alexa. I've got clients waiting in the outer office." He paused. "But it'll get done and I'll stay on it."

"I'm counting on it," she said. "I'll give you a call from Canada when I know what the story is on Frank."

"Good. I'll be waiting." He cleared his throat. "Alexa, good luck. I mean that."

"Thanks," she said, and hung up. "Elvira, make sure you get a second bag. If I know Frank, Harold won't have any luggage of his own."

"*Ya lo creo*," she agreed in her worldweary manner.

"And get me a thousand dollars from the office." She knew that she would need some cash and was afraid that if she left it behind that it would increase her difficulties.

"You do not need so much," said Elvira as she brought a snifter to Alexa.

"Get it." She was checking through the business cards she carried and at last found Jeff Taji's. "I got one more call to make. Then I want the car ready."

"I will tell Emilio." Elvira left Alexa alone for her call.

"This is Alexa Porter in Golden, Colorado," she said to the woman who answered Jeff Taji's phone. "I have to talk to Doctor Taji at once."

"Please hold on while I locate him," said the woman. Immediately the phone began to play a mushy version of *Uptown Nights*.

Alexa had taken three sips of brandy and finished the coffee when Jeff came on the line. "This is Doctor Taji, Missus Porter. What can I do for you?"

"My son just called from Canada. He's in trouble. I'm about to leave to do what I can to help him out. I thought you'd like to know."

"Yes, I most certainly do," said Jeff. "Where in Canada?"

"Penticton," she said. "I'm heading for the airport."

"What about the boy? Is he all right?" Jeff said, doing his best to instill calm in Alexa.

"No, he's not all right. Frank's sick and in the hospital and my boy's on his own." She heard how shrill her voice was and apologized at once. "Sorry, Doctor. I'm pretty wired right now. I didn't mean to yell at you."

"You didn't yell." Jeff gave them both a couple of seconds to change gears and said, "I can arrange to have someone to help you in Penticton, if you require it."

"I don't think I will. I have my lawyer on it. But if it looks like there's going to be red tape to cut, I'll call you. I can do that, can't I?"

"Yes, of course," said Jeff. "I'm going to be traveling myself during the next few days, but my office can always find me in thirty minutes or less." On impulse, he offered, "Would you like to be able to reach the Divisional Coordinator? I can give you her name and number. You remember Susannah Ling, don't you? Do you have her card?"

"I . . . don't remember," said Alexa, her thoughts elsewhere.

"Well, write it down and I'll warn her that she may be hearing from you. She's my superior and she can cut red tape faster than I can. In fact, she's the one I go to when I need red tape cut." He listened to the sound of Alexa's voice, trying to determine how prepared the woman was.

"The lady who was with you is the boss," she repeated, not quite believing it. "Give me the number, Doctor Taji." She read it back as Jeff recited it. "Okay."

"You call her if you need her," Jeff told her firmly. He added, after a brief hesitation, "If you can get to Salt Lake City, we can arrange a charter plane to get you to Penticton."

Alexa was startled. "A charter plane?"

"Yes. We have two of the NCDC planes there right now. I can authorize the use of one. Would that help you?" He did not want to push her, but he was concerned for her and the boy.

"Sure." She had the last of her brandy and decided that she would have to have a bite to eat before she got on the road. "I know it isn't right to say yes to the offer. I do know that, Doctor Taji, but I'm—"

"Why isn't it right, Missus Porter?" Jeff interrupted. "The NCDC is funded by the government"—he had almost said controlled instead of funded—"and you're a taxpayer. Let me make the necessary arrangements for you."

"All right," she said, squashing all the years of training that had told her to be reliant on no one but herself. "Who should I see in Salt Lake City?"

"Good for you," Jeff approved. "You speak to a Cory McPherson in the FAA office in the main terminal. He'll be waiting for you. One of the jets will be ready. You'll have a pilot and a doctor from the regional office of the NCDC, so that the trip can be official. If that's all right?"

"Sure. Sure it's all right. I'll call before we take off." She was surprised at how helpful Jeff was, though it also made her apprehensive.

"Look for a physician named Dien Paniagua, I'll arrange for her to be in Salt Lake City by morning." He hoped he would be able to convince Dien to accompany Mrs. Porter to Canada, for the only other physician he could think of who was available was also an arrogant fellow given to issuing orders to show his importance.

"Chicano?" asked Alexa. "I know some Spanish."

"And Vietnamese," said Jeff. "I'm sure you'll do very well together."

Alexa shook her head. "I'll call you from Salt Lake. I got to get going, Doctor. Don't think I'm not grateful, but—"

"I understand. Good luck, Missus Porter. Please keep me informed."

As Alexa collected her luggage, Jeff placed a call to Dien Paniagua in Idaho.

Irene Channing, Jeff Taji and
General Barton Warren

"—and therefore we are requesting that all of you take the Standard Public School Blood Screen when your children return to classes in September. This is to enable us to offer early treatment for those who have been exposed to TS but have not yet shown outward symptoms. While we have yet to discover a vaccine for this killer—though I am absolutely confident we will—we have treatment. Those with type-O blood—and you type-Os constitute almost half the population—can be easily and completely cured. For the rest of you, we now have treatment available which can arrest the progress of the disease while a cure is being developed. And it will be developed; doctors and scientists are working on it now." On the TV screen, President Franklin Hunter looked over the enormous crowd in the Tulsa Civic Auditorium. "Every one of you has lost friends and relations to this dreaded killer. I share your grief, and I know you join with me in mourning those dedicated public servants who have been stricken by this fatal disease. Vice-President Arthur Ling was a terrible loss to the nation and to this administration."

"He's quite an act to follow," said Irene to Dale as she watched the President. "But I suppose the General insisted."

"Of course," said Dale, looking quickly at Jeff Taji. There had been more to it than that, but neither man wanted to go into it with the time for the interview so close.

"During this administration," President Hunter went on,

"we have seen losses to this disease unprecedented in this
century except by the ravages of war. Make no doubt about
it, we are facing the most implacable of enemies, and only
our single-minded purpose will bring us the victory we all
long for. I pledge to you, to every one of you living now,
and to the memories of those struck down before their
time, that in my second term, we will see this scourge
wiped off the earth. We were able to stop AIDS; we will
stop TS."

As the Tulsa audience applauded, Irene began to pace.
They had been provided a good-sized dressing room that
was actually a three-room apartment, and she went from
the sitting room to the make-up room and back, her face
tense with concentration. "Damn it, I wish we could have
found one other survivor, one other person who could back
me up."

Dale went and put his arm around her. "Irene, don't
work yourself up. Save it for facing the General." He
kissed her cheek.

"I am living proof that we can conquer TS," President
Hunter intoned. "Those who have type-O blood and have
received the treatment have all recovered. The health of
this nation must always be the first priority of this or any
administration. I promise you that I will not be satisfied
until we have abolished TS just as we have abolished slav-
ery and weapons proliferation." The applause was accom-
panied by whoops and cheers this time.

"What do you think?" Dale asked Jeff, watching Hunter.

"About the President? He's a competent man. And just
now he's very grateful. He's lost two children, his Vice-
President, his Secretary of Commerce, three Ambassadors,
twenty-two Senators, two Supreme Court Justices, one
hundred thirty-six Congressmen, three nieces, four
nephews, a sister, and two brothers-in-law to TS. The
chances are excellent he'll be reelected because he has
never dodged the issue. I met him a couple of times while
he was in Atlanta and I know that he takes TS very seriously. Will I vote for him over Booth Stanhope? Yes."

Dale had guided Irene back to the sofa. "Have you found out anything more about the research in the Seventies and Eighties we can use?"

"Not as much as I'd like," said Jeff. "You've seen most of the material. I have a few other references." He took the folded sheets from his jacket pocket and handed them to Irene. "Here."

"Thanks." She opened them and began to read. "I wish I knew what I was looking for."

"So do we all. I circled those that happened about the same time you and the other women became pregnant, but there's no saying how significant that is. It's entirely possible that the agents that caused the mutation were developed before that, possibly as far back as the Sixties." He sat down where he could not see the TV screen. "I think you'd better limit yourself to those, though. Otherwise it'll look too much like you're taking a scattered approach."

"Which I am," said Irene. "How much documentation do you have on the PK?"

"Very little, but there are enough eyewitness accounts to establish that it is the standard result in survivors of TS." Jeff looked over at Dale. "How many other survivors besides Irene have you heard of?"

"I've seen two, heard of another dozen in the Dallas area. From what one of the nurses said, there are a few more, but not a great many. They all agree about the psychokinesis." He held Irene's free hand between both of his own. "Other than Irene, I've only seen one other instance of it."

"And you have information on the substitution of drugs when you left the hospital?" Jeff asked, wishing he could rid himself of the doubts that consumed him now that a confrontation was looming.

"I have it here, with the lab reports," she said, touching the large handbag. "Along with the reports from the hospital."

Dale brought his valise out from under the sofa. "I've

got most of the corroborative evidence in here. I hope you don't have to use it."

"I hope so, too," said Jeff.

There was a muted roar from the TV and a band, reduced to a tinny toy whisper, launched into "The All-Out March" from *High Street*.

"When I was a kid," Irene said, part of her attention on the TV, "it was 'Happy Days Are Here Again.'"

"Styles change," Jeff said, aware that she did not want to discuss their material any more.

There was a knock at the door. "Missus Channing, Doctor Taji, ten minutes, please."

"I guess we'd better get out there." Irene swallowed. "Have I eaten off all my lipstick? That make-up lady will be furious."

"You look beautiful," said Dale, rising and helping her to her feet.

"You say that at seven in the morning; you're no judge," she teased, doing her best to smile through her nervousness.

"I think you look fine," said Jeff. "I keep looking to see if there's a grease spot on my tie."

"You're fine," said Irene, appreciating his effort to put them both at ease.

Dale opened the door and held it for them. "Be careful of General Warren. He's known to be a sneaky bastard."

"Gee, thanks," said Irene as she kissed him on the cheek.

"Good luck. I'll be waiting," said Dale, waiting in the open dressing room door as Jeff and Irene walked down the hall.

"Is Steve handling things okay?" Irene asked Jeff in an undervoice as they went down the stairs to the next level where the studio was located.

"He's doing as well as any of them. He manages pretty well most of the time, but he has bad days. They all do. Ever since their psychiatrist died, they've all been depressed and withdrawn. They aren't doing very well with the new shrink. Be glad he isn't like Harold Porter—"

"Is that the one they just found?" Irene asked.

"That's the one," said Jeff. They were almost at the bottom of the stairs. "He's run away twice. We've been able to find him and bring him back fairly quickly both times, but it doesn't look like he's going to take to this isolated living very well."

"Poor kid," she said. "The other parents?"

"Two survivors other than you: Susan Ross and Brandon Harmmon. Neither of them had more than the first stages of the disease. Harmmon is type-O. Susan Ross is doing Public Benefit for those with type-A blood."

Irene was about to say something, but the assistant producer came up to them and their conversation ended.

The studio was enormous. The *Plain Talking* set occupied only a fraction of its space. The moderator, Stewart Thayer, divided his time between this program and his professorial post at Haverford. He was already seated at the oval table where his interviews took place; he was wearing a tweed jacket in spite of the heat of the day, and his black skin glistened under the lights.

"Doctor Taji," he said, taking Jeff's hand. "And Missus Channing. I'm very glad you can be here, especially in the wake of the President's speech."

They both made neutral, cordial noises and sat down at the places Thayer indicated.

General Barton Lewis Warren arrived five minutes later, his uniform immaculate, his greying hair perfectly in place, the lenses of his glasses bright as an insect's eye. He acknowledged each introduction with a single nod and he sat down as if his chair were covered in uncooked eggs. "I want you to know, Professor Thayer, that there are areas of national security that I am not at liberty to discuss."

"Oh?" said Thayer with deceptive calm.

"I am sorry to inconvenience you and your guests. If there are matters that they ought not to discuss, I will have to ask them to desist." He was used to being obeyed and so did not notice the expression in Irene's eyes or the lift to Thayer's brows. "I'm sure you understand," he said, looking around the table.

"Better than you think," said Stewart Thayer, handing a letter to the General. "We're two minutes to air time. I suggest you familiarize yourself with the contents of the letter. Doctor Taji has a duplicate copy with him."

It was on Presidential stationery, embossed with the Great Seal of the United States and was handwritten: it specifically and completely removed all security restrictions from any information directly or indirectly related to Taji's Syndrome. It was signed by the man who had written it, Franklin Hunter, and was countersigned by the Chairman of the Joint Chiefs of Staff.

"I . . . I should have been informed of this," General Warren stated, his handsome face darkening.

"There wasn't time," said Thayer. "Your mike, General. We're just about on." He sat down and checked the papers on the table in front of him.

General Warren was still trying to argue while the assistant producer attached the button mike to his lapel and stepped out of camera range.

"Good evening; I am Stewart Thayer and this is *Plain Talking*." For the next three minutes, he succinctly recapped the known information and history of the last ten months regarding the appearance and spread of TS. "What has added to the mystery, and what we are concerned with tonight, is the fate of those who have survived TS. Current statistics suggest that twelve to fourteen percent of those who catch TS survive it, yet of those fortunate few, most have disappeared." He let this statement sink in. "To address this question, we have with us this evening Doctor Jeff Taji, of the National Center for Disease Control, Environmental Division. Doctor Taji was the first to isolate and describe the syndrome that bears his name, and was part of the team that developed the current treatments for TS."

As the camera focused on him, Jeff lowered his head.

"With him is one of the survivors of TS, Missus Irene Channing of Dallas, Texas. Missus Channing is also the mother of one of the known carriers of TS. Welcome to *Plain Talking*, Missus Channing."

"Doctor Thayer," she said, though she was watching the General as she said it.

"And last, General Barton Warren. General Warren is with the Army Counterespionage Task Force."

"Professor Thayer," he said, sounding as if there were crumbs caught in his throat.

"Tell me," Thayer said, looking directly at Irene, "how does it feel to have survived TS?"

"Lucky," she said at once. She gave a short description of her illness. "I didn't think I'd get well. I thought anyone who got TS died. But it didn't turn out that way. Eventually I began to get better."

"What about side effects?" Thayer was being deliberately provocative, both to Irene and General Warren.

"Well, apparently the changes that TS creates in brain chemistry continue even after recovery, and it results in . . . in emerging abilities that no one fully understands yet." She looked over at Jeff. "It seems that those who survive TS become capable of moving things . . . objects, with the power of thought."

"Psychokinesis," said Thayer helpfully.

"Yes."

"And you can do this?" He was determined to drive his point home.

"Yes. I haven't much control over it, and when I do it, it leaves me exhausted. It's easier to pick up the front end of a truck with your hands than a dish towel with your mind." She tried not to look at General Warren but she could feel his irate disapproval across the table.

"Doctor Taji," Thayer said, turning his attention to Jeff, "you've been closely identified with this disease since its first appearance last fall. How do you account for this?"

"Frankly, Professor Thayer, I don't. We know very little about TS. It's been a puzzle every step of the way."

"Why is that?" Thayer all but pounced on the question.

"Speculation at this stage might be irresponsible," the General interrupted.

"But there has been so much speculation already, General," Thayer said, silencing his infuriated guest. "Please, Doctor."

"The reason we know so little about TS," Jeff said, speaking with care, "is that we have every reason to believe that we are dealing with a disease that is the result of genetic manipulation. Through some accident—we haven't been able to determine what accident—the altered genetic material was introduced into the carriers before they were born."

"Deliberately?" Thayer asked with a quick glance at General Warren that stopped his objection before it was spoken.

"Probably not," said Jeff. "I did say accident. These carriers then became . . . 'active' might be the best word, when they reached puberty. This is a highly communicable disease, and once it started . . . well, we all know what happened."

General Warren could contain himself no longer. "If you are suggesting that the Army or any branch of the Armed Forces had anything to do with—"

"We're not suggesting that," Thayer soothed. "However, you will admit, General—won't you—that various branches of the Armed Forces were and are actively involved in genetic research."

"That's—" He was about to claim security, but Thayer touched the President's letter which was on the table.

"General?" Thayer said.

"Certain amounts of such research have been undertaken," he said stiffly.

"Is such research continuing?" Thayer asked.

"I am not aware of any specific projects," he evaded.

"But you do know it hasn't been discontinued," Thayer persisted.

"You could say that." General Warren glowered at the

letter. "It would be irresponsible for me to say more at this time."

"Would it?" Thayer had a way of smiling that was not at all pleasant. "Missus Channing, in the course of your illness, how many tests were made on you?"

"You mean while I was in quarantine?" she asked. "I really don't know. I had a high fever and I was very disoriented. As you probably know, many people with TS suffer from hallucinations during the . . . terminal phase."

Jeff supplied the answer. "Since Missus Channing had signed a Public Benefit contract, over one hundred thirty different tests were carried out on her before she began to improve. Once the PK was confirmed, another sixty-seven were administered before she left quarantine."

"That's a lot of testing," said Thayer. "And after you left quarantine, what then?"

Irene felt suddenly very exposed, almost shamed. She stared down at the polished surface of the table. "I was . . . I was transferred to a private hospital for study and recuperation."

"And while you were there, what happened?" Thayer had that eager, predatory look to him now.

"Well, I was approached by two agents from the ESA, the Executive Security Agency, asking me to volunteer for their work. When I refused, they placed agents in the hospital to keep an eye on me. I have documentation on this," she went on, looking the General directly in the eye.

"There are copies on file with the producers of this program," Thayer added.

"The ESA is not part of my service," General Warren said stiffly.

"Tell me, Missus Channing," Thayer went on as if General Warren had not spoken, "did the agents placed in the hospital make any attempt to interfere with you?"

"While I was there, no; once I left it was another matter." She glanced at Jeff. "We have records to support this; I'm not rambling and I'm not making it up. When I left the hospital, I took certain prescription drugs that supposedly were the same as the ones I had been given in the hospital. I was still in my personal physician's care"—that was one way to describe her time at the cabin with Dale—"and it was through him that we discovered that substitutions had been made at the hospital. The investigation that followed revealed that the ESA agents were responsible for the substitutions."

"If you had not been under your personal physician's care, what would have happened if you'd taken those drugs?" Thayer asked, leaning forward.

"I don't know. But at the least I would have been semiconscious and hallucinating because of them." She stopped. "I know that the PK is the reason. I know that's why you can't find the survivors."

Thayer did not linger with Irene Channing. "Doctor Taji, would you agree that survivors of TS are difficult to locate?"

"I've said that," Jeff said. "And there are increasing indications that the decision to isolate the survivors is a military one." He looked at the General, his mind alive with questions he longed to ask. This opportunity was so tempting that Jeff had to force himself to keep still, to control his urge to challenge General Warren to explain why the survivors were being sequestered. "We need to find these survivors," he made himself say. "If we're going to find a cure for all TS victims, we must have the survivors."

"General Warren? What's your response to that?" Thayer asked genially.

It was a moment before the General replied. "I don't think any of you appreciate the potential of psychokinesis. We have here a defense so enormous that you cannot begin to grasp its full implication. A country with people with this . . . ability, can render itself invulnerable. The people who can move objects with nothing more than the power of thought give us an incalculable strength."

"And the people who have the ability? What about them?" Thayer asked. "You are detaining them. We do have habeus corpus in this country. It seems to me that you and your colleagues are in violation of the law. There is also the matter of the Public Health contract most of them signed, which exempts their participation in military experimentation." He sat back and waited to hear General Warren's response.

"That was to protect us from biological warfare," snapped the General.

"The reason why that was necessary is obvious," Thayer interjected.

General Warren turned on him. "You smug, self-satisfied prick! You're treating this like the people were immune to rabies or anthrax. This isn't like that at all; it's something brand new and we have an obligation to see that it is put to the most effective use!"

"Which you are to determine?" This was not Stewart Thayer but Irene Channing who asked. She had risen to her feet. "You are speaking about the people who have survived TS as if they were soldiers in your army, part of your weapons system to be programmed for the best field application. Well, General, *I am one of those people, and I say to hell with you*, to hell with your vision of a psychic secret weapon. None of us owe you anything. We've been through enough." She sat down suddenly and turned to Thayer, prepared to apologize for her outburst.

"Missus Channing, you are wonderful." Thayer addressed the camera. "The question seems to come down to whether people who possess special abilities—ESP, PK, or any of the rest of them—can or ought to be compelled to employ those abilities for the government. By extension, anyone with special attributes, either biological or intellectual, might be required to put those attributes to work at the whim of the state or its branches. And that, ladies and gentlemen, is totalitarianism at its worst. If we are going to portray ourselves as the champions of liberty and the helpers of the oppressed, the least we can do—that we *must* do—is see that these survivors of TS are released and permitted to resume their lives, however they see fit." He paused, his intent stare now on General Warren. "Well, General? What is it going to be?"

"It's not my decision," General Warren said, for the first time his authority appearing more like bluster than strength.

"Whose is it?" Jeff asked.

"Well, ultimately, it's . . . it's the President's decision."

Thayer tapped the letter. "Oh?"

General Warren refused to look at it. "President Hunter was very ill. We had to take action. We had to be prepared." He rose. "That's all I'm going to say. You are not an official body and you have no power to—"

"Make you speak?" Thayer finished for him. "No, we don't. What you decide to do is up to you. Pity you didn't give the same options to the TS survivors."

"Break," said the producer's voice from speakers. "It's a very good start."

"Start?" General Warren bellowed, now driven past his limit. "There isn't going to be any more of this . . . this—"

"You needn't stay," Thayer said, and winked at Irene. "I think we've covered the pertinent points."

General Warren stood, rigid with wrath. "You haven't heard the last of this."

"Good God, I hope not," said Thayer. "And General, neither have you."

Mason Ross

It was a sticky night, hot and clinging. The others were indoors, but Mason sat by the swimming pool, his feet in the water, as he played back the interviews with the latest batch of released survivors. Most of them were relieved, a few were angry. He listened closely, paying attention to every word as if seeking a coded message.

"Mason?" Ace Hardy asked as he stepped outside.

"I'm okay," he said, sighing.

"Doesn't sound like it to me," Ace said.

"Well, I am. I was just... listening to some more of those guys the Army sent home. Hey, it sounds like they were in a war, doesn't it." He held up the tape recorder. "It's like what they do at the front, or when the refugee train pulls into the station. Isn't it."

"A little; you could say that," Ace answered carefully.

"Also," Mason went on a short while later, "I was thinking about Loren Protheroe. I wish I'd known about... about how sick he was. Maybe I would have worked harder to understand TS, you know?"

"We all miss Loren," said Ace. "There's lots of people to miss."

"I know," said Mason. "They told me my Mom's still alive. That's something. She won't talk to me, or answer my letters, at least she hasn't yet."

Ace came a few steps closer. "Give her time."

Mason did not look at Ace; he stared out over the roof of the stable to the waning moon. "Yeah. Everyone says give it time, just wait, eventually everyone will forget, something else will happen and TS won't matter anymore. Isn't that what you're telling us? Everyone will be treated and then we can all go home again." He lowered his head. "Of course, that isn't real easy to do anymore, is it? The twins don't have anyone left except a couple old relatives who are as nuts as the twins are. Steve Channing can go back to his Mom; he's lucky. Laurie doesn't have anyone left. Gail's Dad's a little like my Mom. He never answers her letters. Harold—who knows what will happen to Harold. He'll probably run away again, and one of the times you won't find him." He kicked his feet slowly, watching the crinkle of the water.

"And you? Don't you think your Mom'll want to have you with her, once the worst of this is over?" Ace dropped his voice so that it was just above a whisper. "Mason, you're a very bright kid. Surely you can look beyond what's going on right now?"

The sigh was unsteady. "Sure. You bet. I can look beyond now, and all I can see is this place. No one's ever going to forget we're TS carriers. No one. Before we're anything else, we're TS carriers. Hell, it isn't safe to let us out in public yet, and not just because people can get TS from us, but because we might get lynched." For a short while it appeared that he was trying not to laugh, or cry; his breath rasped in his throat.

Ace had seen Mason depressed before, but he realized that the despair that had claimed the boy was more intense than before. Though he felt out of his depth, Ace wanted to help the boy. "It's a risk. There are people with long memories, and some of them aren't very sensible."

"Who can blame people for being mad at us? We might not have done it deliberately, but TS happened because of us." Mason looked at Ace for the first time. "Nothing's going to change that."

"It didn't happen because of you," Ace said firmly. "It happened because someone screwed up a genetic experiment and somehow your mothers were exposed to it. You've got to keep a sense of perspective about this, Mason. You can't let this wear you down."

"Right. Right right right," Mason said, the sense of the word lost in its repetition. He stared down at the blue-green light from the pool. "Pretty, isn't it?"

"Not bad," Ace said cautiously.

"Not bad at all," Mason agreed. "I've been listening to those interviews, the ones with the survivors, with the PK? They sure got a rotten deal: TS and then military experiments. One of them said that they thought the carriers ought to be killed for the good of everyone else, that we were too dangerous to be permitted to live. She called us mass murderers, even though she said she knew we didn't do it on purpose." He kicked his feet again, more slowly than before.

"She didn't mean it that way," said Ace, wondering if he ought to get more help.

"Yes, she did," said Mason. "She meant every word of it. She wasn't angry or vindictive, she was . . . she was tranquil and sensible. I was thinking, you know. She could be right." He looked at Ace again.

"Mason—"

"I mean, six, seven kids against a quarter of a million people? You don't have to be good at strategy to know where the best odds are. I mean, more kids get killed in traffic accidents every day and we don't ban cars, do we?" He cleared his throat.

"Mason, come on. It's late and the weather's awful." He started toward the boy.

"We don't get nights like this in Seattle. Even when it warms up in the day, it cools off at night. This is like taking a bath in warm pudding." He took his tape recorder in his hand. "You come any closer, Ace, and I'll hit this on your shins."

"Hey, Mason!" Ace chided, more concerned than ever.

"Let me talk a while, okay? You don't have to listen, if you don't want to." The tape recorder was still in his hands, and although he looked away from Ace, it was evident that he was aware of where the tall physician was. "When this started, when Kevin died, Dad and I made a pact: we were going to hunt down TS and wipe it out. We were serious about it, you know?"

Ace wanted to find the words that would purge Mason of his anguish, but he could think of none; he knew before he spoke that he had no real solace to offer the boy. "I'm listening, Mason," was all he was able to say.

"Thanks." He was staring into the distance again, seeing other times and places now. "Kevin died so slowly. It was like watching something in slow, slow motion. And then the others started to die, too. That made it harder to take. By then TS had a name and you could feel how frightened everyone was of it." He continued to kick the water at a steady walking pace. "No one's ever going to forget. Not ever. It's like that lady, the one that *Alice in Wonderland* was written for. Even when she was real old, that's what people remembered about her, that she was this little kid. That was just a book. TS kills people. No one's going to forget that."

"It'll get better," Ace said, hoping it might be true.

"When I'm an old, old man; then I'll be a curiosity, a little old man who was a deadly kid, like some kind of mass murderer who got away with it." He leaned back, braced on his elbows. "That's the whole future, isn't it?"

It was all Ace could do not to agree. "It might go that way, but it doesn't have to. There are measures we can take?"

"You mean like the protected witness thing, where they change your identity and move you across the country? That kind of measure? How long would that work? It's not gangsters that we're talking about, it's Taji's Syndrome." He turned on the tape recorder.

"*—and they wanted us to try to work together, to make things move, always bigger and bigger. They didn't care that it exhausted us, or that we were all getting over a bad, bad illness. They only wanted us to do the mind trick. After a while I wanted to have a stroke, or a heart attack, or something to stop it for—*"

"You see? That's why no one will forget. Because there's always going to be someone who wants one of those PK guys. It isn't only the military. It might have been that way at first, but by now, you know that there are politicians and corporations who are itching to offer those survivors all kinds of goodies if they'll do a few tricks." Mason was quiet. "I'm going to bed."

Ace sighed with relief. "You want to talk some more, you give me a call. I'll be in the lab until five A.M. and then I'm going to get some sleep myself."

"Oh?" Mason did not bother to towel his legs as he stood up. "Maybe I'll talk to you tomorrow night. If it's like this again, I'll probably be up."

"Give me a little warning, and I'll arrange for a snack."

Ace thought about giving Linda Harris a call; she was the new psychiatrist assigned to the carriers.

Mason gave a slight, brief smile. "That sounds too much like a schedule. Everything here is on a schedule." He started away from the pool toward where his quarters were. "No matter how you slice it, Ace, it started with us."

"It started with an altered gene," Ace corrected him. He decided he had better write up the gist of his conversation with Mason; Linda Harris would want to have a report on it.

"In us." The door of his apartment opened. *"G'* . . . *i."*

"Yeah, good-night," called Ace as the door slammed.

It was almost dawn when Mason's body was found in the pool.

EPILOGUE

November, 1998

Laurie Grey

It was chilly; a low fog hugged the ground, seeping into everything and sapping its warmth. Laurie had put on her heaviest britches and a down vest over her sweater and still she was shivering as she lifted the saddle onto Sampson's back.

"You're up early, missie," said the stablehand as he came out of his quarters.

"Nothing else to do and I'm fidgety," she said as she buckled the girths.

"You pick out his hooves?" the old hand asked.

"Of course," snapped Laurie.

"Right," said the old man before heading off for his morning coffee.

Sampson sidled in the crossties; Laurie gave him a slap and an order to move over. She secured the breastplate to the D-rings and took his bridle from its rack. "Just a couple more minutes." These days she spent most of her free time with the horses. She was becoming an expert rider, which pleased her. At first she had ridden out of loneliness, then out of the realization that she would never give a horse TS. None of the horses was afraid of her.

In the covered arena, she spent five minutes with Sampson on the lunge, warming up the leggy black gelding. Then she vaulted into the saddle and gathered up the reins.

After half an hour she and the horse were doing the low jumps, lifting and falling, rising for a brief soaring flight. It let her escape.

It helped her to forget she was no longer dancing.

Adam and Axel Barenssen

On the floor between them lay what was left of a chicken. Feathers drifted around them and the scent of bloody innards was heavy in the closed room. Adam, his dark blue eyes glowing, bowed his head to the inverted cross on the wall and began to chant the Lord's Prayer backwards. Beside him, Axel held up the chicken's head.

"We forsaken children come before you, Mighty Lord Satan, Ruler of Hell, Master of Destruction. We who were made in Your Malign Image offer up the symbols of our mortality."

"Satan is Mighty," Axel declared.

"We accept Your burden of Sin and Death. We welcome it. We know we are outcasts and we bow before You, giving this life and the countless other lives—human lives— we have taken to You, for homage."

"Satan is Mighty," Axel repeated.

"We who have sinned beyond all forgiveness come to You as instruments of Your Power." Adam held his arms out to the side, a small knife in one hand, a riding crop in the other. "We give you our pain and our deadliness."

Axel pulled off his shirt and lay prone between the inverted cross and his twin brother, waiting for the new tokens of his devotion. As the first blow struck him, he called out Satan's name. In two more blows fresh blood ran over old scars as the twins chanted the Doxology backward.

_____ *Steven and Irene Channing* _____

"Will Dale be here at Thanksgiving?" Steven asked as he built up the fire in the wood stove.

"I don't know yet," Irene answered. She was quite thin now, and when she painted, her manner was hectic, fervid.

"Do you think he will?" Steven persisted.

"I hope so. I miss him. Living out here, it makes it difficult, sometimes." She was being evasive and both of them knew it.

"Does he mind my being here?" He closed the door against the renewed blaze. "I'll clean out the ashes in a while."

"Thanks." She was staring at her latest canvas, not sure it conformed to her inner vision. The trouble with painting, she told herself as she had been doing increasingly of late, was that it lacked real depth. There was only the illusion of depth, and no longer satisfied her.

"What about Brice? Will he be here?" Steven took great care not to sound excited at the prospect of seeing his younger half-brother again.

"Oh, yes. That's certain."

"Good," said Steven. He had grown in the last year and was close to six feet tall. He looked more like an adult than many other teenagers, but that was the result of his somber manner rather than anything outwardly obvious. "I miss him."

"So do I," said Irene. "I miss so many things, so many people. But I have a second chance that most never got, and I've acquired another . . . talent. I suppose that's something."

Steven said nothing.

"You know," Irene went on as she sank down in the old armchair near the fireplace, "Dale got me through everything. He was as staunch and true as you could want anyone to be. He helped me, Steve. God knows what would have happened to me without him. But now," she said, her face showing her sadness, "he can't help me any more, and . . . I don't think he knows how to deal with that."

Steven stacked the rest of the wood in a metal bin beside the stove. "You'll work things out, Mom."

"I suppose so," she said. "One way or another. At least as long as President Hunter keeps his word and we're left alone."

"You don't think we're going to have more trouble, do you?" Steven asked, trying to be shocked.

"Not for a while. But eventually, I think . . ." Her voice trailed off.

"We'll handle it, Mom." Steven wanted to shake her, but he knew she was speaking the truth.

"Um-hum," said Irene, though neither was convinced.

Gail Harmmon

For the last year, Gail had been obsessed with the lute. She had three now, and twice a week her instructor drove out from Atlanta and worked with her, bringing her more music and making occasional recommendations.

"I thought I'd try some of those late Renaissance dances," Gail said to Wendy Tyler early one windy afternoon.

"I'll bring some," said Wendy who, at fifty-three, had long since outgrown her first name. "There are some interesting Hungarian dances from that time."

"Anything," said Gail. Her hair was getting long and the

shape of her body was changing. "I'm getting bored with these English things. I need something else."

"The English pieces are very demanding work," said Wendy.

"They're dull." Gail picked up her best lute and plucked out the melody of the Dowland madrigal she had learned recently. "Listen to that. Dull."

"Whatever you say," Wendy responded, feeling sympathy for this pretty teenaged girl who was kept in such strict isolation.

"And I want to see if you can find one of those old kind of lutes, with the extra drone strings. You know the ones I mean."

"A theorbo," Wendy guessed.

"That'll do," Gail said. "One of those. And the music to go with it. I need to learn something new."

"Something new?" Wendy echoed.

"Yes!" She flung her hand toward the window. "I sure as hell can't swim in this weather, and there's no one I can swim with in any case. What else can I do?"

Wendy had no immediate answer. "Surely one of the others would—"

Gail shook her head in scorn. "Them! What do I care about them. I care about my lutes. So bring me something new."

"If you like," Wendy said, and was puzzled when Gail started to laugh loudly.

_____ *Harold Porter* _____

He found a phone booth in a small town more than thirty miles away from the Control Facility, and when he was certain no one was watching him, he entered it. "I want to place a collect call to Alexa Porter in Golden, Colorado," he told the automated operator. He gave the number and waited while the phone rang and rang. He always gave it twenty rings before he hung up. This time he gave it twenty-four. As he left the phone booth, he promised himself he would try again later that night. "She's probably not home from that show in Flagstaff yet," he said to himself.

After buying a cheap dinner in a small cafe, he went out to the main road, walking slowly, thumb out, waiting for a ride heading west. He was colder than he wanted to admit, and his fleece-lined denim jacket did not keep him as warm as it was supposed to.

As he walked, he thought about the Control Facility. It wasn't that he didn't like the place, he reminded himself, but he had always hated being cooped up. And those other kids—Jesus, they were weird. Especially the twins, with their prayers and the crazy things they said. Laurie only cared about horses, and the other girl was so angry at everyone that there was no talking with her at all. It was time to get away for a while, to go see his Mom on her ranch, help her with the ponies for a while, get a little time on his own. And Thanksgiving was coming up soon—it was time he went . . . home.

He was so lost in reverie that he paid little attention to traffic, so that when he finally noticed the half-ton pickup driven by a high school junior who was on his fourth beer, he had neither the time nor the space to avoid it.

The bumper and headlight smashed into him, tossing him onto the hood, where he bounced once, scaring the living shit out of the driver. By the time he hit the pavement, both his back and skull were broken; he had been dead for five seconds.

Jeff Taji and
Weyman Muggridge

When Weyman and Sylvia finished their guided tour of their new house, they were back in the lanai which opened onto a wide patio filled with large semi-tropical plants. This afternoon the glass doors were closed against the first spitting of rain.

"We hope it clears up in time for the wedding," Weyman said to Jeff.

"If you're determined to get married in the garden, I can see why," Jeff said, looking around almost wistfully. "It's lovely here."

"We like it," said Weyman. "I told Sylvia when we found it last March that I'd move back to Atlanta if she didn't agree to buy it."

Sylvia took a playful punch at his arm. "You mean I said I'd send you back there if you didn't agree to buy it."

"We miss you in Atlanta," said Jeff thoughtfully. "It isn't as much fun with you gone."

"You mean that no one has learned how to handle Drucker yet?" Weyman asked in mockery.

"Dien does a pretty good job. And there's always Susannah when Drucker gets out of hand. But it's not the same." He caught sight of his reflection in the windows, as insubstantial as a ghost. His hair was white now, and his face was very lean.

"So leave NCDC-ED and take a job here with PHES, or work in the NCDC regional office. Drucker would probably be delighted to transfer you." Weyman grinned easily. "Let up on yourself a little, Jeff."

"I can't, yet," said Jeff. "We're still getting reports of TS in third world countries and . . . you know."

"You feel compelled to go there and tend to them. I know." Weyman looked at his friend in sympathy. "Just because the shit has your name doesn't mean you're responsible for it."

Jeff nodded. "It's"—he sighed—"complicated. I know I've botched being a father. Looking back, I probably wasn't much of a husband. I don't want to waste . . ." His voice trailed off.

Weyman was about to say something, but Sylvia stopped him. "You can't take on the world by yourself, Jeff. You've done so much already. You've paid your dues."

"Have I?" He watched the raindrops spatter on the glass and slide down, spangled by the light inside the house. "And what about next time?"

"Hey," said Weyman, getting up and going to the bar to open a bottle of Pinot Noir, "you can't do that to yourself. You can't spend the rest of your life waiting for something else like TS to happen." He sniffed the cork. "Heaven."

"I'm afraid it won't take the rest of my life, that's the trouble." He looked from Weyman to Sylvia. "I'm sorry. I shouldn't be dwelling on this with your wedding two days away."

"And you the best man," Sylvia chided him affectionately.

"Quite an event. We're thinking of hyphenating our names, so she won't have to give hers up. Kostermeyer-Muggridge. You got to admit it has a ring to it." He poured the wine and gave the first glass to his bride.

"Muggridge-Kostermeyer," she corrected him, laughing.

Jeff tried to shake off the gloom that enveloped him. "It smells wonderful," he said as he took the wineglass.

Weyman lifted his glass to propose a toast, but stopped himself. "Jeff, it was a million to one chance, that altered

DNA doing what it did to those kids. The chances of that happening again are . . . well, astronomical."

"I know." He tried to smile. "I don't mean to be the spectre at the feast."

"To tomorrow; may each one be sweeter than the one before." Weyman chuckled as the wineglasses touched.

"Happiness to both of you," Jeff added, with an extra salute to his friends.

Weyman clapped his free hand on Jeff's shoulder. "We're through the worst of it, Jeff. Remember that."

"Are we." Jeff looked away, past the bright rain on the lanai window to the oncoming dark.